"Rowdy" Randy Cox, a woman staring down the barrel of retirement, is a curmudgeonly blue-collar butch lesbian, who has been single for twenty years and is trying to date again.

At the end of a long, exhausting shift, Randy finds her supervisor, Bryant, pinned and near death at the warehouse where they work. Upon the news of his death, she battles to find a balance between the joys of an exciting new relationship and the struggles of processing her supervisor's unexpected passing.

The manner of her supervisor's death leaves Randy unsettled and suspicious as she gets sucked into both a criminal investigation led by the police and an administrative investigation conducted by her employer.

As Randy seeks the truth, trust erodes, key friendships are strengthened, and more loss awaits her.

PINNED

RANDY COX, BOOK ONE

LIZ FARAIM

A NineStar Press Publication
www.ninestarpress.com

Pinned

First Edition, March 2023

ISBN: 978-1-64890-635-0

Also available in eBook, ISBN: 978-1-64890-634-3

CONTENT WARNING:
This book depictions of violence, death of a secondary character, and cancer death.

Chapter One

Warm Beer Chaser

THE FIRST RAINSTORM of the season had drawn me out of my house. Local radio news had said something about a bomb cyclone and an atmospheric river. Either way, the whole area was getting hammered in a way I hadn't seen in over a decade.

I'd had the wise idea to go out and watch the storm rage instead of sitting on the couch at home waiting for the power to go out. Rain pounded the roof of my truck with a constant *rat-a-tat-tat*. Massive drops splattered on the roiling surface of Marshtown Strait, and runoff flowed down the boat launch in sheets. Dusk turned to darkness under thick clouds, casting everything in shades of gray.

A lanky great egret tried to take flight from the shoreline, its wings spread wide, but the gusting wind swooped it up and blew it toward the frenzied tides. I leaned back in my driver's seat, its padding and springs worn down to the point where the seat had a hollow that hugged me, and watched a tattered American flag savagely whip about, the halyard's counterweight clanging.

Through sideways rain, the shadowy form of a person scrabbled up from the rocks below Archer Point. Sitting forward, I turned on the windshield wipers to get a better look. Sure enough, a tall figure made it up to solid ground and loped along the walking path. The person wore a hooded rain slicker, a familiar orange backpack, and clutched two fishing rods in their hand. They made their way down to the boat launch, passing briefly under an overhead streetlight, before fading to a silhouette at the end of the dock. I wasn't certain but thought it might be my friend Darcy.

The person, seemingly unbothered by the rain and wind, baited their hook and cast the line out into the void. I settled back into my warm seat and gazed out across the water, spotting the tiny headlight of a train flashing at the base of the hills. My mind wandered around thoughts of a time years ago when I had been caught out on a motorcycle trip during similar conditions.

Looking back at the dock to check on the person who was fishing, all I saw was their orange backpack in a limp pile on the dock.

"Frick," I grumbled and slapped a faded ballcap on my head.

I pulled the keys out of the ignition and pushed open the door of my truck. The wind ripped it from my fingertips. Hopping out, I fought the wind and slammed the door, then tucked my hands into the front pocket of my hoodie and made my way down the slippery boat launch, eyes squinted against the weather.

At the end of the dock, I leaned over the railing and

saw someone sitting in waist-deep water, rubbing their elbow.

"Hey! You all right down there?" I hollered.

They stood up, the water barely up to their knees, and felt around in the murk. Eventually, they came up with a fishing pole. I waited, the deluge soaking through my sweatshirt and jeans, running down the back of my neck and between my shoulder blades.

Rather than trying to climb up the slick wooden pilings, they walked around to the boat ramp and up the pavement. I grabbed their bag and spare pole and jogged back the way I had come. We met up under the streetlight and they took their pole graciously and shrugged into their backpack.

"That you, Darcy?" I asked, wiping water out of my eyes.

At the sound of her name, Darcy raised her eyes and looked at me. "Well, hey, Randy, what're you doing out in this weather?"

Not wanting to talk about myself, I dodged her question. "I was wondering the same about you. What happened? Are you hurt?"

Darcy heaved a sigh. "My line got caught and I leaned over the railing to try and free it. My shoe slipped and over the side I went. Stupid move. I know better."

"Dang. The water is so shallow with the tide out right now. You're lucky you didn't break your neck."

She nodded, rubbing at her elbow again.

A train horn echoed. Across the water another headlight cut through the sooty darkness along the tracks. A huge gust of wind nearly blew us both over, sharp rain pelting my cheeks.

"You need a ride?"

She stopped, considering. The back of her jacket hood shifted with a nod. "Yes."

"Come on, then."

I strode to my truck and unlocked the passenger side with a good old-fashioned key. I didn't have one of those cars with automatic locks or a key fob. The door flung open when the wind caught it, and she maneuvered her rods into the cab while I got in on the driver's side.

Slamming my door, I was grateful to be out of the wind and weather. I fired up the engine and cranked the heater. I cupped my hands in front of one of the dashboard vents for a minute, then took my hat off, turning in my seat.

"Long time, no see, Darce."

"I suppose it has been a while. Thanks for the ride. Sorry I'm crapping up your seats with low tide sludge."

She did smell awful. The silt and muck on the bottom of the strait was full of slimy nastiness, and some was still stuck to her rain pants and shoes.

"No problem. You know I've had to clean worse off my interior before."

We both chuckled, remembering other adventures that had stunk up my truck.

*

WE SAT QUIETLY for a few minutes, relaxing in the growing warmth of the cab as the rain pounded down relentlessly. The windows fogged up and the stink of low tide and bait bloomed even more.

Even though it was pitch dark out, it was barely six

o'clock and I was hungry. The smell of a soaking wet fisherwoman in my truck didn't ruin my appetite. I sat up in my seat, ready to head out.

She startled a bit, coming out of her thoughts. "I'll help you clean up your upholstery this weekend. But in the meantime, let me make it up to you. You hungry?"

"Yeah, I could eat."

"How about we pick up something from the Thai restaurant on the main drag? My treat."

"You don't have to ask me twice." I swiped at the fog on my windshield, toggled the worn-out dial on my dashboard to turn on the defroster, and pulled carefully out of the pier's parking lot.

There weren't many other cars on the road, which was a good thing since the streets in our waterfront town were narrow, making the bad weather and darkness more dangerous.

The restaurant was deserted, so we didn't have to wait long for our takeout. Lands End was a small town, just a speck on the map, so I was home and in warm, dry sweats and wool socks soon enough. Darcy had on proper rain gear over her clothes and was dry underneath despite her little dip in the strait.

I hadn't been expecting a guest, so my place was a bit more cluttered than I would have liked, but I stifled the urge to make apologies. I had spent the first five decades of my life apologizing for things that didn't need apologizing for, and at fifty-three years old, I wasn't doing it anymore.

I put on a Melissa Etheridge record and pulled chipped plates and bowls from the cupboard. Darcy was well acquainted with my kitchen and grabbed silverware and napkins, humming along to the record as she set the table.

I served up piles of bami and miang kham, then ladled steaming Tom kha into bowls. I split a bottle of Singha beer between two small mason jars. We tucked in at the booth I had built into the corner of the kitchen. It was a tight space, and her knees bumped mine under the table.

"Gets me every time," she said around a bite of noo-dles and scooted down a bit so we weren't directly across from each other.

I tapped my toes along to the record as I ate the savory,

crunchy vegetables. I let out a satisfied groan as I popped a miang kham into my mouth, the heat, sour, and sweet of it hitting all at once. I chased that with a spoon full of coconut broth and a sip of beer.

As usual, Darcy was so calm and quiet that I slid into the same level of comfort as if I were home alone. I hadn't seen her in a while and snuck looks at her between bites of food. She looked well. Her big brown eyes were clear, and her long, windblown brown hair fell wildly around her face.

She was exceptionally slim, which was also normal for her. Slim enough for her tall narrow frame that when we first met, I had worried for a moment about her health, then scolded myself for having an opinion about her body. *None of your business, Randy.*

"Mmm," I said as I licked my spoon with relish and got up. "You finished?" I pointed at her empty plate and bowl.

"Yes," she said with a small nod, though she put her hand around the mason jar which still held a few sips of beer. "Need some help?"

"Nah. Take a load off."

I gave the dishes a quick wash and stacked them neatly in the dish drainer, then piled some Oreos onto a little tea saucer before stepping into the living room and flipping the record to the B side. Darcy doodled quietly on the back of her napkin with a carpenter's pencil.

"Come on in here, that old wooden booth bench isn't good for much longer than a quick meal before it'll start hurting your ass."

Darcy collected her beer glass and made the trip from kitchen to living room in three strides. I flopped down in my recliner, and she settled into the love seat. My living room was too small for my recliner plus a full-sized couch. Cozy was the word my realtor had used when we had originally toured the place before I bought it.

It seemed like conversation was in order, though I was never too good at getting one going. I searched around for an easy topic.

"What were you fishin' for tonight?"

"Striper, but I kept pulling up Dungeness crab when I

was down on the rocks at the Point. You know they are il-legal to keep this time of year." I nodded and she went on, "So, I moved over to the dock to see if I'd have better luck. And…well, you know the rest." We both chuckled.

"You been snagging a lot of fishing lately?"

"Oh yeah. Most days. I'm usually out at the cove. More room to get out on my own, away from the other hordes of people at the pier, many of whom I have had issues with."

"Ugh, fuck those guys. Bunch of haters."

"I'd rather not, thanks. I'm not naïve or anything, but you know about how when I transitioned…and things didn't go well at my job after that?"

I nodded, watching as she picked unconsciously at a hangnail. She sat up straighter and went on. "The crew I worked with in Oakland made it impossible to stay on there and I used to come to Lands End a lot to fish and hike, so I figured I'd give this little town a try. The rents here are almost as stupid as they are in Oakland, but I love the small-town feel and had hoped I could just kinda be left alone, but there are some assholes here too."

I nodded and we both sipped our drinks.

She tilted her glass toward me. "What's going on with you? How's the retirement countdown going?"

"I'm still at the warehouse over in Diablo. Two years till retirement. Thank goodness." I scrubbed at my shaggy hair and nodded. "It's a good thing, cuz I don't think my body can handle much more manual labor. Been working in warehouses for thirty-three years. Being able to retire at fifty-five is a blessing these days." Darcy nodded in agreement. "Aside from being harassed by ignorant-ass fishermen, how's work going for you down at the port?"

She grinned. "It's good. Can't complain about it. I mean, not many people can say they get to unload brand spanking new cars from cargo ships. It's kinda cool driving 'em off the ship and over to the storage lot or loading them up into auto transport trains. It's good work, fast paced. And it's fun to see the insides of all the new cars. Everything from minivans to sports cars. And it keeps me moving and mostly outdoors, which you know is what works for me. I couldn't stand having a desk job." She paused, tilting her beer glass at me. "Professionalism is classist bull-shit."

I paused, Oreo in hand, suspended midway between the plate and my mouth. "Huh. I never thought about that, but it makes sense when you put it like that. They've tried a bunch of times over the years to make me a supervisor and I always turn them down. I don't want to leave the protection of the union. And besides, I figure I don't want to stress out about production numbers and all the logistical stuff." I looked down at the cookie in my rough hands. "All I have to do is show up and move boxes till the buzzer rings. I'd be miserable in a desk job too. I move boxes, you move flashy cars. I'd say we are doing just fine." I used my teeth to pull one side of the cookie into my mouth, crunching on the chocolatey goodness.

She nodded. "I like that I only see my coworkers in passing. We ride in vans together down to the port and around the storage lots. But mostly I am on my own, driving car after car from point A to point B. That's the way I like it. I just go in, keep my head down, do my job, and leave. Then all I have to worry about is where I wanna go fishing after work. Keeping it simple."

I tilted my head at the cookie plate, but she shook her

head. I popped the other side of the cookie in my mouth and washed it down with the dregs of my beer and cringed.

"I don't recommend Oreos with a warm beer chaser."

We cackled before settling into another comfortable silence. Darcy closed her eyes, nodding along to the tempo of the song. I leaned back, listening to the rain pattering on the roof and window. When the last song ended, the record player shut itself down with a click.

My cat slid out from under the couch and took a moment to stretch his legs. After shaking his head, he let out a curious *mrow* as he sniffed at Darcy's pant leg. Losing interest, he came to me, giving another *mrow* as I reached down to pet him. He rubbed the sides of his face along my hand. Darcy smiled, watching us.

"Dammit, Porkchop," I growled. I had made the mistake of taking my eyes off him and he had bitten me. I shook my finger, admonishing him. He purred and tried to rub his face on my stern finger. "God, you're such a jerk."

Unphased, Porkchop halfheartedly licked at his messy black-and-white fur. I admired his extra-long white whiskers but disliked his bad attitude and shedding. I shooed him away.

"He's always been a sweetheart to me," she said with a little laugh.

"Little bastard. I love him anyway." I checked my watch and grumbled. It was almost nine. "Ugh, it's past my bedtime. Do you need a ride?"

"Yeah, if you don't mind."

She slid into her rain gear, and I pulled on a dry hoodie. I drove the few blocks down to the last row of houses just before the massive fences for the port. After a quick hug she disappeared into the dark alley that led to the in-law unit she lived in.

Back at home, I set my alarm and groaned again. Two a.m. would be there before I knew it.

Chapter Two

The Crow's Nest

THE ALARM CLOCK on my cell phone wailed and I slapped at the touch screen to make it stop. Squinting, I switched on the small bedside lamp. Two a.m. had come quickly. I lay in bed for a moment, listening to the rain fall, waiting for my gluey mouth and burning eyes to clear.

Eventually Porkchop began clawing under the door and howling. I got out of bed with a grumble, shuffled down the hall and through the shadowy living room with Porkchop underfoot, tripping me along the way, and scooped some food into his bowl.

"If you trip and kill me, you won't get fed, ya dummy." My voice came out in a rattling croak.

I worked on clearing my throat, then stood in the darkness, listening to him crunch his kibbles. I had lived in that house for fifteen years and didn't need light to show me the way. Cold seeped from the floor through my socks and chilly air nipped at my ears, but I didn't bother turning on the heater because I'd be leaving for work soon.

After a quick shower to wake up, I swiped at the fogged-up mirror with my hand and ran a brush through my salt-and-pepper hair. Deodorant and face lotion were next before digging around in the hamper for the pants I had worn to work the day before.

Back in my bedroom I put on clean boxer briefs, thermal underwear, and the filthy jeans. Next up was a thermal top, a turtleneck, and a long-sleeved T-shirt. The shirt had been a heather gray once, but years of wearing it to work had made a permanent brown stain across the belly, and the cuffs of the sleeves were badly frayed.

I slid my feet into a fresh pair of thick wool socks and sat down on the bed to lace up my work boots. They were scuffed beyond recognition, and I was on my third pair of replacement laces, but the soles were still good. To top it all off, I slid a black beanie over my damp hair and pulled on a thick canvas work jacket.

Clomping out to the kitchen, I smiled as I was greeted by the smell of coffee. Technology had come a long way since I was first starting out, and the programmable coffee maker was by far one of my favorite things. I flicked the light switch and nearly jumped out of my skin because of a loud grinding noise. I shut the switch off and the sound stopped. I flipped the switch next to it and squinted as the overhead lights came on.

"Who installs a damn garbage disposal switch so close to a light switch?" My heart glubbed along at double time from the scare.

I poured some half and half into a travel mug, then filled it almost to the top with coffee, before dumping in three heaping spoons of sugar. I gave it a stir, snapped on the lid, and took a sip, scorching my tongue.

"Dammit."

Mee-rowww.

"When will I learn, Porky? I burn my smart-ass mouth every morning."

Porkchop went back to his kibbles. *Cronch purr cronch purr cronch purr.*

I pulled out two shelled hardboiled eggs from the container I kept in the fridge. The smell of sulfur filled my nose as I leaned against the counter and ate the eggs, thinking about how I'd run into Darcy the night before, glad we had reconnected.

"Wasn't it good to see Darcy?"

Porky didn't respond. The last bite of egg gone, I shoved a handful of smoked almonds into my mouth, grabbed a pouch of Pop-Tarts from the cabinet, and headed out of the door.

"Bye, Porkchop. Guard the house."

Stepping out into the pre-dawn darkness, I was greeted by gentle rain. The door to my truck let out a loud metallic squeal as it opened, and the engine roared to life on the first try. I sipped coffee until I deemed the engine warmed up enough to not die at the first stop sign I came to.

The roads were still empty and the trip across the strait to the industrial section of Diablo was uneventful. I drove through the open gate of the employee lot and wound up having to park way in the back. The night shift hadn't wrapped up yet, so the lot was jammed full of older beat-up cars and trucks, mixed in with a few shiny sports cars and fancy, high-end SUVs.

I sat, windshield wipers slowly blurring across my view of the yard through the rusty chain-link fence. The yard was lit up bright as day by massive overhead lights. Yard trucks darted about hauling fifty-six-foot trailers, backing them skillfully up to the unload doors, then picking up fully loaded trailers on the load side of the building. Our building ran twenty-four hours a day, so there was constant activity in the yard.

A woman I recognized as an unload supervisor from night shift stepped out of a pedestrian door into the yard as she shouldered her way into an orange vest. She stood in the crosswalk, hollering at a driver, waving her clipboard for emphasis. The driver just shrugged her off and got back into his rig. Face grim, the supervisor started to walk toward his rig, realized she had stepped out of the crosswalk, and stepped back into it. The driver pulled away from the wall, a fully loaded trailer in tow, and left. The supervisor looked up at the night sky, lips pursed, clearly trying to tamp down her temper, before yanking off her safety vest and storming back inside.

"See. I don't need that bullshit supervisor stress in my life," I mumbled to myself as I locked up my truck. Taking a sip of coffee, I made the long walk across the parking lot to the employee entrance and stood in line with the rest of the morning shift folks, waiting to pass through security. The waiting area was not covered, so we all got wet. My watch said 2:55 a.m.

"Damn," I grumbled, knowing I would make it to the timeclock in time, but not to my workstation.

A few other huddled figures acknowledged my complaint with their own mumbles. I kept shuffling forward until I had made it into the tiny security shack. There was the familiar repetitive *clack* of people dropping wallets, cell phones, and car keys into the basket, then the inevitable *beep* as they passed through the metal detector. The security guard would pass a wand over them, which would also beep, and she'd wave them through without further fuss.

The inside of the guard shack had a low, worn, brown countertop, a beige walk-through metal detector, and white-painted walls that hadn't been white in forty years. Countless dirty bodies moved through that shack twenty-four hours a day, and it showed.

"Mornin', Granny," I said to the guard as I emptied my pockets into the basket. She was only ten years older than me, but all the young guys who worked there called her Granny, and it had stuck.

"Hey Randy. Rainy day, eh." She clasped the wand metal detector in her wrinkled, age spotted hand. A wedding ring threatened to slide right off her slim, bony finger.

"Yup." I stepped through the metal detector, which beeped. She passed the wand over me, and it beeped at my waist, like it always did. I pulled up the front of my shirt and showed her my belt buckle. She waved me through. I collected my belongings and headed out.

"Next," Granny said as I rushed out of the back door and followed the painted stripe on the ground leading to the pedestrian door, which was right next to a wide-open bay door. Walking through the bay door was asking for trouble. Your options included getting run over by a truck or getting yelled at by a supervisor. Yard control and safety were a big deal there, and I was close enough to retirement that I wasn't interested in chancing my luck.

Inside the warehouse, I was greeted by noise from miles of conveyor belts running and high-pitched horns from the electric carts that whizzed around the building. There was also the inevitable *creeeeeeeiikk* of tape guns. And shouting. Lots of shouting. Anybody who wanted to be heard in there had to holler over the machinery.

Warm mug in hand, I waited my turn to punch in at the timeclock, ignoring all the buffoonery and grab ass the young guys ahead and behind me were doing. After punching in, I walked over to the board to see what station I had been assigned to. I found my name, which was written on a thin magnet stuck to the board. My name, among so many others. It took a lot of bodies to make that building run.

The place was a maze of machinery and people. Packages fell, people shouted, and I tucked my chin into my collar until I reached my work area for the day. On the dark concrete wall, neatly stenciled in white paint, was the number 76. I closed the spout on my mug, tucked it into my inside jacket pocket, and hoisted myself up the sturdy metal ladder, which was bolted to the concrete ground at the bottom, and welded to my workstation grating at the top.

Up I went, rung after rung, until I reached a little spring-loaded gate. I pushed it open and stepped though after making the dizzying transition from the ladder. The gate clanged shut behind me and I pulled the warm mug out of my jacket, took a satisfying sip, and placed it in the corner so I wouldn't trip on it or kick it over.

My workstation was called "The Crow's Nest," because it was so high up, and all by itself, not connected to the metal grating walkway the folks on the other side of the conveyor belt had. It was a solo workstation, which suited me just fine. My platform fronted about ten feet of conveyor belt. The floor was metal grating, with a view to the concrete floor far below. There was a waist-high metal railing on all sides except for along the conveyor belt. Chutes on my left and right led down to twisty metal slides, like the kind you find at a playground. Directly over the belt was a tube light that had a cage over it, so packages wouldn't break the bulb. And that was it. It was dark, dirty, and cold.

I flinched as a horn blew. It sounded like the kind they use at basketball games. After the horn stopped the whole building shut down, the machinery falling quiet, the noise replaced with hoots and hollers of the night shift crew calling it a day. Somewhere across the warehouse I heard one guy bellow: *"Freeedom!"* like Mel Gibson from *Braveheart*, which made me chuckle.

I dug around the inside pocket of my jacket and pulled out my custom fit earplugs. By the timeclock was a huge container of those crappy little one-size-fits-all disposable foam ones, but I had invested in some proper earplugs awhile back and was glad I had. Having worked in warehouses and ridden motorcycles my whole adult life, my hearing wasn't the greatest.

There was a lot of playful jostling down below as the night shift crew flowed out from every dingy corner of the building. Hearing a sharp whistle, I leaned over the railing to see one asshole in particular smirking up at me. He had stopped walking, as had his entourage. I recognized him as a sorter from the night shift, someone I'd had issues with before when I worked double shifts on nights.

"Hey. Look who's here. What's up, Randall!" He cackled like a middle schooler and elbowed one of his buddies. I rolled my eyes. He thought he was so damn hilarious with his weak-ass attempt at razzing me.

"It's Randy, idiot," I said, speaking clearly, to make sure he heard me. "Short for Miranda. Not…Randall."

"Huh. I thought for sure you had a dick."

That statement echoed up to me through the bustle, and a couple more people stopped to watch the exchange, adding to the sea of men below me dressed in various shades of ragged denim, their dirty faces turned to look up at me, beanies askew.

I cleared my throat and spoke clearly again. "Why don't you work on paying more attention to your sorting and less attention on what's in people's pants? That way you won't missort half the packages you touch. Have a nice day in your parents' basement playing video games, loser."

He scowled and his buddies let out a chorus of "Ooohhh."

"Oh, and if you do decide to take a shower this month, don't forget to wash your balls. Nobody likes musty balls."

His friends cracked up, clapping their hands and bouncing up and down on the balls of their feet.

I smirked as a frowning supervisor hustled up behind them, shouting. "What the hell, you guys, go clock out. Now!" He waved his clipboard at them, as if to waft them away.

I turned back to my station and put in my earplugs before checking the sheet clipped to the overhead light, which told me I'd be splitting packages for the central valley. The tiny print listed the cities, zip codes, and what load door they were going to. I slipped on my reading glasses, a cheapo pair I had picked up at the drug store, and got my-self familiar with my split for the day. Once I had it down, I watched below as my supervisor, Bryant, held a huddle with the loaders before sending them each off to their trail-ers.

Unlike the other supervisors, Bryant spoke calmly and respectfully to the crew, his voice low enough that the guys had to lean in a bit. When Bryant had first come on board about ten years prior, he had started out as a loader and had gone about his work calmly and efficiently. He never seemed to be caught up in the jeering and arguing many of the other loaders got involved in.

He was so diligent in his work that he almost never had misloads, and he was always courteous to me, even when I accidently sent the wrong packages down the chute to him. I was so proud of him when he got promoted to load supervisor and was glad he hadn't turned mean with the stress of the job.

I slid on my work gloves. The buzzer overhead sounded, and the conveyor belt started up, as did the con-stant low vibration of the grating under my feet. The belt ran empty for almost five minutes as the packages were unloaded from trailers on the other side of the building, sorted, and made their way to my load wall.

As the packages flowed by, I checked the zip codes on their labels. I had four options: push the package across to the far side of the belt, pull it close to my side of the belt, push it down the chute to my left, or push it down the chute to my right. Being the splitter was simple enough, once you got your zip codes down and figured out how to keep up. Push, pull, push, pull, push, push, push, chute, chute.

As the unloaders got into their rhythm, the number of items coming down the belt grew. Several times, I had to press a button to stop the belt because it was so bogged down with packages, all piled on top of each other and spanning the whole belt, that I couldn't split them. Each time I stopped the belt, Bryant stood below me, hands on his hips, deep-brown eyes fixed on me, waiting. Any other supervisor would have been screaming.

Every belt stoppage counted against the shift's production numbers, so I knew he was anxious about it, though after working together for years, he trusted me to only stop the belt when it was necessary. Some jackasses would do it just to give themselves a break; I was not one of those jackasses.

At break time the control tower shut down the machinery. I climbed gratefully and carefully down the ladder to solid ground, though my feet and legs still had phantom vibration from the grating. There were only two women's restrooms in the whole damn place because so few females worked there. The hike to the bathroom took up most of my break.

*

AS THE SHIFT wound down, the trailers were packed full like giant Tetris cubes and most of the crew either clocked out or was in cleanup mode. My final daily task was to walk the entire length of the conveyor belt from my load wall to the unload, in search of any packages that might have gotten stuck.

Walking on the belt, I heard the familiar thump and rumble of yard trucks hooking up and pulling trailers away from the building. The sun shone bleakly through the yawning maws left behind after the trailers had been pulled.

I hadn't found any stray packages on the belt and was almost back to door 76 when I had to get down on my hands and knees to crawl under an overhead light. I tried to enjoy my job every day, and usually I did. But the wear on my body was something I couldn't ignore, and after the long shift my body was tired, and my knees ached. It irked me that I was crawling along a conveyor belt, thirty feet in the air, while all the young, lower seniority guys had already clocked out and were headed to the bar.

Shouting below caught my attention. From my perch I could just make out Bryant outside the open load door, yelling into his cell phone. Something about process flow, package counts, and "…shove it up your pooper!" I didn't bat an eyelash at his language, since that was just how management talked to each other. In fact, Bryant wasn't being nearly as foul as the rest of them usually were, though it was still out of character for him to yell.

He didn't have a safety vest on, and I didn't see a warning cone out on the concrete yard. He bent a few times as he made his way along the wall and grabbed packages that had fallen into the yard from the dock.

He thumped a package on the chest-high dock and rested his forearm on the metal grating. The sleeves of the turtleneck he wore under his polo shirt were dirty, and his hands were too. That meant he had handled a lot of packages during the shift, which he shouldn't have because he was management. I was sure somebody would file a grievance against him for it.

He leaned his forehead down on his arm resting on the dock as he listened to his phone briefly before his tone completely changed, switching from frantic production-obsessed management to what I imagined a lawyer sounded like.

"Let me be crystal clear. It is completely unacceptable for you to be discussing this with me, and you know it. Stay in your lane. You'll be hearing from my attorney."

Mind your business, Randy, I told myself and stood up, immediately smacking my head on an overhead support beam. My vision flashed and I found myself back on my hands and knees on the belt. I sat on my ass, touching my aching head. I was grateful to have fallen on the belt, and not over the side. I peered down at the concrete floor far below as I rubbed at the tender goose egg growing there. I waited for my vision to clear and listened to the usual sounds from the yard; honks of yard trucks backing up, clangs of metal on metal as they picked up and dropped off trailers. With a rumble, the wall shook as a trailer parked at the load door.

The buzz of Bryant's phone call abruptly stopped. Hand shaking, I grabbed the metal guard rail, rolled up onto my knees, and peered over the side. An empty trailer was parked at door 76, ready for the next shift. And there, shuddering, mouth moving silently, was Bryant pinned between the building and the trailer.

"Shit!" I grabbed my hat and crawled quickly to the crow's nest, my knees bruising on the metal. No time. I jumped onto the platform and hustled down the ladder as quickly as I dared. "Help!" I shouted out to the warehouse, hands sweaty inside my gloves. "Help! Shit."

My feet slapped on solid ground, and I ran over to door 76, climbed the short ladder to the dock grating, and knelt in front of Bryant. His mouth moved like a fish on dry land, eyes bulging, his arms extended in front of him stiffly, fingers plucking weakly at the grating.

Clenching my jaw, I leaned forward and peered down over the side of the dock. Sure enough, the trailer bumper was smashed into his back and the Mansfield bar pressed into the backs of his thighs, pinning him. His chest was pressed up against the rubber bumper on the outside of the building.

"Help! Door seventy-six! Help!" *Shit.*

His brown eyes began to flutter and roll back, and his arms fell limply onto the grating.

"Supe. Bryant. Hey."

He didn't respond. Using my teeth, I pulled off my glove and took his hand in mine. His eyes fluttered open, though his grip didn't respond to mine. I saw the remote microphone speaker for his walkie-talkie clipped to his collar and snatched it.

"I'm gonna use your radio to call for help, okay?"

I pressed the button on the side and a staticky sound come from somewhere below. He usually wore the radio clipped to his belt. I pressed the button down again and paused for a second as words escaped me.

"Hello. Hello. We have an emergency."

I released the button and waited. Nothing. I tried again.

"Emergency on door seventy-six. Does anyone hear me?"

Silence. Then a faint *click* and a voice. "Who is this?"

"Randy Cox is who this is. It doesn't matter. There's an emergency. We need an ambulance at door seventy-six. Bryant is pinned. Do you hear me?" I released the button.

"Did you say Bryant is pinned?"

"Jesus fuck! Yes! Call nine-one-one, numb nuts."

Within seconds, the morning shift office door burst open and there was the sound of boots sprinting toward us. I put down the radio mic and continued to hold Bryant's hand…the hand of a hardworking man and one of the few people in the company who had treated me with respect, rather than the usual indifference.

His body shuddered and foamy pink drool trickled from the corner of his mouth. His head lolled, eyes closed, his breath so impossibly shallow. And no wonder, his lungs had to be flattened under his crushed ribs and spine.

I murmured to him, stroking the top of his hand with my calloused thumb. "Bryant. Hang on, man. Help is coming."

I memorized the dirt under his fingernails and pressed into the creases of his skin. The frayed cuff of his sleeve. The color as it drained from his face. Then the moment was scattered as the other morning shift supervisors scrabbled up the ladder and flooded the grating with their frantic energy.

"Oh, shit, Bryant. Dude. You okay?" asked one as he squatted down on the grating, trying to push me out of the way. I hunkered down and held my grip, keeping Bryant's hand in mine.

The guy turned to me. He had a black smudge on his cheek and the same worn-in dirt on his clothes and hands as the rest of us. "What happened?"

"Do you really need to ask?" I said, motioning at Bryant's situation.

The fire station was literally a block away and sirens

had started up as they rolled out. There was also the sound of a truck racing through the yard toward us, its engine growling and tires screeching.

"Hey, you might want to radio to the yard truck and tell him not to hook up to the trailer yet," I said to the cluster of supes all staring at Bryant, their faces set in varying degrees of terror.

"What? Why the hell not?" grumbled the one closest to me.

"Because he is pinned, and his back is probably shattered. When the yard truck tries to hitch up to the trailer it will roll back more. Do you really want to crush him even more? Wait till the firefighters and paramedics get here. They will know the right way to do this."

"Huh. Yeah." He yanked the radio mic clipped to his own collar and began shouting into it to halt the yard truck driver, who had pulled up just outside.

Firetrucks drove right through the main bay door and into the warehouse. One of the supes hustled away to wave them down. The supes cleared out and made way for the paramedics, but I stayed where I was, not yet willing to let go of Bryant's hand.

A highly polished boot and perfectly creased navy-blue pant leg stopped next to me. "Sir, I need you to back away and give us some room."

I craned my head up, realizing that some tears had silently slipped down my cheeks, and met the eye of the paramedic.

He flinched and cleared his throat. "I'm sorry. I mean ma'am, can you please give us some space here."

A firefighter was already on his belly on the grating, his arm shoved down between the wall and the trailer.

"Sure." Reluctantly, I released Bryant's hand, stood, and backed down the short ladder to the floor. I headed for the time clock, but it didn't feel right to leave. I watched the flurry of activity by door 76 and numbly remembered that I had left my travel mug up in the crow's nest, so I walked back over there and started the long climb when one of the firefighters turned and saw. He called out to me and came down from the dock.

"Sir...I mean, ma'am, I am going to have to ask you to please come down from there. The police will be here any second, and they will want the scene undisturbed."

"No problem. I just left my travel mug up there. That's my workstation. Can I go grab it?"

"No. Please don't touch anything."

Everything closed in on me and nausea rose in my belly. I drew in a deep breath and closed my eyes.

"Ma'am, I think the police are going to want to talk to you. Why don't you come sit over here?"

He steered me toward the rear bumper of the fire department's paramedic rig and I sat on it; my knees throbbed and my legs had grown weak, so I was grateful. Police cars pulled into the warehouse and parked three abreast, so no other vehicles could get in or out. I watched as one officer took some yellow tape and roped off the entry area including the pedestrian door and the big bay door. I blew out a breath and rubbed the sore spot on my scalp.

The firefighter standing next to me bounced his leg and kept snapping his head in the direction of his crew. I leaned forward and looked past him to see for myself. The trailer was still parked, and between a few sets of legs, I caught glimpses of Bryant. His skin was gray, his eyes closed, neck and arms limp.

"Why the heck haven't they pulled him out of there yet?"

"It's a delicate process, with not so delicate equipment. They are trying to figure out how to pull the trailer off the door without it jostling him."

"Jostling. Sure. Well, that means he is alive still then, right?"

"So far."

I heard the uneven click of high heels on concrete. I turned and saw Shelly, the Human Resources manager, and an entourage of other suits trying to bypass the yellow caution tape and police cars. A police officer blocked her path and wouldn't let her or any of the other corporate stuffed suits pass. I watched as she spoke with the officer for quite some time, but the cop wouldn't yield.

At my side there was some murmuring between a cop in a suit and the firefighter who'd been standing with me. They both paused and looked down at me. I met their gaze with what I hoped was a rock-solid glare. All I gave a shit about was them helping Bryant, and I didn't feel like sitting around waiting for the cops to decide to talk to me.

"Hey. Officer." I stood, my legs still wobbly.

He turned to me. "Yes?"

Holy crap, this guy is massive. He was easily six foot five and looked to have spent plenty of time injecting steroids and lifting enormous piles of iron. The collar of his dress shirt was so tight around his tree trunk of a neck that I thought the button might explode at any moment.

"Am I being detained? Because if I am, can you please give me some info on my status here? And if not, may I leave?"

He paused, and I figured he was trying to use that trick I'd seen on TV where if they are quiet long enough, you'll blurt out something that might be important. Well, I wasn't gonna fall into that trap. I crossed my arms and waited. The firefighter shifted and scratched his neck.

"No, you are not being detained. But depending on what happens today we may want to speak with you."

"Great," I said and immediately took a step around him, intending to go clock out.

"Hang on. Hang on. I need some information first."

I paused and turned to him, casting another glance at Bryant. Nothing had changed. "Jesus Christ! Would you guys get him out of there already?"

The young firefighter blanched for just a moment. "It's a delicate process" was all he said.

"That kid is suffering," I grumbled and turned back to the cop, annoyed.

"So, uh…" He gave me a once-over, his eyes narrowing for a moment. "Ma'am?"

I nodded.

"Your name, please."

"Miranda Cox. But I go by Randy."

"Contact information and address of your residence?"

I gave him my cell number, email address, and home address. He scribbled it all down in a notepad that was tiny in his massive paws.

"ID card, please."

I frowned at him.

"Whaddya need that for? I don't think I need an ID on me to stand here."

"ID, please." He held out his hand and I decided to give in, since my concern was for Bryant. I loved messing with the cops as much as the next guy but recognized that the time wasn't right for it. I dug my wallet out of my back pocket and handed him my ratty old driver's license.

He handed the ID to a uniformed cop who had joined us. No doubt he was going to run me for warrants and whatnot. I had none, so I stood and waited, watching the paramedics hover around Bryant, who was hooked up to several devices and appeared to have an IV in, delivering some sort of fluids in a bag. In that moment I was grateful Bryant was unconscious, because I could not imagine the agony he would have been in had he been awake.

Eventually, the cop returned and handed my ID back to me. He whispered in the big cop's ear and walked off.

"Okay, Miss Cox, you are free to go. But…what you saw today, you are not to discuss with the press, your employer, or anybody else, for that matter. I will follow up with you later."

"Okay. Oh, hey." I jabbed my thumb up toward the

crow's nest. "I left my travel mug up there. I am sure one of your guys will find it if you do an investigation. It's fine if you need to keep it, I just wanted to let you know that it's mine, so there isn't some big hunt later trying to solve the mystery of the mug."

We looked deadpan at each other. I shrugged at him, thanked the firefighter, and clocked out. A line of company suits stood across the bay from me, behind the yellow tape. They all watched me go and murmured to each other. I imagined the public relations and safety shit storms that were brewing. It wouldn't take OSHA long to get wind of what had happened either. And the highway patrol would probably show up since they regulated the company's Class A drivers, which the yard truck guy was.

What a mess.

I ducked under the yellow police tape and passed through the pedestrian door to the painted pathway. The front gate was closed and there were easily a hundred people lined up outside the chain-link fence, gawking, trying to see what was going on inside. I recognized most of them as the next shift's crew. I opened the door to the guard shack.

"Hey, Gus," I said to the afternoon guard as I emptied my pockets into the basket and lifted my jacket to show my waistband. There wasn't a metal detector on the way out, but they still wanted to half-assedly be sure we weren't stealing packages or company property when we left.

"Hey, Randy. What's goin' on in there?"

"Bad accident. I'm not allowed to talk about it though."

"Yikes. I'm hearing all kinda rumors. Like that some-body fell off the belt and broke their neck. Or somebody got their arm ripped off in the belt motor gears. And some-body else said one of the electricians got hisself killed and his arm exploded by touching one of them high-powered fuses or something."

"Nah. Something else."

"Hm."

I jammed my wallet and stuff back into my pockets and left. As I pushed open the door, I was mobbed by guys from the next shift. They peppered me with questions, but

I put my chin down and pushed my way through them until the crowd petered out and I made it to my truck. Slamming the door, I let out a big breath.

A van from the local news station rolled by on the main road and parked across from the guard station. I shook my head, glad I had made it out before they had arrived. Exhaustion hit me and I took a moment to let it be, though my gaze wandered to the rusted chain-link fence, then through it to the yard until my eyes came to rest on door 76, the trailer parked there, just like all the other doors. But I knew Bryant was fighting for his life in that exact spot.

Crying wasn't something I did much, but my throat was thick and my eyes got hot. I rubbed away the tears and flipped down the sun visor. A pack of smokes landed in the palm of my hand. I shook one free and ran it under my nose, inhaling the nutty scent of tobacco and paper. I had been cutting back and had been good about only smoking a couple of times a day. I pressed in the cigarette lighter on my dashboard and waited, my brain spinning, until the lighter popped. Cigarette between my lips, I pulled the searing hot lighter from the dash and was about to light my smoke, mouth already watering for that first drag, when someone knocked on the window.

Turning, I saw a man standing outside my truck. I put the lighter back in the dash, tucked the filter of the unlit smoke up under the band of my beanie, and used the hand crank to roll my window down.

"Randy, right?"

"Yeah, Dwight, what's up?"

Dwight worked the second shift and was one of the shop stewards for the union.

"I dunno what happened in there, but word has it you're involved."

"Involved." I let the word roll off my tongue, weighing it.

"What can you tell me?"

"Nothing."

"Who is hurt?"

"Can't say."

"Seriously? You're siding with management?" He bumped his fist on the roof of my truck.

My blood warmed at the accusation. "No, man. It's the cops who told me not to say anything. So, for now I'm gonna play ball. And just so you can stop worrying, the person who had the accident and is fighting for their life in there is not in our union, but the person who probably caused the accident, is. Good luck with that." *Dick.*

He let out a sigh and pushed up the edge of his beanie to scratch his forehead. I rolled my window up as he considered that tidbit. I jammed the key into the ignition and gave it a turn. The engine fired up and Dwight stepped away as I backed out and pulled carefully from the lot. Workers were spilling from the sidewalk out onto the street, locked out and not sure what to do.

Dusk was falling and it was spitting drizzle. Traffic at the toll booths was backed up, but the FasTrak lanes were flowing smoothly, my toll token beeping as I sped under the sensors and up onto the bridge, which arched up high and gave panoramic views of the Marshtown Strait, the bluffs, and the Marshtown Bridge in the distance.

As I reached my exit it was finally settling in that I was shaken by what had happened to Bryant and going home was the last thing I wanted to do. I drove down to the water, spotting several anglers, but none with Darcy's posture or orange backpack. I drove farther down to another spot I knew was good for fishing, and there she was, away from the parking lot and far from the other anglers.

I wound down the window just a little and finally lit my cigarette, drawing in the smoke as the tobacco and paper crackled. The taste lay thick on my tongue as I blew smoke out of the window and watched a cormorant dive bomb the water.

I looked back down the waterline to where Darcy had been fishing, but she was gone. I scanned the beach and rocks, but there was no sign of her. Hopefully she was walking home and not going for another unscheduled swim. As I exhaled, a pang spread in my chest, which I thumped with my fist, and I started my truck. I stopped at a drive thru for a burger and fries on the way home.

As expected, Porkchop was beside himself and piled on the drama as soon as I opened the door. Howling, he wove between my legs as I walked to my chair and sat heavily, where I unlaced my boots and kicked them off.

Porkchop threw himself on the floor and began a rapid series of meows, telling me off the way a squirrel chatters down at a pesky human.

"Oh my gawd, Porky, you are ridiculous." I stood slowly, using the arms of the chair to push myself up. As I bent over and poured kibble into his dish, he started eating before I could finish, and half of the kibble bounced off the top of his head and scattered on the floor.

"Dummy."

I washed my hands and put on an old U2 record before sitting down with a tall glass of beer and my dinner. I flattened the burger wrapper and squelched out a pile of ketchup on one corner. I scarfed down the burger and fries, not tasting any of it. Some animal part of my brain kicked in and it was just about getting the food in my mouth as quickly as I could.

After finishing dinner, I sat back, sipped on the beer, and hummed along to the familiar songs, pushing away all my worried thoughts about Bryant.

As much as I tried to ignore it, I was both nauseated and still hungry. Hungry like I hadn't even eaten yet. I got up and opened cupboards and the fridge, looking for something easy and quick. I stood over the sink and ate leftover bami, forking it into my mouth mechanically. Next, I opened the freezer and spotted a box of pumpkin pie flavored ice cream sandwiches. I ate two of them, hunched over the sink.

"Enough," I said to myself, grabbing my glass of beer and slumping in the recliner. Porkchop hopped onto my lap and circled around a few times before finally settling down.

The minute he got comfortable I realized I couldn't sit still. Unsettled was an understatement. But I forced myself to sit there and finish my beer. Porkchop was disagreeable about my bouncing leg and tapping toes and told me so.

Draining the last of the beer, I shifted Porkchop so that after I stood up, he was still comfortably on the chair, minus a warm lap. I turned off the record player and switched on the TV. I flipped around the channels as I stood in front of the screen but couldn't concentrate on anything.

I put the disc for *Jeremiah Johnson* in the DVD player and sat on the love seat. I called Porkchop over, but he gave me a dismissive *prrbttt* and settled back into his napping position on the chair.

I tried to force myself to watch the movie and push away thoughts of what had happened. Screams kept rising in my throat, but I didn't let them out. I fantasized about breaking things or getting hammered and passing out in a drunken stupor. All things I would have done in the past to dull my feelings. But, no more. My fifty-third birthday had been the day I chose to knock that shit off, and to change by accepting myself as I was and not making excuses to anybody.

And sure enough, I eventually fell asleep on the love seat. I woke briefly when the first disc ended for intermission. I shut the house down and stumbled to bed, not even bothering to get out of my filthy work clothes.

*

MY ALARM WENT off at 2:00 a.m., bringing me out of a foggy dream about snakes. I picked up my cell phone and the screen lit up, nearly blinding me. I dialed the call-in number for work. It rang nineteen times before someone answered.

The person who answered grumbled two words. "Pre-load office."

"Hey. This is Randy Cox; I won't be in today."

"Whut? Why?"

"I don't have to tell you why. I only have to tell you I won't be in. The union contract says I have to call in at least one hour before my shift starts, and that's what I am doing."

"No, no. We need you here up in the crow's nest splitting."

"Sorry. I am not coming in today."

"Randy. Dude. You're the only one who can do it right. We'll end up with a bunch of missorts and misloads. And it's a clusterfuck here because one whole load wall is shut down by the cops."

"Hey man, that's not my problem. Cross-train your people better. Bye."

I hung up, annoyed…and awake. So much for sleeping in. It was chilly in my room, so I pulled the comforter up to my chin and watched the shadows of tree branches dance across the ceiling. Rain pelted the window, wind gusted, and real tears finally fell.

Seeing Bryant pinned there had shaken me to the core and reminded me that not being vigilant about safety for one second could end it all. While I didn't talk to anybody at work much, I had heard Bryant speaking with pride about his new baby daughter at home.

Will he ever hold his baby again?

Staring at the ceiling, I listened to the rain and cried for Bryant. And then I slept.

Chapter Three

Corporate Policy

SURFACING FROM A deep sleep, my thoughts muddled, I rubbed my eyes. I had no idea what time it was, or even what day it was. Outside the sky was gray and judging by the shadows it was late afternoon.

I padded down the chilly hallway and used the toilet before going to the kitchen and turning on the coffee maker. Friends had teased me before about how I could drink coffee at any time of day. It didn't matter whether I drank it at 4:00 a.m. or 9:00 p.m., it didn't do anything to keep me awake. Drinking it was just out of habit and because I liked the taste.

The cat door flapped, as Porkchop came inside. I raced him to his food dish and dumped in some kibble before he could read me the Riot Act. He crunched away happily, purring as he ate.

The smell of coffee bloomed in the kitchen. Impatient, and before it even had finished brewing, I splashed some half and half into a mug, poured in some coffee, and topped it off with sugar.

Leaning my hip against the counter, I listened to voice mails and read a handful of text messages. In my voice mail I had a message from the tree-trunk-necked police officer I had dealt with the day before. Apparently, his name was Sergeant Cleese. There were also calls from the union and work. I had one text from Darcy:

I'm off at 4. Dinner tonight?

I smiled. Spending time with a friend was exactly what

I wanted to do. But I decided I should call Cleese first. I took a sip of coffee, burning my lips and tongue, and hit the button to call him back.

"This is Sergeant Cleese." His voice was gruff and gravelly. He sounded tired.

"Hi, sergeant. This is Randy… Miranda Cox, returning your call."

There was some shuffling of papers, and he cleared his throat. "Ah. Yes. Miss Cox. I wanted to set up a time to talk to you about the incident at your work yesterday."

"Sure. I work tomorrow from three to one. I can meet after that."

"I need to talk to you today."

It was already late in the day, and I wasn't interested in being bossed around by a cop. I'd had enough bad inter-actions with law enforcement in my early twenties when they had busted up private lesbian parties, not to mention all the times I'd been picked up for fighting. I poked at Porkchop with my toe, sipped on my coffee, and made the sergeant wait.

Eventually I relented. "Sure. Where should I meet

you?"

"Why don't I swing by your place. Make it easier on you."

Fuck no. I didn't want an investigator in my house. I had nothing to hide but didn't want him sticking his nose around the place either.

I decided to fib. "I'm actually about to head into Marshtown to run an errand. Why don't I just swing by your office?"

"Yeah. Sure."

He gave me directions on how to get there and where to park. Afterward, I shuffled around getting ready, not rushing. I changed out of the filthy work clothes I had slept in and put on some fresh jeans and a hoodie, ate a granola bar and finished my coffee, then brushed my teeth. I texted Darcy back, apologizing that I couldn't meet up.

It was barely five o'clock, but it was already getting dark, and the drizzly weather had stuck around. As soon as I got on the bridge, I realized it was evening rush hour. I hated traffic. Avoiding it was one of the perks of working the early shift. So, whether the freeway was like a parking lot, or I got stuck crawling along as it took five cycles of a stop light to cross one damn intersection, it made me mad.

I was nice and grumpy by the time I reached the neighborhood where Cleese's office was. I parked a few blocks away because I needed the walk to clear my head, and I didn't want to park in a law enforcement lot, which was no doubt covered in those closed-circuit video cameras, logging every car.

Big Brother can kiss my ass.

Striding along the damp sidewalk, hands tucked into the front pocket of my hoodie, I breathed in the rotten egg stink of the refinery and stepped over a stray high-top sneaker.

At his office building, I found the lobby to be standard issue worn-down public building, painted that specific shade of beige most old government facilities seemed to use. The walls were filthy from years of people leaning on them; scuffed-up tile floors; rows of chairs with stained seats, and of course, the bulletproof glass window with an annoyed clerk behind it.

I stood next to a pedestal with a sign that said: "Wait

here until called forward." Black footprints were painted on the floor, showing me exactly where to stand. The clerk had her head down, the sound of a keyboard clacking away. Eventually she looked up, saw me, and waved me over, her lips pinched.

"State your business," she said, her eyes cold as pebbles as she adjusted her bra strap through her uniform shirt.

"Good evening. I have an appointment with Sergeant Cleese."

Without a word, she pointed to the row of chairs. I didn't feel like sitting, so I stood at the end of the row and leaned against the wall to wait. The clerk went back to her typing, a stray clutch of hair coming loose from her bun as she tilted her head down.

Several low, murmured conversations took place around the lobby. The types of conversations people had when a loved one was locked up, and they were trying to figure out how to post bail for the first time.

Across the lobby a woman with wild hair and filthy clothes cradled a phone handset to her ear. She kept trying to pace, but was tethered by the phone cord, so she had to stay put, and did a jig in one spot instead. Before long, her voice grew louder and louder, until she was shrieking.

The clerk peered through the glass at her, unphased, and spoke into a radio. Two uniformed officers emerged from a corridor and framed the woman in between themselves and the wall. She shrieked at them too, total gibberish at that point.

"Come on, Carlene, let's go outside and get some air," one of the officers said as they each grabbed an arm and steered her toward the lobby doors. She kicked at nothing in particular as they made their way across the room. One of her grubby shoes came off, and an officer booted it along ahead of them as they went. It was similar to watching animal control try to get a feral cat into a crate. Carlene was going to be put outside, but she wasn't going to make it easy on them.

Good job, Carlene.

The lobby fell back into unsettled murmurs once the trio had made it outside. The phone receiver Carlene had been using dangled from its cord and I watched it sway, resisting the urge to pull out my cell phone and scroll through Facebook or Instagram.

Sergeant Cleese called out to me from the corridor, and I followed his bulk through a series of hallways before ending up in a small conference room. I was glad to see he hadn't brought me to one of their actual interview rooms. I had a small fear about something going horribly sideways and him arresting me while I was there.

"Have a seat," he said as he shut the door.

I did as I was told, settling into an old threadbare office chair. He sat across the narrow table from me. I wondered if the chair would be able to hold his mass. He was even more humongous in the little room than he had been the other day at the warehouse.

His thick fingers flipped through a packet of papers, his hands massive, veiny, and calloused. Same as the day before, the button at the collar of his dress shirt threatened to pop off and put my eye out. His face and neck were the kind of red when someone is an alcoholic or has high blood pressure. The kind of red that means unhealthy. I wondered if he used steroids, and how he found suits to fit over his muscles. I figured being that huge couldn't be of much use to a police officer. He certainly wouldn't be fast enough to chase down somebody, and probably barely fit in a patrol car. *Window dressing.*

As I sat there, waiting for him to get started, acid gurgled up the back of my throat and my eyes grew hot. I thought back to the last time I was questioned by an investigator. Just a small girl in a jumper and saddle shoes, chubby legs so short my feet didn't touch the floor. Just a small girl who had to tell a terrible story about how she lost her dad.

Dad.

I cleared my throat, swallowing down the tears and stomach acid, putting back on the tough blustery front I had used most of my life.

Finally, Cleese seemed to get settled and cleared his throat.

"Miss...uh—" he flipped through his notepad. "Miss Cox. I would like for you to walk me through your shift yesterday. Then I'll have some follow-up questions."

I walked him through everything that had happened

at work leading up to Bryant's accident. He scribbled down notes with a silver pen. His handwriting looked like nothing but upside-down chicken scratch to me. I peeked again and saw that he was using shorthand.

Holy crap, who uses shorthand anymore?

"Would you like some water?" he asked.

"No, thank you." I had seen enough crime shows to know that was how cops stole your DNA for their case. I wasn't about to just hand it over to them. *Pfft.*

"Okay. So, it sounds like you were in the area, but didn't see the actual incident as it happened? Is that correct?"

"That's right."

"Was Bryant wearing a safety vest?"

Nope, he certainly was not. "I don't recall."

"Did he place a safety cone out in the yard to alert yard staff to his presence?"

Nope. "I have no idea. I was up in the rafters, remember."

"Do you know who he was talking to on the phone?"

"No."

"What was he saying?"

"It was the usual stuff I hear supes yell about all the time. Process flow and package counts." I left out the other part.

"What is your impression of Bryant as a person?"

"He is one of the only supervisors there who treats staff with respect. He has a newborn baby he is proud of. He is a hard worker, and he cares. Beyond that I don't know much."

"Did you spend any time with him outside of work?"

"No."

"Do you know anything about the yard truck driver who parked the trailer?"

"I have no idea who was driving. You'll need to check with dispatch or the supervisor for that crew."

"Does Bryant have any enemies? Anyone who would want to do him harm?"

"Not that I am aware of." I rubbed my thumb against my bottom lip. "Do you think someone crushed Bryant on purpose?"

Sergeant Cleese, not blinking, shifted his eyes slowly

from mine to his notepad, and spoke down at the table.

"These are just the standard questions. Nothing to concern yourself with."

Liar.

If anything got under my skin, it was liars. I realized I was picking at my cuticles and forced myself to put my hands in my lap, stop fidgeting, and keep my mouth shut.

Sergeant Cleese shuffled his papers again.

"So, Miss uh…" He looked down at his notepad again.

Jesus Christ, how does he not remember my name?

"Miss Cox. Do you own a cell phone?"

"Yes."

"And did you have it with you at the time you discovered Bryant pinned?"

"Yes."

"How did you call for help?"

"When I first found him, I shouted out into the warehouse. Sound carries and the machinery was all shut down, so the guys in the office should have been able to hear me. Once I got to Bryant, nobody had come out, so I used his radio to call the other supervisors."

He leaned back in his chair and rubbed at his earlobe for a moment. His suit jacket fell open and I saw the butt of his service pistol on his hip.

"Why didn't you use your cell phone to call nine-one-one immediately?"

"Corporate policy. Staff aren't allowed to call nine-one-one. We have to get management to do it, especially if it's medical."

Still leaning back in his chair, he used his silver pen to itch his scalp just above his ear. The short hair made a gritty sound.

"Hm. You can't call nine-one-one?"

"Nope."

"Corporate policy?"

"Yes."

"Can you get me a copy of that policy?"

"Talk to Human Resources."

"Okay. I know how to get ahold of her. Shelly, right?"

"Yeah, Shelly uh…Barstow, I think."

The chair creaked as he leaned forward and scribbled

down a note. "Okay, so can you at least tell me your understanding of the policy, the part about why staff aren't allowed to call nine-one-one?"

"It's because we have an on-site medical clinic. So only management or the clinic staff can make the decision to call for an ambulance, or not."

"Did the on-site medical clinic staff show up?"

"I didn't see any of them. It was just other morning shift supervisors, police, and paramedics there. I saw a bunch of management suits outside the police tape, but that's it."

"Who did you speak with after the incident?"

"Hm. The supervisors who came running out once I got them on the radio. I think it was Marco, Jamison, and Juan. The paramedics, I didn't catch their names. The evening shift security guard, Gus. A shop steward named Dwight. And you. I didn't tell anybody any details, but those are people I talked with during and after."

"Anybody else?"

"Nope."

"Anything else coming to mind that you think I should

know?"

"No."

He wrote the case number on his business card and slid it across the table. "If something does come to mind, give me a call or shoot me an email. Okay?"

"Sure," I said as I put his card in my back pocket.

He walked me back through the labyrinth of hallways to the lobby.

"Thanks for coming down today," he said, not offering me a handshake.

"Sure."

*

THE LOBBY WAS far more crowded than it had been earlier, and smelled of weed, unwashed bodies, and coffee. I had to pee, but wanted to get out of there, so I wove through the lobby and out through the glass doors to the sidewalk.

A gust of chill wind hit me, and I pulled up my hood, snugging my shoulders up nearly to my ears. Grit crunched under my boots on the sidewalk, and the stink of refinery sulfur and low tide hung in the air. It was already dark out, there was only a handful of functioning street-lights, so I squared up my shoulders and balled my hands up into fists in my front pocket.

My grumbling stomach sent me on a detour, cutting over a block to the main drag, and pulling open the glass and chrome door of my favorite barbecue joint. The place was warm, crowded, and filled with the welcoming smells of roasting meats and garlic. My mouth watered as I stood in line. I ordered a pulled pork sandwich with extra sauce, a side of coleslaw, and an Arnold Palmer, then used the re-stroom and found an open stool at a counter along the wall.

Most of the tables were full of workers from the nearby refineries. They were easy to spot because they wore cov-eralls, knee-high rubber boots, and had name badges sewn to their breast pockets next to the company logo. A couple of other tables were full of longshoreman from the Marsh-town port. I felt at home surrounded by them since I had spent my whole adult life working shoulder to shoulder with guys like that. I knew what to expect from them.

I was sure if I went to that same restaurant during daylight on a weekday the place would be full of people in suits and ties from the nearby government buildings, the types of people who made me uncomfortable.

My meal arrived and I dug in. The sauce on the sandwich was sweet and spicy, the meat tender, and the bun melted in my mouth. The coleslaw had just the right amount of vinegar and wasn't overdressed. I leaned into the meal, not giving a damn about table manners. That was the good thing about those sorts of places; nobody cared. I could be myself, mostly. Course, not everybody knew what to think about being around a big ole butch dyke. But that was their problem and hopefully, they didn't make it mine too.

Once I had cleaned my plate and finished my drink, I bussed the dishes and headed back out into the cold. Carlene, the lady from the police station, was somewhere nearby shrieking gibberish that echoed through the darkened downtown blocks.

I got back to my truck and drove by the stink and blight of the refineries, grateful I didn't work there. Sure, I probably would have made more money and had a better pension, but it wasn't worth it to me to work in a place where it could blow up at any second and you're surrounded by chemicals and fumes all day. I was happy working a conveyor belt and moving packages.

*

AS I PULLED into my driveway, everything came back to me, and I realized I hadn't asked the sergeant the one question I had been holding on to. I pulled out my cell phone and his rumpled card from my pocket and dialed with a shaky finger.

"This is Cleese."

"Hi, sergeant. This is Miranda Cox. I just met with you about my supervisor Bryant being pinned by a trailer at my work." I felt like I needed to give him an intro since he seemed to always struggle with my name.

"Yes?"

"Do you know if Bryant is okay?"

A chair creaked through the phone, followed by the scratch of stubble. I imagined him leaning back in his chair.

He cleared his throat and spoke. "He did not survive his injuries."

My hand shook on the wheel and my stomach dropped. "Oh." Mouth flooding, I hung up, opened my truck door, and threw up my dinner in the flower bed.

Chapter Four

Nickel and Diming

ARRIVING AT WORK early, I was glad to see that the night shift had wrapped up on time, which meant I didn't have to park in the boondocks. I walked through damp fog, under the floodlights, and stood in line at the guard station in the freezing drizzle. I shuffled up slowly until it was my turn. I kept my hood up and nobody seemed to notice me until I got inside and numbly dumped my pockets into the basket.

"Hiya, Randy," Granny said.

"Howdy, Granny. How're you?"

"I'm good. We missed ya yesterday."

"Hmph," I grunted as I shuffled through the metal de-tector, setting off its shrill beep. I lifted the front of my jacket and shirt to show her my belt buckle and she waved me through, not bothering to wand me down. She slid the basket and my spare travel mug down the counter to me and I started putting things back into my pockets.

"There's a lot of buzz about you around here."

While curious, I didn't want to listen to a bunch of gos-sip. I shrugged my shoulders at her. "You hear it all, I bet."

"Sure do," she said, clicking her tongue.

"Have a good day, Granny."

"You too, Randy." She turned toward the line of peo-ple behind me. "Next!"

My gut tightened as I walked over to door 76 and climbed the ladder up into the dizzying heights of the raft-ers. Once safely up top, I unzipped my jacket and pulled my travel mug out from where I had tucked it. I took a long sip to chase away the sudden urge to go home.

People on the dock below were hustling around preparing for the shift. Pallets slammed down on the concrete floor, a *clang clang clang* as the conveyor chutes were lowered down and the *whoosh as* roll-up doors were raised, revealing the dark mouths of empty trailers waiting to be filled.

The buzzer went off directly overhead and I jumped, nearly dropping my mug. I put in my earplugs, settled my glasses on my nose, and checked the sheet of zip codes clipped above my station. It was a split I was familiar with, so I didn't have to study it long.

My eyes flicked back down to the dock below. There was a shadowy image of Bryant, pinned, his head bowed down on the grating, arms stretched out, twitching. A loader hustled past the spot and Bryant was gone.

Boxes came my way at a steady pace, and I mechanically pushed and pulled them to where they needed to go. As the morning wore on and the package flow grew thicker, my stomach became unsettled and acidic as my chest tightened. Normally comfy under my layers of clothes, instead I felt feverish as my ears burned and my thoughts jumped around without landing anywhere. I worried that I was coming down with something.

I did my best to stay focused on the zip codes and splitting the packages to the right places, while trying to figure out what was going on with me. The closest thing I could tie it to was when I sometimes felt nervous. But I told myself I didn't have anything to be nervous about. So, I gnawed on the *why* of it until the buzzer blew and the machinery stopped for break.

I climbed down the ladder and flipped my hood up as I took the usual route across the warehouse to use the toilet. I wasn't much interested in talking to anyone, not that I had many pals at work, but hiding in my hood helped with whatever it was I was feeling. I walked past clusters of exhausted, filthy young men slouching on the docks drinking from tall cans of energy drinks and eating junk food.

I made it to the bathroom, did my business, and thawed my hands out under the hot water at the sink. Shouldering my way out the door, I pulled a crinkly silver packet of s'mores flavored Pop-Tarts from my pocket and ate them while I walked. Being that it was just before sunrise, the temperature in the warehouse had dropped, and I shivered, zipping my jacket up.

Leaning against the ladder below my station, I finished off my snack, the chilled concrete and icy metal of the ladder blooming through my boots and pants. I crumpled the Pop-Tart wrapper, tossed it into the trash, and started climbing back up to the crow's nest. The sounds around me picked up as people got moving again, going back to their stations as the two-minute warning buzzer blipped. Over the sounds of chatter, boots on grating, and pallets being dragged, came the sharp sound of heels clicking. That caught my attention because it was so rare on our side of the warehouse. The load area was far away from the management offices.

A woman's voice spoke, but I didn't pay any attention to it. The voice came again, louder. I stopped and tossed a glance down, always a bad idea when up on a ladder that high. I gripped the rungs tightly in my hands as I swooned for just a second while the ground below spun. I blinked a few times to clear my eyes. When I opened them again, I saw Shelly Barstow standing directly under me, which was stupid of her. A hand reached out, grasped Shelly's arm gently, and pulled her a few steps away so she was in a safer spot.

I was about to continue climbing when Shelly pointed directly at me and shouted again. I still had earplugs in so I couldn't make out what she was saying.

"I have earplugs in," I hollered down at her. I was about to point at my ears but didn't want to let go of the ladder. Her lips pursed and she motioned at me to come down.

What the fuck does she want? I grumbled and made my way back down to the concrete floor. As soon as I turned to face her, she stepped up close to me. Too close. I tried to move back but was blocked in by the ladder, so I side-stepped, pulled out my earplugs, and looked at Shelly with a raised eyebrow, readying myself for whatever management nonsense she was about to throw at me.

"Hi. Miranda. I'm Shelly." She stuck out a rigid hand at me and I shook it, not taking off my filthy work glove.

"It's Randy. And we've met."

"Ah, well… Randy. I am sure you can imagine how many people I have to keep track of, so if we have met before I apologize." She gave an insincere grin that didn't reach her gray eyes and smoothed her matching gray skirt.

The buzzer went off far overhead, causing her to jump. I chuckled.

"Nice to meet you, again. I have to get back to work," I said, pointing a thumb up at the crow's nest and turning to the ladder.

Through my thick jacket, I felt a strong hand on my shoulder. Rage boiled up inside me out of nowhere. *Don't fucking touch me.* I turned to her, biting back my anger. "Please do not touch me, Shelly. Was there something else?"

She dropped her hand to her side. "Yes. I need you to come with me, please."

"What for?"

Her eyes narrowed. I bet as the human resources manager the line staff didn't question her much.

"It's not something I can discuss out on the floor. Please, come with me." She motioned toward the side of the building where the management and executive offices were, what us hourlies called the "Golden Aisle."

I wasn't a frequent flyer when it came to the disciplinary process, but I had gone to enough union meetings to know what my rights were, and to know that whatever Shelly wanted to talk to me about could mean my ass was in trouble. I had to let her know from the get-go that I wasn't going to let her walk all over me.

"In that case, I am enacting my Weingarten Rights, and request to have a union rep present."

Shelly clenched her jaw, her lips in a tight smile. "That won't be necessary. What I want to talk to you about isn't something that would result in discipline."

I shoved my hands in my pockets and squared up to her, holding her gaze. The safety manager, who still hadn't said a word, squirmed next to Shelly.

The belts were moving again, and I knew that packages were flowing past my workstation untouched. The sorters further down the line began yelling in protest and calling out my name.

"Randy! Ran-nan-a-day-dayyy!" I looked up briefly

and saw them shouting playfully, grins on their faces.

I met her gaze again. She crinkled her brow as she considered her options. A *clonk* of boots came down the short ladder from the dock, followed by grumbling and cussing. A man's voice approached behind me.

"What the *fuck,* Randy? Why aren't you at your station? Packages are going to the wrong doors. You're missing your splits. Get up there, goddammit."

I turned and saw Justin, the supervisor who was taking Bryant's place for the day, stomping up to me. I gave him a *this is bullshit* expression and held out a hand, trying to show that Shelly was the hold-up. "I'm trying. Talk to Shelly, dude."

Justin and Shelly went back and forth a bit. Shelly repeatedly insisted on pulling me out while the operation was running, and Justin held firm that there was no one available to take my place, and he needed me up top, working. Eventually Justin won out and I was released to go back to my station.

Shelly turned to me. "I will send someone to get you at the end of your shift. Wait for them right here."

"Just a reminder, I want a union rep present."

Visibly miffed, Shelly stormed off toward her office, the safety manager following in her wake.

What the fuck is her problem?

The nervousness—I didn't know what else to call it—which had shrunk back during my talk with Shelly came back and stuck with me for the rest of my shift. One thing I liked about my job was that, even though it was boring and physically demanding, it was pretty mellow. I wouldn't say I actually enjoyed my job, but I didn't mind it either. What I did mind was being upset about Bryant and then having Shelly up my ass.

Eventually, the machinery shut down and I walked out the belt. I found a few small packages stuck in a seam where two belts merged. I handed them off to Justin, then stood by my ladder for about five minutes, waiting for whoever was supposed to take me to Shelly. No one came.

Justin shouted at me. "What the hell, Randy. You're not approved for overtime. Go clock out and leave."

I shrugged my shoulders and did as I was told.

*

ON THE WAY home, I stopped at the grocery store up the street from my house and got a box of beef stroganoff mix and a pound of ground beef to go in it. I also got coffee filters, toilet paper, and beer.

Aside from missing rush hour, another perk of working the early shift was grocery shopping in the afternoon after the lunch rush, but before the schools got out. No crowds blocking aisles or making me rush to pick something.

The customer service at that store was always terrible, not to mention the place was cluttered, and the produce, dairy, and meat were usually a few days past their prime. I knew I had to sniff the meat and check expiration dates before putting things in my basket.

Even though it was a big chain grocery store, the one in Lands End was bleak and seemed to have gone rogue. The staff, without fail, seemed to hate every second of their job. Not that I was the type of customer who needed to be waited on hand and foot, not at all, but even my low standards for customer service were not met.

Though, on that day, it was a customer who was behaving badly. A man the next aisle over was bragging about his boat, then about his recent mountain biking trip, then invited himself to a party the lady he was talking to was shopping for. As the guys at work would have said, he was a real douche canoe. I rolled my eyes hard and headed to the checkout line. Somehow that jackass got there before me and cooed to the checker.

"Hey, Carly. Carlyyy."

Carly ignored him and rang up his items with a straight face.

"You got a man at home, Carly? I know just how to take care of you, Carly. I got just what you neeed."

She continued to ignore him, but the rest of us in line grew uncomfortable, shifting our feet and shaking our heads at each other. As the dirtbag continued harassing the young checker, the nervousness I had been pushing down at work bloomed into anger. *Who the fuck is he to talk to her like that?*

I wanted to step up and looked to Carly to see if she was putting out any signs that she wanted help, but she bagged up his groceries as if he wasn't even there. The guy swiped his debit card, got his receipt, and tossed a few gross comments over his shoulder as he left.

Moving up to the register, I didn't quite know what to say, but needed to say something. "Do uh…do you know that guy?"

She looked at me, surprised to find me standing in front of her. She started running my items across the scanner.

"Kinda. I used to work at another grocery store over in Valle and he would always come to my check stand and do that. Then I moved stores, and he started shopping here. Today wasn't too bad. He's said way worse things than that."

"Jesus, what a creep."

She nodded, her face still flat and unperturbed. "Did you find everything okay?"

"I did. Thanks." With that, I took my things and left.

I got in my truck, glad to have some residual warmth coming out of the heater vents. I sat for a moment, watching a group of classic cars pass by on the main drag. My cell phone started to ring. Grumbling, I dug around in the deep front pocket of my jeans and pulled it out. The number was not one I knew, but I recognized the prefix as being a number from work. I hit the answer button.

"Hullo?"

"Uh yes. Is this Randy?"

"Who is speaking?"

"This is Shelly, from Human Resources."

"Yes, Shelly, what can I do for you?" I pulled off my beanie and ran my fingers through my hair, then massaged my aching stomach.

"Uh, well…" Her voice had an edge to it that I didn't like. "…you were supposed to meet with me after your shift."

I also didn't like the accusatory way she worded that, so I turned it around on her. "And you were supposed to send somebody at the end of the shift to take me to the meeting. I waited right where you told me to."

"Well, they couldn't find you."

"Not my problem."

"It is of the utmost importance that I meet with you,

Randy." It was clear, by her choked voice, that she was trying hard not to yell, and I couldn't grasp why she was so aggravated with me. I was just another cog in the corporate wheel.

"Okay. I can come by after my shift on Monday."

"Come back to the building."

"No. I am off and was told I am not approved for overtime."

"Overtime. Jesus. You hourly employees insist on being paid for every second. Just nickel and diming the company."

I didn't like how Shelly was being so dismissive of what was so clearly spelled out in my union contract, as if she was above it and didn't have to follow the rules. I wasn't about to let her get away with that.

"I sure do, which is my right. And by the way, if this call lasts any longer, I am going to file a grievance because you are contacting me off the clock to discuss work."

As she stuttered, I imagined her narrow, tanned face turning red. I hung up and smiled. I decided that pushing her buttons was fun.

Smile fading, I realized didn't want to spend the evening home alone, so I shot a text to Darcy asking if she was available to come by for dinner. She replied before I could even slip the phone back in my pocket.

Yes, dinner sounds great. I'm just off work. Will go home and shower first. See you soon.

Relieved to have company coming, I hustled on home, fed Porkchop, and showered. In a fresh hoodie and jeans, I hit play on a Loretta Lynn CD and sipped beer as I cooked the noodles and browned the ground beef, adding in a few tablespoons of my beer to the mix along with the seasoning packet.

Despite good music, decent beer, cooking, and a friend on the way, I just couldn't shake the tightness in my chest, the butterflies in my belly, or the sweaty palms.

"Dammit." I fussed when I realized I hadn't prepared any vegetables. If it had only been me eating, I would have left it as it was, but with a guest coming over I figured having something green would be a good idea. There weren't any fresh vegetables in the fridge, so I opened the freezer and spotted some frozen peas. I dumped the peas straight into the stroganoff pan, turned down the temperature, and put a lid on it to let them simmer in the sauce.

I sat in my recliner and stared at the only painting on the wall, which was a custom piece my friend Bear had painted for me as a housewarming gift when I had moved to Lands End. It was painted on a rectangular sheet of scrap wood. There was a black background spattered with white, and three colorful circles staggered on it. I had always thought of it as being a picture of the universe, with three planets. For fifteen years I had contemplated the painting, its whorls of color on the surfaces of the planets and delicate splashes of white, like glimmering stars.

A knock at the front door broke my concentration. "Come in," I hollered and started to stand, expecting Darcy. Instead, I heard the click of high heels in my entryway, making my hackles go up. Darcy wasn't a high heel wearing kind of gal.

Shelly strode into my living room with a man following close behind her. Placing my beer on the coffee table, I stood up tall, folded my arms across my chest, and frowned deeply.

"Shelly. Not at all who I was expecting."

"Hello, Randy. This can't wait until Monday." She flicked her hand, motioning at the man in a way which made his introduction seem like an annoyance to her. "And this is Joe Rawlins. He is the Loss Prevention and Security Manager for our building."

I took in his faded polo shirt, wrinkled slacks, and scuffed boots. He was dressed like an operations supervisor, not at all what I would expect of a non-operations manager. He held out a hand to me.

"Hi, Randy. Nice to meet you." He gave me a small smile. Flecks of chewing tobacco were lodged between his yellowed teeth, showing beneath a shaggy mustache. I did not shake his hand.

There was another knock on my front door. *That better be Darcy.*

"Come in."

Darcy's narrow, stooped silhouette came down the hall. "Mmm, it smells great in—" She froze as soon as she spotted Joe and Shelly. My small living room was cramped with all four of us bunched up in it.

Darcy must have sensed my anger at my uninvited guests because she came and stood shoulder to shoulder with me, feet wide and hands on her hips.

Shelly pursed her lips as she took in Darcy. "Randy, I need you to ask your" —she gave Darcy another top to bottom scan—"friend…to leave."

I scoffed. "That's a fucking laugh riot. Not a chance, Shelly. What the hell are you doing here?"

"Like I said, this can't wait. I need to interview you about the accident you witnessed. So, let's just sit—"

"No. How do you even know where I live?"

"I'm HR."

"Just because you're HR and can see my info, doesn't mean you can just show up at my house unannounced, off the clock, and without a union rep. *Which I have asked for.* I know my rights. Weingarten. Look it up."

Shelly put a hand up to interrupt me, but I was not about to be silenced by her.

"No! You will not shut me up. You are in my goddamn

house. Now get out." Flecks of spittle collected at the corners of my lips as I growled at her.

"I am well versed on Weingarten, Randy. I really must insist on speaking to you. Corporate wants a full report, and you may be the only witness."

My anger turned to downright rage and my growl turn to a snarl. "I already told the police everything I know. Fuck you. And fuck Corporate. How dare you. Get out of my fucking house." Balling my fists at my sides, I leaned in toward Shelly. Her chin wavered for just a moment, but her eyes stayed as sharp as flint.

Joe took Shelly by the arm and gently shepherded her out of the door before closing it silently behind them. I waited five seconds and blew out a gust of air, releasing my fists and sitting down heavily on the recliner. Darcy locked the front door and handed me my beer before sitting on the love seat.

"Wow. Randy. What was that?"

Running my hands through my messy hair, I waited until my heart slowed and took a few sips of beer.

"That was Shelly. The HR manager where I work. I

uh… I witnessed a really terrible accident the other day. My supervisor ended up dead. And that lady from HR wants to talk to me, apparently. I asked her earlier for a union rep… You can see she doesn't give two flying fucks about that."

"So, that guy who was with her isn't from the union?"

"No. She said he is the security manager, though I've never seen him before. She probably brought him along as her bodyguard. Good thing he had the sense to pull her out of here."

Taking another sip of beer, I sat back and looked back at Bear's painting, doing my best to calm down.

"How dare she just show up here like that," Darcy said softly.

"Sorry you had to walk in on it. I thought it was you knocking on the door, so I just told 'em to come in, and they sure did." My voice lost its fury, leaving behind only exhaustion.

"No need to apologize for those jackasses."

My hands and thighs started to shake. "Hey, how about some dinner? I made stroganoff."

"Yum. Let's do it."

During dinner, the elephant in the front of my brain was stomping around and I pondered telling Darcy what I was feeling after Bryant's death. I scooped up a mouthful of food and chewed it slowly while I weighed my options. The peas and boxed stroganoff didn't taste like anything at all.

"What's on your mind, Randy?"

"That obvious, huh?"

She raised her eyebrows at me.

"It's just, since seeing my supe get killed, I'm just…so nervous all the time now. I don't even like being at work anymore, which is weird. I always want to go home, but I also don't want to be home and alone. My chest hurts, my stomach feels like I drank acid, my hands are sweaty, and I can't focus. Closest thing I can think of is when I get nervous."

Darcy met my gaze, face creased with concern and her head tilted just a tad in a way that I hoped wasn't pity. She put her spoon down. "Randy. I think the word for what you're feeling is anxiety."

We sat at my kitchen table in silence while I let the word sink in. Anxiety.

"Is that what this is?"

"Sounds like it, though I'm no mental health professional. Do you have a therapist?"

"A therapist? No. Can't say that I've ever been to a shrink before."

"Maybe now is a good time to check out therapy. You've been through a lot this week. It might help to talk to someone."

"I'm talking to you."

"Yeah. And I am happy to listen. But therapists have tools friends don't."

"Hm." I shoveled another tasteless spoon of food in my mouth. "I have great insurance. Course I never use it. Healthy as that X-Men Wolverine guy most of the time. Guess I'm lucky to have hearty genes. But I've heard the guys talking about how their kids and wives get unlimited therapy and don't have any co-pays or anything."

"Wow. That kind of insurance is hard to come by."

"Yeah. Only because the union has the company by the

balls. Otherwise, we'd have some crappy benefits that'd cost us employees a fortune. The union reps bargain hard and get what they want every damn time. They call our contract the 'Cadillac Contract,' and for good reason. It really is." I took a swallow of warm beer, grimacing. "I guess I'll call my insurance tomorrow to see about getting a therapist. Thanks."

She nodded and took her last bite of stroganoff and peas. "Thanks for dinner, Randy. It was really good."

I let out a bark of laughter and slid my plate away. "Good? If you say so."

We listened to rain come down for a while, the patter only interrupted by Porkchop's muffled snoring from under the couch.

Darcy drew in a deep breath, crossing her arms as if she were hugging herself, a small smile on her lips. "Psithurism and petrichor," she said faintly, her eyes distant as she gazed out of the darkened window.

"Define sithu-rism and petree-core, please." I stumbled over the words but refused to be embarrassed about it.

"Psithurism is the sound of wind in the trees and rustling of leaves during a storm. Petrichor is the smell of rain."

I smiled to myself, happy to have learned those words and glad to have the kind of friend who would share them with me.

Chapter Five

Rockslide

THE NEXT MORNING, I sat on an Adirondack chair on the back patio, bundled in my jacket, looking out at the water through the trees. A recording on my phone told me my insurance office was closed for the weekend. I had hoped to get information on therapists covered by my plan, but it seemed that would have to wait till Monday.

While I didn't have a clear view of the strait and bluffs,

I sure did enjoy what little view of them I did have. Years ago, my realtor had called it a "peekaboo water view."

The recent rain had turned the dusty brown bluffs across the strait a bright green. We were having our first sunshine in a week, and everything seemed fresh and new. The earth in my yard steamed where the sun hit it and the air smelled of damp leaves, petrichor, and wood smoke.

I lit a cigarette as Porkchop tried to wrap himself around my pant leg before wandering off to sniff around the patio. He couldn't find a warm dry place to lie and gave up, squeezing through the cat flap to go inside.

"Don't you dare lay on the furniture, Porky," I said to him halfheartedly.

I took a long drag on my cigarette and warmed my hands around my coffee mug. All was good and well until the image of Bryant's limp arms on the grating seeped into my head.

"No," I whispered as I blew plumes of smoke out of my nose. When I closed my eyes, the view of swaying trees, beautiful green bluffs, and choppy gray water disappeared. I wanted the image of Bryant to go away, but it held fast in my brain. Instead of Bryant vanishing, thoughts about his wife and newborn baby at home poured in. My throat tightened and face grew hot. I couldn't imagine the long-lasting impact his death would have on their lives, and the pain his wife had to be in at that very moment.

That thing Darcy said was anxiety started piling on. I couldn't catch my breath. My heart raced just above my acidic stomach, while my hands grew clammy. It was all topped off with the urge to get up and go. *Where you gonna go?*

My cigarette had burned down and the cherry bit at my fingertips. I snapped my eyes open and snuffed out the butt in the coffee can full of sand that I used as an ashtray.

I needed to move and to not be alone. Grumbling, I pulled out my cell phone and dialed a number from memory. The line rang a couple of times before a groggy voice answered.

"Yeah."

I lowered my voice, apologetic. "Hey. Buck. It's Randy. Sorry to wake you."

"Hey, Randy." Through the phone came the sound of

sheets ruffling and Buck groaning as she sat up. "What's up?"

"I…you wanna go for a ride today?"

"Yeah. Sure."

"You worked last night, huh? Shit. Sorry. I didn't even think about it."

"Don't worry about it. Usual spot? Bear's around. You wanna call and invite her too?"

"Yeah. Sounds good. Thanks, Buck."

She grunted and hung up. I dialed up Bear. Her phone rang a bunch before she answered with a flourish.

"Bueno, bueno, Ran-day."

"Hey, Bear."

"What can I do ya for?"

"I'm taking a ride with Buck today. We're meeting in Dairy Glen. Usual spot. You wanna join us?"

"You know it. I'm just kicking back doing that thing I do."

"Sitting around in your underwear playing video games?"

"You know it," she said, chuckling.

"Man, you never change. Get some coffee in you and I'll see you in a bit."

We hung up and I sent a text over to Darcy.

Hey Darce. I'm going go for a ride with Bear and Buck. I can't remember if you've met them yet or not. You want to come? We're going to hit the canyon.

Waiting for her to respond, I took a moment to watch the choppy water of the strait again and pondered the new words I had learned from her: psithurism and petrichor. I said them out loud a couple of times before going inside.

Porkchop sprawled out across the entire love seat.

"You are such a lump. I told you to stay off the furniture."

He didn't bother opening his eyes or acknowledging that I had entered the house. I stood at the sink and ate some Pop-Tarts, a hardboiled egg, and a microwaved breakfast burrito, before finishing off my coffee.

My phone pinged. It was Darcy.

Thanks for the invite. I'm at sea on a chartered fishing boat today so I can't make it. Have fun.

I shot a quick reply to her.

> *Chartered fishing boat, eh? I look forward to hearing all the stories when you get back. Don't forget the Dramamine!*

I inserted a little, green-faced sick looking emoticon and sent off the text. Next, I used the toilet, brushed my teeth, and gathered up my riding gear from the hall closet.

On the way to the garage, I gave Porkchop his directive for the day: "Guard the house, Porky."

He didn't reply.

The garage was cold, and the clunky wooden door creaked and shuddered on its springs as I raised it, a stiff breeze blowing leaves in. I draped my gear over the pillion seat of the bike, bent, and disconnected the battery from the trickle charger. I slid the key into the ignition, popped the transmission into neutral, and flipped the power switch on. The fuel injectors made a small, short whining sound. When that stopped, I pressed the ignition button and the bike started on the first try, as always.

As the engine warmed, I shimmied into my riding

pants and jacket, and tied a bandana around the bottom half of my face like an old timey bank robber, which worked to block the chilly road wind from freezing my neck and blowing down into my jacket collar.

I pulled on my helmet, a full faced unit with a secondary Bluetooth I had installed. I dug around in my pants pocket, pulled out my cell phone, and synced it to my helmet, then launched Spotify so I could listen to music while I rode. I pressed play on the Tom Petty station and grinned as "Free Fallin'" started.

Finally, I pulled on my winter riding gloves. Back in my early twenties, as a new rider, I had put my gloves on before my helmet so many times, only to have to take them off again. You can't secure the helmet strap with bulky gloves on. At fifty-three, I was proud to have learned that lesson.

Ready to go, I pushed my bike out into the driveway and closed the heavy wooden garage door with a *thump* and big gust of wind.

I looked at my bike, a Honda ST1300, with appreciation. I'd ridden many motorcycles over the years and the

ST1300 was my all-time favorite. The engine purred smoothly as it warmed up. The black paint looked fresh even though it was over fifteen years old. It helped that the bike had always been garaged by both me and its original owner. When my old 1982 Honda took a dump a few years earlier, Buck had put me in touch with her friend who was selling the ST1300.

Eyes closed, I listened to the engine until its pitch lowered, telling me that it was warmed up and ready to ride. Grinning, I clapped my hands together, threw my leg over the saddle, and rolled out.

Merging onto the freeway, I barely felt any of the bumps and creases in the aging pavement. I had heartily cursed those same bumps and creases while riding my prior bikes, especially the one Bear had nicknamed the "HAA," which stood for Harley Anal Assaulter, due to how bad the suspension was.

It was early enough that the Bay Area's weekly mass exodus to Lake Tahoe wasn't in full swing yet, so there weren't many cars on the road. I listened to Tom Petty through the speakers in my helmet and tried to watch my speed as the ST1300 ate up the miles with zero effort. After blurs of orchards and outlet malls, I pulled into the parking lot of the PJ's grocery store in Dairy Glen.

Climbing off the bike carefully, I made sure my feet were solidly under me before letting go. My legs, ass, and hands were numb with cold. Unbuckling my helmet with frozen fingertips was a challenge, but after a moment of fumbling I managed it.

Walking through the automatic doors of PJ's, I was relieved by the warm air that greeted me. My core relaxed and I lingered inside the store to thaw out and use the restroom. Compared to most suburban grocery stores, this one was small and had an odd triangle-shaped floor plan.

I took my time choosing some snacks, dodging the occasional blurry eyed college kid, until I heard the throaty rumble of motorcycle pipes closing in. I headed to the registers up front and found one that had no line. Placing my snacks on the little shelf at the register, I was distracted, thinking about eating the little round salty rice crackers, chocolate bar, and string cheese I had picked out. Head down, I dug in the back pocket of my jeans for my wallet, which was hard to get to because of the heavy riding pants I had on over them.

"Hi, find everything okay?" the checker asked, her voice chirpy and friendly.

Wallet in hand, I looked up and paused, drawn in by her bright-blue eyes, which beamed at me as she rang my items up with experienced hands. It wasn't just the shade of blue that smacked me, but also because her eyes were clear and vibrant…so alive. I was so struck because most of the people I saw at work had dull, bloodshot eyes.

She tilted her head at me, waiting for me to answer her.

"Hi," I said back, my gaze flicking down to the PJ's daisy logo on the front of her sweatshirt. She had done a clean job of using Sharpies to turn the white daisy logo into a rainbow flag. *Huh.* I wouldn't have clocked her as LGBTQ, but there she was.

"Would you like a bag?"

"No, thank you." I woke back up and inserted my debit card into the reader.

"Going for a ride?" she asked, a smile still broad on her lips, and delicate crow's feet crinkling around her eyes.

Trying to guess her age, I figured her for probably ten years younger than me. It was ridiculously hard for me to find words in that moment. *Jesus, come on Randy.* "Uh. Yes. Riding up through the valley and the canyon."

The card reader squawked at me that it was time to remove my debit card, which I did and gathered up my items clumsily before heading for the door. On the way out, I turned to look back at her. She was peering over her shoulder at me, that hundred-watt smile still on her face. I gave her a lopsided grin, raising my chin at her as I passed through the glass doors.

Bear and Buck had parked their bikes next to mine and were pulling off their helmets as I approached.

"Wow, Randy, what's that look on your face for, bro?" Bear asked as she pulled me into a massive hug, pinning my arms and snacks between us.

"Nuthin'," I squeaked out as she squeezed me. We both laughed until she released me.

"Mh-hm." Buck squinted at me, deep creases forming around her mouth as she grinned. She fussed with the zipper of her weathered leather riding jacket.

"You guys have a good ride over from Sacramento?"

"Yeah. You wanna ride the canyon?" Bear asked as she ran her fingers through her wild salt-and-pepper hair. Buck and I both nodded.

I stowed my snacks and slid on my helmet. "Okay. Everybody's all gassed up, right? Last gas station before the canyon is at the casino."

"We're good. Filled up before crossing the causeway. Now stand back," Bear said as she did a Jackie Gleason style windup before hoisting her short leg over the saddle of her bike.

We'd ridden many miles together and I was happy to see that her bike, a massive 1600cc Road Star, which she had lovingly named Champagne, was still on the road.

Buck fired up her Harley with a bone rattling rumble. I reminded myself to ride in front of her. When I rode behind her the engine noise was too much. I paired up the Bluetooth and Spotify again and picked a 1980s hits channel. Van Morrison sang to me about tupelo honey as I pulled out behind Bear, with Buck taking sweep behind us.

As we rolled slowly by PJ's, the checker was walking

out of the front door, gazing down at her cell phone. She looked up just in time to knock me out one more time with her bright eyes and toothy smile, making my heart race. I had to force myself to focus back on riding as we pulled out of the parking lot onto the main road.

We dodged big groups of college kids on bicycles as we passed through intersections until Dairy Glen turned back into farmland. Long, ramrod-straight county roads that ran between tomato and sunflower fields took us to the next county. The coastal mountains rose in the distance, the only thing to break up the scenery of the flat valley floor except for the occasional barn, well pump, or windmill.

Before long the three of us were weaving our way through the green rolling hills of Capay Valley, the two-lane road gently curving around orchards and dormant row crop fields. I saw some farms with livestock, including a few llamas and emu. We passed through the small towns of Madison, Esparto, and Capay.

Around the bend we got to Brooks, where the small farmhouses gave way to the casino, looming large, overlooking vineyards and the foothills. A massive banner strung across the front advertised an upcoming big-name concert. After the casino we passed through Guinda, and the road narrowed further as the terrain changed from wide-open valley floor to canyon, with steep wooded hillsides. The temperature dropped several degrees in the shade of the hills.

I did my best to stay focused on the ride and the road, but the heart-stopping smile I had gotten earlier in Dairy Glen, those blue eyes locked on mine, were a big distraction. I hadn't given any woman a second look in years, let alone have one get my heart and mind racing.

Bear cruised along, never in a hurry, taking the curves with ease. I checked my side mirror now and then to make sure Buck was still with us, her aftermarket exhaust pipes echoing through the narrow canyon. There were hardly any other vehicles on the canyon road, though we did pass a few packs of cyclists decked out in spandex, riding fancy road bikes. As we rolled by a group of bikes on a steep climb, I watched one guy's chiseled leg muscles working hard to pedal. The lady in front of him blew a snot rocket over her shoulder and he didn't even flinch. I was glad to have an engine between my legs and opened the throttle to climb the last bit of the hill.

At the top of the hill, we zoomed by another gaggle of cyclists, resting after their climb. They were all off their bikes, panting and sweating even in the cold. One lady was throwing up in the bushes. Her jersey said "Veni, Vidi, Vomiti." The slogan rattled around in my brain, drawing me back to my father trying to teach me Latin as a kid. I figured it meant something like: I came, I saw, I barfed. Another lady stood by, leaning on her bike frame, totally unbothered, sucking on one of those goo energy tubes.

My fingers and toes had started to go numb from the cold despite wearing thick socks and boots, and winter riding gloves. While on a short, straight stretch I took my eyes off the road again to turn on the heated grips. I pressed the button and looked up just in time to see Bear dump her bike over farther than I thought possible. Champagne, nearly on its side, cut over into the opposite lane and back.

I scanned the road for the hazard and had just enough time to register a small rockslide, scree and baseball-sized chunks of rock bouncing down the steep hillside and onto the road. I spotted a small gap and rode straight through, pebbles pinging off my helmet and shooting out from under my tires. I checked my mirror and watched as Buck, who'd had the most time to respond, swung out wide and avoided the whole thing with little fuss. That was Buck for ya.

Bear parked in a turnout a few hundred yards up the road. I pulled in behind her to catch my breath. I yanked off my helmet and pulled the bandana down off my mouth, heart doing somersaults.

Bear slapped her chest and let out a roar that reverberated through the hills and down the canyon.

"Awooo! Jesus Christ! Did you see that, Randy?"

"I can't believe you didn't dump it. That was some fine goddamn riding."

"Wasn't my first time, won't be my last." She gasped and shook her hands out.

"Good thing you've been riding since before you could spell motorcycle."

We laughed wildly, which helped me relax and steady myself as the adrenaline rush faded. Buck pulled in behind us, tires crunching on gravel, and killed her engine. Without the rumble of wind and motors, I was left with the sound of the creek thundering past below.

I shivered as wind whipped through the canyon, cutting through my layers of riding gear. "Fuck, it's cold out here. Ey, I don't have phone signal in the canyon so I can't call public works or whoever about the rockslide."

Bear nodded, trying to blow rings with the steam that came from her mouth. She seemed nice and cozy in her balaclava and insulated coveralls.

"Good job on not dying, guys," I said with a chuckle.

"I'm getting' too old for this sheeyat," said Buck, with her usual gruffness. Bear snorted.

I chuckled. "You are so full of shit, Buck. You'll be sporting that mullet and riding a motorcycle till the day you die, and you know it."

"Pfft," Buck said and waved me off.

Bear looked up at the treetops as they swayed in the wind. I wanted to share the new word I had learned from Darcy, psithurism, but I let the moment pass.

"Okay. Everybody good? Nobody gonna have a heart

attack?" asked Bear and she did something akin to a karate kick to get her leg over her bike saddle again.

"All good," said Buck. I nodded and pulled my bandana back up over my nose and gratefully pulled my helmet on, insulating my head and face from the wind. Our bikes roared back to life, and we pulled onto the deserted road.

When we reached our turnaround point, we doubled back through the canyon, taking extra care when passing the rockslide. As we turned the last corner out of the canyon, Capay Valley sprawled out before us, bursting with sunlight, a warm breeze, and green grasses. Though only November, the first massive rains had spurred new growth. Farmers were out on their tractors, plowing the damp earth. Cows, goats, horses, and sheep grazed near the road. The smells of soil and sweet cut grass along with the tang of manure made me feel right at home. Being outside and away from the bustle of the Bay Area was the distraction I had needed.

*

BEAR PARKED AT a restaurant in Capay that catered to the biker crowd. We piled into a booth and ordered right away. Bear and I ate piles of nachos while Buck tucked into a warm bowl of chili.

Buck and I had been friends since the '80s, coming up as young lesbians in Sacramento back in the day when the women's socials had to happen in private. We met Bear when she moved to town in the '90s, and the three of us quickly formed a bond that, while it had been put to the test plenty of times, persisted. Buck, with her Marlboro Man aesthetic and quiet, strong disposition, was steady and reliable. Bear had a big personality and was the best storyteller I knew, though she was also prone to weeks long quiet spells. She drifted between Northern California and Arizona, falling off the radar for months on end. It was good to have the group back together again, even if just for a few hours.

Looking back and forth between the two, I sat back from my plate, stifling a belch.

"Quit making eyes at me, Randy," Bear said, cackling.

Buck wiped her mouth with a crumpled paper napkin,

grinning.

"I just love you guys, that's all. I been feeling the distance more lately. I love Lands End, but have been a damn hermit in that little town."

Buck pressed her lips together, contemplating, as she fluffed up her hair.

"Buck, you still working at the lesbian night club?"

"Sad to say it's not a gay bar anymore. Owner sold out a while ago. It caters to the hets now, mostly. But yeah, I still work there. Lead security officer. The new owners kept me on. The frat boys from the university don't know what to make of me when they come in."

I caught a glint from our bikes through the front window. "Whatever happened to that chick who sold me my bike? She used to work at the bar with you. What was her name? Valerie?"

Bear cut in. "Vivian. Viv, yeah, she's doing good. She's a big shot firefighter now."

"She still ride?"

"Yeah. I still can't get over her selling her ST1300. She *loved* that bike."

"Well, her loss, my gain. It's my baby now, and I love it. Best bike I ever had. We should do a ride with her some time. She seemed nice."

They both nodded. "Yeah. She's a good one," Buck said as she scraped the last bits of chili from the bowl with her spoon.

We finished off our drinks and settled our tabs. The ride back to Dairy Glen on the back roads was nice and easy. Bear and Buck split off with hearty waves, taking the freeway on-ramp when we got to town.

My bladder was bursting, so I decided to head back up the street to PJ's for more snacks and a bathroom break. It was a nice afternoon, and the store was busy. There were zombified college students filling the aisle, shuffling along buying frozen pizzas and premade salads. It must have been finals week or something. Though what the hell did I know? I had been in the workforce since I was fifteen. College wasn't something people in my family did. My dad taught himself everything he wanted to know by studying books from the library and yard sales.

I ducked and dodged my way through the crowd and

was grateful there wasn't a line for the bathroom. It took me longer than usual to use the toilet because I was piled up in riding gear. When I came out there were two people waiting, arms crossed and frowning.

The riding gear kept me warm and protected when out on the road in the winter elements, but in a grocery store in the afternoon it was too heavy and hot. Sweat trickled down between my boobs as I clomped toward the cracker and chip aisle.

"Welcome back," came that same sweet, friendly voice. I stopped in my tracks and turned, seeing the woman who had rung me up that morning. She was standing at a demonstration table, giving samples of some sort of stuffing. It occurred to me that Thanksgiving was around the corner.

I stepped up to her table, pulling at my collar to get some air circulation under the heavy jacket.

"Thanks. Stuffing, eh?" *Jesus Christ, Randy. Really?*

She gave me a patient smile. "Yup. Want to try some?"

"No. Thanks. Just had lunch. Smells good though."

Something about her radiated kindness and I wanted

to dive into her like a warm pool of water. I had been single for over twenty years and realized I was off my game and had no idea what to say to her. I shifted my feet. Still smiling, she raised her eyebrows at me. "Can I help you find something?"

"No. Thanks. I—uh…" *Oh god. I'm an idiot.*

"Did you have a good ride?"

The ice broke and I found my words. "Sure did. That canyon is cold as a witch's tit today, but we had a blast aside from almost getting taken out by a rockslide." *Okay, now you're just bragging. Stop it.* "So, do you ride?"

"Bicycles, yes. I have the same beach cruiser I've been riding since high school. But I've never been on a motorcycle." She paused to hand another customer a sample. "You want to take me on a ride some time?"

I hadn't expected that and stammered. "I… I'm not local." *Idiot.*

"Oh. Where are you from?"

"Lands End. I just came down for a ride with my friends."

She frowned a little, considering.

My brain raced, trying to find words to bring her smile back. "But Lands End isn't all that far away. Maybe an hour if traffic is behaving."

She nodded. "I'm familiar with Lands End. I live over in Marshtown."

I felt myself frowning and did my best to replace it with a smile. "Uh, wow. That's a big commute to work here."

"Oh, well, this isn't my regular store. I am just here picking up an extra shift today. My main store is the one in Diablo."

"Huh, how about that."

Someone bumped their shopping cart into the back of my heel. I ignored them.

"You have a cell phone?" she asked, handing out another sample.

"Yeah."

"Put my number in your phone, if you want."

I dug around in my pockets and pulled out my phone. Her nametag said KRISTEN, which I typed into my contacts along with the number she gave me. I sent her a quick text, so she had my number too.

"Thanks," I said. "Name's Randy." I extended a hand to her, but she held up her hands, showing that she was wearing neoprene gloves. "Oh, right. Serving food. Well, I better let you get back to it. Nice to meet you, Kristen."

"Nice to meet you too, Randy." She smiled and turned to a customer, who asked her what she was serving despite there being a big, clearly visible sign that said "STUFFING" on it. She gave a patient smile to the customer and told them about the stuffing.

*

THAT EVENING I fiddled around with a jigsaw puzzle, with the TV on in the background and Porkchop sleeping on top of my feet. He was a royal pain in the ass, but when I needed comfort, he usually showed up. I tried hard not to think about Bryant's death, or the suffering his family must have been going through. I tried not to worry about meeting with HR the following week. I did try to hold on to the happiness and freedom I had felt while riding with Buck and Bear, and the butterflies that came when I thought about Kristen.

Leaning forward, I rested my chin on my knee and pet Porkchop's head with a shaky hand. He meowed and lifted his chin, allowing me to continue petting him. His long fur was smooth and soft under my rough fingertips.

"What am I gonna do, Porky? I feel so outta whack."

He purred and closed his eyes. My phone pinged and its screen lit up, saying that I had a text message from Kristen.

"Holy shit, Porkchop. She texted me."

I held my breath and read her message.

Hi Randy. This is Kristen from PJ's. I am off Sundays and Mondays. Want to go for a ride tomorrow?

I reread her message a few times and thought about what to say. I didn't have any plans the next day, so I could take her for a ride. But I had an ounce of hesitation, like it was too soon. I texted her back, poking at the touchscreen keyboard with my pointer finger.

Howdy. Yes, I am available for a ride tomorrow. Do you have a motorcycle helmet?

She responded quickly, clearly a fast texter.

No. I don't have a helmet. I guess that's kind of important huh.

Well damn. I felt a tiny bit of relief that she didn't have a helmet, and I didn't have a spare, so there was no way we could go on a ride. While I thought about how to respond she sent another text.

Well, I guess a ride isn't going to happen. I love Lands End. Maybe we can check out Main Street and the pier. Or go on a hike?

I hesitated again. *A date? Is it the right time?* I recognized that I had been single for so long that changing it up terrified me, and I worried about how messed up I was over Bryant. *What if the anxiety gets to be too much during the date?* I closed my eyes and drew in a deep breath, leaning down and stroking Porkchop. I considered what advice Bear and Buck would give me if I asked them what to do. They both would tell me to go for it. I picked up my phone and wrote back.

Sure, sounds great.

From there we figured out a time and place to meet and said good night. I turned off the TV, kicked back in my chair, and stared at Bear's painting of the universe until I was tired enough to go to bed.

*

THE NEXT MORNING, I was up early, fretting about what to wear and trying to brush my unruly hair into something presentable. I ended up wearing my newest blue jeans, a white button-up dress shirt, and a brown leather belt. I slid on a pair of perfectly polished cowboy boots. After some more thought, I slipped on a silver ring and matching neck-lace with a turquoise pendant on it. I thought about con-versation topics and what sort of questions to ask her, which made me nervous and sweaty. I had to put on more deodorant and change my undershirt twice before it was time to go.

Just before lunchtime, I shrugged into my trusty leather jacket and took the short drive to the main drag. I snagged a lucky parking spot out front of the restaurant we had chosen. After a moment of looking at the people milling around, I spotted her peeking in the window of a shop that sold succulents and antiques. I watched her for a moment and realized I didn't know her at all.

She wore a flowing burgundy cotton dress that fell just below her knees, and cream-colored leggings with a bunny ears design showing above her low-top Converse All-Stars. She shivered under her light sweater, crossing her arms over her chest.

Hands tucked into the front pockets of my jeans, I walked up behind her, my boot heels loud on the sidewalk. Kristen turned and gave me the biggest damn smile. Her arms spread wide, she came in for a hug. I pulled my hands out of my pockets just in time and hugged her back. She smelled clean, like laundry soap and some sort of fruity lotion. As we separated, she looked up at me, her nose red and teeth chattering.

"Hey. Let's get you inside. You must be freezing."

She nodded. "Yeah. I'm not always the most prepared." She motioned toward her outfit and light sweater, which wasn't suitable for how cold it was.

I held the door of the restaurant open for her. The place was warm and only half full. The hostess led us to a booth in the back. I was relieved to be tucked away in a quiet corner, instead of out in the busier front room. I had only eaten at that restaurant once before, so I picked up a menu. The words were too small, so I mostly saw the blurs of the words that were next to pictures of food. *Dammit.* I squinted and tried again, but the low light and small print worked against me.

"You okay?"

"Yeah… I just…" I sighed and pulled my readers out of my jacket pocket and perched them on my nose, embarrassed. Then I remembered I was done apologizing for myself and sat up straighter. Kristen smiled and squirmed a little. "Oh, you wear glasses. That's hot."

I didn't know what to say, and thankfully she looked back down at her menu. With the help of my glasses, I saw that the place served a mixture of Mexican and American foods. I ordered an iced tea, and carne asada tacos with a side of rice. Kristen ordered a chicken pot pie and a Shirley Temple.

I paid attention to how she spoke with the waiter, because how someone treats waitstaff and folks in the service industry tells me a lot about them. I was relieved that she was kind and friendly with the waiter.

I'd always assumed that all people who work in the service industry would be kind to others in customer service, but I had dated a woman back in the day who was an absolute monster with waitstaff despite being in customer service herself. That one didn't last long.

"So, you mentioned being familiar with my little town here. You've been here before?"

"Yeah. I grew up just across the water in Diablo. I come here a lot."

"You grew up in Diablo? Did you go to the central high school?"

"Sure did."

"If you graduated, when was that?"

"Are you trying to figure out how old I am?"

I chuckled. "Guilty."

"All you have to do is ask. I'm forty-two and yes, I graduated. And what about you?"

"I'm fifty-three. So, how long have you worked at PJ's?"

"Fifteen years."

"Impressive. So many people bounce around jobs these days…not that that's a bad thing. It's just not often I run into someone who sticks it out that long anymore. That's about how long I've been at my job too. You like working there?"

"Yeah, I love it." Her smile seemed genuine, and the corners of her eyes crinkled.

The server placed a plate of steaming tacos and rice in front of me, and Kristen beamed down at her pot pie. My mouth watered at the smell of chili, onion, and cilantro. Kristen cracked open the top of her pot pie, scooped out a big spoonful of chicken and vegetables, and savored her first bite with her eyes closed. We took a break from our conversation to eat.

After I had finished my first taco and half of the rice, I took a long drink of iced tea and dabbed at my mouth with a paper napkin. The booths around us were still empty, but there were the whoops and laughter of a rowdy group in the front room. Somebody shouted, "Another pitcher of margaritas, *por favor*." The *por favor* was said in the most obnoxiously American way possible and I was glad not to be in the same room as them.

I turned my attention back to Kristen. "I have to be honest, I have so many questions I want to ask you, but I don't know what's impolite to ask on a first date."

"Like I said earlier, all you have to do is ask. If you ask something I don't want to answer, I'll just say so."

"All right. Uh, do you have any children?"

"No kids. You?"

"Just my dummy of a cat."

She let out a squeal that took me by surprise. "Aw! You have a kitty?"

"Sure do."

She leaned forward, her face beaming. "Oh my gosh. I want to meet him. I love cats."

"Ha, well, glad to hear it. He's pretty grumpy though. You've been warned."

"He sounds sweet," she said chirpily, not fazed by my description of his attitude. "Do you have a picture of him?"

I pulled my phone out and flipped through the pictures until I found one of him sprawled out across the love seat, his long black-and-white fur glossy in the sunlight.

She let out another squeal. "Ohhh! Look at how long his whiskers are. I love him!" Taking my phone, she grinned at his picture. "I wish I could have pets where I live. It's been hard not being able to have a kitty. I volunteer at the cat shelter when I can."

"That's really great. What else do you like to do when you're not working?"

She gave a last glance at Porkchop's picture and slid the phone back to me. "I like to play, push my body, and get dirty. I do things like mud runs and obstacle course races. Other than that, I volunteer for hospice, and since I don't have any family, on holidays I usually volunteer as a Bridge Angel."

"Well, damn. Remind me not to mess with you. Sounds like you're one tough gal doing those obstacle races." I paused. "What's a Bridge Angel?"

"It's a volunteer group called Bridgewatch Angels. We

walk the Golden Gate Bridge on holidays to try and pre-vent people from committing suicide there. Golden Gate Bridge has a long history of being a place people go to jump…especially on holidays."

"Wow, that's really good of you." I wondered why I hadn't done any volunteer work. During the off season I had plenty of time to spare.

"Yeah, I guess. It just feels like the right thing to do. So, what do you do for fun?"

"I mostly fish or catch a movie. Though sometimes I meet up with friends to go on motorcycle rides or bowl-ing."

We paused to eat some more, and I thought about the conversation so far. Her easygoing, upbeat personality helped take the edge off my first date jitters.

"Tell me more about you, Randy. Where'd you grow up? Any family?"

I cleared my throat, considering how much I wanted to share. "I grew up in Sacramento, don't have any family, and I've been single for over twenty years. That's me in a nutshell." I chose to leave out the enormous detail about witnessing my supervisor's death just a few days before.

"Sacramento. I've had some fun times in Midtown."

I liked that she didn't really press me for more right then. I nodded and finished off my iced tea. The waiter swooped by and cleared our plates. He came right back with the check, and I settled the bill on the spot, making sure to give the guy a decent tip.

Kristen took the last sip of her Shirley Temple, fished out the bright red Maraschino cherry, yanked the stem off, and tossed the cherry back into her glass. She put the stem in her mouth, a focused expression falling over her face. A few moments later, her eyes cleared as she plucked the stem out of her mouth and placed it on her napkin. We both looked down at the cherry stem, which was tied in a tidy little knot.

She grinned at me, and I grinned back. My heart rate picked up just a tick. "I haven't seen that trick since my days back in the bar scene. Do you have any other, uh, talents you'd like to share?" *Oh my God, did I just say that?*

She leaned in conspiratorially and gave a little laugh but didn't say anything more. A gray cloud passed through me, stealing away the happiness and thrill I was feeling. After a beat I realized the anxiety was nipping at the back of my brain, bringing frustration with it. I resented the anxiety for trying to ruin my date. I had been enjoying myself and didn't want reality to come crashing in like the Kool-Aid Man.

I shook my head, trying to push the bad feelings away, and drummed my hands on the table a couple of times. "Hey, how about a walk down to the pier?"

Her eyes lit up. "Sure!"

She slid lithely out of the booth. My hips and knees protested, so I moved a bit slower. Pushing open the restaurant door, I was glad to find that the temperature, while still cold, had risen a few notches and the sun had broken through the clouds.

We meandered down the main street, chatting and peering into the windows of galleries, art studios, wine bars, and antique shops. She coyly hooked her arm through mine and gently pulled my hand from my pocket. Butterflies took flight inside my belly as I intertwined my fingers with hers and we walked the rest of the way hand in hand, my boots clunking and her soft soled Converse gliding along silently. The street dead ended at the water, where there was a parking lot and public pier.

At the pier the wind was fierce, rumpling us. Kristen's light-brown hair blew around her face until she stopped for a moment, produced a hair tie from who knows where, and pulled her hair into a loose ponytail. We continued to the end of the pier where groups of tourists mingled. I felt the worn wood and protruding nail heads of the old pier through the soles of my boots.

Clusters of people fished on the rocks, the tips of their rods bent by the pull of the current on their nearly invisible lines. I scanned each person on the rocks, checking to see if Darcy was one of them, and sure enough, there she was. She gave me a sly smile and raised an eyebrow before turning back to her tackle box. I was surprised that she had chosen to fish at the crowded pier.

I leaned against the railing and looked across the water toward the small collection of houses and brick buildings of Gallery Bluff tucked into the hills. A boat slipped by on the choppy water, its sails snapping sharply. Kristen wrapped her arm around my waist and leaned into me. The side of my body that was pressed against hers was nice and warm, protected from the chill wind, though she began to shiver.

"Let's head back. Want my jacket?"

Before she could respond I had the jacket off and draped it over her shoulders. She put her arms through the sleeves and zipped it up, smiling. It was far too big for her small frame and we both chuckled about it.

"Thanks. It's nice and toasty."

The wind blew right through my thin dress shirt, and we hustled along the path and back up the main street to my truck.

"Hop in," I said and held the passenger door open for her.

She got in with no hesitation. I closed the door for her once she was in her seat and walked around the bumper. I got in on my side and slammed the door, grateful to be out of the renewed wind and cold. I fired up the engine and turned on the heater.

"Your nose and cheeks are bright red," she said with a

little laugh. She reached over and placed her warm palm on my cold cheek.

"Thanks so much for coming across the bridge to see me," I said as I turned in my seat to face her.

"Of course! I love it here, even when it's cold and cloudy."

She gave me a small grin and looked out of the windshield as huge raindrops began to splatter. "We made it back just in time."

I took her hand and was relieved when she immediately gripped mine in response. Her hands were slim and warm, though her palms were nearly as rough as mine. I turned her hand over and ran my fingertips along her callouses. She didn't shy away from the attention I gave them, and in fact seemed proud.

"Many years of carrying boxes at work, plus pull-ups, and kettlebells at the gym," she informed me.

I nodded. "That'll do it."

She turned her eyes back to me from the deluge on the windshield. "So, Randy, are you going to kiss me or what?"

A firecracker went off in my chest. She was bold, and

I liked it. "I…uh. I've been single a real long time. I can't even remember the last time I went on a date."

"I know. What does that have to do with you kissing me?"

She has a point. My dark eyes locked on her blue ones, and I reminded myself I was moving forward, breaking out of my old patterns. I took a moment to ask myself if kissing her was what I wanted to do, and it was.

I leaned across the center console and slid my hand along her jaw until I was cupping the back of her neck under her smooth hair. I pulled her in gently until our lips met. The storm of sensations that had been going on in my chest and stomach launched into a full-fledged tsunami.

I pulled back slightly, our lips separating, and opened my eyes to find that she was looking back at me. She closed her eyes and kissed me. Self-doubt and anxiety did their best to try to ruin the moment for me, but I shoved them down and leaned in. I just wanted to be present in that one moment, and I succeeded.

Chapter Six

Do 'Em Both

WORK WAS BUSY, and we would continue to get more and more packages flowing through our building right up until Christmas. Before Bryant's accident I had been pretty carefree at work. Afterward, there was a gray cloud over the whole place for me. During my shift that day I did my best to let my mind go blank and focus only on the task at hand: zip codes and working safely.

At the end of my shift the building had fallen into silence and by the time I finished walking out the belt, my muscles and soul were tired. I put away my earplugs, collected my belongings, and climbed down the ladder.

I sighed as my feet touched the solid concrete floor. Turning from the ladder, I was annoyed to find Shelly from HR standing there.

"Hello, Randy."

I gave her a tight, forced grin. "Howdy, Shelly." I walked past her, heading for the time clock.

Her high heels clicked rapidly behind me as she stammered. "Randy. I need you to come with me."

I didn't slow my pace, speaking over my shoulder at her. "I don't see a union rep around. So, no."

Her hand grasped my shoulder, and I stopped in my tracks. Anger boiled up inside me and I spun around to face her.

I spoke clearly and quietly, through clenched teeth. "Once again, Shelly. Do not touch me." My cheeks shook with the anger I was trying to stuff down.

She stared at me, her eyes huge, showing true fear for

the first time. She quickly wiped it away, her expression closing up and shifting back to her HR poker face. She dropped her hand from my shoulder.

"I insist, Randy. In fact, I instruct you to go to my office. This cannot wait any longer. If you refuse to meet with me, I will issue discipline against you for insubordination."

I fought hard not to shout and not to put my hands on her. *She's not worth losing your job and your retirement, let alone jail time.* I'd done a few short stints in jail back in my twenties for bar fights and drunk and disorderly, but those days were long over.

I glared at Shelly in her skirt suit, high heels, and peacoat. Her short hair was perfectly styled, and her hands looked soft and clean. I had no doubt her job was challenging, but I didn't care to make it any easier for her since she had repeatedly disrespected me.

Hearing boots approaching, I broke off our stare-down and saw a fellow long-time morning shift employee round the corner. He pulled a pallet jack loaded up with empty pallets. It clicked in my head that he was a shop steward for the union.

"Brody!"

Looking up, he took in the scene, parked his pallet jack, and strode over, chest puffed up. He didn't even acknowledge Shelly. "Randy. What's going on?"

"I've enacted my Weingarten rights. Can you come with me to talk to HR?"

"You know it."

"Finally," Shelly said and walked toward her office in a huff.

Brody and I walked far enough behind her that we could speak quietly.

"What's this about?"

"She wants to question me about what happened to Bryant."

"Oh man. Okay. Don't give her anything more than what she asks for. You know the drill."

"Yeah."

"I'm gonna record. But don't say anything about it." He pulled out his cell phone and started an audio recording.

We followed Shelly into her cramped office. She shut

the door behind us and took a seat at her desk. Brody and I sat in the visitor chairs. It was a tight squeeze, our knees pressed against the back of her desk. Brody placed his phone face down on his thigh. With how common cell phones were, it didn't seem to raise Shelly's suspicion that he might be recording.

She straightened some papers on her desk, picked up her pen, and gave it a twirl. "For the record the time is 12:17 p.m. We are in the Human Resources manager's office in the Diablo hub facility. My name is Shelly Barstow, and I am the Human Resources manager for the East Bay District.

"Miranda Cox, you have been asked to come to this meeting to provide information about an incident you were involved in while on the job...." *Involved in?* "There is the possibility that the information obtained through this meeting could lead to disciplinary action against you, up to and including termination—"

Brody interrupted her, as I knew he would. "Hold on, Shelly. Hold on. These are the admonishments you normally give to the subject of an investigation, not a witness.

What's going on here?"

Shelly clenched her jaw, clearly annoyed at being interrupted and questioned. "This is merely a formality."

"Formality? No. I have heard your various admonishments over the years, and I know darn well you have different ones for subjects and witnesses. Explain."

"Until we get to the bottom of this incident, these are the admonishments I choose to give. Now, let's move on—"

I stopped her. "No, let's not. I already spoke with law enforcement, and they are treating me as a witness."

"Well Randy, they are doing a criminal investigation on behalf of their agency. I am doing an administrative investigation on behalf of the corporation. The two are separate and running parallel to each other. What they do and what I do may differ—"

Brody cut in again. "And what about Lybarger? Are you giving her Lybarger rights?"

Shelly scoffed. "No. Certainly not."

What the hell is Lybarger?

"We need to step outside for a caucus. Excuse us." Brody stood up, so I did the same.

"Make it snappy. This whole thing has been delayed far too long already."

"That's out of line, Shelly," Brody said as he frowned and led me out into the warehouse. He closed the door behind us. We walked about fifty yards away, so she wouldn't be able to overhear. A few folks from the next shift had arrived to start setting up, but they were across the aisle from us, and out of earshot.

"Randy. If she won't Lybarger you, and law enforcement is already involved, I don't know if the union can represent you—"

"Wait, back up, Brody. What's Lybarger?"

"It stems from case law. Basically, if you are being investigated by your employer about something that the cops are involved in too, the employer can provide you Lybarger rights to get you to talk. Basically, they can promise that whatever you say during your employer's administrative investigation, they won't turn over to the cops. But, see, Shelly is refusing to Lybarger you, which means she can turn over whatever she gets out of you to the cops, if she wants."

Annoyed and impatient, I hissed at him. "So what! I didn't do anything! Let's go get this over with. You coming with me or not?"

"You're sure? There's not one single thing that might pull you into a criminal investigation? Cuz if I sit in on this meeting today and then stuff from today ends up in the criminal courts, you're gonna drag me and the union in with you, and that's not something we are interested in."

I saw that he still held his cell phone in his hand, recording our conversation. "Brody. We have worked together for fifteen damn years. Have I ever been a problem? Given you any reason to doubt me?"

"Nah."

"Okay then. Let's get this over with."

He sighed and rubbed the back of his neck. "Man. All right."

We returned to Shelly's office. As soon as I sat down, I launched a question at her.

"Have you interviewed the yard truck driver yet?"

She narrowed her eyes at me. "I will be asking the questions here today. Now, please allow me to finish the admonishments. Where did I leave off?"

"Termination," Brody and I both said flatly.

"Ah yes…" She continued reading from a script. Informing me that my attendance in the meeting was mandatory, that I was required to answer all questions and be honest, and that I wasn't allowed to talk about the interview or incident with anyone besides my union rep or attorney or law enforcement. After she finished reading, she opened a folder and pulled out a small packet of papers neatly stapled together.

"I am going to start with the standard introductory questions. Please state your name."

"Miranda Cox. Randy."

"What is your job title here?"

"Outbound Load Splitter."

"How long have you worked here?"

"Fifteen years."

"Who is your immediate supervisor?"

"It was Bryant. A couple of other people have been filling in since the accident."

"Incident."

There it was again. "Ooo-kay."

"Are you left or right-handed?"

I squinted at her, wondering why that mattered.

Brody spoke up. "How is that relevant?"

"It just is."

"Well, not like it's any big secret. Anybody could figure that out just by watching me for a minute or two. I am right-handed."

"What station were you working on the date of the incident?"

"You know where I was working."

"Just answer the question, Miss Cox."

Brody nodded at me that it was okay.

"I worked the crow's nest above door seventy-six."

"And on the date of the incident did you walk the belt out at the end of your shift?"

"Yes."

"What time did you do your belt walk?"

"I am not exactly sure. I didn't check the time because I was busy working. It was just like any other day. After the belt and machinery shut down, I waited for the all-clear and then walked the belt."

"And you were up on the belt still when that trailer was parked at door seventy-six, correct?"

"Correct."

"Did you see anyone else in the yard or on the dock at the time of the incident?"

I paused, thinking back. "I…I don't think so."

"That's not good enough. Did you see anyone or not? I need to know for certain."

I thought back to that day. I hadn't really been paying attention to what was going on down below. I was more focused on my task up on the belt, and not falling off, and still managed to hit my head. I had heard Bryant yelling; had seen he wasn't wearing a vest and hadn't put out a cone. *Was there anyone else?*

Shelly leaned forward in her chair, her face tight and fingers clamped down on her pen.

"I can't say for certain."

"Randy, that's not good enough. It's a yes or no question."

Brody interrupted. "Shelly…she has answered your

question."

Shelly pursed her lips angrily, scribbled a note, and underlined it three times. I tried to see what it said, but her handwriting was tiny and even with my glasses I couldn't read it from across the desk.

Brody shifted his feet and patted his knee. "Are we done here?"

Shelly sat back in her chair and clicked her pen a few times, gazing at the wall over my head. I looked at a picture of her at the golf course with the other managers, where she had on a visor and sunglasses, and held a putter in her hand.

"Just a few more questions and then you can be on your way."

I returned my attention to her. "Yes, please ask everything today. I want this to be the end of it."

"You don't get to decide that. I can call you in here every day and question you if I need to."

I wasn't about to take that from her. "If you want a grievance for harassment, go ahead."

Brody spoke up again. "Listen, Shelly, we are cooperating. Go ahead with your questions."

Shelly's lips had a smug curl to them as she launched into another volley of questions about the rest of what happened after the trailer parked on door 76. As we went through the questions, the sound of the buzzer echoed through the warehouse, followed by the rumble of machinery starting up, letting us know that the next shift had started. I was relieved when Shelly finally wrapped up her questions and released us.

As soon as I stepped out of the office I sucked in a deep breath, only to get a lungful of diesel exhaust. Brody tugged on my arm, and I walked with him toward his abandoned pallet jack. He turned off the recorder on his phone.

"Jesus, Randy, I've never seen her get like that. Something was different about her this time. I mean, she's always a bitch. But this was unreal."

"Maybe it's cuz someone died? I'm sure an on-the-job fatality is a serious amount of work for HR."

"Nah. I've been in the room when she has interviewed

witnesses of a fatal accident before, years ago. Do you remember when Bobby's sleeve got sucked into the box line?" He shivered. "Anyway, this was different. Can't put my finger on it."

I shrugged, anxiety boiling up in me as nausea and a hot flash. I was surprised it hadn't shown up during the interview. Seemed there was no rhyme or reason to when my new pal anxiety showed up.

"Hey, I am going to forward a copy of this recording to your cell phone and email. Save it. Store it somewhere safe. Do you have a thumb drive?"

"Yeah."

"Okay, download it on the thumb drive and lock it up."

"You sure? That sounds a little paranoid."

"Something's weird here, Randy, and this company has a lot of resources. Do it, just in case, okay?" He patted my shoulder.

"Yeah. Okay. Hey, thanks, Brody."

"No problem. I gotta run. Take care."

"You too."

Steering his pallet jack, he walked away, his long strides covering the expanse of the warehouse. My hands started to shake, and I swallowed back some bile as I clocked out and drove myself home. I slept the rest of the day away, only waking up for my alarm the next morning.

*

I FOUND THAT the previous day I had missed a handful of text messages from Kristen and realized I should have checked in with her after our date. Since it was 2:00 a.m., too darn early to respond to her, I waited until after work.

We had a text conversation with a lot of stops and starts because she was still at work. At one point she sent me a picture of her gloved hands holding a hummingbird, its iridescent breast feathers a shiny fuchsia color. I sent her a text.

I have questions. Call me on your break?

Eventually, my phone rang.

"Hey there. Looks like you're having an adventure at work today."

"I sure am." She was winded, her voice cheerful and excited. "That sweet little bird flew into our back work room and got caught up in the corner in some cobwebs. The rest of the crew just stood around watching him struggle, but didn't do anything to free him, so I climbed up on a U-boat cart and got him down. I didn't have a free hand to climb down since I was holding that delicate little cutie, so I just jumped down and my crew caught me. Can you be-lieve it!"

It was easy for me to picture her doing something like that. "Yup, that definitely sounds like something you would do. I'm glad you made it down safely. Cuz, you know me and safety…"

"I had to wipe away the cobwebs from him because he was tangled up tight…his wings, feet, and beak. Once I got him cleaned up, he rested on my hand and then flew away."

The whole story spoke to the sweetness and bravery I had started to notice in Kristen as I got to know her. My heart squeezed and I realized I was developing feelings for her.

An old quote I had heard once, something about how you ought not wait for the conditions to be right to do something, because the conditions would never be right, floated through my head. I realized that I wanted to see her again.

"So…would you like to go on another date next time you're off work?"

"Sure!" She was still a bit winded, and I could hear the sound of shopping cart wheels on pavement in the background.

"I'll gladly come to you this time."

"Sounds good. Hey, I gotta get back to work though. Talk to you soon."

After we hung up, I stroked Porkchop's fur, and watched the trumpet flower tree outside the living room window shudder in the wind. The twinge of happiness I had felt while talking to Kristen fell away and something like loneliness took its place.

I decided to call Bear. She was one of the most insightful people I knew and cut through all the bullshit. She never candy-coated anything.

"Bueno, bueno, Randeee."

"Hey, Bear. How's it going?" My voice sounded flat and hollow to me.

"Ahhh, what's on your mind? Did somebody poop in your cereal this morning?"

That got a chuckle out of me. "Things are weird right now, is all. Good things and bad things all colliding. Tell me about you."

"Me? Just your friendly neighborhood circus Bear, doing tricks for treats."

I gave another halfhearted chuckle.

"Oh…it's bad, eh? You want me to do story time?"

"Yes, please."

"Hm. Okay. Let me think." There was a pause, then a crackle as she took a drag off her vape pen, which made me want a cigarette, but I forced myself to stay on the couch rather than go outside to smoke.

"Okay, did I ever tell you about how my mom used to send me out for firewood?"

"No, I don't think so."

"So, you already know that we were poor as shit when

I was a kid. My mom would send me out to collect wood scraps to burn to keep the house warm, cuz half the time we didn't have electricity. I used to ride my skateboard out behind the industrial complexes and steal pallets. The pallets were damn near as big as me, so I'd load them up on my skateboard and push it down the street. I'd go at night, even though I was just a kid, so there would be less people to see or catch me. I'm lucky I didn't get disappeared, you know?" She paused again, taking another drag. The sound of her blowing out the smoke in a big plume gave me comfort. I stroked Porkchop's head.

"Those were some shitty, hard times, Randy. I mean, it was real bad. But you know what? I still found things to be happy about. I would steal the weekend newspaper from the gas station and read the comics section and just laugh and laugh. And listen. I am not blowing smoke up your ass or trying to minimize or invalidate whatever you've got going on. All I am saying is that it's okay to be happy, even when things are fucked up. One thing I know about you is that you're tough as fucking nails."

I took a moment to think about what she had said and

listened to her breathing for a few beats. She didn't push me. Bear was never in a rush about anything.

"Thanks, bud. I didn't realize it 'til now, but I guess I kinda needed permission to do the things that make me smile while also wading through the shit."

"Yup. Do 'em both. Hey. I gotta go. My edible is kicking in and I have a date with my Xbox."

We laughed and said our goodbyes. As night fell, I watched the faint outline of the trumpet flower tree still swaying, its leaves brushing up against the window.

Chapter Seven

Come On, Randy

THE WEEK WAS a balance of work, hanging out with Darcy, texting with Kristen, and plenty of time spent under the thumb of anxiety. I had left a few messages for therapists but hadn't heard back from any. I was stuck in a rut of coffee and takeout food because I didn't have it in me to cook. My battle to cut back on smoking was in the toilet.

The following Sunday, I rode my motorcycle through

a light drizzle to Kristen's place in Marshtown. A storm was coming, and I should have driven my truck, but I wanted to ride, so I did. The excitement about seeing Kristen put a smile on my face as I followed the red glow of taillights down the freeway. The usual view of the strait as I crossed the bridge was hidden by heavy fog.

I found her address easily. To its credit, Marshtown had done a pretty good job of making sure their street signs weren't hidden behind tree branches.

She lived in a little studio on the second floor of an old brick building in the downtown district. I climbed stiffly up the creaky wooden stairs. My knock echoed on the metal door. Through the small side window, I saw her skip to the door from the sink. I tried, and failed, not to watch her breasts bounce. She opened the door, her trademark toothy grin spread across her face.

She raised her eyebrows. "Oh my gosh. You rode in this weather?"

I nodded and stood awkwardly in the doorway, feeling like I took up too much space in my riding gear. The place was tidy, decorated with a few nature prints on the walls and succulents in petite pots along the windowsill. A row of hand weights and kettlebells stood next to a shoe rack, and a hook by the door hung heavy with medals from all the mud and obstacle runs she had done. They didn't look to be on display so much as she just put them on the hook to give them somewhere to be in her utilitarian space.

She pulled me into a big hug.

"I'm soaking wet from the road. You're gonna get wet."

"I'm already wet," she whispered in my ear.

My heart leaped into my throat. Before I could think of something to say, she ended the hug and gave me a truly innocent grin, tucking a stray bit of hair behind her ear.

"You want some tea? It'll help warm you up."

"Tea. Sure, that sounds good."

I peeled off my layers of gear and placed it all in an organized pile by the door and put my big boots on the shoe rack next to her running shoes and Converse. I stood in the doorway, hands in my pockets, stockinged feet half on the entry linoleum and half on an area rug.

She plugged in an electric kettle and pulled down two

mugs from an open shelf. They appeared to be her only mugs. She also had two plates, two bowls, two glasses, and a cup with a handful of utensils in it.

"I know you like coffee, but I don't have any and the teas I have are all decaf herbal. Your choices are chamomile, rose mint, peppermint, lemon ginger, and ummm, oh, red rooibos."

"Rooi—what?"

She smiled patiently. "Rooibos. It's made from a bush from South Africa. Kinda sweet and nutty. My customers seem to love it."

"Maybe next time. I'll go for the peppermint. Thanks." *Next time? That's awfully presumptuous, Randy.*

"Sure." She turned back to the worn countertop, placed tea bags into mugs, and poured over the boiling water. The cabinets under the counter didn't have doors, but she had hung some makeshift curtains to conceal what I assumed were pots and pans, and maybe some dry goods.

It was cold in her studio, yet she only wore a tank top, pajama bottoms with polar bears on them, and little ankle socks. I was a bit surprised by her choice of clothes for a date. *Who are you to judge her choice in clothing? If she wants to be comfortable, more power to her.*

Kristen carried the mugs over and handed me one that had a tagless teabag floating at the top, the water swirling a greenish-brown color. We stood in the entryway for a moment, holding our mugs, looking at each other.

"Oh. I guess I should invite you in. Come on. Make yourself at home."

We took the three steps from the door to the futon couch across the living room and sat down. I placed the mug on my thigh, holding the handle so it didn't spill. The mug had a painting of owls on it, and hers was painted with rabbits.

She gave me a little grin. "I like to keep things minimalist. I don't like having a lot of *stuff*."

"No shit. Well then, you'll hate my place. Heck, I still wear twenty-year-old socks and sweatshirts." I blew on the tea and took a sip, burning the hell out of my mouth, which was already sore from burning it on my coffee earlier. I rubbed my scorched lip with my thumb, realizing I shouldn't have butt into her sharing with my own stuff.

Unphased, she went on. "I just don't like to get attached to things that can be taken away from me. I know that about myself now."

Her eyes on me, she blew on her tea but didn't take a sip. She showed no emotion about what she had said. I was sad for her and the matter-of-fact way she'd said it. Those two sentences told me a lot about her childhood. I was no psychologist but based on my own background I understood where she was coming from.

I took another scorching sip of tea and watched the bare treetops whipping around outside. I wondered if her desire not to get attached to things carried over to people and relationships, and wanted to ask, but didn't. The color of the thick clouds shifted to a deep gray. The talk about possessions dropped like a lead weight.

She finally took a sip of tea and smiled. "You know, I used to hate tea. I always thought it tasted like warm dirt water. But it's growing on me. My coworkers always seemed to enjoy their tea so much that I decided to really give it a try."

"Well, I can say for certain that this peppermint tea

does not taste like dirt."

We smiled and a comfortable silence strung out between us. The walls creaked and rain spattered the window as the storm arrived.

"Hey, do you want to go for a walk?"

I looked at her, surprised since there was a storm crashing around outside. I eyed my weatherproof riding gear stacked by the door, and realized it was a chance to do something outside of my regular old routine.

"Sure. Let's do it."

I put my mug on the coffee table and slipped on my riding pants, baseball cap, boots, and jacket. I spotted a small, framed photo of Kristen on a low shelf. Bending down to peek at it, I realized that it was her twenty years earlier walking naked on a beach, a spray of her mousy-brown hair blowing across her face.

She saw me looking at it. I straightened up quickly, embarrassed.

"I like to be naked," she said with a smile and wriggled into a lightweight windbreaker before pulling on a pair of tall rain boots that had a ladybug pattern on them.

"You're going to get soaked!"

She shrugged and opened the door. The wind blew in fiercely, bringing fat raindrops with it. We picked our way down the rickety wooden stairs and out to the sidewalk. Kristen took my hand, and we walked up to the main road. The gutter was full of fast-flowing water, and without hesitation Kristen stepped down into it. I walked by her side, getting doused with sprays of water as she kicked it up. She seemed to be truly enjoying herself.

After a few more kicks at the water, she joined me back up on the sidewalk and we strolled on, eventually reaching a train station and park. We did a big loop along a paved trail that took us past a boat repair shop, the marina, baseball and soccer fields, tennis courts, and a playground. Past the marina the path led us along the frothing waterline and back inland again.

The downpour beat leaves down from the trees, and we had to step over a few small tree branches that had been shaken loose by the wind. My nose ran and my head was soaked, the ball cap totally saturated, its bill dripping.

Kristen turned to me, smiling, her hair plastered to her

cheeks. That smile shot straight into my chest, and I wanted to dive into her eyes, which were bright and alive, even in the sparse light cast through storm clouds. I took her hand and we walked on.

We finished the loop and hoofed it back up the stairs to her studio. I checked the doorknob. It was unlocked.

"Your door isn't locked."

"So? I never lock it."

"Really?"

"Really."

"Huh." The thought of just leaving my own house unlocked gave me the willies.

My hand ached from the cold as I turned the knob and stepped inside. We stood in the calm of her studio for a moment, dripping on the small linoleum patch of her entry, while the wind beat on the closed door.

"You can just put your wet stuff here on the tile."

She kicked off her boots and shrugged out of her jacket, which hit the floor with a splat. Next, she peeled off her socks, pajama bottoms, and panties, then wriggled out of her tank top. I stood there, jacket half off, staring at her.

She looked at me and I quickly turned away, cheeks hot.

"Let's go," she said and disappeared through a door off the side of the living space. The sound of a shower turning on spurred me into motion.

I removed my hat, riding gear, and boots and stood on the area rug. My clothes were bone dry, but my hair, face and hands were frozen and soaked. I wasn't sure what I was supposed to do next. Wait for her to finish her shower? I started to sit down on the futon when I heard her say something from the bathroom, but I didn't catch it. After a pause, she repeated herself.

"Come on, Randy, don't you want to get warmed up?"

I drew in my breath, realizing that she wanted me to join her in the shower. I hadn't planned on getting naked in front of her on our second date, but…*what the hell*. I stripped down, making a neat pile of my clothes on the low shelf, next to the picture of her on the beach. I stepped through the narrow door and saw that she was waiting for me, her face peeking out around the shower curtain.

As I hesitated, she looked me up and down and I beat back the shyness I was feeling. Hardly anybody had seen my naked body for years. *Randy, you have nothing to apologize for. Your body is what it is, and she'll either like it or not.* Straightening my shoulders, I stepped over the edge of the tub and joined her in the shower. I tried to be polite and not stare at her and was relieved when she pulled me into a hug. We stood there, under the hot water, holding each other until we had both warmed up enough to get out.

She only owned one towel, which we shared to dry off before sliding into her futon bed under piles of blankets. She had switched on a tiny heater unit built into the wall. It warmed up the small space quickly. Nice and toasty, we cuddled, skin to skin.

Within minutes Kristen was asleep, her cheek on my shoulder and lithe body pressed against mine. I looked up at the light fixture and popcorn ceiling, thinking about our date. It was certainly not like any other date I had been on, which wasn't a bad thing. I had spent my forties a grumpy old bitch and had promised myself to be more open to new experiences in my fifties. I decided that my date with Kristen fell under the category of new things.

I listened to her slow breath, feeling the occasional puff

of air on my throat. Every few breaths she gave the most delicate little snore I had ever heard. Even Porkchop snored louder than her. Her skin was so warm and smooth pressed up against mine, and I took a minute to try and remember the last time I had lain naked with someone. It was 1999. Nineteen-fucking-ninety-nine.

I smiled, pretty damn proud of myself for being right there, in that situation, in that moment. I decided I liked trying new things and promised I would keep pushing myself out of my comfort zone.

Just as I was feeling good about myself, the anxiety stuck its head up and nausea landed in my belly and crept up my throat. I fought the urge to get up and leave, knowing that however much my body and brain wanted to run, I wanted to stay. I clenched my jaw, suddenly mad as hell at the anxiety ruining my moment. *Fuck off.*

I reminded myself to call some more therapists when I got home. Then I lay there, caught somewhere between anger and helplessness. Overwhelmed, I closed my eyes, a tear of frustration rolling down my cheek as a branch scraped rhythmically on the side of the building. Through all of that came the sound of a muffled cell phone ping. It wasn't a sound my phone made, so it must have been hers. The phone pinged again. Kristen shifted and let out a little moan. I hastily wiped away the tear on my cheek and watched as she opened her eyes. She smiled up at me and drew a hand from under the covers to rub her eyes before stretching her arm up in the air. Her elbow let out a meaty crack that made me cringe.

"Nice nap?"

"Yeahhh." The word drew out as she stretched.

"Your phone made a noise."

"Well, the only person I want to talk to is right here," she said, snuggling up against me.

"Hm," I mused, grinning at the ceiling fan. It was nice to be a priority to someone. Then I remembered her earlier comment. "May I ask a question?"

"Of course. Ask me anything."

"So, earlier, you said you don't like to have things in your life that can be taken away from you." I paused, struggling with how to word the next part. "So, is that just about stuff…possessions, or does it carry over to people too?"

She turned over and rolled up on her elbows. "No."

I waited for her to go on, but she didn't. "So…" What was I trying to say? "So…you're okay having people in your life that are close to you, just not things?"

"Yeah."

I gave that a moment of thought as I worked up the nerve to tell her what I had gone there to say. The butterflies in my stomach woke up, fighting with the anxiety nausea that was already there. Bear had said it was okay to have good stuff in your life even when things were bad, but my body didn't know what to do when the anxiety and good stuff happened at the same time. My armpits grew damp.

"So, I think I mentioned that I've been single a long damn time. It's hard for me to open up to people when it comes to dating. But I just wanted to let you know that I really like you. You're on my mind a lot and it makes me happy. And I recognize that this is only our second date, but I'm trying to say what's on my mind more."

I held my breath, hoping she wouldn't pull away, and was relieved when she gave me a big grin and kissed me.

"I like you too," she said, her lips moving against mine as she spoke. Then she raked her fingers through my damp hair and shifted her body on top of mine.

*

BY ALL RIGHTS I should not have survived my ride home that night. The storm raged and blew, there were areas of standing water on the freeway, and I hydroplaned several times, which is scary as shit in a car, and twice as bad on a motorcycle. The side-wind gusts blew so hard I had to lean far over to stay upright. Ignorant drivers changed lanes into me a few times, and the wash blowing up from big rigs as I passed them was like riding through a waterfall. Rain-water got in the collar of my jacket, and ran down my neck, soaking my shirt and bra.

By the time I rolled into my garage, I was exhausted and wrung out. It was late, well after my bedtime for a work night, but I couldn't go to bed yet. I still had to feed Porkchop, set up the automatic coffee maker, and get into some warm pajamas.

As I went through the motions, I thought about my

date with Kristen, and mostly felt good about it, though something tiny tugged at the back of my mind. Some sort of hesitation. I didn't know if it was me being scared to possibly get into a relationship again, or if it was something about her that had me worried.

When I finally hit the sack, I fell asleep right away. My dreams flitted back and forth between Kristen laughing in the rain and snuggled up on my chest, and Bryant pinned against the loading dock, head hanging and pink spit bubbles collecting at the corners of his mouth.

Chapter Eight

Is That What I Think It Is?

IT WAS THE week before Thanksgiving and the package flow picked up so much at work that the machinery and staff could barely get the job done. The conveyor motors and belts groaned and squealed, straining to keep up. The number of belt stoppages and jams were higher than ever, and a big group of seasonal new hires were released from the orientation classroom to do their hands-on training.

The anxiety was with me nearly nonstop at work that week, so I was glad my position wasn't suited for having a trainee. I wouldn't have been much of a mentor since I had to keep my mouth clamped shut for fear of puking or sobbing, or both.

The day before Thanksgiving, I crawled along a low spot on the belt on my way back from the end of shift belt walk, pushing a few stray packages ahead of me. I paused under the spot where I had hit my head the day Bryant had been pinned and rapped my knuckles gently against the metal beam I had cracked my head on. I caught movement below and spotted Shelly watching me from the dock. As soon as our eyes met, she hurriedly looked down at a clipboard she was carrying.

What the hell does she want? I dreaded talking to her and my nausea doubled itself. I just wanted to go home and enjoy the holiday without any of Shelly's bullshit. Steeling myself, I pushed the stray packages down the reject chute, collected my stuff, and stiffly climbed down the ladder, expecting Shelly to get in my face when I made it to solid ground. But when my boot hit concrete, she was gone.

The roads were jammed with holiday travelers doing a mass exodus out of the Bay Area, and it took me twice as long to get home. The traffic made me grumpy, so I sat on the back porch, drank a beer, and smoked. The cigarette made me feel sick, which annoyed me.

I snubbed out my cigarette, ran my hands over my face, and blew out a big breath. I hated how my quiet little life had been turned upside down. *Knock it off. Focus on the positive, Randy. Get your shit together.* Looking around my yard, I saw that the wet ground in the yard was spotted with little green shoots poking up here and there in the soil. *That ought to give me some hope, right? Nature has its cycles. Things'll get better.*

I recalled a saying I'd heard a few years back, which I always thought was gaslighting bullshit, but I said it to myself anyway. "You can start your day over at any time."

I took another breath and thought about what I had to do before bed; iron my dress shirt, brine a turkey, and bake pumpkin pies for Darcy's Friendsgiving gathering.

I didn't have any family left and Darcy had a close circle of friends who had become her family since she'd transitioned. Her "chosen family," she called them.

Back inside, I put on a Garth Brooks CD, and two-stepped into the kitchen. By the time I had a turkey neck-deep in brine, and pumpkin pies in the oven, I'd cheered up and was singing along with Garth. My little kitchen smelled of cloves and buttery pie crust, and I was excited about having somewhere local to go for the holiday. I had spent the last fifteen Thanksgivings home alone.

Buck always invited me, and sometimes Bear would too, when she was in California, but I never could make the trip because they ate late and I had to be up at 11:00 p.m. for work. Black Friday marked the start of the true "peak season" at work, and my shift start time switched to midnight.

Darcy planned to start her gathering at noon and lived right up the road, so I figured it'd be a great chance to meet some folks and be home in time to go to bed by 4:00 p.m.

Kristen didn't have much family either and didn't celebrate Thanksgiving, so she would be on the Golden Gate Bridge with the Bridgewatch Angels, talking to people who might be contemplating jumping. When she told me about it, it sounded like she had made some good friendships with the other Bridge Angels, and enjoyed spending holidays with them, walking the bridge and helping people.

I set the timer for the pies, cracked open another beer, and sat down gratefully on my recliner thinking that it was nice to be able to break out my dad's pie recipe. A little grin pulled at the corners of my mouth as I remembered being a tot standing on a stool at my parents' old Formica kitchen counter watching him roll out pie crust, oldies music on the radio, and the smell of creamed onions in the air.

Porkchop, who was napping on the back of the couch, opened an eye to peer at me, then went back to snoozing. Sipping the beer, I resisted the urge to pull out my cell phone to scroll Facebook. I was hooked on it almost as bad as I was hooked on smoking. I tapped my pocket, checking that I had the phone on me, but didn't pull it out. I turned to Bear's painting instead. Every time I looked at it, I saw a new bit of spatter I hadn't noticed before; the painting always revealed more of itself to me. I was grateful for it, and to Bear for making the painting just for me.

My meditation was interrupted and I damn near

spilled the beer in my lap, startled by my phone ringing and vibrating in my pocket. Porkchop glanced up, disapproving of the shrill sound of the ringer. "Yeah, yeah. Wouldn't want to interrupt your beauty sleep, Your Highness," I said to him, pulling the phone out of my pocket with some difficulty.

I didn't recognize the number, but the prefix was out of Marshtown.

"This is Randy."

"Miss uhhh…Cox?"

"Yes. Who is this?"

"This is Sergeant Cleese."

"What can I do for you?" *Nothing, I hope.*

"You've worked at your job a long time, and I figure you're what we would call a subject matter expert on the equipment and materials in that building."

I liked how he didn't try for small talk and cut right to the chase. "Yes, I probably am a, what did you call it? Subject…"

"Subject matter expert."

"Yeah, that. For anything having to do with what goes

on with the workers inside. I don't know anything about what management or the drivers do. But load, unload, and sort? Yeah, I know all about that."

"So, let's say that we gathered up a bunch of stuff that was on the floor inside, under the loading dock grating. If I had you look at the stuff we found, do you think you could tell us what it is all used for?"

"Probably. The trash under the dock grating is supposed to get swept up twice a day, but it often piles up like snow drifts 'til it is spilling out in the walkway. Hub snakes, plastic wrap, foam peanuts, markers…yeah."

"Hub snakes. Huh. Well, I'd like to meet up with you to get your input on what we have."

"Are you sure that's allowed? I mean, with me being your only witness and all. Will it cause any problems with me also being your subject, uh, whatever?"

"No. I assure you we aren't doing anything that will jeopardize this investigation. Can you meet tonight?"

Jeopardize this investigation. I repeated it to myself, knowing there was more to it than what he was telling me.

"No. I have pies in the oven, so I am not going any-where."

"Great. I will come over."

"No. Not to be rude, but I am not comfortable with that." I started getting nervous that maybe this was all just set up as a way for him to get into my house to snoop around. "I am still being considered only as a *witness*, right?"

"Of course. Well, it would be really helpful for us to have you take a look at this stuff as soon as possible. I realize that tomorrow is Thanksgiving, but I will be working. Any chance you can meet up with me tomorrow?"

I had plenty of time in the morning, before going to Darcy's, but paused before I responded. I liked making him wait. I sipped my beer and watched Porkchop, his long whiskers twitching along with whatever dream he was having.

"Sure. Yeah. I have some time in the morning, before eleven. Can you meet me here in Lands End though, maybe at a café or something else that is open, cuz I will have a turkey in the oven and don't want to go too far or be gone too long. It's that or you'll have to wait till Friday after I get off work."

"Sure thing."

We worked out the details of where to meet the next morning. I hung up and tapped my stubby fingernails along the side of the beer bottle, wondering what the heck they had found that they couldn't figure out for themselves. The piles of trash they had collected was probably just loose packing materials that had fallen out of boxes.

The timer for the pies beeped, drawing a fresh glare from Porkchop. I pulled the pies out of the oven and checked with a toothpick to make sure they were cooked through, then put them on cooling racks on the countertop.

Before bed I covered them with a clean kitchen towel. Porkchop wasn't one to jump up on the counter, he was too chubby to get himself up there, but I didn't want to risk it.

*

THE NEXT MORNING, I was up early and pulled the turkey out of the fridge to take the chill off it. I set the oven to preheat while I showered and had my coffee. I did my best to tame my hair into something presentable for Darcy's party. I dressed up a little, with an abalone snap front shirt, new Wranglers, boots, and even put on a ring that had a wide silver band with turquoise set in it. I didn't wear it much because wearing a ring to work was a surefire way to get a finger ripped off by the machinery, and I didn't exactly go out much, so Darcy's Friendsgiving party seemed like the perfect time.

I rolled up my sleeves and put an apron on, then rinsed the brine off the turkey and trussed it up before rubbing it with butter, lemon, and seasoning. I went outside, clipped a handful of rosemary and sage sprigs, and pulled a couple of lemons off my tree.

I pushed the rosemary and sage into the cavity along with halved lemons. All of that done, I put the turkey into the oven, set the kitchen timer, and got washed up, then set a second timer on my phone so I wouldn't lose track of time while out of the house.

I shrugged into a comfy old leather jacket and drove down to the cafe, which was open for a few hours despite the holiday. Cleese was at a table, his bulk making the tiny chair look like something from a child's tea party. The place had a long line but many of the tables were empty because most customers were getting their drinks to go.

"Hi, Miss…uh. Cox." He extended his enormous hand, and we shook.

"Hullo."

"You want something to drink? It's on me."

More like it's on the department and the taxpayers. "Thanks, but I'll get my own."

"Suit yourself," he said and sipped on an espresso.

I ordered a rooibos tea, going off Kristen's recommendation from our last date. Scorching hot paper cup in hand, I sat down across from Cleese.

"Thanks for meeting with me on short notice, Randy."

"Sure." I sipped the tea and instantly regretted it. It was the temperature of magma. "Shit."

"A little hot, eh?"

"Yeah." I took off the lid to let it cool down. "So, you need some help identifying garbage you found on the floor at the warehouse?"

"One man's trash is an investigator's treasure." He

chuckled at his little joke. I just shrugged at him. "So, since I couldn't haul it all down here, I have pictures of individual items, and would like for you to identify them, if you can. But first I have a quick question. Sound good?"

"Sure." I looked at the tea, which was still steaming angrily. *Wait, dummy. You'll burn your tongue.* I lifted the cup and took a sip anyway, and decided I was an idiot as I flinched. "Jesus. How can they even sell it this hot?"

He gazed up from his notepad. "So are there rules about what you can and can't wear in the warehouse?"

"Yeah. We have to wear closed-toed, sturdy, slip resistant shoes. No sneakers. Most of us wear boots. I skip the steel toes though. I saw a guy lose a toe one time when a huge pallet dropped on him and bent the steel toe into his foot." I paused as that memory swam up. "Oh, and our clothes can't be too baggy, cuz the last thing you want is to get your shirt sucked into a conveyor motor or caught up on machinery." I cringed thinking about the time Bobby got pulled in by his shirt.

"That all makes sense." He pulled a sheaf of papers out of his shoulder bag. "Okay, I am going to show pictures to you one at a time. Take your time, all right?"

I nodded. He set down a picture of a yellow packaging strap. The strap was on a brown tabletop and had a ruler lined up with it.

"That's what we call a hub snake. It's a thick plastic or nylon strap that shippers use on their heavier packages. We call that kind a yellow-bellied hub snake." I chuckled to myself.

He smirked at our lame warehouse humor and placed a new piece of paper down. It was a rat's nest of plastic wrap.

"That is exactly what it appears to be. A giant wad of the plastic we use to wrap up pallets of packages."

He nodded and put down the next picture. It was a red permanent marker, missing its lid, the plastic casing scraped up and filthy, the fat felt tip smashed down and dried out. "Now, of course we know that is a permanent marker. But what is it used for? We found several."

"The loaders have to use a ring scanner to scan the package barcode and then visually double check the zip code on the package shipping label before they load them into the trailer. As they check them, they use the marker to write the door number on the box. That way the supe can go in the trailer later and check to confirm that the loader is paying attention. Checks and balances, I guess."

"So, you mean they have to wear the scanner strapped to their finger, scan the box, hold this marker, and write on the box, all while picking up and carrying the box?"

"Yep."

"Jesus. Talk about having your hands full."

We went through several more pictures, which were mostly discarded supplies and tools the loaders and supes used. It was stuff I saw every day and was able to identify for him immediately. Plus, there were a few items that had clearly fallen out of packages. The company called the loose items "overgoods." Things like a sealed bag of colorful children's marbles, and some sort of little HVAC tool still shrink wrapped to its cardboard backing.

"Okay, last one." Sergeant Cleese placed the final picture on the table, and I didn't immediately recognize it. I pulled out my cheapo reading glasses from my jacket and slid them onto my nose as I leaned over the picture.

"Huh." The image was the same as the others in that it was taken on a brown countertop and had a number marker next to it, with a little ruler. But the item itself was not something I'd expect to see on the floor at work. I turned the picture to see it from another angle.

I met his gaze. "Is that what I think it is?"

Chapter Nine

Peak Season

AS I PARKED in the alley behind Darcy's place, she slid out through a gate in the fence, a huge smile on her face. She waved at me enthusiastically with both hands. She wore a long flowing dress that had stripes of purple and white tie dye and she had well-worn Birkenstocks on her feet.

"Hey, Darce. You look great."

She gave me a warm hug as I stepped out of my truck.

"Thanks for coming! Here, let me help you."

I passed two pumpkin pies to her, before putting on my work gloves to carry the big, smoking hot tray that had the turkey in it. I was careful not to spill any of the juices over the side. The aluminum foil I had placed over the top threatened to blow off as I walked.

Darcy led me through the back gate. I had to go slow as we walked on stepping-stones through the damp grass. We rounded the corner to the front of her cottage and a roar of greetings went up as her friends saw me.

"Are you guys cheering me or the turkey?" We laughed heartily.

Darcy and I went inside and put the turkey and pies on her small countertop, which was already buried in covered food dishes. I had prepared the turkey because she didn't have a full-sized oven in her little kitchen.

Back outside, I sat on a folding chair with a beer and followed the conversation as it flowed along. From what I picked up, the folks at the party lived all over the Bay Area and had known each other a long time, though they didn't make me feel like an outsider as they greeted me warmly and did their best to include me in the conversation.

They seemed edgy and cool in their trendy outfits, and from what I picked up they had jobs like software engineer, author, café owner, esthetician, and surgical nurse. A couple from Oakland had perfectly shaped and trimmed eyebrows and razor-sharp mustaches. I had a moment of feeling dumpy, with my shaggy hair and stretched-out sports bra that was probably older than they were, but I sat up taller in my seat and took a deep breath to push that away.

We sat in a loose circle of folding chairs on the concrete that ran from the front of Darcy's in-law unit to the main house. We were under a gorgeous wooden awning with jasmine weaving itself up the posts and through the trellis overhead. Even though it was November, the jasmine bloomed, leaving its heady scent in the air.

Darcy brought out a few trays of snacks and placed them on the wobbly card table in the middle of the circle. She got a lot of "oooh"s and "aaah"s as she described the snacks. There was a spinach and artichoke baked brie with little rounds of baguette, asparagus spears wrapped in prosciutto, sausage stuffed mushrooms, and something she called "crack on a cracker." I had seen Bear make that before. You put a spoon of brown sugar on a butter cracker, then wrapped it in bacon and baked it.

I could have filled up on the appetizers alone but chose to only have one of each so I would still have room for turkey, potatoes, and pie later.

The boys from Oakland chatted animatedly about the new queer-owned bagel shop in Berkeley, which sounded like it was really popular. According to them the shop usually sold out by 10:00 a.m. I nodded, following along, but at the mention of bagels I remembered that Bryant ate a bagel with cream cheese every day on break, and that sent me down a rabbit hole of worry for his family, having their first holiday without him. I didn't even know if they had had his memorial service yet.

"Hey, Randy. You okay?" I looked up from my paper plate and saw one of the men looking across the table at me with genuine concern, his mouth creased and eyes questioning.

"Yeah. Just thinking about work stuff. I'm good."

"Oh honey! You are off the clock. They are not paying you to think about work right now. Try and relax."

I nodded and took a big bite of a stuffed mushroom so I wouldn't have to talk. I was relieved when Darcy announced it was time for supper. Everyone lined up, piling their plates with turkey, rosemary roasted potatoes, brussels sprouts, and green salad.

Darcy's place was too small for us all to fit inside, so we went back outside and pulled our chairs up to the card tables. A few had to put their plates on their laps because they couldn't fit at the table, though nobody seemed bothered by it. The group was easygoing and jovial. Thankfully nobody said grace.

It was unseasonably cold for California, so Darcy pulled out a propane heater, which took the edge off the chill, and we dug into our food with gusto. Everybody made conversation, and compliments on the food flowed freely, as did the drinks. I started to relax and enjoy myself enough that after we had finished desert and cleaned up, I went to my truck and grabbed my Bluetooth speaker. After

I synced it up to my phone, I launched the classic country station and grinned at the group, rubbing my hands together.

"Who wants to two-step with me?"

The boys looked at me in surprise, which I liked. I was feeling more daring since I had a few drinks and a good meal in me.

Darcy sidled up and we had a moment of giggly fumbling because we both tried to take the lead. Once we got sorted, we started two-stepping and I found that she was one hell of a good dancer. Her friends smiled from the sidelines for a moment, then joined us.

We danced the afternoon away, all smiles and chatter, taking breaks to sip on our drinks, and talk. Before I knew it, it was time for me to go home. A 4:00 p.m. bedtime seemed ridiculous, but I had learned the hard way my first year at the job not to fuck around with it. As temping as it was to stay and keep partying, I knew I needed to get my ass home and in bed. I said my goodbyes, getting lots of hugs on my way out, which I hadn't realized I needed. The hugs helped chase out the sadness about Bryant that had been lurking.

Once home and settled in, I checked my text messages. Kristen had sent me a few pictures, including a group shot of her with some of the other volunteers on the bridge, the turbulent gray water of the San Francisco Bay in the background. A selfie of her glowing face grinned right at me, cheeks and nose red from the cold. We texted for a little bit, then I fed Porky and went to bed. All in all, it was the best day I'd had in years, and for that I was grateful.

*

WHEN MIDNIGHT STRUCK on Black Friday, I was up in the crow's next above door 76. The place got up to full swing in no time. It was easy to spot the recently recruited seasonal workers as they hustled around below, their new boots and hesitation being the most obvious signs.

I got into a steady rhythm and did my best to stay focused on the zip codes and splitting as a way to fend off the anxiety, though my coffee wasn't sitting well while my mind and stomach fought.

Through the roar of machinery and my earplugs I

heard the unique *clang* made by the metal gate at the top of the ladder to my crow's nest. I couldn't stop what I was doing to turn and see who was behind me because there were no gaps in the packages coming at me.

Someone stepped up next to me and hit the button to stop the belt. *What the hell?* It was unheard of to stop a belt at such a busy time unless there was a jam or an emergency. I turned and saw my supervisor, Justin, and someone new.

"What's up, Justin," I grumbled, pointing toward the packages that needed to keep moving.

"I will be real quick, Randy. I've got a trainee for you. Can you show her the ropes?"

"On splitting? Seriously? This is one of the highest seniority jobs in here, aside from clerk. Newbies should be down in the unload or sort."

"Randy. There's no time to argue about this. The HR lady insisted. Can you train her, please?"

"Whatever. Somebody'll file a grievance about this. You know that, right? It won't be me, but one of these guys will see her up here and file."

Justin shrugged and climbed down the ladder. The

guys farther down the belt were watching us, sipping their energy drinks and taking advantage of the unscheduled break.

I hated training in the crow's nest. It was too loud to really talk anyone through the task and there wasn't room for two people to split side by side. It was truly a one-person workstation.

I stuck out my gloved hand. "Randy. What's your name?"

"Mikela." She took my hand and shook it confidently.

Mikela looked like she was maybe twenty years old. She had short dark hair and the squat, solid build of a wrestler or gymnast. She'd be fine with the physical demands of the job, I just hoped she was up for dealing with assholes.

"Okay, Mikela, we gotta get this belt moving pronto. Where are your gloves?"

"They didn't give me any."

I grumbled and dug out a spare pair from my jacket pocket.

"How 'bout your earplugs?"

"They didn't give me any."

"Oh, for fuck's sake." I dug out a set of the cheap-ass foam ones the supes handed out. I always kept a few sets handy.

Mikela put in the earplugs and slid on the gloves, which were snug on her.

I hollered so she could hear me, pointing to the piece of paper taped to the light over the belt, "These are the zip codes we are splitting today. Stand to my side and just watch for a little bit so you can get an idea of how this works."

She nodded, her expression open and confident. I looked up and down the belt. "I'm checking to make sure the belt is clear, and nobody is on it. Next, I'm gonna hit the warning buzzer a few times to alert people that it's going to start, then press this here green button, see?"

She watched as I went through the motions. I knew they covered all the belt stoppage and start-up protocols in orientation, but since she was training under me, I wanted to be sure I said it too. The guys down the belt gave loud, mock groans as the belt started.

As packages passed my station, I pointed to the zip

codes on the package labels, to show Mikela, then pushed them down the chutes or across the belt where they needed to go. She watched me until the building shut down for break.

"Break time!" I flipped open the gate and started down the ladder.

"Where's the bathroom?"

I chuckled. "Follow me. It's a bit of a hike since there are only a couple women's restrooms in this place."

She followed me down the ladder and we struck out for the toilets. I walked at my usual quick pace, and she kept up just fine.

"Wow, you weren't kidding. It's crazy that they don't have a bathroom closer."

"Plenty of men's bathrooms between here and there, but so few women work here they don't really bother. I usually eat my snack on the walk back." I patted my pocket to make sure I had my Pop-Tart in there and was relieved to hear the crinkle of the wrapper.

After using the toilets, we stood at the sinks washing our hands. When I looked at Mikela in the mirror, she had that look on her face people get when they want to say something but are holding back, lips pursed and forehead wrinkled.

"Spit it out, Mikela. What's on your mind?"

We dried our hands and started the walk back. I pulled out my snack and offered her one of the pastries, which she took gratefully.

After chewing on a big bite, she clicked her tongue. "Fuck it. I know it's probably tacky to ask about something like this, but I heard so many rumors during orientation I figured it'd be better to hear the truth from a full-timer like you."

"I'm not one for gossip, but let me hear what it is."

We passed a group of guys sitting on a stack of packages.

"Hey. Idiots," I snapped. "Get offa them packages! You know better. Go sit on a pallet or the dock. Somebody paid a lotta money to ship those through us and they don't need your ass print on 'em."

The guys lowered their eyes, ashamed, and stood up.

"Okay, sorry. Go ahead, Mikela."

"Well." She lowered her voice. "I heard some guy got killed in here. Like, got crushed by some boxes or something a few weeks ago. Is that for real?"

My appetite immediately left me, and I chucked my half-eaten Pop-Tart in a trash can as we passed by.

"Yeah. Sorta. A supervisor got pinned between the load wall and a trailer that was parking."

Her mouth dropped open. She stopped walking and grabbed my shoulder. "Are you for real?"

"Yeah. Come on, we gotta get back before the belts start rolling." I shook loose from her hand and started walking. She caught up to me and was silent for a moment, biting her lip.

"So. Like. A supe really died? Holy shit."

"Yeah. So, I hope you were paying attention in class about all the safety stuff. They aren't teaching you that just for shits and giggles. Take it all seriously and follow it."

"I'm not really new, ya know. I transferred over from the airport like a month ago. They wanted me to go through the new hire orientation since I haven't worked in a package hub like this before."

"Huh. You worked on the tarmac with our jets? That must have been fun. You'll have to tell me about it some time. Anyway, when we get back up top, I am going to have you split for a few minutes. We will take turns so you can start to get some hands-on practice. Sound good?"

"Yeah. Sounds good. But, like did you know the guy? Were you here?""

"Jesus, Mikela. I really don't want to talk about it. Yes, I knew him. He was my supervisor. Yes, I was here. I am the one that found him. Now, that's it. I'm done talking about it." I sped up, not wanting to talk to her anymore. I heard her boots slapping the concrete behind me as she tried to keep up.

Once the belts got rolling, I stood next to her and watched as she did her best to split the packages. I was standing downstream from her so I could fix any mistakes or snag any she missed, though it was a really tight squeeze. We kept bumping elbows and I'd hear her apologize over the din of machinery. Eventually the flow got too heavy for her, and I had her stand aside and watch while I worked.

I wondered how the hell she landed a spot training as a splitter. It really was not a position that newbies or transfers ever got to do. It took about ten years to get enough building seniority to be promoted to splitter. I got to thinking about her questions about Bryant and started getting suspicious. Not taking my eyes off the packages, I hollered to her over the machinery.

"Do you know anyone that works here?"

She paused before she answered. "Nah. No. Don't know anyone here."

She scuffed the toe of her boot on the grating. My gut told me she was a liar, but what the hell did I know, and I was too busy battling a flood of packages to deal with it right then.

Later, after the belts had stopped and I showed her how to do the belt walk, I got back into it with her.

"How'd you land a spot as a splitter?"

"No idea. I went through class same as everybody else. They gave us some tests at the end where we had to memorize three sheets of zip codes. Maybe I did well on that?"

We crawled under an overhead light and came to a

spot where two belts met. I saw a few fat shipping enve-lopes trapped in between the belts and pointed at them.

"See that there?" I grabbed the shipping envelopes and tugged on them to get them out of where they were lodged.

"Oh shit. Man, they are tore up. Why are they black like that?"

"That's called belt burn. The belt wears against the sur-face of whatever package gets stuck and it rips it up, leav-ing something like skid marks on it." I pointed at one side of an envelope that was completely worn through. The back of the cardboard envelope was gone and half of the documents inside had been burned up or ripped. I flipped it over to look at the shipping label, then at the hole in the back to see the documents inside again.

"Oh no. Shit. It's payroll for one of our customers. This is not good. That's half their pay checks ripped to shit and useless."

"Oh man." Mikela ran a hand over her hair as she stared at the mess I was holding.

"Okay, almost done. This is bad. We need to finish up." I crawled along the belt to the end, then we turned around and went back to the crow's nest.

"So, Randy, do you think I did so well on the zip code test that I got bumped up to splitter?" Mikela asked.

"I hate to ruin your day, but no. That zip code test is for sorter. They don't even test newbs for splitter because—"

"—it's for high seniority. Yeah. Got it."

"Good working with ya today. Best of luck to you during peak. Make sure to work safe. Okay?"

"Yeah. Sounds good. But…" She bit her lip.

"But what?"

"Well, I worked in the load earlier this week and one of the other regular guys yelled at me."

I scoffed, not surprised. "What for?"

"He told me to slow down. Said I was making him and the other guys look bad."

I let out a cackle that was much louder than I had intended. "Yeah. Those guys aren't interested in busting their balls or breaking a sweat. Don't mind them. Just do your thing. 'Kay?"

"Yeah. Thanks for today, Randy."

We shook hands and she climbed down the ladder. I peered over the railing and saw one of the training supervisors from HR waiting down below. When I got to the bottom, nobody was around.

I put away my glasses and earplugs and grabbed the shredded payroll envelopes from the bottom of the reject chute, then walked through the nearly silent warehouse toward the clerks' area, which was clear across the building from my load wall. When I eventually got there, the guy who supervised the clerks held out a hand to me.

"Whatcha got today, Rand— Jesus Christ, is that what I think it is?"

"Payroll? Yeah."

He snatched the destroyed envelopes out of my hand and stared at them, his eyes bulging and his lips moving silently as he read what was left of the shipping labels.

"Fuck, fuck, *fuck*! Why the hell were these even on the belt? The unload and sort know that all the envelopes from the payroll vendors go in a tote, not straight onto the belt! Goddamn newbies. Fuck!" A vein pulsed in his temple.

He grabbed his radio and started speaking into in.

Whoever was on the other end barked out a shrill "Fuck!" in return.

I didn't want to get pulled into that mess, so I waved at him. "Can I get outta here? I'm supposed to be on lunch."

He waved me away dismissively as he angrily tapped the envelope's tracking number into a keyboard, the clerk standing back to avoid his wrath.

Passing through the building, I heard the first noises of the next shift setting up and ran into Brody.

"Hey, Randy. How're things?"

"Busy. First shift was a doozy." I thought about telling him about Mikela being in training with me up in the crow's nest but didn't want to start a whole big thing with the union. He'd find out eventually on his own.

"Yeah, it sure was. Hey, have you heard any more from HR or corporate about their investigation?" He made air quotes with his gloved hands when he said the word *investigation.*

"Nope. Nothing since that meeting we had with Shelly."

"Hm."

"'Kay. Thanks, Brody. Have a good one."

"Stay safe, Randy."

*

AFTER MY FIRST sixteen-hour shift of peak season I was exhausted and not interested in cooking anything, so I grabbed dinner from a drive thru on the way home. As soon as I walked in the door, I stripped out of my filthy work clothes and put on some comfy sweats, then fed Porkchop and sat down to eat. I only had about forty-five minutes before I had to get to bed, so I scrolled through my text messages with one shaky hand, while I shoveled the burger and fries into my mouth with the other.

I responded to a check-in text from Darcy, sending me good vibes for my first double shift of the season and thanking me for joining her Friendsgiving party. Then I opened a string of texts from Kristen, burger suspended in midair in front of my mouth as I read them.

My chest tightened as a zing of excitement hit me at the simple act of reading a few friendly messages from her. I couldn't wait to see her again. Then I remembered it was peak season, and I would spend the next month working sixteen-hour days with about one hour in the evening of personal time before I had to hit the rack at 4:00 p.m.

I took a big bite of burger and my phone starting ringing, the screen lighting up with a selfie of Kristen. I did my best to chew up the food as quickly as I could and slid the answer button with my burger-free hand.

I coughed a little on the huge bite of burger I had swallowed. "Hey!"

"Hiya. Whatcha doin'?"

"I'm eating dinner. You?"

"Just getting off work. And thinking about you. I want to see you again."

I grinned, putting the burger down. "I'd really like that. I'm on double shifts now through the end of the year, so it's going to be tricky, but don't take that as a lack of interest, it's just our busy time at work." I sighed. I was excited to talk to her but was fading fast as the long day caught up with me.

"You sound tired. Go get some sleep. Maybe we can

see each other after I get off work tomorrow?" The excitement in her voice had dropped a notch.

"Yeah, let's do it."

We said our goodbyes and hung up. I was so tired I couldn't finish my burger. I pulled the patty out from the bun, tore it into small pieces, and put them in Porkchop's bowl.

I locked up, shut off the lights, and put myself to bed. For once, sleep beat out anxiety.

Chapter Ten

Tread Lightly

I DIDN'T NORMALLY work Saturdays, but it was peak season, and the facility was running around the clock. I loved the extra hours on my paycheck and would only be missed at home by Porkchop.

Just before midnight on Saturday morning I climbed the ladder to the crow's nest and my heart leaped into my throat when I saw someone else already there. I closed the gate behind me with a clang. When I double checked the number stenciled on the wall, it read "76." I was in the right place.

"Hey, uh, I think you may be on the wrong platform," I said as I pulled my coffee mug out from where it was tucked inside my jacket.

As the person turned from studying the zip code sheet, I realized it was Mikela.

"Hey, Randy," she said, a big grin on her face. She ran her palm forward over her short hair, smoothing it down.

"Mikela. You're up here again today?"

"Yup. Training supe from HR sent me."

"Are you here with me for both shifts?"

"No, just the first shift. Dunno where they'll send me for the second half. Man, this double shift thing is rough. Reminds me of my days at wrestling meets. But I haven't pulled a day like yesterday in a long time. Fuck, I'm sore." She pulled an arm across her chest to stretch. "They weren't kidding in training when they said to make sure you get to bed on time. I was in bed by five, but there were kids playing outside my apartment and they kept waking me up."

She sighed, fresh dark circles under her eyes, then smiled again, dropping her arm to her side.

I sipped my coffee and set the mug in its usual spot, then put on my glasses, earplugs, and gloves. Mikela put on the gloves and earplugs I had given her the day before. I pointed at the zip code sheet, and she went back to studying it. I leaned against the belt and watched her, still suspicious of why they had sent her up to train on splitting. Checking my watch, I saw that midnight had passed, and wondered why the belts and machinery hadn't started up yet.

Down below, Justin was giving his usual pep talk to the loaders, who were circled up around him on the grating right where Bryant had died just a few weeks earlier.

This standing around is bullshit.

I wanted to get busy working before the anxiety showed up. I was also pissed off that I had to babysit Mikela again and the delay with getting the belt running was making my heart twitch. My coffee wasn't sitting well, and I stifled an acidic belch, swallowing hard.

Mikela leaned her hip on the belt and turned to me. "I

think I've got the codes down for today. You think I can try splitting again?"

"Sure, we'll have you start as soon as the belt gets going, before the flow gets too heavy."

"Cool. Thanks." She ran her gloved palm over her hair. "Working here has been crazy. I had no idea what it took to get packages from one place to another. At the airport most of the packages were all sealed up in air containers. It wasn't anything like this."

I nodded at her. "Yeah, seeing these types of warehouses for the first time is pretty neat. I remember my first time. Before they would let us interview for the job, we had to go on a group tour. Mine was at 3:30 a.m. and I was shocked to see how many people were working. I'd mostly worked days and third shift before coming here. We walked all around the place and the HR rep explained how the packages go from the unload, through the sort, and are either loaded into a new trailer or into a truck for same day delivery. Miles and miles of conveyor belts. And now the noise and dirt and weird hours are no biggie to me."

She nodded at me, the corner of her mouth twitching

just a hair. She started to speak and hesitated, touching her hair again.

I resisted the urge to roll my eyes. "What's on your mind, Mikela?"

Mikela opened her mouth to speak just as the buzzer blew. She clamped her mouth shut at the interruption. I shrugged. Packages started flowing and I squeezed in downstream from her so I could check her work, catching the occasional mess-up and shoving it back up the belt to her so she could get it to the right place. We got into a rhythm, and the flow was manageable enough for her that she worked through until our first break. I was impressed with how well she was doing with memorizing the split and keeping up with the flow.

At break time, we climbed down the ladder and started the trek to the restroom.

I gave her a hearty clap on the back. "You're doing great."

"Thanks."

We passed groups of filthy, sweaty guys leaning against the unload docks and sitting on pallets. Some had earbuds in while others drank from tall cans of energy drinks and hollered playfully at each other. I heard a "Wassup, Randy," and gave a small wave in reply.

After using the bathroom, I watched Mikela in the mirror as we scrubbed up. She kept biting her lip. I held my hands under the warm water a little bit extra just to thaw out my aching joints.

"I wanna ask you something but you told me yesterday to drop it."

"Oh. You want to talk about the supe who got killed? Is that it?" The patience I had for her was growing thin.

She nodded and turned to grab some paper towels. We dried our hands and started walking back.

"You gotta understand, Mikela, that's a hard thing for me to talk about."

"Sure. Makes sense. You'd said you were the one who found him, right?"

I stopped walking and turned to her. A group of unloaders were resting a few feet away and stopped their chatter to listen in. "Yes. I found him. I already told you that."

"But. Like. Did you see it happen? Was anyone else around?"

I grit my teeth as my temper rose. The guys who were watching us leaned in.

"Jesus fuck, Mikela. I already told you I don't want to talk about this. No. I didn't see the moment he got pinned. I was doing the end of shift belt walk. Remember when we walked the belts and found those payroll envelopes yesterday? That's what I was doing." My voice lowered to an angry growl. "I didn't see shit." The palms of my hands itched, a sign back in my bar fighting days that I was about to haul off on someone. I realized I was about to explode on her and didn't want to lose my job for kicking the shit out of some transfer, so I turned on my heel and took off toward the load wall.

I found Justin sitting on the dock, chatting with a few loaders. I shouldered my way through the group and stepped in front of him.

"Hey, Randy. What's the problem?"

I drew in a deep breath, doing my best to steady my

tone. "I don't want that new chick up there with me any-more. Send her back to the trainer for a different assign-ment. Please."

Justin narrowed his eyes, looking down at me from his perch, shaking his head. "Randy. You know that's not how things work around here. Whatever it is, work it out. Now get up there and get ready. The belt is going to fire up any second." He waved harshly at the rest of the workers stand-ing around. "All of you, let's go. Move it!"

I climbed up the ladder and found Mikela at the top, looking down at me, blocking the gate. I stopped a few rungs below her, waiting for her to get out of the way. I tried not to think about how high up I was, with no safety harness, just my hands and feet on the ladder keeping me in place.

"Back up, Mikela. Get out of the way of the gate."

She continued to look down at me, eyes hooded and dark, then ran her palm over her hair and clicked her tongue, stepping back slowly. A chill rolled down my spine as I realized that maybe I wasn't safe up there with her. But I wasn't about to let her intimidate me. I climbed the rest of the way up and closed the gate securely behind me.

The railing up there was only waist high. She could easily push me over the side. I had never once, in my fifteen years there, worried about something like that. I had trusted my crew not to do anything to put me in danger. But something wasn't sitting right with me about her.

The buzzer blew and I pointed to show that I wanted her to keep splitting. She couldn't shove me over the side if her hands were full of packages. She stepped up to the belt, gloves on, and got to work. We didn't speak another word to each other.

When the first eight-hour shift ended and we broke for shift change, Mikela met up with her trainer from HR down below. I watched as they walked away, the training supe tossing an occasional look over her shoulder up at me while Mikela talked animatedly to her.

I was angry and didn't feel like talking to anyone, so I stayed up in the crow's nest and ate lunch from my ice chest. Before work I had thrown together some leftover re-fried beans, grated cheese, rice, and chilis in a stale tortilla. I would have liked to throw it in the crusty microwave in the break room but decided to stay put up top.

I folded back the paper towel my burrito was wrapped in, took a big bite, and scrolled through Facebook for a few before checking my text messages. It was just after 8:00 a.m. so I wasn't expecting texts, but I had some from Kristen. She was up early and was on a walk at the Marshtown Marina park.

We texted a little bit and she sent pictures from her walk, things like the water, bluffs, and boats under an overcast sky. I smiled down at my phone and took another bite of my stale, cold burrito. Seeing the scenery calmed me down, and I was grateful for it. I thanked Kristen for the pictures, and we said goodbye since I needed to run to the restroom.

As the second shift started, I was happy to be up in the crow's nest by myself. I thought about my morning with Mikela and didn't know what to make of it. I tried to brush it off as her being one of those people with an obsession with death. Maybe she watched those true crime shows on TV. Either way, I was glad she wasn't training with me anymore and I hoped to never see her again.

*

"THIS DAMN TRANSFER is being nosy and keeps asking what I saw when Bryant died, even though I've told her to knock it off."

I let out a sigh and stroked the back of Kristen's neck as we lay on her bed. The window was propped open with a few books, letting in the cool breeze and the sound of the creek trickling below. Kristen shifted a little, adjusting her head on my chest.

"Sounds like a weirdo. You're not worried, are you?"

"Kinda. I probably just need to let that go. Hopefully they won't pair her up with me again." I blew out another sigh. "Anyway, how was work?"

"It was good. One of my friends transferred back from the store in Dairy Glen. It was good to see her. You'd think with it being a couple days after Thanksgiving that the crowds would have thinned out, but nope. Place was packed. But that's good. It makes the day go by faster."

We paused, listening to the creek some more, and I kissed the top of her head.

"The pack of aggressive turkeys is back at the parking

lot. Today they wouldn't let people get in their cars. I posted video on my Insta of me chasing turkeys away with a shopping cart so a customer could leave." She let out a little giggle.

"Aggressive turkeys the weekend after Thanksgiving. Sounds like payback."

I felt her lips curl into a smile against my skin.

From my spot propped up on her futon bed I admired the crown molding and rounded doorways in her darkened studio.

"I really like your place," I said, wondering how much the rent was. It had to be high.

"Me too." She took in a big breath and let it out slowly. "It was a lucky find. This place has it all. Right downtown, along the creek, and the place is well maintained. The cost of rent is no joke though."

"Well, if you need to pick up some extra hours, we are still hiring hourly seasonal workers at the warehouse."

"Oh yeah?" She popped her head up.

"You interested?"

"Heck yes."

"Well, all right then." I chuckled. "I'll text you the website to apply, if you're serious about it."

"That'd be kinda cool, right? I could work at like midnight with you, then come home and shower before I do my shift at PJ's. And then you and I would kinda be on the same sleep schedule too."

She gave me a huge smile that made my heart melt into a puddle, before resting her cheek on my chest again. I looked out of the window at the treetops and dusky sky, a grin on my face and something close to happiness in my heart.

*

KRISTEN EASILY LANDED a seasonal job at my warehouse. They hired her for the graveyard shift, working from midnight to 8:00 a.m. After two days of classroom training, she started as an unloader, then they moved her to the load. While we didn't work together, it was great to catch glimpses of her hustling around down below.

We weren't able to see much of each other outside of work, aside from the one day a week we both had off. We spent our Sundays under a cloud of exhaustion at her place watching old DVDs, eating take-out, and napping. Somehow the long hours and exhaustion brought us closer together, and pretty soon we were calling each other girlfriend.

She laughed off the fact that practically every dirtbag in the warehouse hit on her or asked her out. We both got satisfaction in their reactions when she told them she was my girlfriend. She easily passed as straight and was such a fresh, sunshiny, youthful person that she drew them in like moths to a flame, whether she liked it or not.

They were surprised first to learn she was gay, and second that she was with me. I figured that was because of how weathered and grumpy I was. It was nice to sling my arm across her shoulders and walk through the warehouse, escorting her out to her car when first shifted ended.

Near the end of December, when her seasonal work was almost over, Kristen's normally cheerful mood abruptly stopped. We sat in her car, eating lunch before she had to leave for her other job and I had to go inside for my second shift. She poked at the chicken and rice in her glass container, a meal she normally wolfed down, hungry after so much physical work.

I put my thermos of stew in the cup holder and placed my hand on her leg. "What's wrong, babe?"

She set her dish on the dashboard, laid her hand over mine, and looked at me. "Something happened today."

I did my best to wait patiently for her to go on, but my heart rate went up and my stomach clenched. She looked out of the window and then back at me.

"This isn't the first time, but I didn't mention it cuz it didn't seem like a big deal. But it happened again today and…I don't like how it's making me feel."

I stopped myself from questioning her about what "it" was and forced myself to shut up and be a good listener, so she could say her piece at her own pace.

"I've been paired up in the load with Mikela a bunch lately."

"Oh?" My free hand clenched into a fist. I forced myself to release it.

"Yeah. And she seems to know that you and I are in a relationship cuz she asks about you a lot. I mean, we are stuck in a huge trailer together almost the whole shift, so it's hard to ignore her when she gets like that, but I try to. You were right that she has a weird vibe. There's something unsettling about her. I don't like it."

I sat up a little and flipped my hand over so I could hold hers. "What sort of things has she been saying that are bothering you?"

"Well. She asks a lot about you. Personal stuff like where you live, if you have family, and how you're handling the whole Bryant thing, like if you're upset at night or in therapy. She wanted to know the name of your therapist."

"I don't have a therapist."

"I know. I didn't answer her questions, so she just assumed and kept asking."

I grumbled, my free hand tightening into a fist again. "What'd you tell her?"

"Nothing. Like I said, I didn't answer her questions. I just either ignored her or told her if she had questions about you to ask you herself. When I ignored her, she started saying stuff to get a rise out of me." Kristen took a breath and held it.

My temper rose, making my temples throb and hands tingle. Kristen wouldn't look at me.

"What sort of things did she say to you, Kristen?"

She tightened her grip on my hand. "Okay. But promise me you won't do anything to get yourself in trouble."

I clenched my jaw and waited until we were making solid eye contact. "I can't promise that. What did she say?"

She hesitated, eyes shifting to a spot just over my shoulder before meeting my gaze again. "Well, today, after really pestering me about you and me ignoring her, she started saying nasty things to me. Talking about how I should dump you and date her. She got really graphic about what kind of sex she wanted to have with me, and said she'd been thinking about me while she masturbates." She paused, a little sniffle escaping her. "She said she likes it rough and wants to grab my throat and push me against the trailer wall, and that it was making her wet just thinking about it."

Kristen hooked some stray hair behind her ear. "Ick, I just… I didn't even know what to say to her, so I didn't say anything. I kept my head down and continued loading the trailer. She kept at it 'til the end of the shift and then used a hub marker to write her number on my arm."

"What? She touched you?" I shouted louder than I had intended, and Kristen flinched. "Sorry."

"Yes. She grabbed my arm and pulled up my sleeve and wrote her number. See?" Kristen pulled her hand from mine and yanked up her sleeve. Sure enough, scrawled in huge red print were Mikela's name and a phone number.

"What the fuck?" I muttered as I ran my fingertips along the bold writing. Kristen pulled her sleeve back down, her eyes cast in her lap, shame creasing her lips.

I chewed on a hangnail on my thumb. My mind raced through what she had said. "I'm going to fucking kill her."

Kristen grabbed my forearm. "No. I just want to leave it alone and pretend it never happened. I'm fine. Really."

"I don't understand why you aren't pissed right now."

"It's fine. Let's just forget it."

"Nah. I hate Shelly, but maybe this is something HR should hear about."

"No. I'm not reporting it. It'll just make things weird."

"And things aren't already weird? Kristen. Seriously. This is not okay." I rubbed my hands over my face, trying to subdue the rage flooding me. I pulled a smoke from a crumpled pack of American Spirits in my jacket pocket and held it, unlit, between shaking fingers.

"I only have a week left of my seasonal gig and then I'm done. Let's just leave it alone."

I rubbed my chin, thinking about how to handle Mikela.

"Randy. You're not listening to me. It's my call, and I am not going to report her. If they stick me with her again, I'll just keep ignoring her. It's only a week. I remember in school when I got teased, my teacher told me the kids were just doing it to get a reaction out of me, and if I didn't react, eventually it wouldn't be fun anymore and they would stop."

"Yeah, that's some gaslighting bullshit, and it may work on a second grader, but she is a grown-ass adult and who knows what her motivation is. But…if you don't want to report it, fine. Doesn't mean I won't fuck with her a little though."

She huffed. "Just don't get yourself in trouble or endanger your job. She isn't worth it."

"Fine." My head pounded from holding my temper in. "I'm gonna have a smoke and then get back to work. You have a good day at your second shift too, okay?"

"I will." She paused. "I really wish you wouldn't smoke."

I gave her a quick kiss and climbed out of her car. I lit up my cigarette and leaned against the chain-link fence. Kristen gave me a wave and pulled away, her car's muffler rattling and serpentine belt squealing.

I watched the line of employees pass slowly through the guard station. Most were dressed in blacks, browns, and grays since anything else would show the filth of the job. I took a long drag and realized for the first time how depressing my workplace could be. The interior of the building was all concrete and metal, no color or soft edges. In the winter it was literally freezing, and during the summer it was like being inside an oven. I had never minded it before and wondered why it had started to matter to me. I told myself thinking like that was of no use and flicked the cherry off my cigarette before stowing the butt in my breast pocket.

On my way to the guard station, I spotted Mikela getting in the back of the line. She had her hood up, but I recognized her squat, solid body and what bit of her face was showing. The rage at how she had treated Kristen bloomed again. She wasn't in the guard station yet, still on the public sidewalk, and we were both off the clock, so if we had a scuffle technically it wouldn't be workplace violence or anything the corporation could get involved in.

I walked up and cut in line between Mikela and the person in front of her. Mikela gave my back a little shove, and I grinned at how easy it was to rile her. Straightening my face, I turned around.

I jammed a finger at her, just short of touching her, and spoke loudly so other people in line heard. "What the hell was that shove for, Mikela?"

"You cut in front of me, Randy."

"I don't know what you're talking about. But keep your fucking hands off me."

Mikela shoved me again, not hard, but enough to

make me stagger back a pace. The guys in line started mur-muring.

"What's your problem, Mikela?"

"You, Randy. You're my fucking problem."

"Pfft. I'm just here to do my job, earn a paycheck, and go home. I don't need any of your drama."

Knowing it was risky to take my eyes off her, I turned around and got back in line. The guy in front of me, another salty long-timer, mumbled something to me about Mikela being a dumb kid. I nodded and shuffled forward as the line moved.

There was the scrape of boot on concrete behind me. I braced for whatever Mikela was about to do. Both her hands slammed into my back. She shoved me so hard that my whole body rammed into the guy in front of me. I spun on Mikela, glad she had ratcheted it up enough that I would be justified in hitting her in self-defense. I got into a guarded fighting position, my hands up near my face, ready to strike. Being in that stance felt natural to me. It had been a long time since I had gotten into a scuffle, and I wel-comed it.

"You fuck with my girl, you fuck with me," I growled at her, bringing up Kristen on purpose to try to spur Mikela on.

As she was a wrestler, I knew she'd have me pinned on the ground in no time, but I was hell bent on getting a few strikes in before she did. Mikela smirked and got into a low stance, arms wide. I took that as my only chance and struck her square on the ear with a hammer fist. Heat bloomed in my hand and Mikela staggered. Her ear immediately bloomed red and began to swell.

She shook her head like a dog with water in its ear, and before she could get back into her low stance, I whacked her again in the same spot. The skin along her earlobe opened up more and blood flowed freely. Not as phased by the second hit, she charged at me. I tucked my chin into my chest, loosening my body, and let her take me down easily. When we hit the ground, I didn't put up any resistance as she pinned me.

A few of the guys grumbled, and one spoke up. "Hey. Knock it off."

Mikela had me pinned in such a way that she was basically hugging me, and somehow, she also had her knee on my chest, grinding into my sternum. Cheek to cheek with her, trying to manage the pain from her knee, I looked up at the sky and spoke into her ear, keeping my voice low so the guys couldn't hear.

"What do you want from me, Mikela?"

"Nothing, old lady."

She rubbed her cheek against mine, painting her slick, hot blood on me.

"Stay the fuck away from Kristen, then." I coughed as the pain from her knee digging into my sternum peaked.

"I don't give a damn about her either."

"What's your deal then? Why are you digging for info about me and Bryant?"

"Maybe I just like twisted shit." She loosened her grip on me a hair and raised her face until we were chin to chin. She smirked and ran her bloody cheek across my open mouth and nose.

Disgusted, I squirmed under her weight as she ground her knee into my chest even harder. I groaned and raised my voice. "Somebody get this bitch off of me!"

Two guys from the jostling crowd grabbed Mikela and lifted her up so quickly it was like she weighed as much as a toddler. She didn't resist them, and got in line with no fuss, as if nothing had happened.

Brody squatted down next to me, extending his hand.

"Whoa, Randy. What's going on? Can you get up?"

"Yeah, I'm fine." I took the hand he offered and stood up. My head swam and I leaned over, resting my hands on my knees, seeing stars for a few seconds.

"You need to go get cleaned up."

"Don't worry, none of it is mine. But yeah, I need to go wash my face in case she has any diseases or something." I spat into the gutter, trying to get her blood off my teeth and tongue.

The security officer let out a startled cry when Mikela stepped into the guard station, her face bloodied. A group of guys in line ahead of me huddled around a cell phone hooting and whooping. One turned and looked at me.

"Randy! Dude, you're about to go viral!" He chuckled.

"No way. You little shits took video?"

A couple of them pulled out their cell phones and snapped pictures of my face, which was a mess. I smiled so they could get the bloody teeth too.

"Damn, Randy. You may be older than my momma, but you are one tough chick. Pow, pow." He acted out the punches I had thrown and laughed wildly as he bounced on his toes.

I nodded, excited from the scuffle. "You got that right."

Brody stepped in. "Okay, guys, the buzzer is about to go. Let's get moving. Hey, send me the video and pics, would you?"

"Yeah, you got it."

We got into line and Brody leaned into me. "Hey, don't be surprised if Shelly pulls you in to HR for this. Come find me if she does."

"She may, but we were off the clock and off property, so there's not much she can do. And Mikela put her hands on me first." I shrugged.

"Even so." He thumped me on the back, and we stood in silence, waiting for our turn to pass through security.

My belt buckle set off the metal detector and Gus, the guard, let me pass unchecked as he gave my bloody face the side eye.

Brody's phone pinged a few times from text messages rolling in as we walked into the building to clock in. He was chatting about having holiday plans with his kids and grandkids when I caught the sound of high heels, practically at a run.

"Is that Shelly coming up behind me?"

"Sure is, and man, does she look pissed."

I turned, a big smile on my face. "Good morning, Shelly."

Shelly's face was flushed, her lips pressed tightly in a flat line of anger, though she blanched briefly as she took in the blood drying on my face and coloring my teeth. She gathered herself quickly and narrowed her eyes.

"You. My office. Now!"

"Come on, Brody," I said. He nodded and grinned at me. Sometimes I thought the shop stewards got off on pushing back on management. Either way, I was glad he was on my side.

As we trailed behind Shelly we passed by Justin, my supervisor, who took in the scene.

"Nope. Hey, come on, Shelly. I need Randy up in the crow's nest. The belts are about to start rolling. Shelly!"

Shelly didn't slow down or miss a stride. I gave Justin an *I'm sorry, what can I do?* shrug as I passed him.

"Fuck," Justin grumbled, throwing his arms up in frustration.

We trundled along behind Shelly, not rushing the way she was. Her perfectly styled pixie cut didn't move despite her brisk pace. Her suit skirt, tight and tailored to her body, moved with her.

"Hey, Shelly. I'd like to go wash my face first."

She ignored me.

Brody spoke up. "Shelly, I'd like a quick caucus with Randy before we begin." She ignored him too.

Just outside Shelly's office I spotted Mikela leaning against a drinking fountain, watching us with a smug grin on her face. She looked pretty pleased with herself, blood smeared down her cheek. She pulled out her phone and snapped a selfie with a fake distraught look, her bottom lip pouting out and eyebrows crinkled as if she were about to cry.

I raised my voice. "Hey, Mikela, don't you have a trailer to load?"

Brody bumped me with his elbow lightly and shook his head. Taunting her was fun, but he was right.

At her office door, Shelly bent over a bit to unlock the handle with a key that hung on her ID lanyard, then motioned with a rigid hand for us to go in.

"We'll join you in just a moment," Brody said, holding his ground. "This will be quick."

Shelly frowned even harder and stepped into her office. She slammed the door in my face. Brody pulled me away from her door by the elbow and eyed Mikela until she left. We were in the middle of the hustle of shift change, so there was no private place to speak.

Brody looked at his cell phone and scrolled through the pictures that had been sent to him. Then he held the phone out to me. "Here's the video of your fight. You want to watch it with me or not? I need to know exactly what happened before we go in there."

I nodded and he pressed play. The video started right as I told Mikela to keep her hands off me, followed by her shoving me, then it went on from there.

"Well, that doesn't look good for Mikela. I am going to send you copies of the photos and video real quick, and then we will go in. For now, let's not tell Shelly that we have video."

I sighed, unzipping my jacket roughly as sweat formed under all the layers of clothing I had on. Brody pressed his finger to his lips and showed me as he pressed the record button on his phone, then opened the office door. He let me go in first. We squeezed into the visitor chairs.

Shelly's eyebrows were drawn down and her lips formed a thin line. Her jaw clenched and unclenched. Brody placed his phone facedown on his knee. Shelly's expression changed, looking more drawn and exhausted. While her hair and clothes were on point, underneath all that polish, she didn't look well.

"Randy, it's been reported that you have committed an act of workplace violence. I am informing you that I will be opening an investigation into this matter. I will not be interviewing you today, as I still need to gather more information, but for the time being I am placing you on administrative leave—"

Brody cut in. "Whoa, whoa. Shelly. On what grounds?"

She hissed back at him, clearly annoyed at being interrupted. "*I just told you*. Randy has committed workplace violence. We cannot have her in the workplace until we know she is not a danger."

"Allegedly. Randy has *allegedly* been *involved* in workplace violence. That's a hell of a lot different than what you just said, which is that she has committed it. How did you determine that she is not safe to be in the workplace? On what authority are you placing her on admin leave?"

"Brody. It was reported that she attacked a fellow employee. I mean, just look at her face."

"I ask again, on what authority are you placing her on admin leave? I've been through this dance with you before with other employees, and you and I both know darn well that you can't just put people out. You have to get approval from the district HR director. This confrontation literally happened five minutes ago. There is no way you got approval from the district already."

Shelly paused and looked intently down at the dish of paperclips on her desk.

Called out, motherfucker. I wanted to celebrate this small victory.

I turned to Brody. "May I speak?"

"Tread lightly."

"Shelly. Aside from who did what, I would like to point out to you that this all happened off property and off the clock. To me that means the corporation shouldn't be involved at all."

She raised an eyebrow at me, a flicker of surprise on her face that she quickly covered up.

"I'd also like to add that I've been here fifteen years with zero disciplinary actions. If you try to do this, it will drag out through the progressive discipline and appeals process for months. And that's all assuming you do have enough findings to put me out on admin leave or suspend me in the first place. I—"

"Enough. I don't need you to tell me how to do my job, Randy." Shelly's voice dripped with condescension and disgust. "You don't know the first thing about how Human Resources works—"

Brody cut in. "Be that as it may, Shelly, I do. And even Randy can see that this is unreasonable."

The buzzer rang outside, and the sound of machinery and conveyor belts began rumbling. I shifted in my seat, hoping Justin had found someone to sub in my spot until I could get up there. Shelly stared at the wall just over my shoulder again. We sat in silence for a solid two minutes before Brody cleared his throat.

"Shelly, with all due respect, Randy and I both are needed in the operation."

"Fine. Go. I'll follow up with you both later."

Brody and I left, walking quickly toward my load wall.

"What the fuck was that?" I asked.

Brody clicked his tongue.

"I don't get why she would jump straight to putting me out on leave like that. Did she really just take Mikela's word for it?"

"This isn't like Shelly. She is normally very composed and does her due diligence before making any big decisions."

"Can you send me the recording of the meeting?"

"Sure. If she calls you in again, don't go without a shop steward."

"You know it."

We shook hands and I climbed up the ladder to the crow's nest. Nobody was there, so the packages were flowing by without being screened or split off. As soon as the sorters further down the line saw me, they cheered. I stripped off my jacket, put on my PPE, and got to work.

*

BREAK CAME QUICKLY and I was glad to get a moment to rest, since I was twelve hours into my workday. My cheek itched. I rubbed it on my sleeve, which came away with a mixture of gluey blood and sweat. "Shit," I muttered, remembering that I hadn't had a chance to wash Mikela's blood off my face yet and was sweaty from working. I turned on the camera on my phone and grimaced at the sight of myself, then snapped a quick selfie just for the fuck of it. I hustled to the restroom to wash my face, waving off questions from the guys as I passed by.

I used the toilet and washed my face, alternating between dousing my cheeks and mouth with water and rubbing at my face with damp paper towels, doing my best not to splash water all over the place.

Stooping down over the sink, I rinsed one last time and dried my face off with more rough paper towels. Opening my eyes, I had to hold back a flinch. Mikela was reflected in the mirror, standing right behind me.

Her top lip curled, and I knew right away that she had bad intentions. I hesitated, not sure if I should turn and face her or stay as I was. Trapped between her and the sink, there was no room to maneuver. I drew in a breath, choosing my words carefully.

"Mik—"

The door flew open and Brody stormed in. "Come on, Randy, time to get back to work."

Mikela startled and stepped out of Brody's way as he

placed himself between us and ushered me out of the bathroom. I exhaled, grateful for Brody saving my ass.

"Shit, who is the dangerous person now?"

"Yeah. I'm going to go back to Shelly now and demand that Mikela be taken off the schedule, maybe even angle to have her transferred back to the air hub. You might actually want to go to the cops with this."

I groaned.

"Look, Randy, I know cops aren't your thing, but she is proving to be a threat at this point. Who knows what she would have done if I hadn't pulled you out of there."

"Yeah."

"File a restraining order. Press charges. You have the video."

I scrubbed at my shaggy hair and grumbled some more. "I'll think about it."

"Okay. I'll text you when I'm done with Shelly. Head on back to your workstation."

"Thanks, Brody."

As I returned to door 76, the buzzer blew but the belts didn't start up right away. Everyone stood at their stations, ready to get back to work, but nothing happened. Justin's radio crackled down below as the unload, tower, and operations supes all started yelling at each other. I leaned my hip against the belt, took off my gloves, and pulled out my phone.

I sent off texts to Kristen and Darcy, then a group text to Bear and Buck. Down below the supes circled up, shouting at each other, so I knew I had more time. I opened Facebook and made a post with the pictures the guys had taken of me earlier and the selfie I'd taken, along with a snarky "You should see the other guy."

I was energized by my run-in with Mikela, enjoying how hot my blood had gotten. *Slow it down, Randy. You aren't some youngster anymore.* Getting into fist fights at fifty-three was not a great idea, especially when the other person was a twentysomething wrestler.

My phone pinged with a text from Brody.

> *Spoke to Shelly. You will not be put out on admin leave. You shouldn't see Mikela around work anymore. If you do, call Joe Rawlins in security.*

I scraped around in my memory, trying to remember who Joe was, then it came to me that he was the one with Shelly when she showed up uninvited to my house.

The buzzer blew again, and the belt finally started running so I got back to work. My cell phone vibrated several times in my pocket as people responded to my texts, but they would have to wait till the end of shift to hear back from me.

Chapter Eleven

Case Closed

"RANDY, I JUST don't like it. Violence goes against every fiber of my being. You getting into fist fights at work…over me, no less. It's just not okay," Kristen stammered, searching for words. "I can't be with someone who thinks getting into a fist fight is fun. It's battery! You could be in jail right now."

I wanted to tell her it should be Mikela in jail, not me,

but I let it go. I knew enough to know when to shut the hell up and listen, especially when the person talking is your girlfriend.

I clasped my hands on my lap and nodded to her.

"I just…Randy…" She didn't finish her sentence.

"I hear you. Message received. I didn't know how you felt about it, and now I do."

Kristen turned in her spot on the futon, facing me. Her voice softened. "No more fighting, okay, honey?"

"Agreed…unless it is for self-defense. Okay?"

"Fine." She smiled and slid over to me. I put my arm around her, and we cuddled up. I enjoyed how her body was a combination of strength and softness. Her smooth skin, sinewy muscles, and curvy hips fit against me perfectly.

That had been our first tense conversation. I was happy with how well Kristen handled it, and that she let it go once we had come to a compromise. I'd had ex-girlfriends who would stay angry for days, and that was a miserable thing to be on the receiving end of.

I let out a big sigh and listened to the creek, easing into

the futon. Too soon, the alarm beeped on my phone, telling me that it was time to go home and sleep.

We had one last big day at work before the Christmas holiday. "Time for me to go. You rest up tonight so you can kick ass at your last double shift of the season." I stroked her back.

She tightened her arms and legs around me, giving a mock groan. "Nooo. It's so hard to let you go. But yeah, I won't miss going to bed when the sun is still up. Overall, it's been fine."

"Really? Figures. You're just a youngster and still have energy to spare."

Kristen gave me a little smack on the shoulder, and I chuckled. "I'm not that much younger than you."

"Babe. There's a big difference between forty-two and fifty-three when it comes to energy."

"Fine, fine." She kissed my neck and released me.

"See ya at work." I shrugged on my jacket and grabbed my keys off the table. She blew me a kiss as I closed the door.

Driving along the frontage road toward the freeway, I

lit up a cigarette. The refinery smokestacks and holding tanks marred my view of the waterfront. The stacks and massive holding tanks were painted an orangey-yellow color and had big rust stains streaking down their sides. The stench of sulfur flooded my truck through the heater vent, which was blowing on high.

I took a big drag on my cigarette and tapped my fingers on the steering wheel to a Diamond Rio hit playing through my scratchy old speakers. The lyrics reminded me how important it was to compromise, to give a little and meet in the middle. I was proud of how Kristen and I handled our first disagreement, given how upset she was at me for fighting. I knew it was time to knock that shit off.

I took another drag on my cigarette, then watched it as it smoldered between my fingers on the steering wheel. Kristen had asked me to quit smoking, and she was right about that too. I had been halfway quit for a while, so figured I might as well give it up altogether. I snuffed out the butt in the ash tray and blew out my last drag as I pulled onto the tight cloverleaf ramp to get up to the freeway.

My cell phone rang loudly from my pocket, but I

wasn't about to try to dig it out and answer while merging across six lanes of traffic to get to the FasTrak toll lanes. As I drove under the toll canopy my FasTrak token beeped, and my cell phone stopped ringing.

A few minutes later I was home and so exhausted I kicked off my boots, fed Porkchop, and fell into bed fully clothed without checking my phone.

*

ELEVEN P.M. HIT hard. Not bothering to shower or change, I stood swaying in the dark kitchen, scorching my mouth on hot coffee. My clothes stank from a sweaty sleep and the sixteen-hour shift the day before. Squinting down at the bright screen of my phone, I saw there was a voice mail from a number similar to Sergeant Cleese's.

"Later," I said, my voice gravelly.

I rubbed at my burning eyes. The light from the phone was too harsh in the darkness, so I shoved it back into my pocket along with a pouch of Pop-Tarts. I tossed some food into the cat bowl, though Porkchop was nowhere to be seen. It was too early for breakfast, even for him.

I didn't bother packing myself a lunch since the company usually gave us an end of peak season meal on the last day. Just as well, since I hadn't cooked or been to the grocery store in a few days.

On the way out, I doubled back to my bedroom and pulled my gun case from under the bed. I looked at the black box, giving myself a moment to really think about what I was doing. Carrying a weapon into work was grounds for automatic termination, but I wasn't about to get cornered by Mikela again.

When I placed my thumb on the scanner, the lock popped open with a sharp *clack*. I sat on the bed and opened the lid. The matte-black paint of the pistol glinted dully. I checked that it was loaded and sighed. I pulled my waistband holster from a drawer. It took me a few minutes to get the elastic holster around my waist and tucked it under my jeans, then I did a bit of rearranging to make sure there wasn't a bulge where my trusty little Sig Sauer P365 sat snugly against my body. I knew I was breaking all sorts of rules and laws. Weapons were strictly forbidden at work, and I did not have a concealed carry license. Heck, it wasn't even legal for me to own the sub-compact pistol in California.

Would I really shoot her? I blew out a big breath and scrubbed at my face, then yanked the pistol and holster out of my waistband and put them away. As I placed the holster back in the drawer, I saw my old fixed-blade knife. I had worn it on my belt for most of my twenties, thinking I was some hot shit tough chick, which maybe I was.

I decided I was more comfortable carrying a knife and fidgeted around with the sheath so that it was hooked on my belt but tucked down the inside of my jeans instead of outside. I slid the knife into the sheath. Its cross guard dug into my skin just above the elastic of my boxer briefs.

I needed to hustle or I'd be late. Heart rate up, I drove across the bridge through darkness and fog. Tracy Lawrence sang on the radio about time marching on, and damned if he wasn't right about that. The busy season was ending, and I realized with a thrill that I only had two more to go before retirement. But the worry that I was not safe at work sickened me. Having to resort to carrying a knife on the job was something I had never imagined possible. Of course, the place was filled with box cutters, but carrying a long, fixed-blade knife was a different thing entirely.

At work, I passed through the guard station, nervous that I'd be found out for the knife, but despite me setting off the metal detector, Granny just wished me a Merry Christmas and waved me through.

Christmas music blared from a portable speaker by the time clock. I kept an eye out for Mikela and Kristen but didn't see either one of them as the shift ran its course in a blur. Occasionally, grill smoke would drift through the open roll-up doors. The managers were cooking for us. My stomach rumbled and mouth watered as the smoke carried the smell of tri-tip and chicken.

When the belts shut down, signaling the end of my first shift, I hustled outside and got in line for food. I zipped up my thick jacket, shivering in the misty morning. The digital thermometer on the front of the building told me it was 42 degrees out, which was pretty damn cold for me, having grown up in Northern California.

When it was my turn, I grabbed a paper plate, napkins, and plastic utensils. As I shuffled down the line, managers piled my plate with potato salad, tri-tip, and rolls. I also grabbed a bag of chips and a granola bar from the next table and stuffed them in my pockets. I dug around in a tub of ice and grabbed a soda, the chill hitting my already cold joints and sending pain up my hand and forearm. I put the soda can in my other jacket pocket and lowered myself down onto a low concrete parking barrier, the chill of it immediately passing through my jeans and into my haunches.

The sun hadn't yet penetrated the low overcast. Watery gray light seeped through the fog as I dug into the food, shoving a huge strip of juicy tri-tip into my mouth. It was seasoned well and cooked perfectly, tender and smoky. I swallowed and scooted over on the parking barrier, making room for Kristen as she came up, balancing her plate.

The two of us barely fit, but I didn't mind at all having her side pressed up against mine.

I turned and looked at her, proud. "You did it. You survived your first peak season."

She smiled back. "Hey wait. My *first* peak?"

"You know you'll be back," I said, chuckling. I took a big bite of potato salad, enjoying the tang of the dressing and the crunch of celery with creamy potatoes. "Mmm, this is good." I pointed at the potatoes with my fork.

Kristen only had rolls and a little dollop of potato salad. She didn't eat red meat.

"You gonna come over after second shift?" she asked. "I probably will have to stay late at PJ's, but you're welcome to take a shower and a nap while you wait for me."

I loaded up my fork with more food. "Yeah. That sounds good."

I took a big bite, not wanting to rush the meal but knowing the next shift would be starting up soon.

Kristen put her plate on the ground and dug around in her pocket. She pulled out her key ring and fiddled with it for a minute until she had freed the key to her studio and dropped it into my palm. At my insistence she had begun locking her front door. I tucked the key away in the inside pocket of my jacket, for safe keeping. The warmth inside my jacket was a nice relief to my aching, cold hand. I exhaled and steam came out of my mouth.

We watched the rest of the crew as they screwed around, playing grab ass in line, and sneaking extra bags of chips and sodas. Once I'd finished up my meal, I walked Kristen to the security station and gave her a long hug.

"Have a good day at work," I said. "I bet you guys will be slammed with all the people buying food for their holiday meals."

"Yeah. It's been nuts all week. See you tonight."

I kissed her on the cheek, and we went our separate ways.

My second shift was intense. The package flow was so heavy that the belts got overloaded and jammed a bunch of times. It was a rough day, and I was glad when it was over. The crew streamed out of the building, hooting and hollering, excited to be off the next day for Christmas.

Clocked out and sitting in my freezing cold truck waiting for the engine to get warm, I pulled out my phone and saw that I had a few texts from my friends and the voice mail still waiting from the night before. Something dug into my side, and I reached down, surprised to find that I was armed. I blew out a sigh, a vague memory of putting the knife in my pants the night before. I was thankful that I hadn't been caught armed at work and even more thankful that I hadn't needed the knife.

I pulled off my gloves so I could use the touchscreen and dialed up my voice mail. Balancing the phone between my ear and shoulder, I dug around in the inside pocket of my jacket for my pack of cigarettes. It wasn't there. Instead, my fingertips grazed the key to Kristen's studio. I nodded to myself, remembering that I had quit smoking.

The message was from Sergeant Cleese. He said he had news and asked me to call him back. I dialed his number, put the phone on speaker, and placed it on the dashboard so I could warm my hands at the heater vent.

"This is Sergeant Cleese."

"Hi sergeant. This is Randy…uh, Miranda Cox. I'm returning your message from yesterday."

"Oh, hm." Papers shuffled in the background. "Oh. Yes. Right. Miss Cox."

Jesus Christ, how does he keep forgetting who the hell I am?

"Just a courtesy call. I wanted to let you know that we have closed the case on Bryant's death."

My heart leaped. "You did?"

"Yes. We determined that it was an accident. The yard truck driver has been arrested and charged with PC one-ninety-two c, felony vehicular manslaughter."

"Oh shit. An accident. Huh." Suspicion flooded my brain, which made me wonder why. *He said it was an accident, so that's what it was.* I rubbed my forehead and shook my head, not fully buying his explanation but not knowing why.

"Yup. That's a wrap. Hopefully, this is some good news to make your holiday a little bit brighter."

I looked out of my windshield, through the chain-link fence to the yard, where the yard truck drivers were busy pulling full trailers and parking empty ones, getting ready for the next shift. One of their crew members was sitting in jail at that very moment.

"Thank you, sergeant."

I hung up and drove numbly to Kristen's studio in Marshtown. The commute traffic combined with holiday travelers was ridiculous, so the drive took triple the usual time. I was agitated and exhausted when I finally closed her door behind me and placed her key on the kitchen table.

I stripped down, leaving my clothes in a filthy, stinking pile on the floor, and got into the shower. The water was too hot, but I stood under it anyway. My frozen hands and feet burned painfully as they thawed out and turned a deep shade of purple. I used Kristen's shampoo and body wash, which lightened my mood a tick because they smelled liked her, floral and fruity.

After toweling off, I used her brush to tame my hair. I found some lotion under the sink and rubbed it on my arms and face, then massaged it into my rough, calloused hands. Hands that had dirt still ground into the creases, along with swollen joints, cuts and scars, wrinkles and age spots and bulging veins. They were not attractive hands on a woman, according to society, but they told my story, and I was proud of them.

In her closet I found some sweatpants, socks, and a long-sleeved T-shirt that fit me. The soft fabric was cool against my warm skin and made me shiver.

I folded the futon out into a bed and curled up under

the quilt and fell asleep immediately.

*

MY BRAIN WAS foggy as I woke to the sound of a door opening and closing, and Kristen's key ring clinking on the table. I heard rustling as she slid out of her jacket and shoes. The room was dark and cold, and my eyes burned from exhaustion.

"Hey," she said as she climbed into bed beside me, cuddling up under the quilt. She pressed her freezing cold nose into the nape of my neck with a giggle.

"Hi," I said as I wrapped my arm around her and pulled her in closer. "How was work?"

"People are crazy. Some lady spit on my boss and called him a little bitch."

I chuckled. "What? Why?"

"Because she walked in the store empty handed, picked up three huge cuts of expensive meat and some booze, and tried to return it all for cash. She got mad because he said no."

"Guess she wasn't really in the holiday spirit."

"Nope. And probably mad cuz she needed that money for presents or drugs or something. It's okay. He gets spit on all the time."

"What the—how is that okay? I am so glad I don't work in customer service. You're a saint. I commend you for it."

"Don't."

"Don't what?"

"Commend me for it. I hate it when people get all appreciative of me for working the front lines of customer service, especially during the holidays. Like, it is literally my job and I do it because I need money and benefits to survive."

"Fair enough."

"So anyway, what are you going to do tomorrow for Christmas?"

"Sleep."

"Heh, yeah, it's been a long couple of months, and you have worked really hard."

"We both have. What about you?"

"I'm volunteering with the Bridge Angels again. But I

should be back in the afternoon. Want to get together?"

"Yeah, I'd like that. I haven't bothered to decorate or anything, but it would be great to have you over. You don't have family or somewhere else to go?"

She pulled the blanket up over her shoulders. "No, you know that…and I prefer doing Bridge Angels."

"We've never really talked about what happened to our parents. Just glossed over it on one of our first dates. Can I ask what happened to yours?"

"Mom died young of a heart attack. And my dad… I don't know where he is. It's better that way."

I slowly stroked my hand up and down her back as I thought about what she had said. She had mentioned before that she'd had a really difficult childhood, but we hadn't gotten into the details, and I figured if she had wanted to talk more about it, she would have. I wasn't going to pry.

"Well, I'm always here if you ever want to talk about any of that."

"Thanks. What about your parents?"

"Simple. Mom killed Dad, and then Mom died in

prison." Anxiety crawled up the back of my throat and I swallowed it down.

"That doesn't sound simple at all."

I shrugged. I hadn't told the full story about my parents out loud in a long time and when I did, I'd wished I hadn't. It was like what I had heard someone at work say one time: "Once you squeeze the toothpaste out of the tube, you can't put it back in."

Exhausted silence fell between us, and soon Kristen rolled over and fell asleep. As sleep tried to take me down, I realized I hadn't been invited to stay over, so I slid on my work boots, gathered up my stinking pile of clothes, and slipped out. I locked the door behind me.

*

BACK AT HOME, I was bone tired but wide awake, so I started up a load of laundry, and tended to the chores that'd been neglected since my double shifts had started. I scrubbed the bathroom, picked up all the random stuff that was left out around the living room, then washed dishes, dusted, swept, and mopped.

When the washer wound down, I switched the clothes to the dryer and stripped my bed. I tossed the sheets in the wash. I couldn't remember the last time I had washed the sheets and was a bit ashamed about it. As I put on fresh sheets, I reminded myself that I had been working extra-long hours, and not to be ashamed if I had gotten behind on cleaning.

From his napping spot in the living room, Porkchop watched me come and go. When I finally sat down on my comfy chair, he padded over and hopped up into my lap. I pet him with one hand and scrolled Facebook with the other. It was nice to see all the posts my friends had made about their holiday plans. I enjoyed seeing pictures of friends gathering with their families, or of little kiddos in the snow for the first time or opening one special gift for Christmas Eve. I grinned, glad that even though I lived over an hour away I could still keep up with what everyone was up to.

The dryer buzzer went off and I flinched because it was too much like the buzzer at work. I transferred Porkchop back to his bed and pulled the clothes out of the dryer, inhaling the floral smell of detergent and warm fabric, which was so much better than the stench my clothes had had before the wash. I shuffled down the hallway, trying not to drop anything and enjoying the warmth of the laundry against my body. I went back and put the sheets in the dryer, then locked up the house and returned to my room, where I folded the freshly washed clothes and put them away. Afterward, I sat on the corner of my bed and realized how cold and quiet my house was. There was not a single sound inside or outside.

I shut off the light, silenced my phone alerts, and climbed into bed, pulling the heavy comforter up to my chin. Sleep finally caught up with me.

*

I WOKE JUST before noon on Christmas Day. I lay in bed for a bit, responding to holiday texts from friends.

Muscles and head aching, I finally peeled myself out of bed and turned on the heater before stumbling to the kitchen, happy with myself for remembering to set up the automatic coffee maker during my cleaning frenzy the night before. I poured myself a mug, added a splash of half and half that smelled a bit suspect, then took a scorching hot sip, swallowing down a few Tylenol with it.

I considered going to a drive thru for breakfast but settled for some oatmeal and scrambled eggs. Afterward, I rinsed my dishes and headed to the back door to smoke a cigarette, remembering as I saw the ashtray that I didn't do that anymore. Smoking had become a part of my routine over the years, and I hadn't even realized it. I stood in the doorway, a brisk afternoon breeze blowing by, when the phone call with Sergeant Cleese came back to me.

In my exhaustion at Kristen's the night before, I had forgotten about it. I put on a jacket and sat down on the Adirondack where I had smoked in for years. I looked out past the trees at the strait and ran through the conversation again. As I recalled it, Sergeant Cleese had said they'd closed the case and arrested the yard truck driver for vehicular manslaughter. He'd decided it was an accident and not a murder.

The last few leaves on the trees rattled in the cold wind, and I tucked my hands into my jacket pockets. I had nothing to go on, but just couldn't believe that Bryant had died by pure accident. *Why can't you just accept it? Industrial accidents happen all the time, which is why you've been so focused on working safely lately.* I wanted to retire in one piece and not spend my days in pain from years of manual labor wear and tear.

My phone pinged; it was a text from Kristen.

Just finished volunteering on the bridge. On my way.

That news got me moving. I took a shower, put on clean clothes, and finished wrapping her gift. She had said she didn't want a gift, but I had found something I thought she needed at her place. I didn't believe in using wrapping paper, so I wrapped her present neatly in newspaper and tied it up with some colorful yarn.

She pulled up just as I placed the present on the coffee table. Porkchop ran to the door before Kristen had even knocked. She grinned when I opened the door, and we shared a long hug in the entryway, the cold still clinging to her clothes and cheeks. Porkchop meowed loudly and wove himself between our legs.

"Well, come on in. Let's get you warmed up. Can I make you some tea? I got the rooibos stuff you like."

"Sure, thanks," she said as she walked through the living room. She paused in front of Bear's painting before taking a seat in the kitchen booth.

She watched as I put water on to boil and put tea bags into mugs. I tried to do it all with confidence and not let the anxiety show through, but realized I needed to knock off the machismo bullshit. I paused, looking down my hands on the counter.

"They closed the investigation. Said my boss was killed in an accident."

"Oh? That's good, right? That it's closed now?"

"I just…can't seem to let it go."

"Yeah. That sounds really rough." She paused long enough that I turned to her. "Have you heard back from any of those therapists you called?"

"Nah." I ran my fingers roughly through my hair. "They must not be interested in new clients during the holidays. Whatever."

I stood there, allowing the anxiety to run through me

and resenting every second of it. I knew it wasn't Kristen's job to help me work through it, but I realized in that moment I wanted a little more support from her. *Nothing to be done about it, Randy. Just handle your shit.*

Once the water boiled, I pulled the pot off the burner and poured it carefully into the mugs, then carried them to the booth. I took a seat across from Kristen. We bumped knees, so I scooted down a bit farther. We sat quietly, watching the tea steam as it whorled with the color seeping out of the tea bags. Water gurgled faintly down the drainpipe outside.

Kristen pulled up the sleeves of her pullover. It was one of those fancy quarter zip things athletes wear over their clothes and was a deep purple color that made her light-blue eyes shine.

I sipped my tea, burning my tongue and lips. "Dammit," I grumbled and laughed at myself.

"You never can seem to wait, can you," she said, looking at me in a way I could only describe as adoringly.

"I'm never gonna learn." I reached across the narrow table and took her hand. As I did, I saw faint red marks on the skin of her forearm. I turned her arm so the light hit the marks better and leaned in to get a closer look.

"Well, fuck me. Is that still Mikela's phone number on your arm?"

"Yeah, she used one of the permanent hub markers, remember? I have scrubbed at it for days, but it's not quite gone yet."

Anger rose in my chest. I clenched my jaw and looked at the faint marks, memorizing the phone number…just in case.

"You're still mad about that, aren't you?"

"Yes. Aren't you?"

"Nah."

"All that gross shit she said to you, and then she wrote on you in permanent marker and you're not angry?"

"No. Being mad isn't going to help anything."

How can she take it all so lightly?

It hit me how protective I was becoming of her, and it seemed off that I was more upset about her being harassed than she was.

She quickly changed the subject. "I think I stopped a

jumper today."

"Oh?"

"Yeah. My partner and I came up on a guy on the bridge who was staring down at the water for the longest time. I walked up and started chatting with him. I can't go into details about it, but we got him some help. I think he was ready to jump if we hadn't shown up."

"That's incredible." I squeezed her hand. "I am so impressed with you. You really do get out there and make a difference in the world."

She shrugged and sipped on her tea. I wondered why she was so nonchalant about Mikela sexually harassing her and about the possibility that she had just saved someone's life.

Kristen looked over my shoulder into the living room. "That had better not be a gift for me."

"It is."

"Babe. I told you no gifts."

"Oh well. I guess you had better open it at least, then decide if you want it or not."

We moved into the snug living room. I sat on the love

seat and Kristen sat on the floor on the other side of the coffee table. She untied the yarn and removed the newsprint wrapping paper. She read the label on the side of the box and a slow smile spread across her face, crinkling the corners of her eyes. Her gaze flicked to me and she laughed. "Yes, I'll keep it. Thank you!"

I chuckled. "Good. I noticed that you hate turning on your oven just to cook one little thing. I figured a toaster oven would make your life easier. And the stainless steel will match the appliances in your studio."

She came around the table and sat on my lap. She hugged me and kissed my cheek. "It's perfect."

Chapter Twelve

You Remember Vivian, Right?

THE DAY AFTER Christmas I was back to my usual grind, though it was light and carefree because I worked one shift instead of two, and I did not have to be at the warehouse until 3:00 a.m. The shift was over before I knew it. On the way home, I grabbed a sandwich and some chips from the deli and drove down to the Lands End marina.

I parked facing the shoreline and bluffs across the

water. The waves were choppy, and a commuter train sped by on the tracks running along the far side of the strait. I took my time eating the huge sandwich and wondering where all the people on the train were going. Work? Coming back from visiting family for the holidays? Just riding the train as a way to get out of the house and be around people? It seemed like I didn't ever take much time to look outside of my own little world and see what else was going on. Having Kristen in my life had helped me start looking out more.

I leaned back in my seat and sipped on a bottle of iced tea. Craving a cigarette, I patted my empty breast pocket. Grumbling, I dug a toothpick out of my cup holder and popped it in my mouth, letting out a throaty sigh.

My phone vibrated in the center console. Fumbling around, I grabbed it and saw it was Bear calling.

"Howdy, Oso. How are you?

"Randayyy! I am fucking amazing, dude. Good to hear your voice."

"You have a good holiday?"

"Yeah, you know it. We did it up right with some

wings and barbecue. Man, I stuffed my pie hole. Any excuse to have a party, you know me."

"I sure do."

"Hey, me and Buck are going up to Guerneville with Vivian for New Year's. Wanna come? We are going to do some riding up Highway 1 and just chill."

"Vivian?"

"Yeah, you remember her. She's the one you bought your bike from."

"Oh, yeah. That's right. Sure. That sounds good. I can get the time off now our busy season is over. We gonna get a cabin or camp or what?"

"Vivian stays at some cottage she visits a lot and says she's got us covered. I'll email you the address and stuff." She paused and I heard a slight hissing sound, followed by Bear exhaling.

"Man, are you smoking a vape pen?"

"Yep. Got me some sweet ass CBD cartridges for it. Sour apple flavor, and tomorrow I'm trying out the pumpkin pie one. Hey, it's gonna be good to hang with everybody and do some riding. I'll bring Cards Against Humanity and weed." Bear cackled.

"Oh Jesus. It's gonna be like that, is it?"

"Don't sound so surprised."

"Heh, yeah. Sounds good. I'll see you guys in a few days. But uh, don't mind me if I'm a bit grumpy. I quit smoking."

"Whaaat? Good for you, Riz-andy."

I ran my hand over my mouth. "Thanks."

After we hung up, I texted Kristen and Darcy, asking if they wanted to go to Guerneville. Kristen couldn't get the time off work, but Darcy was game.

Dusk had settled, so I drove up the hill to my house. I wanted to leave for Guerneville right after work the next day, so I threw some clothes in a bag and went into the garage to check the fluids and tires on my bike. I also took time to clean the bike's windshield and the visor of my helmet. Safety at work was important, and I also wanted to be as safe as possible on the road, which starts with well-maintained equipment.

Satisfied with the condition of the bike, I went inside,

washed up, and put myself to bed. Exhausted as I still was from peak season, it was hard to sleep because I was excited to spend time with my friends. There I was, a fifty-three-year-old woman, feeling like a five-year-old before their birthday party. All I could do was chuckle and watch the dripping eaves outside until I fell asleep.

*

WITH MY EXCITEMENT about the trip, my shift flew by in no time. I was pumped full of a giddy energy I hadn't felt in years and couldn't wait to get out of the warehouse. It was tempting to rush through my final belt walk at the end of the shift, but I reminded myself to be safe up there, and slowed down. After clocking out, I hauled ass home, changed into riding gear, ate a quick lunch, set up Porkchop's auto-feeder and water dish, and paced until Darcy texted me that she was on her way.

I packed my travel bag into the hard luggage case on the back of my bike, checked the tires and fluids again, and sent a text to Kristen letting her know that I was hitting the road. I made one last trip to the bathroom, turned on the radio to discourage any would-be burglars, and locked up the place.

The roar of motorcycle pipes coming up the road gave me a thrill, and I raised the heavy garage door, smiling as Darcy pulled right up into the garage on her bike. She killed the engine and yanked her helmet off, a huge grin on her face. I gave her a hug.

"Feels like forever since I saw you."

"It has been. You survived the busy season at work, I see."

"Barely. Damn, this trip is just what I need. I'm glad you could join us." I stood back and checked out her motorcycle. "That's a hell of a bike. Did you build this yourself?"

"Yup. Been tinkering around with it for a while."

I shook my head in amazement. "It's like a cross between a Mad Max build and Daryl's bike from *The Walking Dead*. Is that what you were going for?"

Darcy touched her finger to the tip of her nose. "Bingo. That's exactly right."

"Dang. Wow." I squatted down to peer at the engine,

suspension, wheels, and racks. It had knobby tires, a brown banana seat, and mock rusted paint job just like Darryl's bike, plus Mad Max style touches to the sissy bar, forks, and leather saddle bags. Her helmet was styled like a leather covered pith helmet, and she wore fighter pilot goggles and a bandana around her throat like a bandit.

I straightened back up, my knees popping loudly. "You look like a badass there, Darcy."

"Thanks. You ready?"

"Yep." I rolled my bike out onto the cracked, uneven driveway and Darcy backed hers out. She closed the door behind her with a thump.

I started my engine, which purred and was no louder than a sewing machine. Darcy listened and let out a bellowing laugh, making me laugh too.

"Is that thing even on, Randy?"

"Listen here, bee-atch. It may be quiet, but it is a precision machine. It's fast, and agile—"

"Save the sales pitch. I'm just yanking your chain. Let's go. I'll follow you since I dunno where we are going."

I nodded to her, synced up the Bluetooth in my helmet

to my phone, and launched the Tom Petty station. As we rolled out into the chilly afternoon, I kept an eye on Darcy in my side mirror. She was a solid rider, but I always kept an eye on my friends when they rode with me. Soon enough we were cruising along Lakeville Highway toward Petaluma, then the slow twists of Old River Road.

We made it to Guerneville just before dark and crossed over the river to the address Bear had sent me. I had partied in Guerneville many times with Buck and Bear when we were in our twenties and thirties, but we'd always camped near town. I'd never been down the little road where we would be staying, and I was pleasantly surprised as we pulled into the driveway. In the parking lot I spotted a row of motorcycles and parked next to Bear's bike, Champagne.

When we cut off our engines, the sudden silence of the redwoods was startling. My ears rang loudly, interrupted only by the gentle swish of trees in the breeze. Darcy and I took a moment to shake out our numb hands and legs.

Ringing the small parking lot were gardens that seemed tended, but only just. Fruit trees were surrounded by wild grasses, herb plants, berry bushes, and chard. Another area had some early bulbs sprouting naked ladies and what I thought would soon be daffodils.

It took a moment for the vibrations of the ride to leave my body, then it dawned on me that the cottages were all built up high on stilts, way up in the treetops, with single parking stalls underneath. I figured the place was designed like that due to the river flooding every couple of years.

"Nice ride, eh?"

"Hell yeah," Darcy said, her eyes glimmering. "I haven't been on a ride in so long. Been staying close to home." She turned her face up to the gently swaying treetops far overhead. "It's nice here. I mean, we already live in paradise by the water in Lands End, but it's good to get a change of scenery too."

"Yep." I nodded and started unpacking my bike.

The sound of boots clomping on stairs made me pause and turn. Bear was coming at me with her arms open wide. The gap in her front teeth was visible as she smiled, her whole face beaming.

"Ran-day. Get over here, fucker." She cackled and

pulled me into a proper bear hug, thumping me on the back and rocking us side to side.

"Man, you look old. What's your secret?" I asked with a laugh as she released me.

She waved me off. "Good ride up?"

"Yep. Had to lane split a few times on Highway 101, but otherwise we made good time. I'm freezing my tits off though."

I turned to Darcy, who was leaning on her bike, watching us. "Bear, you remember Darcy."

"Of course! Bring it in, Darce."

Bear gave her a big hug, then turned to look at Darcy's bike. I knew Bear well enough to know that the kind of bike someone rode told her a lot about them. "Ooh! Holy shit, did you build this?"

Darcy gave a coy grin. "Sure did."

"Shit. It's cold. Here, lemme help you with your stuff. Tell me all about your bike."

They walked on ahead, chattering about Darcy's bike. I followed behind, carrying my bag and dilly dallying, looking around at the grounds and layout of the cottages.

A few of them had lights on inside, and laughter drifted out of one.

I climbed the flight of creaky wooden stairs up to the elevated walkway. It had been a long day of work and riding, so the stairs made my legs burn, and my knees protested under the extra weight of my travel bag, but I made it. Bear and Darcy stood talking in the open doorway of a cottage halfway down the walkway. Light spilled out into the gray dusk.

Bear waved me in. "Come on, old lady."

The cottage was rustic but well maintained, with polished wood from floor to ceiling. There was a tidy little kitchen and a large living room with two futon couches, and a long dining table surrounded by wooden chairs. Up a short ladder was a sleeping loft over the kitchen.

A woman sat on the couch reading, the lamp pulled close. She placed her book and reading glasses down on the coffee table and rose. She was solidly built, her long-sleeved T-shirt tight enough to show off her muscles. She had short, salt-and-pepper hair and eyes just a tad deeper blue than Kristen's, with a haunted intensity. There was a big, jagged scar on her cheekbone and another on her temple, which I remembered from when we had met years ago.

"Randy. You remember Vivian, right?"

"Yeah. Of course." I shook the hand she offered me, which was stronger and more calloused than mine. *Impressive.*

"Good to see you again, Randy. How's the bike treating you?"

"It's still the best bike I've ever owned."

"I'm glad to hear it."

Vivian and Darcy shook hands as Buck climbed down from the loft, the wooden ladder squeaking under her.

"Caught me napping," she said gruffly, and gave me a hug before shaking hands with Darcy.

Bear gave us a tour of the cottage. I was surprised to see that not only did it have the two futons in the living room, but also a bedroom, four more beds up in the sleeping loft, and two little bathrooms.

Buck started up a fire in the fireplace and we settled down in the living room. I was grateful to be able to take off some of my cold weather riding gear once the fire got going.

Bear, Darcy, and I chatted away about motorcycles and our favorite riding routes, while Buck listened and nodded every now and then. Vivian stayed on the couch reading, earbuds in her ears. She had pulled out a high-lighter and pen and was switching back and forth between highlighting in her book and writing notes on a big pad of paper that was thick with weathered pages.

The four of us eventually moved into the tiny, one-person kitchen to cook dinner and give Vivian some quiet. There was a little table pushed into the corner, and I sat down at it just to get out of Bear's way as she pulled out food from the fridge, and pots and pans from the cabinet. She assigned me to peel and chop carrots and onions, Buck to cube up the beef, and had Darcy peel and chop potatoes and celery.

"What're we making?" I asked, and nearly stripped a layer of my fingertip off with the peeler.

"My beef stew," Bear said as she dumped cubed-up beef into a smoking-hot pan. The meat sizzled and Bear did a little tap dance as she watched it sear.

"Mm. Man, it's been a long time since I've had your stew." I turned to Darcy, keeping half an eye on the peeler so I didn't cut myself. "Darcy, you're in for a treat. Bear's food is damn good."

"Looking forward to it."

A shoe scraped on the floor behind me, and I turned to see Vivian standing in the pass-through between the kitchen and living room. She leaned her hip against the pony wall and rubbed her eyes.

"Hey, guys. How can I help?"

Bear grinned over the pot she was stirring. "Don't you worry, Vivi. We got it covered."

"Cool. Thanks." Vivian crossed her arms, her body loose and relaxed as she watched us. I chopped up the carrots but couldn't help wondering about her.

"Whatcha reading in there?"

Vivian's face was creased with fatigue, her eyes drifting, but when I spoke, they snapped back in to focus.

"Studying."

"Oh, you going back to school?"

"Nope. I'm up for a promotion at work and need to

prepare for the assessments."

"Oh, wow. When I first met you, you were a brand-new firefighter. That was a long ass time ago though. What position are you trying for?"

"Battalion chief."

"Wow. Battalion chief. That's a big deal. Aren't you a little young to be a chief?" As soon as the words crossed my lips, I regretted it. Bear whistled through her teeth and Buck clicked her tongue.

Vivian bristled and stood up straight, the relaxed looseness of her body gone.

"No. I am not *too young* to be a chief. I've been busting my ass, climbing the ranks for damn near thirteen years. I've been a firefighter, an engineer, and am currently a captain. I am right on track and have earned it, not to mention my time in the military leading troops before that."

"You're right. I'm really sorry, that was ignorant of me. I apologize."

Vivian nodded at me and her body relaxed. She leaned her hip on the pony wall again. I stood and carried my cutting board of chopped carrots and onions to the countertop.

"Here you go," I said. I wanted to go outside and have a smoke but reminded myself that smoking wasn't my thing anymore.

"How's Porkchop doing?" Bear asked, turning to me from the stove.

Vivian laughed heartily, cutting through the tension in the room. "Who or what is Porkchop?"

I smiled at her. "My jerk face cat. He's doing okay. Fat and sassy, as always."

"He sounds delightful."

Relieved that Vivian had moved beyond my stupid comment, I got bowls from the cupboard and spoons from the drawer, then folded five paper towels into napkins. Vivian took the stack of bowls and led the way to the dining table in the living room. We set the table and pulled some chairs up to the fireplace.

I rubbed my hands together, warming them, then pulled off my riding boots and crossed my feet on the hearth so my frozen toes could thaw out. Vivian stretched her legs out toward the fire too.

I cleared my throat. "Didn't realize how long I'd had

that bike till you said how long you've been a firefighter."
I clicked my tongue, amazed at how time had flown.
"Whatcha riding now?"

"I just bought a Motto Guzzi MGX-21. My wife, Audre, persuaded me to give up the fast bikes and slow down with a cruiser. My job is already dangerous enough. She worries about me riding since I am prone to, uh…exceeding the speed limit and taking risks to get adrenaline boosts. I miss my speedy street bikes…but don't get me wrong, that Motto Guzzi outside has got plenty of power." Vivian pointed her thumb toward the parking lot.

"Well, I can hardly wait to check out your bike out in the daylight tomorrow. And you've got a wife now? Congrats. Sounds like things have been moving along well for you."

She nodded, leaning farther back in her chair and massaging the scar on her cheekbone. We fell into a comfortable silence, watching the fire crackle and listening to clinking dishes and low chatter from the kitchen. My eyes started to burn and sag as exhaustion swept over me. I let my chin drop to my chest and was just drifting off when

Bear bumped my shoulder with her hip and hooted, "Wake up you two, it's dinner time."

Clearing my head, I cracked open beers for everyone except Vivian, who poured herself half a glass of red wine. I scooted my chair up to the table, buttered a few rolls for myself, and smelled the bowl of steaming beef stew that was placed in front of me. The rich aroma had hints of bay leaves, wine, and onions. The cottage was filled with the sound of utensils on bowls as we plowed through our meal.

After everyone had refilled their bowls with second helpings, the conversation picked up and we had a great time regaling Vivian and Darcy with stories of our sordid twenties and thirties in Sacramento. In turn, Vivian had us rolling with laughter as she told us stories of her years bartending at the only lesbian night club in town, and Darcy shared the antics of the guys who worked at the port with her.

Buck, who was normally a woman of few words, piped up several times. She had run the streets with us back in the day, and she'd also been the head bouncer at the bar where Vivian had worked, so she added key details to our stories.

It was good to see my friends smiling and chatting and I laughed until my face and stomach hurt. As the evening wound down, I sent a few group selfies to Kristen, and she sent a selfie back of her smiling with her work buddy for the evening. Her picture made me grin and I wished wholeheartedly that she was there at the cottage with us.

We planned to get up early for a breakfast ride, so we washed up the dishes and got ready for bed. Bear took the bedroom, Buck and Darcy took the futons in the living room, and Vivian and I took mattresses on opposite ends of the loft. The roof sloped down low up there, so I had to be careful not to sit up too fast, otherwise I would knock myself out on the wood paneled ceiling. It was cold up in the rafters, but I bundled up in sweats and had plenty of blankets. Once settled in, I looked out of the little skylight, past the swaying tops of the grand redwood trees, to the twinkling stars, and sent up one fleeting thought about Bryant and his family.

Chapter Thirteen

The Ax Forgets, But The Tree Remembers

MY NOSE AND toes burned from the icy air in the loft. The faintest gray-orange rays of sunrise seeped through the skylight. I sat up slowly, careful not to hit my head on the ceiling, and noticed a blue glow coming from Vivian's bed. She was propped up on a pillow looking at her cell phone.

"Mornin'," I whispered, my throat gravelly.

"Good morning," she said, looking up briefly from her

phone, the glare of the bright screen reflecting on the lenses of her reading glasses.

I crawled along the carpeted floor to the ladder and cautiously climbed down, the rungs creaking under my feet. Chill seeped through my socks as I reached the main floor and felt my way through the dark to the bathroom. I sucked in a sharp breath as my butt cheeks rested on the frigid toilet seat.

Finished in the restroom, I tiptoed across the living room to stoke up the fire but gave up trying to be quiet when I saw that Buck and Darcy were both sitting up on their futon beds in the dark, scrolling on their phones.

"Howdy," Buck said, putting her phone down. "You sleep okay up there?"

"You know me. I can sleep good anywhere. You?"

"Yeah, I slept okay till the cold woke me up, and that was that."

"It sure as hell gets a lot colder up here at night than I am used to."

Buck nodded and got out of bed. Together we got a roaring fire going, which cast our shadows along the far wall.

The rental came with complementary coffee grounds from a local roaster, and the cottage soon filled with the smell of it. I poured three coffees, adding a splash of half and half and a spoon of sugar into mine. We joined Darcy in front of the hearth and chatted quietly until the ladder creaked as Vivian joined us.

Buck, normally the quiet one, spoke up right away. "Hey, Vivian. You want me to pour you a cup?"

"No, thanks. I don't drink coffee." She went to the kitchen, speaking to us over the low pony wall. "Tea for me. I'll just heat up some water." There was a clang of pots as she dug around in the cabinet.

"Tea?" Buck asked, under her breath, and stuck up her pinky as she sipped some coffee.

I winked at Buck. "Now, now. Normally I'd be joking along with you, but my lady likes tea and I've gotten partial to it lately too,"

"Well, look at you." Buck chuckled.

Vivian strode into the living room with a steaming mug and a banana. She pulled up a chair and we sat quietly while the smell of her peppermint tea and banana mingled with the strong scent of our coffee. I poked at the logs now and then to keep the fire going. The sun rose gently, but didn't break through the fog layer, and the gray light didn't do much to brighten up the dark innards of the cottage.

Through the thin wall came the sound of Bear waking up, which included some grumbling, a loud yawn, an even louder fart followed by a giggle, which set us all to laughing.

Bear shuffled out from the bedroom, her long hair wild, a quilt around her shoulders.

"Good morning, princess," I said as I stifled my laughter.

"Wazzup Randay. Jesus, it is cold. Not so great for riding. I hope the sun breaks through soon." She sat down heavily on the couch and peered out of the window.

Vivian turned in her chair to face Bear. "So, what's your plan today?"

Bear shook her head. "That early morning ride to get breakfast may get squashed cuz it's too cold. Maybe we have breakfast here and then ride out for lunch later?"

We all nodded. I wasn't a fan of riding in cold weather, and if I didn't absolutely have to be out in it, I wouldn't.

Vivian had arrived at the cottage a day before us and gone into town to stock up on groceries, so we were well supplied. I turned on an '80s classic rock station and stepped into the kitchen where I threw together some vegetable omelets, ham and cheese omelets, and oatmeal.

We ate and had a nice lazy morning, taking our time showering and getting ready. Vivian studied in the loft while the rest of us played cards at the dining room table until the sun broke through the fog.

As soon as the first sun ray hit the floorboards, Bear perked up and howled. "Viviii, get your ass down here. It's time to ride!"

Vivian flew down the ladder, showing off that she was a hell of a lot spryer than us, still agile and nimble. I piled on my winter riding gear, laced up my boots, and shoved a packet of Pop-Tarts into my pocket.

"Good?" I asked as everyone else finished zipping up jackets and chaps.

They all nodded, and we clomped along the elevated

walkway and down the stairs, to discover our bikes were dripping with dew. I pulled a handkerchief from my back pocket and wiped the moisture off my seat and hand grips. One by one we fired up our bikes. The ruckus brought a few people to the windows of their cottages to watch. One cottage had a little kid bouncing in the window waving. I waved back to him.

While our bikes warmed up, we huddled in a circle to talk about our route and decide what our riding positions would be. Bear knew the route best, so she was the road captain up front, and, as usual, Buck took position in the back as sweep. I got the number two spot, behind Bear with Vivian and Darcy in the middle of the pack.

Once we had finished fidgeting around getting our gloves and helmets on, we finally got going, taking the wide, sweeping curves of Old River Road until we reached the dense canopy of the redwood trees, where the road nar-rowed, and the curves grew tighter.

It was much colder under the redwoods, where the sunlight hadn't reached yet. Occasional runnels of water washed across the tarmac as it drained from the steep hills above toward the Russian River below. We came out from the cover of the redwoods and passed through little towns like Monte Rio and Duncans Mills. Then we took a quick left onto Highway 1, and the Pacific Ocean opened up across the horizon.

Highway 1 was narrow and twisty, so I did my best to be careful when gazing at the ocean view to also keep an eye on the road. I also watched Darcy, Vivian, and Buck in my side mirror and Bear up ahead. My heart swelled until there was a lump in my throat. Moments like these made everything else worthwhile. I just wished that Kristen was there with me to enjoy it too.

By the time we reached Point Reyes Station the temperature had risen just enough that my hands, feet, and ass weren't painfully frozen. At Bolinas Lagoon, Highway 1 dipped down to ocean level and I was taken aback by the sights. The tide was out, and massive flocks of waterbirds waded and perched in the shallows practically within arms' reach. A group of brown pelicans swooped by, making a flashy entrance to the lagoon.

Bear eventually pulled us into town at Stinson Beach

and wound around the streets until she found a spot big enough for us all to park. Shutting down my bike, I was grateful for a break from the vibration and noise of the road. I pulled off my helmet and scrubbed at my face and hair to get the blood flowing again.

I got off the saddle slowly, making sure my legs were awake and ready to support my weight, and watched as my friends did the same. Vivian hopped off her bike like an energetic youngster and thrust her arms in the air over her head to stretch. I pulled off my riding pants, hopping on one foot as the hem caught on my boot heel. Buck put a hand on my shoulder to steady me.

"Thanks, bud."

She nodded in response. We stowed our layers of gear in our saddlebags and shook our legs out. The fresh ocean air whipped through the streets in low gusts and seagulls swooped down in flocks, aiming for tourists with snacks.

We talked over one another excitedly about the ride as we walked into the bar Bear had chosen. We took a table in the back near the pool table. The space was nice and warm, and I rubbed my hands together as I read the menu.

"Oh man, gonna be hard to choose," I said, seeing they had a decent menu for a backstreet dive.

The bartender came out from behind the massive wood plank bar, a notepad in hand. Her arms and hands were covered in tattoos, her earlobes stretched with big plugs, and she wore a bandana in her hair like Rosie the Riveter. She looked just like the kind of gal I would have tried to date in my earlier days.

"Hey all. You guys have a good ride?"

We all nodded and responded with "yes," "yup," and a "yes, ma'am," from Buck.

"Before you leave, be sure to sign the ceiling." The bartender pulled a thick red marker from her back pocket and put it on the table. I looked up and saw that the ceiling was covered, wall to wall, with drawings, tags, and names with dates. "What can I get started for you?"

We put in our orders, all of us getting something heavy and greasy, except for Vivian, who ordered a turkey club. We skipped the alcohol, since we had a long ride back, and went for iced teas all around. Darcy came back from the jukebox grinning as a Journey song came on. We sang along and kept going when it switched over to Jefferson Starship.

The bar was mostly empty, so we weren't really bothering anyone with all the carrying on we were doing. When the next song ended, Bear got up and stood at the end of table, her iced tea held aloft.

"I think a toast is in honor."

We raised our glasses, turning to her.

"I am so glad to have my two groups of friends together again. And of course, I welcome Darcy into the fold. You can't choose your family, but you can choose your friends, and I'm glad that I get to spend my New Year's with you ugly ducklings. Cheers."

We sent up a chorus of "Cheers," and clinked glasses.

Our food arrived and I dove heartily into my bacon cheeseburger and onion rings. Buck crumbled crackers into her bowl of chili, and Darcy squeezed a lime over her battered fish tacos. I tapped my foot along to a Steve Winwood song and wiped my greasy fingers on a napkin. Vivian pulled a little bottle from her jacket pocket and squeezed something out on to her hands, which she rubbed together.

It smelled like rubbing alcohol.

"What's that?" I asked, pointing to the bottle.

Vivian looked at me, her face frozen like she was trying to cover up some sort of expression. She spoke slowly, carefully, as she answered me. "It's hand sanitizer. Have you not seen it before?"

"I've heard of it, but I guess I've never seen anyone use it. So, is that supposed to kill off germs or something?"

"Yes."

Around the table, everyone was staring at me, their eyebrows up.

"What?" I asked.

Bear spoke up first. "Randy. Have you seriously never seen hand sanitizer before? Do you live under a rock?"

Darcy held up a hand. "Easy now. No need to shame her." Everyone fell silent, because it was unheard of to correct Bear. Darcy grinned.

"Jeez, you guys. I just wash my hands in the sink," I said. "Haven't had a need for that fancy stuff."

Vivian's lips twitched with the effort of keeping her face blank. "Randy, let's think about all of the things you have touched since you last washed your hands." She held up her hand, counting off the items on her fingers as she spoke. "Riding boots, jacket zipper, bike keys, your helmet, the inside of your riding gloves, which are probably filthy, cell phone, the door handle coming into the bar, the menu, the table. And that's probably being conservative. Lots of opportunity to pick up something nasty that'll make you sick."

"I'm not worried about it," I said and shrugged. "A little dirt is good for ya."

Vivian blinked and turned to her sandwich. We went back to eating and carousing. After I finished off my burger and onion rings, Bear challenged me to a few games. She beat me at pool, and I beat her at air hockey, then we spent some time playing the pinball machine and singing along to more of Darcy's jukebox DJ-ing while Buck and Vivian sat in the corner having a quiet conversation.

I saw the pen on the table and remembered that we still needed to write something on the ceiling.

I held the pen up. "Hey guys, anybody want to join me?"

The bartender saw me and brought over one of those rolling ladders with narrow stairs and a small platform on it. I climbed up and read what was already scribbled on the ceiling. There were crude drawings of breasts and of a dick squirting, some lewd poetry, a few names with dates, and in bold black marker was the quote:

The ax forgets, but the tree remembers.

I reread that line a few times and worked my brain around what it meant. Wanting to remember it, I snapped a picture with my phone. I was at a loss for what to write myself, not having anything witty to share or desire to draw anything, so I just wrote *Randy C.—12/31,* then I climbed down and handed the pen to Darcy. One by one, everyone in my surly group climbed the ladder and wrote something on the ceiling.

Things wound down, so we settled the bill and filed through the bathroom, taking turns using the toilet. Back at the table we did the usual sweep to make sure we hadn't left anything behind. When I pushed open the heavy wooden door, the bright afternoon light hurt my eyes. We stood on the concrete out front squinting as we put on our jackets.

I pulled my phone out again. "Picture time."

Everyone grouped up around me in a tight clump. We wrapped our arms around each other, and I held my camera above us. We all looked up at it, and instead of telling them to say cheese, I said, "Say 'big fat wiener,'" and snapped a few pictures of us cracking up.

I scrolled through them quickly and sent one off to Kristen.

"Hey, Randy, start up a group text and send that out to us, would you?" said Bear.

"Sure thing." I poked around on my phone, grumbling as I tried to figure out how to add everyone's numbers to the text. I scratched my chin, holding the phone farther away since I hadn't brought my reading glasses.

Darcy spoke up. "You need some help with that?"

"Nah. Got it!" I puffed out my cheeks, glad I had figured it out. I hit send and moments later everyone's pockets started pinging.

The temperature was dropping again, so we stopped dicking around and followed Bear out of town, taking the faster route back to Guerneville.

*

BACK AT THE cottage we all napped, except for Vivian, who studied quietly at the kitchen table. For dinner we made burgers, rosemary roasted steak fries, and green beans, though I skipped the green beans. Chilly air seeped through the window glass as I stood at the sink washing up our dinner dishes.

I smiled to myself as I listened to the murmurs of conversation floating in from the living room. Bear, Buck, and Darcy sat on the couches, passing a pipe around. The smell of pot mingled with wood smoke from the hearth. I got lost in my own thoughts as I scrubbed a baking sheet that was crusted with the remnants of potatoes, and wondered what Bryant's wife was doing, as yet another special occasion passed without her husband at home. My throat grew hot as tears threatened to well up, and I tried to swallow down the sensation. I startled as someone placed their hand on my lower back.

"Hey, sorry. Didn't mean to scare you. Did you want

help with those dishes?"

"Hey, Viv. No, thanks. I got it."

She leaned her hip against the counter, pulling off her glasses and rubbing her eyes.

"Taking a study break?"

"Yeah." She let out a long sigh.

"Hey, sorry again for making that dumbass comment about you being too young for that promotion."

"It's okay. I am not mad at you about it. I just hear that kind of garbage a lot from the guys at work, so I get pretty defensive about it."

"I get it… Being a woman working around a bunch of men, that is. Always having to prove yourself, even having to work harder than them to prove the point that you deserve to be there."

She nodded. "Yeah. That about sums it up. A story as old as time," she said, chuckling.

I placed the baking sheet in the drying rack and scrubbed at the frying pan. Vivian picked up the baking sheet and dried it with a kitchen towel.

"Hey, uh…as a firefighter, do you just deal with fires,

or do you also do medical stuff and extrications…or extractions? I dunno if I am saying that right."

"I am a firefighter paramedic, so I do all of those things. Why?"

I shut off the water and looked down at the dish rag in my hand, trying to figure out what it was I was trying to ask.

"Well, uh, let's say someone gets pinned between a trailer and the loading dock, and they are still alive. What's the right way to, uh…" I felt like throwing up and squeezed the rag as hard as I could.

Vivian put her hand on my back again. "Hey. Randy. What's going on?"

I swallowed down the bile that was burning the back of my throat. "What would you do, if you went on a call and there was someone pinned like that. How do you get 'em out without hurting them worse?"

"Hm. Hang on." Vivian walked out of the room and came back with her weathered notebook in hand. I squinted as she turned on the light over the table and sat down with a spark in her eyes. "Sit down for a sec."

I sat next to her and watched as she opened the notebook and grabbed the pencil that was tucked behind her ear. Her voice had a bit of excitement as she spoke. "Okay, so it's funny you ask that, because I was just at a training session last week and we talked about this exact thing. It was a great workshop. Our facilitator is incredibly talented and has been in the fire service like forever."

She paused, the excitement dropping from her face and her expression growing serious as she registered the pain on my face. I desperately wanted to go outside and have a cigarette but picked at my cuticles instead.

She nodded and started sketching a diagram on the sheet of paper. "Okay, so you see here how the loading dock is about chest height?" Without waiting for my reply, she continued running the tip of the pencil along the paper. I watched as she made a rough drawing of an area from inside the warehouse looking out through the loading door, and a separate drawing outside the warehouse looking at the trailer from the side. She drew a stick figure in both diagrams to signify her patient.

"Okay, so what we talked about in the training was

how do you hitch up the trailer to pull it away from the wall without crushing the patient further. We talked about jamming some high-powered spreaders in the gap to literally shove the trailer away from the wall and create a gap big enough to pull the person out. So" —she used the tip of her pencil to point to the stick figure—"what we would do is…"

"No, that's wrong." I put my fingertip next to the drawing of the stick figure. There was dirt under my nail. "His arms weren't pinned down at his sides like that. They were up in front of him on the dock." My throat closed up and I forced myself to take in a deep breath.

Vivian's sharp blue eyes were trained on me with a focus I had never seen before.

"Wait. Are you saying you have seen this happen before?"

I nodded; my throat too tight to speak.

"Oh shit. Randy." She put her hand on my forearm and lowered her head. We sat like that for a moment while I shuddered, doing everything I could to hold in the sobs that wanted to explode out of me.

"It's okay for you to cry, you know."

I swiped at my eyes. "I don't wanna."

"Okay. How can I best help right now?"

"His arms…they were up on the dock. And he was un-conscious, but alive." I drew in a shaky breath. "How long can someone stay like that, I mean, how long is too long to be like that? It seemed like they left him pinned there for far too long." I blew out a long sigh and swiped at my damp eyes again.

"Do you happen to work at a warehouse in Diablo?"

I nodded. "Yeah."

"Well, shit. I think they used the accident at your ware-house as a case study for my training."

"Why do you say it was an accident?"

She paused, looking me square in the eye. "Do you think otherwise?"

I shrugged. "It's just not sitting right with me, them deciding it was an accident, I mean." I thought back to the evidence photos Sergeant Cleese had shown me on Thanksgiving Day, and the one picture that just wouldn't leave me alone.

"I know this is direct, but were you there when it happened?"

"I am the one who found him."

"Shit. That's a lot."

"Yeah, but hey, I figure you see horrible stuff all the time at your job, so me seeing one accident isn't a big deal, right?"

"Wrong. It is a big deal. Try not to minimize your own experiences, Randy. I wonder…have you spoken to a therapist about this?"

I waved my hand like I was shooing a fly. "I tried. None of them called me back. So, that's that. You said something about a case study. What does that mean?"

"It means they used the accide—I mean incident—at your workplace as an example of how to handle that type of extrication. We read some of the details from the police report, saw a bunch of photos taken by the investigators, were given all the details about the weight of the trailer, how much space was between it and the loading dock, stuff like that, and then broke out into groups to try and work out the best way to get the patient out. Then we had to present our plans to the class, and answer questions." She raked her fingers through her hair. "Man, based on what I learned and saw, it was bad. I am sorry you had to see that, and that you lost one of your crew."

"Thanks." I picked at my cuticle some more. "Based on what you saw, do you think it was an accident?"

Vivian pursed her lips and let a huff of air out of her nose, looking down at her hands. I watched as she considered my question.

"We weren't presented with all of the facts. Only what was pertinent to our workshop, which was not an investigation workshop. We were talking about extrications. But..." She squared her shoulders and looked directly at me again. "Are there supposed to be packages on the outside of the building on those load doors?"

"No. When the empty trailer backs up to the building, there are those foam pads all around the door that should seal it off, to keep the rain out and the packages in. But there are plenty of times where there is a gap off to the side when the trailer isn't parked straight enough, or the foam pads are flattened down over time. And when the loaders can't keep up, packages start falling over the side of the conveyor belt and piling up around the load door. Plenty of times I've seen packages fall through the gap and end up on the ground outside in the yard."

Vivian ran her calloused thumb across her bottom lip. "And who picks those packages up so they don't get lost or destroyed?"

"After the trailers are pulled, the supervisor does. While I walk the belt inside on the hunt for stray packages, the supervisor walks along the load wall outside looking for dropped packages. They have to follow yard control of course, with the vest and cones and stuff."

"Yeah, that's pretty standard. The cones and vest, I mean."

Bear came into the kitchen, pulled a six-pack of sparkling cider from the refrigerator, and did a perfect impression of Vivian. "Yeah, that's pretty standard yard control blah-dee-blah. I dunno what you're talking about in here, but that's enough doom and gloom for tonight. Come on."

She padded out to the living room, her floppy My Little Pony slippers nearly silent on the wood floor. Vivian nodded to me and closed her notebook. "Shall we?"

We followed Bear outside and down to the screened porch under our cottage. The flimsy door clacked closed behind me, and I waved my hand, trying to clear the cloud of pot smoke I had walked into. Darcy, Bear, and Buck all giggled.

"Jesus, you guys," I said as I settled down onto a camp chair with a grunt.

It was frigid outside, so we huddled our chairs around a small propane space heater. There was the glow from a bonfire and loud chatter and laughter from the campground next door.

"I sure am glad not to be tent camping in the cold tonight. Thanks, Vivian, for putting us up in your cottage."

Everyone nodded silently as Bear passed the pipe to Darcy.

"My pleasure. I'm glad to have the company."

A bottle of hard cider hissed as I twisted the top off. Taking a long sip of it, I enjoyed the burn of the carbonation and tart bite of apple flavor. I smacked my lips and let out a satisfied belch. "That's good stuff. I might have a new favorite drink." Holding the bottle up to the faint light, I tried to memorize the label so I could look for it at the store when I got home.

Bear stood up, holding a bottle of cider in one hand and vape pen in the other. "Hey, gimme your attention. As midnight and the new year approach, it's time for another toast."

I groaned sarcastically. "Two toasts from you in one day? Here we go."

Bear *tsk*ed at me. Looking up at my dear friend, I recognized with warmth how time had aged her. She wore her graying hair, double mastectomy, and wrinkles with pride. She took a small hit from her vape pen and blew smoke up toward the ceiling before speaking.

"I just want to take a minute to acknowledge. To let you know that I see each of you, like… I really see each of you and I welcome you as you are. I've known some of you fools for over a quarter of a century, and I am so glad you are still alive and kicking and being a bunch of pains in the asses. And I welcome you, Darcy, if you'll have us."

Darcy nodded to Bear and raised her drink. I gave Darcy a grin and turned back to Bear, ignoring the pain in my knuckle joints as the chill from the bottle of cider bit down.

Bear went on. "I wouldn't want to welcome the new year in with anyone else. I know some of you are skeptical…Vivi…but my ancestors told me that this is right where all of us are supposed to be tonight–"

Vivian cut in. "Bear, your *ancestors* sent me on a wild goose chase across multiple states back in 2006. Remember that?"

"Zip it, Viviana. That happened for a reason. It all does. Now just let me finish. They told me that next year will be a hard year for each of us, for different reasons, and that some of us might not survive it. So, rather than wasting my time worrying about that, I want to be in this moment with you guys. Right here. Right now."

"You are hecka high," I said, chuckling. The others joined me in the laughter. "Did you pop some shrooms, too?"

"Ey, I'm fine. What I'm trying to say is I love you guys, even though you're a bunch of dirty bastards. Happy New Year."

Bear raised her drink, and we all did the same, clinking bottles and hugging each other as the clock hit midnight and someone farther down the river set off fireworks while the campers on the next property howled at the moon.

Chapter Fourteen

Joe Rawlins

THE NEW YEAR dawned overcast and cold. I rolled over and saw Vivian sitting propped up on a pillow, studying with a head lamp on, her pen busily scratching a diagram in a notebook.

"Mornin'," I said. She flipped her head lamp up so it didn't shine in my eyes. I let out a rattling cough and her eyebrows creased with concern.

"Sorry about that. I quit smoking and I think my body is clearing things out."

"I'm glad to hear that you quit smoking. Good for your body and your wallet."

I sat up on my elbow and raked at the knots in my hair. "Yeah. It's for the best, but it took my girlfriend pushing me to really do it."

"I like her already."

I grinned. "She's pretty great. I can't wait to get back and see her."

"Is that who you were texting last night after we came back upstairs?"

"Yeah. Hey, I think some of us are heading back home today. When are you goin' back to Sacramento?"

"My next tour doesn't start for a couple more days, so I am going to stay here a while longer to study and get in some trail runs."

"You mentioned having a wife. May I ask why you guys aren't spending the New Year together?" I felt like I was intruding, but it was something I had been wondering since we got there.

"She's spending the holiday with her boyfriend."

I tilted my head and ran what she'd said through my brain a few times to be sure I had heard her right. My face must have shown what I was thinking because she smirked and went on.

"Don't stress on it, Randy. We are in an open marriage and have been polyamorous since the very beginning. In fact, I am happy she had a chance to get away with him. They haven't seen much of each other lately and it's good for them to reconnect."

I chewed on a hangnail, considering. "Well, whatever floats yer boat." I sat up a bit more and yawned, stretching my legs out. Knees and ankles popping, I let out a groan of relief. "Sorry for all of the old man noises."

She chuckled. "You're fine. I live in a firehouse half the time, so you can imagine some of the noises I hear from the sleeping quarters and latrine. Not as bad as what I used to hear in the barracks when I was in the army, but still."

We both laughed, covering our mouths so as not to wake the others. Darcy's voice drifted up from the living room below.

"Are you two up there telling fart jokes, cuz you're giggling like a couple of eight-year-old boys."

I stifled a laugh. "Sorry if we woke you."

"No worries. I'm about to get the fire and coffee going. Come on down when you're ready." Her voice trailed off as she padded toward the kitchen.

Vivian put down the notebook and took off her head-lamp and glasses. She placed them neatly on top of her backpack. Lowering her voice, she turned to me. "So, I've been thinking more about what happened with that person at your work getting killed."

"Oh?" I put on a beanie and turned to her.

"I made some phone calls."

"Really? You didn't need to do that."

"No problem. Holiday or not, they owed me favors." She flicked her hand. "Anyway, I talked to a friend of mine over at the station where that Sergeant Cleese works. Here's what I found out…"

*

AFTER BREAKFAST, DARCY and I said our goodbyes and

rolled out. I had hoped to ride part of the way with Bear and Buck, but Bear wanted to stay behind to go geocaching with Vivian, and Buck wanted to do some river fishing.

Darcy took the lead, and I cruised along behind her, lost in thought, too distracted to notice the beautiful views of Sonoma vineyards, redwood trees, and rolling hills; things tourists travelled from all over the world to see. My stomach burned, my teeth ground against each other, and my hands ached from white knuckling the grips.

What I'd learned from Vivian dredged up a level of anger I had not experienced in decades, and it boiled inside me. We rode straight on home, but when Darcy took the ramp toward Lands End, I continued over the bridge to Kristen's studio in Marshtown.

Since it was a government holiday, the streets of downtown Marshtown were nearly empty and parking at Kristen's place was easy. I bounded up the stairs to her door, weighed down by my bag and heavy riding gear.

She opened the door before I could even knock and pulled me into her arms so abruptly that I had to drop my bag. I wrapped my arms around her, nuzzling my face down into her warm neck.

She giggled. "Hey! Your nose is cold." I burrowed my icy nose deeper into her collar. She tossed her head back and hollered, "Welcome back."

"Thanks," I said, holding her tight as a wave of sorrow washed over me.

My thighs grew weak, and tears filled my eyes before I could do anything about them. My cheek wet against her neck, I tucked my chin in to try to hide it. She pulled back and dipped down to look up at me.

"Randy, are you okay?"

I swiped roughly at my wet cheeks with my palm, wiping the tears on my pant leg, then held my hands up.

"I dunno. This is…" I didn't know what to say.

"Well, come in and sit down. I'll make some of that tea you like."

I stepped inside, took off my riding gear, and used her restroom before joining her on the futon. She handed me a mug and placed her hand on my leg. "What's going on?"

I drew in a long, shaky breath, and blew it out. "I, uh, got some news today about what happened to my boss at work that made me really angry. And for some reason it came out as tears." I took a sip of scalding hot tea, burning my tongue.

"Oh? Did the investigator…Cleese, wasn't it? Did he call you or something?"

"No. It was actually Vivian, a good friend of Bear's… the one who got us that amazing cottage for New Year's. Anyway, she works for the fire district and made some phone calls for me." I used the thumbnail of my free hand to pick at a hangnail, making the skin bleed.

Kristen pulled a tissue out of her pocket and dabbed at my bloody finger, her bright eyes searching mine.

"So, uh, I guess it's easiest to just say it. You remember how Sergeant Cleese said it was an accident and closed the case, but charged the yard truck driver with manslaughter?"

"Yeah. That's not what happened?"

I shook my head slowly, looking out the window. "I don't think so. Do you remember the HR lady from work?"

"Uh-huh. Shelly, right?"

"Yep. Well, get this, she is Sergeant Cleese's sister." I

rubbed my forehead and yanked off my beanie. I shook my hair out to get some air on my scalp.

Kristen looked at me, her eyebrows raised. "So, what does them being brother and sister have to do with all of this?"

I raked my fingers through my hair again and burned my mouth on another sip of tea. "I just… I don't know how to explain it. It just doesn't sit well, right here." I pointed to my gut.

"Okay. I can see this is hard for you. How can I help? I am off work today, so we can do whatever you want."

I blew out a big breath and ran my thumb along my thigh, feeling the tiny ridges of the denim fabric.

"Do you have a laptop? I want to search up some stuff."

"No, you know I don't."

"Oh. Right. I guess it'll have to wait till I get home." I sighed, trying to ratchet down my emotions. "How about we order take out, cuddle up, and watch some TV?"

"That sounds great." She ran her fingertips along my jawline and leaned in to kiss my cheek.

*

THE TEA SETTLED my stomach, so we gorged ourselves on tacos, rice, and beans, and watched hours of a show about hoarding. I rode home at dusk, feeling a tiny bit lighter, the anger mostly gone. I could finally think clearly.

After I closed the garage door and unloaded my bike, I walked into the house with relief, grateful to be home. The first thing that hit me was the smell. I stopped, hand hovering over the light switch, listening and sniffing the air, catching an aroma somewhere between roadkill and swamp decay.

"Porkchop?"

I waited for his telltale chirruping meow, but aside from the hum of the refrigerator, the house was silent. I flipped on the light and strode into the living room. Porkchop was curled up in his bed, his fluffy black-and-white fur disheveled and dull. "Shit. Don't be dead, Porky."

I squatted down and reached out my shaking hand to touch him. The double shotgun sound of my knees popping startled us both, and he flung his head up from where it had been burrowed under his paw. I let out a massive sigh and pet his head as he blinked up at me drowsily.

"You little asshole. I thought you were dead."

He lifted his chin up, rubbed his head against my hand, and stopped mid-yawn to meow at me. I ran my hand over his fur, trying to flatten down the messy parts.

"What died in here, eh?" I asked as I stood and followed my nose to the kitchen. First stop was the trash can, which was empty. Stepping to the sink, I remembered I had done the dishes before leaving, but hadn't run the disposal, and clearly something had rotted down there. I grit my teeth, turning on the sink and disposal, and poured a bit of dish soap down the drain. I ran it until the disposal sounded clear, then shut it all off.

Then I brewed some coffee, turned on the heater, unpacked, started a load of laundry, and changed into some sweats. Once I was ready to focus, I settled down on my recliner with my computer and mug of coffee.

My laptop didn't get much use, so I had to dust off the top with my sleeve before opening the lid. The thing was ancient and out of date, so I did my best to be patient while it went through the motions of booting up. When it was finally ready, I opened a search engine and typed in the name I remembered from the front of his business card: Chester "Chip" Cleese.

Porkchop rested his chin on the edge of his bed and gazed at me with heavy eyes. When I turned back to the screen, I saw a whole list of articles and hits on his name. *Of course, he's a cop and an investigator. He's probably in the news all the time.*

I stroked my chin and scanned the headlines. Then I erased his name from the search field and typed in the name of the Human Resources manager at work: Shelly Barstow. Only a few headlines popped up. The first few had to do with some human resources organizations, which I didn't care about.

I scrolled down a little further and saw a headline that caught my attention:

Brother and Sister Pair Set Another Record at Local Golf Tournament

I clicked on the headline and the article opened. Sure enough, right at the top of the page was a picture of Cleese and Shelly standing proudly in front of a country club, putters in hand and smug grins on their deeply tanned faces. I read the first few lines of the article and learned that they had been playing, and winning, mixed golf tournaments for years.

I shut the laptop, rubbed my cheeks, and looked up at the ceiling. I had no idea what help the information would be, other than I had confirmed that Shelly and the lead police investigator on the case where my boss had died were siblings.

*

AT THE END of the shift, I stood at the gate, leaning against the chain-link fence by the guard station, wishing for a cigarette and waiting for Brody. Not long before the buzzer, he jogged up, his heavy boots thumping on the concrete. I stepped forward and called out to him.

"Hiya, Randy. What's up?"

I kicked at a piece of gravel, not sure where to start. Brody placed his hand on my shoulder. "You okay?"

"Yeah, mostly. I just… I found out some information about the accident with Bryant and don't know what to do with it. It might be nothing, but I dunno."

My nose had started to run, so I sniffed and wiped at it with a handkerchief. Brody waited patiently for me to go on. I pulled him another few steps away from the line of people waiting to go through the guard station.

"So, I found out that Shelly here is the sister of the cop who investigated Bryant's death."

"The big guy?"

"Yeah."

"Huh," he said and sucked air between his front teeth. "Best keep that under wraps for now. We don't want Shelly to know that you know, all right?"

"Yeah. Okay."

"Ey, Randy, chin up."

"Thanks."

"I gotta get going. But let's talk more about this later, okay? Take care."

"You too."

*

SITTING IN MY truck, parked at the marina, I ate another

massive deli sandwich, and watched the choppy water. I picked a few stray pieces of lettuce off my lap and dropped them into the brown paper deli bag as I chewed, enjoying the sharp notes from the salami and mustard mixed with the bread and smattering of limp veggies. A few hearty souls were out in sail boats, and tugboats helped steer a massive cargo ship up the deep-water channel, headed to port.

I finished the sandwich and pulled out my phone so I could reread old texts from Brody and listen to the recordings he had sent me from our meetings with Shelly.

I listened to them over and over until my phone battery died. I was trying to see if there was anything helpful, and all I came up with was how Shelly acted in the first meeting she had with Brody and me. She was so hung up on whether I had seen anyone else around besides Bryant. I remembered how tense her face was, how she leaned forward in her desk, how she kept pushing me for an answer even though I couldn't give her one. I blew out a breath and brushed crumbs off the front of my shirt.

Phone dead and needing to pee, I drove back up the

hill to my house. A truck I didn't recognize was parked out front, but I didn't pay it much mind. Walking up the front path, I noticed weeds in need of pulling and gutters that needed cleaning. It took me a second to realize someone stood on my front porch, leaning against the door frame, and smoking a cigarette.

I froze, hands clenched into fists. After a tick I recognized Joe Rawlins, the loss prevention manger from work. Joe dropped his cigarette on the path and ground it out under his boot. He kept his hands at his sides, his movements rigid, which I took as him being nervous.

"Hiya, Randy. Joe Rawlins." He stuck out a calloused hand toward me.

"I know who you are, and I am not in the mood for your corporate bullshit."

I brushed past him and unlocked the door. As I crossed the threshold, I spoke to him over my shoulder. "You better come on in. But first, pick up that cigarette butt you just littered on my stoop."

He grunted as he bent and picked up the cigarette butt. He had a pot belly and moved stiffly, like a man with a bad back.

"Yes, ma'am," he said as he straightened up, his tone sincere.

I turned away from him and hung my keys on the hook. "Come on, come on. Close that door before you let out all the heat."

He stepped into the dim entryway and shut the door. I turned on the living room light, plugged my phone into the charger, and motioned for him to sit. Still tense, and not trusting that I wasn't going to have to defend myself or run out in a hurry, I didn't take off my jacket.

"I'll be right back."

"Sure," he said, looking around the room.

I made a quick trip to the restroom, then sat heavily in my chair, sizing up Joe, not quite sure if I could trust him or not.

"Things did not go well the last time you showed up here without an invitation, Joe. Shelly's not with you this time, so that's a good start."

He nodded, rubbing at the five o'clock shadow on his jowls and shuffling his worn-down Velcro sneakers.

"That's fair. Listen, you've been around a long time, Randy, and I appreciate your quiet and consistent work ethic."

"What do you know about my work ethic, Joe? You work in security, not out in the operation." I paused, realizing I was being rude. "Sorry. That was uncalled for."

He waved it off. "No worries. And, actually, I see and hear a whole lot more than people in the operation know. That's part of my job. In fact, I spent last night staked out up on the roof watching the trailer storage yard."

"Really? Well, shit. I had no idea you had to do that sort of thing for your job."

"Yeah. Not related to why I'm here, but it's just an example."

"Okay. Well. Why are you here then?"

He rubbed at his bristly jowls again. The raspy sound made me cringe.

"Well, Randy. Uh…as I was saying, you've been around a long time. Almost as long as me. And while you don't see much of me or my crew, we are around, working quietly in the background. Have you heard about employees caught for stealing medications, high value packages, and electronics that get shipped through our system?"

"Sure." I nodded, remembering talk around the building over the years about people getting caught stealing.

"Do you know how we catch thieves?"

I stiffened, suspicious of where the conversation was going. "What are you getting at? Am I being accused of something?"

He leaned forward, clasping his hands in his lap. "No, no. Nothing like that. I was just curious what you know about how things work. What our processes are."

"I have no idea. Snitches? People being dumb and selling stolen things online and getting caught?"

"Sometimes. Yes. We catch people in a variety of ways. How do you think we might catch a loader stealing from the packages they are loading in outbound trailers?"

"Well, I guess that would be one of the hardest places to catch a thief in the warehouse. They are deep inside a fifty-three-foot trailer, buried in packages. Lots of privacy to do some nonsense like stealing."

"Exactly. So, if you were in charge, how would you catch a thief stealing packages from a trailer?"

Bear's painting of the universe hung on the wall behind Joe. I looked at it as I thought about the layout of the building, the placement of the conveyor belts and loading docks, how the work flowed, where people's workstations were, and where the supervisors spent most of their time.

"Well, there's no way to watch a loader who's deep in a trailer without them seeing you. You'd have to stand at the mouth of the trailer door. Nowhere to hide and spy on them."

The anxiety woke up and churned my brain, trying to sideswipe my thoughts. I patted my lap a few times and Porkchop squeezed himself out from under the love seat. He hopped up onto my lap and pawed at my hand until I pet him. His long, soft fur under my rough hand was a comfort.

"Well, if you can't physically stand and watch the loader, I suppose you'd have to hide a video camera or something, right?"

Joe pointed a stubby finger at me. "Bingo."

"Okay, now what? What are we talking about?" My heart raced, and the undigested sandwich sat in my stomach like a brick. I stifled a belch, though a bit of stomach acid bubbled up the back of my throat. I swallowed it down and raised an eyebrow at Joe, urging him to get to the point.

He drew in a breath and reached inside his jacket. I stiffened, causing Porkchop to jump down off my lap and squeeze back under the love seat. I watched Joe's hand closely, relieved when he pulled a tablet out of his jacket pocket.

"Randy, I want to start by saying that I am absolutely not supposed to be here. Showing you this could definitely get me fired." He waved the tablet. "May I pull my chair up next to you, so we can watch together?"

"Sure."

He stood and pulled the wooden chair until it was flush with my recliner, the chair creaking as he sat again. He smelled like an ashtray doused in Old Spice and armpits. I sniffed, swallowing down more bile.

"So, one of the loaders on your load wall has been suspected of stealing prescription meds from medical packages for a while. We finally got the okay to try and catch him. It just so happens that he was loading on door seventy-six the day Bryant was crushed." I flinched at the word crushed. "We sent fake prescription medication packages with dye packs in them to his trailer, so if he happened to open one of those packages the dye would stain his hands and clothes."

I raised my eyebrows and turned to Joe, who nodded at me.

"Jesus. Wait. Does this mean you had a video camera on door seventy-six that day?"

Joe nodded again and keyed a password into the tablet to unlock it. He clicked around, opening an app and scrolling through pictures and videos.

"You need to see this."

"Wait. Wait. This isn't the video of Bryant getting… crushed, is it? Cuz if it is, I don't want to see it."

"Well, that is on this video, but what I want you to see happens before that. I will stop it before Bryant gets hurt, okay?"

I nodded and put on my glasses as he rested the tablet on the arm of my chair so we could both watch. He pressed the triangular play button, and a silent, grainy, black-and-white video began to play. I saw my crew doing prep work before the shift, walking back and forth in front of the camera carrying load stands and sheets of paper with their load guides on them. I caught glimpses of Bryant as he walked back and forth, shouting down the loading docks and up toward the crow's nests.

My chest swelled at the sight of Bryant going about his work so assuredly, no clue that he would not make it home. My eyes grew hot, and my nose ran. I sniffed, and Joe realized that I was getting upset.

"I'll uh, just fast forward here to the important part."

He hit the fast forward button and the whole shift went past in high speed, packages flying down the belt and the loader building load walls deep inside the trailer.

By the angle of the video, the camera was filming from just outside of the load door, probably hung from the side of the chute. From that spot you could see what was going on inside the trailer as well as all the activity on the loading dock just outside the load door.

The video continued whizzing by until the packages stopped flowing and the crew disappeared one by one to clock out. I caught a glimpse of Bryant placing the straps and load bars, meant to hold the packages in place inside the trailer. After Bryant walked away, Joe pressed the play button again, returning the video to normal speed.

My stomach clenched again, cramping a bit, and sweat dripped down the side of my neck. I pulled off my heavy jacket and tossed it on the love seat. The full trailer jerked, which I knew was what happened when the yard truck driver hitched their truck to the trailer. The trailer then pulled away from the load door, leaving bright sunlight pouring through, nearly blinding us.

I squinted and wondered where I was the moment that trailer was pulled. No doubt I was up top, doing a belt walk. The video appeared to have frozen because there was no movement for quite some time, though I knew something was about to happen because Joe tensed and leaned in even closer.

I pushed my glasses up higher and held my breath,

both to keep Joe's stink out of my nose, and because I feared what we were about to see. The loading dock was clear. Nice and tidy, the way Bryant liked it after a shift. No stray packages or tools left lying around. There was a flicker as two people walked on the grating of the loading dock and stopped at door 76. The sunlight streaming through was so bright that only their silhouettes were visible. The first person had a few small packages in their arms. Joe and I watched as the second person spoke and pointed to the ground outside.

The person holding the packages squatted and dropped the packages out of the load door, where they would have fallen onto the concrete ground of the yard outside. They then stood and wiped their hands on their pant legs.

The person giving the orders turned to walk away but stumbled just a bit and the two walked back the way they had come.

The video seemed frozen again as about a minute passed. Joe and I sat as still as the video. I took a shallow breath through my mouth, but it froze in my throat as Bryant's head and shoulders appeared in the yard outside of door 76. He yelled into his cell phone, then stooped to pick up the packages that had been dropped out into the yard.

I shoved the tablet away, not wanting to see any more. Joe caught it and pressed the stop button before folding the screen cover closed and placing the tablet back inside his jacket.

Sitting back in my soft recliner, I waited as Joe scooted his chair back around to where it was before, and gazed at me, his eyes fuzzy like he was deep in thought. I ran my thumb along my bottom lip, replaying the video in my mind.

He pursed his lips and bit at a hangnail. "I think we both know who that was."

Dipping my chin, I blew out a breath through my nose that I hadn't realized I was holding. "Shelly. Fuck. Who else knows about this?"

"Nobody. I am the one who set up the camera, and I am the only one who has had access to the surveillance video from that day."

"When did you watch the video and put two and two together?"

His face tightened as he clasped his hands together over his groin, as if to protect his balls. "Uh, the same day Bryant got hurt."

I clenched my jaw and balled up my fists. "You son of a bitch. You had to know this was important for the investigation and you've been sitting on it. How dare you!"

Ready to take a swing, I stood up and lunged at him. Joe did not make a move to protect himself. I stopped short, fist back and ready to strike. Porkchop bolted out from under the couch and ran between my feet, halting my advance on Joe.

"Whoa. Jesus, Porky."

I dropped my fist and sat back heavily in my chair, the anger dissolving as quickly as it had risen. I remembered my promise to Kristen that I wouldn't start any more fights, which took a bit more of the piss and vinegar out of me.

I wished my phone hadn't died, because I wanted to take a page out of Brody's book and record the conversation.

Joe cleared his throat and nibbled, with his front teeth, on the piece of hangnail he had bitten from his cuticle. "Look, I know I should have brought this forward a long time ago. It was wrong of me not to. But it's complicated."

I scoffed. "You've got that right." I recalled the picture I had found online of Cleese and Shelly, gritting my teeth at what it meant.

"Did you speak with the investigator?"

"Sure did. Couple of times. Guy by the name of Chip Cleese," I said, wondering why he had asked such an obvious question since I was the only witness.

"Well, I have had to participate in a few golf tournaments with folks from corporate. Golf isn't my thing, but saying no was not an option. Anyway, Cleese was there playing with Shelly from HR. Turns out they are sister and brother." Joe pursed his lips and looked directly at me, anticipating another blowup from me, but there was none.

"Yeah. I know."

His forehead wrinkled. "You do?"

"Yup. Just found out. Not sure what to do about it. What do you think?"

"I think Cleese intentionally steered the investigation toward it being an industrial accident."

I tapped the side of my nose twice, letting him know that I thought his suspicion was correct.

He went on. "I mean, can you imagine the fallout if it was proven that an employee did this on purpose? It would be a disaster for the company. I can just see that ball buster, Shelly, pressuring Cleese into compromising his integrity…if he had any to begin with. I have a few ideas on how we can turn this thing around, and I need your help."

We continued talking well into the evening as I shared with him what I had seen in the investigation photos Cleese had shown me on Thanksgiving, and we worked through a few different ways to approach the situation. Thankfully, Joe had a degree in Criminal Justice Administration and was a former police officer, so he knew far better than me how the system worked.

*

AFTER JOE LEFT, I pulled out my laptop and did another Google search of Shelly. There were plenty of articles on the internet about her. It turned out she was involved in several human resources organizations, a sorority, golf leagues, women's business groups, was on the board of two nonprofit organizations, and a mentor for homeless youth. She'd done several fun runs, and even one marathon.

Sipping on coffee, I read every single article and story I could find. Porkchop settled down in his cushy bed and put a paw over his eyes to keep out the light from my reading lamp. Eyes burning from exhaustion and only an hour out before my alarm was due to go off for work, I clicked on a link to read about Shelly's time mentoring homeless youth in the East Bay. As the picture at the top of the page loaded, I slammed the coffee mug down on the side table, making Porkchop jump.

"Well, would you look at this. I fucking knew it," I hissed through my teeth as I zoomed in on the picture and nudged up my reading glasses to read the tiny script below, which said:

Philanthropist and mentor, Shelly Barstow, attends the GED program graduation of her mentee, Mikela Gunnarsdottir.

The picture showed Shelly, dressed in her usual high heels and skirt suit, grinning widely. She had her hand on the shoulder of Mikela, who grinned at the camera. Mikela was dressed in a graduation robe and held a certificate. I zoomed the picture in further, so the only person on the screen was Mikela. Without a doubt that was the same woman who had worked side by side with me and had harassed Kristen. I pulled out my phone, sat back in my chair, and watched the video of our fight, feeling very disconnected from the person on the screen.

Afterward, knowing I had nothing left in the tank, I put the phone down and closed my eyes, but less than thirty seconds later my work alarm went off.

Porkchop shifted, burying his face into the corner of his bed. I closed the lid to my laptop and stretched my arms high up over my head, elbows popping, and got my morning routine going. Since I hadn't had any sleep in two days, I was grateful that it was a Friday. One shift between me and the weekend.

Chapter Fifteen

I Don't Need Your Protection

I SPENT MOST of my shift trying to stay focused on the details of the job but was so distracted by everything I had learned over the last few days that I made plenty of mistakes, causing shouts from farther along the belt and from down below on the loading dock.

"Ay, you having a stroke up there, old lady?"

I recognized the voice as one of my favorite loaders

and knew he was just teasing.

"Shove it, Arturo," I said without even bothering to look over the railing at him.

My missorts got bad enough that Justin showed up in the crow's nest and hit the belt stop button. He fiddled with the coiled cord of his two-way radio, hesitating. Normally when employees were fucking up, he would rage at them, shouting and sometimes even throwing packages. But he knew damn well that wouldn't fly with me.

I could see him trying to calm his temper and choose his words carefully. He took a deep breath and straightened the orange safety vest that hung loosely on him. His cheeks were red and sweat ran down his temples despite the freezing temperature in the warehouse.

This guy is a heart attack waiting to happen.

"Randy, is everything going okay up here?"

"I know I've been missorting all morning. But I have my focus back and promise it won't happen again."

He clapped his gloved hands together once, hit the belt start button, and took off down the ladder in a flash. The buzzer overhead blared through my earplugs, and I took a swig of coffee before turning back to the packages flowing by.

Come on, Cox, get it together.

The rest of the shift I managed to keep my focus until I clocked out. I nearly ran to my truck as the weekend opened up before me, though I wasn't totally free yet and I knew it. I sat in my truck and reached inside my jacket, feeling for a pack of cigarettes.

My stomach grumbled. Despite being so out of sorts I was fiercely hungry. I texted Kristen and asked if she wanted me to swing by her store so we could have lunch together. She replied quickly, saying that her lunch break was coming up and she'd meet me in the parking lot.

My phone rang, and I figured she had butt dialed me by accident, as she often did, but the screen lit up with Joe's cell phone number.

"Hey, Joe." Exhaustion came through in my voice.

"Hi, Randy. Just wanted to give you an update. I went down to the sheriff's administrative office during my lunch break and dropped off a copy of the citizen complaint form I mentioned last night. I made a copy for you too, which I'll email over. I named you in the complaint as a second witness and complainant, so somebody will probably be calling you."

I rubbed my clammy palms on my jeans. "Jesus, Joe. Are we really doing this?"

"It's done. Just tell them what you know when they contact you. Share with them whatever info you have, and then they will do whatever it is they do. I am going to stop by the district attorney's office and give them a copy of the complaint. That way, if the internal investigator at the sheriff's office decides to brush this under the rug there will be someone else keeping an eye on things to make sure the criminal side of this so-called *accident* gets addressed."

I yanked off my beanie and shook out my hair, trying to get some air circulating. "Thanks, Joe, I'm glad you decided to report this. I'll be sure to keep my phone handy for when they call me. I gotta go, but keep me posted, okay?"

"You got it. Bye, Randy."

"Bye."

As soon as the call ended, I jumped out of the truck, yanked my jacket off, and threw it on the passenger seat. I fanned the collar of my flannel shirt to get some cool air on my skin and wondered if I was having one of those hot flashes I'd heard about, or if it was my nerves unravelling.

I leaned against the cold metal fender of my truck and shoved my hands in my pockets to stop from flapping around. A couple of guys from the next shift ran by, cigarette smoke trailing behind them. It took everything I had in me not to call out and ask them for a smoke.

Over the sounds of the road and the yard I heard a faint tinkling. After a few seconds I realized it was the ringer on my cell phone. I jumped back into the driver's seat and dug around in my jacket pockets until I found the phone.

I fumbled with it, sliding my finger across the screen to answer, but my skin was so cold and dry that the touchscreen didn't know what I was trying to do. I licked my fingertip and slid it across the screen a few more times before it registered that I wanted to answer the call.

"Hullo?" I was winded and stressed and my voice gave it all away.

"This is Sergeant Castaneda. Is this Miranda Cox?"

"Speaking. Call me Randy, please."

Sweat dripped down under my layers of shirts. Mind racing and chest tight, I knew I needed to settle down.

"Sure thing, Randy. I am calling because you were mentioned as a possible witness in a citizen complaint that was filed today, and I'd like to set up a time to meet."

"Sure."

"So, it sounds like you know what this is about."

"I do."

We scheduled a time to meet the following day and I hung up. My stomach rumbled and a headache warmed up behind my left eye.

The drive to Kristen's work was just a few minutes, so I swooped by and picked her up. She gave me the sweetest kiss as a greeting, and we drove a few blocks to a noodle place.

I ordered a huge, steaming bowl of chow mein and she got spaghetti with a spicy sauce. We tucked into a booth and spent the first few minutes just eating and grinning at each other. I ate all the vegetables first, then started in on the chicken and noodles.

Swallowing a big bite, my hunger finally settling down, I pointed my fork at her bowl. "How's your pasta?"

She finished chewing. "It's good. But the sauce tastes like it's full of preservatives. Not freshly made."

"Preservatives are good for you," I joked as I slurped a noodle.

"Hey, so I'm having some friends over to my place for a little party in a couple of days. I'd love it if you joined us."

"That sounds fun. I haven't really met any of your people, so yeah, I'd like that."

"It's mostly people from work. They are a fun bunch."

I forced a smile and took a big bite.

She put her fork down and sipped her water. "So, what's on your mind?"

"It's that obvious, huh?"

She nodded.

"There's some stuff going on with the Bryant investigation that's bugging me." I finished chewing and tapped the tines of the fork against the bowl as I thought. I'd taken in so much new information the night before, and after making the connection between Shelly and Mikela, I couldn't stop thinking about that angle. "Has that Mikela been in touch with you since peak ended?"

Kristen's smile faded and she looked down at her napkin. I could barely hear her over the noise of the restaurant as she spoke. "Yes."

I put my fork down with a clatter. "Did she contact you, or did you contact her?"

Kristen raised her eyes. "She contacted me."

"Well…when? How often? What did she want?"

"Jeez. Right after she got transferred back to the air hub. She seemed lonely and I felt bad for her."

I scoffed, wading through my anger to find words. Nothing reasonable came to mind so I kept quiet.

Kristen went on. "She found me on Instagram and sent me a message. We've been in touch now and then."

She gazed down at her napkin, shoulders rounded like a toddler who had been scolded. I gnashed my teeth together, ready to wring Mikela's neck, but knew if I let that anger out around Kristen it would upset her. I shoved it down the best I could and tried to steady myself.

"Uh, wow. That's not good. She's a predator, hun. And

on top of that, she is probably trying to get information from you about me."

She tilted her head and by the look on her face I could see that she thought I was being paranoid. "No, I don't think so. I promise that I don't talk about you to her. She seems genuine. I...I trust her so that should be enough."

"You *trust* her?"

"Yeah."

"What about all those disgusting things she said to you at work? What about when she put her hands on you? What about when she attacked me?" I knew I was being dishonest about the last part, but I didn't care because I was trying to make a point to Kristen. "She's dangerous."

"I know. It sounds bad. She behaved badly. Like I said, she seems genuine, and she apologized."

I raised my hands up in mock defeat. "Oh well then, by all means, let's become her best friend."

"Randy, I don't appreciate your tone right now, or the fact that you don't trust me to make decisions for myself."

"I'm just trying to protect you, babe."

"I don't need your protection."

I blew out a breath, realizing that we were not going to see eye to eye on this. I grumbled, "Okay." I forced myself to release my fists and took her hand, leaning across the table and kissing her knuckles. "Let's finish up lunch. I know you need to get back to work soon."

She nodded and I watched her eat the rest of her meal. I took mine in a takeout carton because I had lost my appetite.

*

DARCY KNEW I was coming and welcomed me at the back gate. She handed me a chilled bottle of hard cider and gave me a hug. She was still dressed in her work coveralls.

"Come on in, you."

"Thanks."

Inside her cottage, I held the carton of food up to her, but she waved it off. I ate the lukewarm chow mein and stared at the wall. After I finished, I put the plastic fork inside the takeout container and crumpled the whole thing up, then sat back in the chair and took a long pull on the bottle of hard cider. "Thanks, this hits the spot."

"You're welcome. You look like shit, Randy. What's going on?"

I ran my hand down my face and patted my breast pocket, wanting a smoke. "A bunch of stuff I can't really talk about right now. The investigation at work. Kristen being kinda shady. Pretty much my life is chaos right now and my nerves are on edge."

She pulled a cigar box out from under the couch and flipped the lip open. She removed a pack of rolling papers, a lighter, and a baggie of weed. I watched her fingers work at plucking away stems and seeds, grinding the nuggets, and sprinkling it on the paper, which she rolled up with a practiced hand. She extended the joint and a lighter, but I shook my head.

"Mind if I smoke this inside?"

"Nah. It's your house. Go ahead."

Darcy switched on a small rotating fan, put the joint between her lips, and flicked the lighter into life. She drew in several times until the joint was lit. She held a long drag and blew it out with a cough. Smoke gathered around the overhead light, then blew away as the fan turned toward it.

"I think I'm not accustomed to the level of stress I'm under right now. The first half of my life was bad. Really rough stuff. I've spent the last twenty years trying to keep things low stress, like…live a low maintenance life. Heck, that's one of the reasons I've stayed single this whole time. I couldn't find anyone I trusted enough to not stir things up. But, just in the last six months, everything has turned upside down. And now I don't know if I can trust Kristen."

Darcy's eyebrows raised slightly. "Really? What's going on with Kristen?"

"Well, there is somebody that I know for a fact is dangerous, and Kristen has been in touch with this person even after they did bad stuff to her and to me. She doesn't like that I don't trust her to make decisions for herself."

"Hm. Is this about trust or is this about control?"

I scoffed. "Control?"

"Yes. Maybe you are frustrated because, despite your cautions, Kristen has chosen to be in touch with this person. So, is it that you don't trust her judgement or is it that you are bothered that you can't control who she chooses to have contact with?"

I took a sip of cider, the cool sweet bite of it lingering on my tongue, and gave Darcy's question some thought. The fact that I might be trying to control Kristen had never entered my mind. To me, it felt like I was trying to protect her.

"I'm trying to protect her."

"Maybe she doesn't need or want your protection."

"That's what she said."

Darcy shrugged her shoulders. "Well, there you have it."

The bottle of cider in my hand had condensation on the outside, and I picked at the corners of the label where it was peeling away from the glass.

"I dunno. I'm an old-school butch. We protect our women. We make sure they have what they need and are safe and comfortable."

"That may be so, but if your partner doesn't have the same outlook on relationship roles or desire to have that type of care from a partner, it's going to cause some friction."

I scoffed. "You've got that right."

Darcy crossed her legs and tapped a forefinger to her lip as she thought for a moment. "There are plenty of relationship resources out there to help you two find out what your relationship styles are. Just go online and search up attachment style quizzes and you'll find a ton. There's one theory out there from a guy named Gary Chapman. It's called five love languages. Have you heard of it?"

"Nope, can't say that I have."

"Well, according to him, each person has ways they show their love, and ways they want to receive love. So, for me, I like to receive love through quality time, and I show my love by doing acts of service. So, if I am with someone who is not into giving love through quality time, we might be a mismatch or at least have some things to work on."

"Hm, so you think Kristen doesn't like me being protective?"

"I can't speak for Kristen, but based on what you've said, she sounds like someone who is really independent and likes to make her own decisions."

"Yep, that sounds like her."

I finished off the cider and cleaned up my trash. We walked out to the alleyway and Darcy gave me a big hug.

"Thanks. I'll get on the computer and check out some of those quizzes. What was it you called them? Attachment styles?"

Darcy nodded. "I'm happy to help."

We smiled at each other through the windshield, and I fired up the truck.

*

BACK AT HOME I spent some time uploading the pictures, videos, and audio recordings I'd collected from Brody, transferring them from my phone into a Dropbox folder online. The hope was that I could have them all backed up in one place, and I figured it would be safest to store them there.

I had beer and pretzels for dinner while I took a few relationship attachment style quizzes online. I wasn't sure how much I could rely on them but figured some of it had to be right. I learned that I liked to show my affection with acts of service and liked to receive love from words of affirmation. It also turned out that my relationship style was something called fearful avoidant.

"Fearful avoidant? Huh," I said, looking up from my laptop to think about what that meant. Lack of sleep combined with hard cider and beer made the room swim. "It's bedtime, Pork-eeeeee."

Porkchop, a pile of fluff on the love seat, didn't bother opening his eyes. I thought about shooing him off, since he wasn't supposed to be up there, but skipped it. I shut off the lights and stumbled down the hallway. I crawled into bed still dressed in my filthy work clothes.

I slept solidly, and woke up late the next morning in the same position I had fallen asleep in. It took a few minutes to get up and work out the kinks in my neck and shoulders. I stripped down and took a long, hot shower. It was cold and foggy out and I was grumpy, so I dressed warmly in carpenter pants, a long-sleeved T-shirt, and my favorite hoodie, hoping that being warm would help my mood.

In the kitchen I was disappointed to see that I hadn't

set the automatic coffee maker the night before.

"Great."

After some rushing around and drinking of scorching hot coffee, I drove across the bridge for my appointment with Sergeant Castaneda. Blustery side winds blasted me, and I had to hold tight on the steering wheel the whole span of the bridge.

I was relieved that the appointment wasn't in the same building where Cleese worked. The address Sergeant Castaneda gave me was on the far south side of town and didn't look like a government building at all. It was a strip mall that was mostly shops with boarded-up windows. Weeds grew up between cracks in the pavement. I checked the scrap of paper I had scribbled the address on. I was in the right place.

I drove around to the back, as she had told me to do, and parked next to a loading ramp. A few cars and SUVs lined up in the parking spaces had the look of unmarked government cars. A woman dressed in khaki tactical pants and a black, long-sleeve polo stood by the door, her thumbs hooked into her duty belt.

I cleared my throat and took a deep breath, trying to get rid of the butterflies in my stomach. She watched me closely as I locked up the truck and approached.

"Randy?" she asked, her hand extended.

"Yes. Are you Sergeant Castaneda?"

I shook her hand as she nodded.

"Guilty as charged. Come on in." She chuckled at her own joke, turned, and swiped a key card over a subtly placed card scanner.

The back of the building looked as abandoned as the front, but they definitely had some sort of operation going on inside. I followed her past a series of closed doors along a dark hallway. Snippets of low conversations and police scanner static came from some of the rooms.

At the end of the hall, she led me through the only open door, which led to a dimly lit conference room that looked like it had been furnished at a government surplus sale. There was a long conference table lined with crappy, old beige chairs, a dry-erase board on the wall, and a pro-jector. The tabletop was chipped and bare aside from one seat that had a laptop, paper cup of coffee, and a notepad.

She pointed to a chair on the far side of the table from the door. "Go ahead and have a seat. Make yourself comfortable."

I wondered how the hell I'd ever be comfortable in the situation I was in, tucked away in some windowless conference room in a sneaky unmarked cop shop. I sat where she told me to, placing my sweaty hands flat on the cool tabletop. I liked that I was facing the door but didn't like that she was between me and the door.

"Can I get you some coffee? A snack?"

"No, thanks. I'm fueled up for now."

"Okay." She closed the door and sat in the chair with the laptop and notepad, taking a sip of coffee.

"How are you doing this morning, Randy?"

"Tired. How about you?"

"I'm great. Thanks for asking."

The sheriff's star neatly embroidered on the breast of her polo shirt gave me something to focus on as she flipped through a few pages in her notepad, pulled out a small digital recorder from the cargo pocket of her pants, and set it down between us on the table.

"I, uh, this is all new to me."

"Of course, no worries. I'm just going to ask you some questions. Please answer the questions as fully as you can. Take your time. I want to be sure we get as many of the details today as we can. Sound good?"

"Sure." I splayed my hands out on the tabletop, my knuckles thick with scar tissue and callouses, and dirt under my nails. Though wrinkled and veiny, I liked my hands. They told my story of hard, honest work.

One thing I couldn't stand was dishonesty, and people not having integrity. Heat rose in my chest as I thought about Shelly and Cleese trying to cover up what had happened. I took off my jacket, hung it on the back of the chair, and pulled up the sleeves of my hoodie.

"All set?"

"Yep."

"Okay, so just to get you up to speed, we received a citizen complaint form from Mister Rawlins...Joe. We've already interviewed him and now want to speak with you, as your name came up a few times. I'd like to start with you telling me everything you know about the death of Bryant, and the investigation afterward. And, if you don't mind, I will be recording this session just to ensure I don't miss anything."

I nodded, agreeing to be recorded. It was easier to talk to my hands, so I kept my eyes down, focusing on a knotty purple scar that ran across the top of my right hand. I explained to her everything I had done and seen the day Bryant had died. I went on to tell her all about my conversations with Sergeant Cleese, then about the video Joe had shown me. And since I had figured out that Mikela and Shelly were connected, I also shared with her how Mikela had harassed Kristen, and my fight with her.

Sergeant Castaneda seemed to be a good listener and jotted down notes as I spoke. From what I could see she was just doing bullet points, relying either on her memory or the recorder for the rest. She didn't interrupt me at all, and I took my time explaining everything. I didn't want to have to go back there for more meetings if it could be avoided.

Eventually I petered out. She smiled at me, her lip gloss shining even in the low light of the room.

"Thank you, Randy. Can I get you some water?"

"Yes, please."

She left the room, notepad in hand, closing the door behind her. I noticed that the digital recorder was still on, the blinking red light telling me it was still running. I wondered if she had left it recording on purpose, or if it was a mistake. Given that she was a sergeant and worked in internal affairs, I figured it was no mistake. I decided she had left it running on purpose.

I checked my watch. She had been gone for quite a while, and I grew fidgety, shaking my leg under the table but trying to stay as silent as possible. I resisted the urge to pull out my cell phone to scroll Facebook. I busied myself by dusting away the cobwebs in my brain and pulling together the words of a poem that my father had made me memorize as a kid. *Jabberwocky* by Lewis Carroll.

> *'Twas brillig, and the slithy toves*
> *Did gyre and gimble in the wabe:*
> *All mimsy were the borogoves,*
> *And the mome raths outgrabe.*

"Beware the Jabberwock, my son!

The jaws that bite, the claws that catch!

Beware the Jubjub bird, and shun

The frumious Bandersnatch!"

He took his vorpal sword in hand;

Long time the manxome foe he sought—

So rested he by the Tumtum tree

And stood awhile in thought.

And, as in uffish thought he stood,

The Jabberwock, with eyes of flame,

Came whiffling through the tulgey wood,

And burbled as it came!

One, two! One, two! And through and through

The vorpal blade went snicker-snack!

He left it dead, and with its head

He went galumphing back.

"And hast thou slain the Jabberwock?

Come to my arms, my beamish boy!

O frabjous day! Callooh! Callay!"

He chortled in his joy.

'Twas brillig, and the slithy toves

Did gyre and gimble in the wabe:

All mimsy were the borogoves,

And the mome raths outgrabe.

I ran through the poem in my mind over and over, remembering my father reciting it in the car whenever we went somewhere, just the two of us. He'd make his voice low and spooky when he spoke the lines about the jabberwock, then triumphant and loud when shouting "callooh callay." It always made me giggle, and when he had me try to recite it back, I'd stumble on so many of the words. I was surprised at myself that, over forty years later, I could still remember every word.

I savored the memories of him as they rose. Tears welled up as I remembered how much I had loved my daddy, and how sad I still was about his death. Anger at my mother soon followed. My mother had murdered the father who loved listening to country and classical music, and usually came out from shaving with bits of bloody toilet paper stuck on his face along with a whimsical grin. The father who shielded me from my mother's fits of rage, and her slapping, tearing hands. In the end they were both dead and gone, and there I was, sitting at a conference table trying to get justice for Bryant.

I figured that stuff all came up because I was feeling mighty vulnerable. I was relieved when Sergeant Castaneda returned. She smiled at me as she slid a plastic bottle of water across the table. I caught the quick flick of her eyes as she checked that the recorder was still running. I wondered why, if I was there to help them, they were being sneaky? I didn't like it.

"Sorry about that. I got pulled into another meeting."

I stayed silent, not giving her an inch, knowing she probably didn't get pulled into a meeting at all, but was just hoping if she left me in there long enough, I'd make a phone call they could listen in on, or say something stupid that they could use. I made a point of looking at the re-corder too, enjoying it as she shifted in her seat.

I cracked the seal on the water bottle, took a sip of the cool water, and continued sitting quietly, watching her fiddle with her pen.

"I'd like to ask you a few questions, now that I have heard your side of things and have a better understanding of what happened."

I raised my eyebrows at her and realized I was being a bitch, but I didn't like that she was playing games. When I had arrived, I was perfectly willing to spill my guts to them but was feeling much more guarded after being left to stew.

I had told her about my conversations with Shelly, but I hadn't told her that I had Brody's recordings of them, and she didn't know I had video of my fight with Mikela. I weighed my grumpiness at her with the bigger picture of what I wanted to accomplish.

"Listen, Sergeant. I don't appreciate you playing games with me. If you want information from me, let's have a conversation. I came here to help. But if you are go-ing to pull some bullshit cop tactics on me, then I am out of here."

As I stood up, so did she. She held out a hand to me, motioning for me to sit.

"Sit, sit. Please. We appreciate you coming down and talking to us."

"After what I went through with Sergeant Cleese, and the cover-up I think he did, I don't feel very trusting toward cops. So, you leaving me in here to cool my heels with the recorder on is not appreciated. I am not interested in playing any of your games. If you want info, let's talk. Or like I already said, I'm done."

She waved toward the chair again. Her tone softened. "Sit, please."

I sat and tapped my fingertips on the table while Sergeant Castaneda looked at me. She clicked her pen a few times and flipped her notepad to a fresh page.

"Why didn't you file a police report when Mikela attacked you outside of work?"

"No point. It was just a little scuffle and was over in a few seconds. She got transferred to another building which got her out of my hair, so I'd say that's enough."

"Do you have pictures of your injuries?"

"Yes."

"Will you show them to me?"

I pulled my cell phone out and scrolled back in my pictures until I found the selfies I had taken at work after our fight. I held the phone across the table so she could see. She reached to take my phone, but I held onto it tightly. She pursed her lips and gave a slight nod after looking at the picture of my bloody face.

"That's her blood though, not mine."

"Any others?"

"Pictures?"

"Yes."

"No, but one of the guys shot a video of the fight, if you wanna see it."

"I do." Her face and tone stayed flat, but I figured she jumped in excitement a little on the inside.

I cued up the video, and leaned across the table, still holding tight to the phone. She watched the short video intently. Once the video ended, I laid my phone face down on the table.

"So, that's Mikela," I said with a grumble. "She's the one I mentioned who sexually harassed my girlfriend, and has ties to Shelly, and was asking me way too many questions about Bryant's death."

"Let's loop back around to Shelly. You mentioned that she showed up at your house unannounced and also pulled you into her office shortly after Bryant's death for her administrative investigation. Did I get all of that right?"

"Yes."

"So, now that I know you have video and photos from your run-in with Mikela, do you have anything similar from your interactions with Shelly?"

"Is there a law in California about recording people when you don't have their permission?"

"Uh, well, penal code six-thirty-two does prohibit recording conversations that would otherwise be considered private or confidential. So, you can record out in public, when privacy is not guaranteed. But recording a private meeting without both parties' consent is considered illegal."

"Okay, good to know. No, I don't have any videos or

anything from my meetings with Shelly. It was just me and my shop steward, and I don't recall Shelly recording the meetings either."

She tilted her head, clearly not buying it that I didn't have recordings, but moved on by asking a few more questions about the night Shelly showed up at my house, then about Thanksgiving Day when Sergeant Cleese had me look through photos from the scene.

Then we rehashed how I put two and two together that Shelly and Sergeant Cleese were siblings. I left out the bit about Vivian telling me they were related, and just explained that I had done an internet search, same as how I found out Shelly had mentored Mikela.

"Okay, Randy, I know this is taking up a big chunk of your day off, but can you bear with me a little bit longer?"

"Sure." I took another swig of water. Even though I was stressed, my stomach growled with hunger.

"Now, Joe Rawlins told me he showed you the surveillance video from the day Bryant died. Is that right?"

"Yes, he showed me a video. Not sure if it's what you saw."

She paused and tapped the end of the pen on her lip. "I'd like to watch it with you and get your take on what is happening. I'd also like for you to name off everybody you recognize as they show up on the screen. Will you do that for me?"

"Yes, but only if you promise to stop the video before the trailer pins Bryant. I can't watch that."

"Deal."

She turned on the projector, which shone a blue loading screen on the whiteboard. It took a few minutes of clicking around for her to find the file she wanted and for the projector and laptop to link up.

The chair creaked as I turned to face the whiteboard. The video was paused at the beginning, showing an empty trailer and loading dock. She pressed play and we watched as my crew got ready for the shift. Each time a person walked past the camera I said their name and she jotted it down. This went on until the conveyor belts got rolling, packages started flowing, and far fewer people walked along the dock. Every once in a while, Bryant would walk by, otherwise we just watched the loader load his trailer.

She put the video on fast forward at that point and only slowed it when a new person walked by so I could identify them for her. Even though the video was mostly on fast forward, it was tedious as we watched an entire eight-hour shift unfold.

Once the shift ended, she slowed the video back to regular speed and we watched the trailer pull away from the wall, the blinding sunlight blasting the lens of the camera. When the two silhouettes stood at the load door, one ready to drop packages out into the yard, Sergeant Castaneda paused the video. She sat back in her chair and patted her hands on the table in a quick drumming tempo.

"Have you seen what happens next?"

"I have."

"I'd like for you to tell me what you think is happening and who they are."

"Well, I…" My throat closed up and tears welled in my eyes. I drew in a few shaky breaths, trying to steady myself.

"Hey, Randy, I know this is tough. I appreciate you having the courage to come speak to me today and for watching this video again."

You can cry later. Just get this over with.

My throat relaxed and my eyes cleared. "Uh, well. Anyone familiar with how our operation flows would know that after the shift wraps up and the trailers are pulled, the wall supervisor checks the yard for any stray packages. What I see here is someone dropping packages out into the yard, which means Bryant would have to go pick them up. I see one person doing the dropping, while another watches and seems to be telling 'em what to do."

"And why do you think someone would want to do that? Tell me as if I were someone who didn't know anything about how your operation runs."

"There could be a bunch of reasons why. Corporate is cutthroat, and packages not making it onto the trailer is a big deal. If some packages got overlooked and didn't make it on the trailer, someone might throw them into the yard to make it seem like they missed being loaded because they overflowed into the yard instead of being missed inside the building. So, if the people throwing them in the yard were loaders or a wall supervisor, I'd think that was what was going on. But that's not who I see here. My gut tells me someone was setting it up for Bryant to have to go out into the yard. I have nothing to prove that though."

I paused, looking at the water-stained acoustic ceiling tiles, hating the idea that someone set things up so Bryant had to go out into the yard.

"I imagine it would be dangerous for someone to walk around in the yard. If someone needed to go out there on foot, what are the protocols?"

"They have to wear a fluorescent safety vest, and they have to put an orange traffic cone in the area where they are working to let the yard truck driver know there is a pedestrian out there."

"And where would someone get these supplies?"

"There are safety vests on coat hooks near each of the pedestrian doors that lead to the yard, and there is also a stack of traffic cones by each door."

"Hm. Okay. Based on what I saw in the video it appears Bryant was not wearing a vest. In your interview with Sergeant Cleese, I see that you told him you weren't sure if Bryant was wearing one or not. Why do you think

Bryant would go out into the yard without taking the necessary safety precautions?"

"I have no idea. I mean, he was a supervisor and making sure people followed the yard control rules was part of his job, so he knew the rules. But how would I know why Bryant did what he did?"

"Hm. Okay." She pointed back to the frozen image of the two silhouettes on the whiteboard. "Can you identify these two people?"

"Sure can. And it all makes sense now, because when Sergeant Cleese showed me the evidence photos back in November, one of the things they found in all the trash under the metal grating of the loading dock was a heel that had broken off a high-heeled shoe. The only person in the entire building who wears heels is her." I pointed at the video image frozen on the wall. "Shelly Barstow."

"And who is the other one, holding the packages?"

*

"CALLOOH. CALLAY," I muttered as I got back on the

freeway and the tears that I had held back during the interview fell in a rush. I stayed in the slow lane because it was hard to see through all the tears on top of fighting the wind gusts. I shook my head, realizing I had cried more in the last couple of months than I had in the last ten years.

Nothin' to be ashamed of, Randy.

I didn't want to go home and couldn't figure out what to do with myself, so I drove to a movie theater and bought a ticket for the next show. It was one of those theaters with fancy new reclining seats and little tables on swing arms. Half of the seats were empty, which suited me just fine. I fidgeted and fussed through twenty minutes of commercials and movie previews, which annoyed me so much that I almost got up and left. Once the film started, I was able to relax a bit. The movie was full of A-list actors and the storyline had a lot of good plot twists, so I was able to put my worries on hold for a couple of hours.

After the movie, I zipped up my jacket and stepped out into the gray drizzle outside. I sat in my truck for a few minutes, waiting for the vents to blow warm air and adjusting back to my reality after being immersed in the movie.

I was still having a hard time accepting what I had seen in the video Joe and Sergeant Castaneda had shown me. It seemed impossible to me that people from work would want to hurt Bryant. What could they possibly gain from harming him?

A family hustled by, heading to their car through the drizzle, shopping bags looped over their wrists and a baby asleep in a stroller. I had never wanted the complications of a family, but in the moment, as I watched the mother and father work together to load up their shopping bags and transfer the sleeping baby to the car, a small twinge of longing pulled at my chest. The pang wasn't that I wanted a child, it was that I wanted more than being alone for the rest of my life.

I pulled out my phone and called Kristen. She answered after a few rings.

"Hey babe. Everything okay?" she asked cheerfully, the buzz of people chattering and shopping carts rattling in the background.

"You working?"

"Yeah." Her voice lowered. "Are you okay?"

I cleared my throat. "Yeah, I'm just tired. Can you stay over tonight?"

"Really? I mean…you've never let me stay over at your place before."

"Yes, really."

"I'd like that. Should I bring some dinner too?"

"That would be great."

"Okay, I have to get back to work. I'll see you later."

"Bye, babe. Be safe driving over the bridge. The wind up there is terrible."

The gray cloud in my chest lifted a little, and I drove home through the blowing winds and drizzle. I took a long shower and puttered around the house until I saw Kristen's headlights flash across the wall as she pulled into the driveway.

When I unlocked the deadbolt, the front door flew open as a huge gust of wind blew rain and leaves into the entryway. Kristen hustled up the walkway and stepped inside. I shut the door behind her and took the bags of takeout food she was holding so she could take off her dripping raincoat.

"Oh my gosh, you weren't kidding. It is crazy out there. Driving over the bridge was really scary," she exclaimed as she wiped rain off her face and hung her drenched jacket in the garage.

"I'm glad you made it here safe. Thanks for bringing dinner," I said as I put the food bags on the counter and pulled her into a long hug. Her cheek was damp and ice cold against mine. I rubbed her back and upper arms, trying to help warm her up.

"I got us a DVD." She ended the hug and started pulling food containers out of the bags. "And I picked us up some dinner from that amazing Hawaiian place downtown."

"Sounds great," I said, though my voice sounded flat.

She stepped up to me, placed her cold index finger under my chin, and raised it so we were eye to eye. "Let's get some food in you, and we can talk about whatever is on your mind, okay?"

I nodded and set the table while she prepared plates for us. Porkchop deemed the arrival of food important enough to climb out from under the love seat. He ambled into the kitchen, stretching his hind legs and blinking sleepily.

Kristen and I tucked in at the booth, sitting staggered across from each other. I ate chicken katsu, Kahlua pork with cabbage, and sticky rice, but didn't taste any of it. The only thing I could taste was the canned peach nectar she brought, though what I really wanted was a beer and a smoke.

Porkchop sat under the table alternating between meowing and purring. I reminded him that human food was not for cats, but he was not convinced. Pushing my empty plate and glass away, I sat back while Kristen finished up her stir-fried udon noodles and vegetables.

"How much do I owe you for dinner?" I asked.

Kristen frowned at me. "Nothing. My treat."

"Thank you for feeding me, and for coming over." My chin slumped down to my chest again, and Kristen pulled it up.

"Hey, Randy. Let's talk."

I made a pathetic attempt to move the conversation away from me. "So, how about this weather?"

She raised her eyebrows at me. "Look, I am happy that you invited me to stay over tonight, but up until now that has always been a hard no for you. So that, plus you are clearly upset about something… What's going on?"

"Bryant, Shelly, Cleese. And…" I met her gaze and took her hand in mine. "I just don't want to be alone anymore. I don't want to live the rest of my days as some grumpy, lonely old hermit."

I realized that what I was saying could have been taken as the beginnings of a marriage proposal, which was not what I was getting at, so I changed course.

"So, dropping my ridiculous rule about no sleepovers at my house is a good place to start."

"I'm glad. What else is going on in there?" she asked, pointing at my head.

I wanted to spill my guts to her but was worried about her telling Mikela. My tailbone started to hurt from sitting on the wooden bench of the booth, so I shifted, trying to get comfortable.

"Before I say this, I want to say I am not asking this to give you a hard time. I just need to know. Are you still in touch with Mikela?"

She frowned. "Yes."

I knew I needed to tread lightly. "May I ask when was the last time you had contact with her? And how often you are in touch?"

"Well, she and I went for a hike while you were away for New Year's Eve. Otherwise, we just text now and then. She mostly just sends me stupid memes and half the time I don't even respond."

"I—I had no idea you went hiking with her."

"Yeah, we did that trail in the hills, the one that goes around the reservoir. She's hella fit. I was impressed that she could keep up with me. We might do some mud runs and a Spartan race together in the spring."

"Has she said anything else inappropriate to you, like she did that day at work in the trailer?"

"Nope, she has been totally normal."

"And has she asked about me at all?"

"I feel like you're interrogating me. I don't see how what I talk to her about is any of your business. But, since you asked, the only time she asked about you was when we were hiking. She just asked how you have been doing."

"I'm not interrogating you; I promise there is a reason why I am asking. And what did you say when she asked about me?"

"Geez, Randy, do you want me to tape record our conversation for you next time? I told her you were fine. That's it."

With disappointment, I realized I couldn't be totally honest with Kristen about what was going on with the investigation, in case she said something to Mikela about it. I hated not being able to be open with my girlfriend. I wanted so badly to be able to just let it all out and have someone listen, but Kristen wasn't the one. It didn't sit well with me that I couldn't fully trust her but I didn't have the energy to dwell on it right then.

"Okay. So, what movie did you rent?"

"Oh, right. It's in my jacket. I'll be right back."

She jogged out to the garage, and I cleared the dishes, getting myself ready to fake a good mood for the rest of the night because I really did want to spend time with her. I shoved down my worries, grabbed a beer, and slapped on a smile as she came back into the kitchen, DVD case in hand.

The windows rattled as gusts of wind blew in from the strait, rain pattering on the panes. I turned off the lights and lit some candles while she turned on the TV and loaded the disc into my ancient DVD player. We cuddled up on the couch and I gladly lost myself in another movie.

Chapter Sixteen

Clipped Hip

THE STORM BROKE overnight, and the morning dawned bright and crisp. Sunlight shone through my window for the first time in weeks. I lay in bed watching water drip from the trees outside and listening to the gurgle of the drainpipe. The roof of the house across the street steamed where sunlight hit it.

The sound of Kristen humming in the shower brought

a smile to my face. I pulled the blanket up to my chin, enjoying a moment of warmth and comfort. It took a few minutes for the shit I had pushed down the night before to resurface. I focused on the ceiling, trying to decide what to do about it.

The water heater made its usual rumbling sound in the service closet down the hall, and only let up when Kristen shut off the water and came out, toweling her hair. Her taut skin and perky breasts spoke to how much younger she was than me, and I gave her a lopsided grin. She spread her towel out over her pillow, climbed under the covers, and wound her arms and legs around me. We lay there cuddling for a few minutes, and I absorbed every bit of her that I could.

"I'm so glad you stayed over last night."

I ran my hand up and down her damp back and she snuggled into me even closer. Her wet hair soaked the front of my shirt, but I didn't give a damn, I was just happy to have her in my bed.

Why the hell did I wait so long to have her stay over?

My dreamy, drifting thoughts were rudely interrupted

by the alarm on her cell phone. She groaned and slapped at the side table until she found her phone and shut the alarm off.

"As much as I am loving this, I have to finish getting ready for work."

She slid out of bed and pulled a few bottles out of her backpack. I watched curiously as she applied deodorant, lotions, and sun block.

"Sun block? It's January."

"Every day, rain or shine. Gotta protect this skin."

"Huh." I ran my hand along the weathered creases of my face. I had never paid my hide much mind and knew that all my years of smoking and motorcycle riding hadn't helped any.

She pulled on panties decorated with designs of little ice cream cones and rainbows. Over those she put on skinny jeans and her work shirt. She had perfect posture, which emphasized her breasts in her tight shirt. I couldn't seem to get enough of looking at her. I was objectifying her body, but she had been clear with me before that she enjoyed it.

After blow drying her hair, she slid on some socks and her low-top Converse All Stars.

"All right, time to go," she said as she zipped up her backpack.

I climbed out of bed, the chill air raising goose bumps on my skin. We shared a long hug at the front door, and she headed out. The sun was shining, and I had the whole day ahead of me. I knew for certain that I did not want to spend it at home, alone. It was too cold and wet to go for a motorcycle ride, and I'd already been to the movies.

Over coffee and my favorite Janis Joplin record, I got caught up on Facebook and watched birds digging around under leaves in the wet soil of my yard. I knew it was too early to get a response back from them, but I sent check-in texts to Bear and Buck, then I messaged Darcy asking if she was free for the day. Darcy was awake, responded that she was free, and invited me over.

I scarfed down a Pop-Tart and bundled up in heavy carpenter pants, a few shirts, and a hoodie. It took some effort to lace up my boots because the joints in my fingers hurt from the cold; a recent change I was not happy about.

Stepping out into the brisk morning, I was glad to have somewhere to go.

On the short drive to Darcy's house, I saw the damage from the storm; downed fences, tree limbs and piles of leaves in the road, and flooded intersections where the storm drains had clogged. Grateful to be in a big shit kicker of a truck, I made it through the mess without any issues.

Darcy met me at the back gate on the alley and ushered me into her cozy little home.

"Have a seat. Coffee?"

"Yeah, I'd love some."

I'd never really paid much attention to how Darcy's place was decorated. I found that she had photographs, prints, and paintings artfully placed around the tidy room.

"Looks like you have a thing for Escher and Warhol."

"Sure do. I've been collecting their prints since the '80s."

I also spotted framed photos of motorcycle trips, gatherings of her chosen family, and a few that left me wondering. I pointed to a grainy picture of a little boy in a small aluminum boat holding a fishing rod; a mustachioed man in a bucket hat grinning behind him. "May I ask, who is in this picture?"

Darcy turned to the framed photo and gave a wistful smile. "That's me and my dad. I always felt like the most important kid in the world when he took me out on the boat to go fishing. Those were some good times."

"That's really great," I said and smiled, happy for her that she had some good memories from childhood. I knew so many people who didn't.

I had a moment of wonder that she had a picture on display that was from before her transition, then I immediately scolded myself for daring to assume anything about how trans folx would or wouldn't display their lives. *What the hell do I know?*

"Now I know where you got your love of fishing."

She smiled and gave a little nod. "I'm going to shift the conversation if that's okay. You're a good person, Randy. It's clear to me that you are going through a lot right now and I just want you to know that I am here for you if you need."

I blew out a sigh and fiddled with the rim of my mug.

"I don't know what I need, or what will make it better. I'm just taking it one day at a time. Heck, sometimes it's one minute at a time." I shifted my feet and looked out of the window. "It's not all terrible though. Things are going good with Kristen at least."

"I'm glad to hear that. You deserve to have some happy in your life."

"But I just can't seem to get past this feeling like…like I'm standing on a motorcycle that's fishtailing. It's scary."

"Do you want to talk about it?"

"No. Hey, you wanna go out and do something?" I looked at her, hoping she'd let me change the subject too.

"Sure, what do you have in mind?"

"I dunno. How about we go bowling or maybe shoot pool?"

"I know a place where we can do both, plus they have food and drinks."

"Perfect. My treat."

"I'll take you up on that! How about I drive? That way I can pay the bridge toll at least."

"Deal."

I waited while Darcy got her jacket and keys and locked up her place. She led me out to the alley, and I climbed into her classic Volkswagen minibus. The entire thing had been completely refurbished inside and out, and it was a beauty.

Snapping on my seatbelt, I checked out the interior. The seats were two-toned leather in white and teal, matching the exterior paint job. The engine fired right up and sounded clear and strong.

"When did you rebuild this?"

"Oh, I guess it was last summer," she said as she turned onto the main road, clicking her tongue when she had to veer around a large branch that had fallen in the middle of the road.

She parked at the curb, and I jumped out so I could pull the branch out of traffic. We had to do that a few times before we reached the freeway onramp.

The minibus hummed along on the freeway, and I enjoyed being a passenger for once, able to check out the scenery.

"So, between your post-apocalyptic motorcycle build

and refurbishing this bus, I'd say you are mighty talented at this stuff. You ever think about doing it as a business?"

"Nah. It's a hobby. I prefer working on stuff on my own time and doing it how I want it. That all changes if you start to build projects for other people."

"Good point."

"Besides, I like my job at the port. It suits me."

"Mine too," I said. "Everything has just gotten so complicated lately. I liked how things were before. No fuss, I would just cruise through work and then had the rest of the day to do whatever I wanted. I was happy, I think." *Stop talking about yourself so much.*

Darcy drove across the bridge, which rose high above the water. I looked down at the port directly below, spying a massive cargo ship docked there.

"That's where you work, right?"

"Yes."

"So, that huge cargo ship is full of brand-new cars?"

"Sure is."

Past the port were huge lots full of tightly parked cars, many of which were covered in white protective plastic film. I had owned several cars in my day but had never bought a new one. I figured all those shiny new cars would be sold some day but had no desire to have one for myself.

"And that down there is where you park them before they get loaded onto the trains?"

"That's right."

"Hm. I think our jobs are kinda similar. We are just moving other people's stuff from one place to another for them."

"Ha. Yeah, that seems to be the gist of it." She nodded. "Hey, open up the glove box, will ya?"

"Sure."

Inside the glove box I found a fully modern stereo system, with satellite radio and all the bells and whistles.

"You sneak! That's really cool."

"Put on whatever you want."

I poked around through the menu of stations and chose one that was playing Dave Matthews Band. We rode along the wet freeway, listening to music and chatting about fishing until Darcy pulled off at an exit and parked in a massive lot that was mostly empty aside from a cluster of Cadillacs and Buicks. The low-slung building was huge and sleepy looking.

"Is this place open?"

"Yeah. It's early so it's probably just the senior bowling league in there right now. It'll get crowded soon with families and stuff. Better to get ourselves set up now while there are still lanes open. Once all the kids start taking over, we can escape them in the bar and shoot some pool."

"Sounds like you know the drill here."

She smirked and patted me on the back heartily as we walked under the deep portico and through the glass front doors. I was slapped with the sound of bowling balls hitting pins, cheers and jeers, and Lynyrd Skynyrd on the overhead speakers.

Darcy was greeted warmly by the person working the front counter, and we got a lane on the far end, away from all the rowdy senior league bowlers. We played two games, and I solidly kicked her ass. I'd bowled many years in the Sacramento lesbian league back in my day, and it all came back.

It irked me just a bit that the aches and pains in my

joints interfered with my normally smooth game, but over-all, I still did great.

As families started arriving for pizza parties we scooted on up to the bar, which was in an enclosed room near the front of the place. The bar was dark and stank of beer and stale cigarettes. The indoor-outdoor carpet was filthy, and my boots stuck to it in a few places. I had been in plenty of dive bars like that and didn't mind.

I nudged Darcy. "Whoever decided it was a good idea to put carpeting in this bar was an idiot."

She let out a hearty laugh and led me to the counter. We ordered hot wings and tacos, plus some stout beers. I picked a few songs on the jukebox, and we got a pool table in the back. While I had plenty of experience playing pool, Darcy beat me over and over until the food and beer were gone.

We didn't talk much, which was fine by me. It was nice to be out of the house and spending time with my friend. The distraction was good. I dreaded leaving, but my watch said it was time to mosey on home. We put away the pool cues and carried our plates and glasses to the bus tub near the exit.

*

WALKING OUT INTO the sunshine was a rough transition from the dingy bar, and I had to stop on the curb and squint for a few seconds, letting my eyes adjust, before I dared set foot in the parking lot.

Tires squealed and an engine revved, moving much too fast for a parking lot. I placed my hand across my brow to shield my eyes from the sun so I could see who was driving like a dumbass. A hand grabbed the sleeve of my flannel and yanked me back just as the car hopped up on the curb and blew past me with hardly an inch to spare. The side mirror bit into my hip and sheared off from the car, dangling from one wire.

Breath caught in my throat and my heart pounded like a jackrabbit as I caught my footing. The car thumped down off the curb and sped toward the freeway. Someone was speaking, but all I could hear was my pulse whooshing in my ears. I shook my head and turned to face whoever had pulled me out of the way. It was Darcy, her face red and twisted up in concern as she spoke. I shook my head again and opened my mouth.

"What the fuck?" was all I could mutter.

Darcy's voice broke through the fog. "Did anybody get a good look at the driver, or the license plate?"

Several older folks shook their heads, standing back from us as if we were on fire, then shuffled off to their cars, bowling bags in hand.

Pain flared in my hip where I'd been hit. "I think I need to sit down," I said, reaching out for Darcy. She took my arm and led me to a concrete bench under the portico. I sat heavily and groaned as a hot poker of pain shot from my hip down my thigh. My hands shook.

"Can you find me a smoke?"

"Sure." Darcy trotted off to get a cigarette from a group of people huddled under a sign that said "Designated Smoking Area." I could see her talking to them and pointing to me. I was worried they were going to give her a hard time, but one of them handed over a cigarette and she came back with a victorious smile on her face.

"Nice guys. They were talking about fishing, so I was

able to slide right into that conversation. Here you go." She handed me the cigarette and I lit it, my hands still shaking badly.

I drew in a long drag, the smoke burning my lungs. I coughed deeply and my mouth filled with saliva. I snubbed out the cigarette and tucked it into my pocket.

"I guess my body doesn't like smoking anymore." I turned to her and took her hand. "Thank you for pulling me out of the way. You saved my ass. Literally."

We chuckled and I flinched as my hip protested. "Well, I got a brief look at the car. Make and model, anyway. I didn't see the driver or the plate. Sorry, Randy."

"Are you kidding me? You have nothing to apologize for. It was probably just some drunk."

"Yeah. Well, how bad is it? Do you want me to take you to the hospital?"

"No. No hospital. I just need to get home and put some ice on it."

She dug around in her pocket and pulled out the key to her VW. It was on a thin keychain, with a lucky rabbit's foot on it dyed the same teal color as the microbus. "Why don't you go have a seat in the bus while I call the cops."

I groaned. "I really don't want to deal with the cops. Can you just not mention me? Just report a drunk driver or something and leave out the part about jumping the curb and hitting a pedestrian."

"Are you sure?"

I nodded and hobbled toward the bus, grumbling over my shoulder to her. "Leave me out of it, please."

Once I was safely inside the bus, I sat back and rubbed my face. It dawned on me that I might be too injured to go to work in the morning, which pissed me off. And never one to leave well enough alone, anxiety was telling me that the whole thing was not an accident and maybe I was being targeted because of the investigation.

I pulled out my cell phone, wanting to call Kristen to tell her what had happened, but I decided not to since she was at work. No point in upsetting her while she was on shift. I unlocked my phone and saw that I had texts back from Bear and Buck. I started up a group text with them:

Hey bitches. Just a heads up that I got hit by a car. I think

I'm okay, heading home to see how bad it is.

A few minutes later, Bear responded:

Motherfucker, what? Whose ass do I need to kick?

Buck pinged next:

Were you on your bike? Do you need a ride?

I responded back, my hands shaking a bit less:

I was just standing on the curb, minding my own business. They jumped the curb, hit me, and took off. Probably just some drunk. Got clipped by the side view mirror. Thank baby Jesus for Darcy, she pulled me out of the way. I'd probably be roadkill otherwise.

Bear: Damn, tell Darcy I'm gonna give her a big ole smooch next time I see her. You mean too much to us to get taken out like that. Send pics if you have some fun bruises.

Buck: I hope the injuries aren't too bad. Let me know if you need ANYTHING. I mean it.

Me: Thanks guys.

I tucked my phone away and handed Darcy her keys as she climbed into the driver's seat. "Well, I called the cops and reported the car. I didn't mention anything about you getting hit, although I really think I should have."

"I have talked to enough cops over the last few months to last me the rest of my life. Thank you."

The drive home was a blur. I was probably in shock. Darcy dropped me off at my place and helped me get inside. She had me sit in my cozy recliner and brought me a big bag of ice.

"I am gonna go home and drive your truck back, if that's okay, so you have it in the morning."

"You sure?"

She waved her hand at me. "Yeah. It's only a few blocks. I can walk home when I'm done."

After she left, I kicked up my feet on the recliner and lowered my heavyweight carpenter pants, the bag of ice situated between my hip and the arm of the chair. Porkchop hopped up and got comfortable between my feet. I pulled the TV remote out from the side pocket of the chair and put on a cooking show, just to have some background noise and feel less alone in the house. I looked at Bear's painting and dozed off despite the pain throbbing down my leg. I woke up to the sound of my truck keys being dropped on the kitchen counter.

"Hey, Randy. I parked your truck in the driveway. Do you need anything?"

I blinked a few times, trying to clear my head. "Nah. Just gonna take a little nap. Thanks for taking care of me and bringin' my truck back."

"No problem. Okay, well if you don't need anything else, I think I am gonna head out. You take it easy. I am only a few blocks away if you need anything."

"I appreciate you, bud. Thanks."

She pet Porky and patted my shoulder on her way out.

I fell right back asleep, pulled down by a level of tired that was impossible to fight. I woke to the faint sound of my cell phone ringing. Groggy, I tried to remember where I had left it. I leaned over to grab my jacket off the floor and a searing pain shot down my leg. I grit my teeth and dug around in my jacket until I found the stupid phone. The screen was lit up with a picture of Kristen's smiling face. I swiped at the answer button, putting the call on speaker-phone.

"Hey, babe. What's up?"

"Hi, Randy. Did I wake you?"

I rubbed at my eyes. "Yeah. But it's okay."

I realized with surprised that it was dusk out and I had slept the afternoon away.

"So, uh, are you coming to my party or what?"

"Oh shit—yes, sorry. I hadn't meant to sleep this long. Are people already there?"

"Yeah. But a couple more won't be here for a bit cuz they are still working."

"Okay. Let me get cleaned up and I will head over. You need me to being anything?"

She laughed. "No, I work at a grocery store, remember? I got it all already. See you soon?"

"Yep. Be there soon. Oh, hey. I am going to need a spot on the couch. I got a little bit hurt today and will need to sit. Is that okay?"

"Ohhh no! Yeah, I will make sure to save you a spot on the couch. Tell me all about it when you get here, okay?"

"You got it. Bye, babe."

We hung up and I pressed the down button on the chair's remote, which slowly lowered the foot of the chair. Porky woke up just in time to hop down before he was dumped on the floor. Throwing me an annoyed glare, he skulked off to eat some kibble.

The bag of ice I had been sitting on was melted and had leaked all over me and the chair. I hobbled over to the sink and dumped it out. I found that Darcy had refilled the ice trays. Appreciative, I dumped fresh ice into the bag and put it on the counter next to my keys.

It was slow going, but I made it down the hallway to wash my face, put on some fresh deodorant and cologne, and brush my teeth. I thought about putting on some dry underwear, but the idea of having to bend my leg enough to get my boots, pants, and underwear off and on again was too much.

The drive across the bridge was quick and I got a parking spot right near the bottom of the stairs at Kristen's building. *Stairs? Shit.* I looked around to see if her building had an elevator. It didn't. I reminded myself that grit was one thing I had in spades, and hauled my ass up that flight of stairs, bag of ice tucked into my jacket. Halfway up the stairs I cursed my grit and muttered to myself. "You stubborn old fart. Dumbass."

Kristen was waiting in the doorway, and the beaming smile she gave me melted my frustration away. She wrapped me up in a deep hug that touched my soul.

We were rudely interrupted by a familiar voice. "Oh my God, you guys, get a room!"

Annoyed, I ended the hug and squinted through the door, clenching my jaw when I saw Mikela.

I whispered angrily into Kristen's ear. "What is she doing here?"

"She's my friend, Randy. Please try to play nice, okay?"

I balked, my hands balling up and core tightening. Kristen gave me a peck on the cheek and took my hand, pulling my fingers gently until I released my fist. She guided me inside. A few people sat around the kitchen table and on the couch. It was snug in her small studio. She waved away someone who was on the couch.

"Scoot, scoot. Randy needs to sit, please."

The guy stood and smiled. "It's all yours. I warmed it up for ya." The bead securing the end of his braided beard jiggled when he spoke. He leaned against the windowsill and sipped from a flask.

Kristen sat on the edge of the futon, putting her arm around me. "Okay, guys, I know you are sick to death of hearing me talk about Randy all the time at work. So, here she is."

She pointed to each person in turn, telling me their names. Most of them gave me a smile and nod. I recognized some of their names from stories she had told me.

One guy raised his soda to me and laughed. "So, you really do exist. We were starting to think you were a figment of K's imagination."

"I'm as real as it gets," I said jovially.

We turned to the last person, who reclined on the floor, leaning back on her elbows.

"And, of course, you already know Mikela."

"Hello, Mikela," I said, playing nice and biting back my urge to pummel her.

"Good to see you again, Randy," she said, a sneer on her face.

"They know each other from the warehouse."

Everyone nodded and went back to their conversations. I wanted to keep staring down Mikela but looked at Kristen instead.

She patted my shoulder. "Babe, can I get you anything? A drink, more ice, a snack?"

"Iced tea?"

"Sure."

As Kristen whisked the few steps to the kitchen, Mikela turned her beady eyes on me, tapping the corner of a plastic lighter on the table, and sizing me up. I held her gaze that time. There was no fucking way I would back down to that little asshole.

"What's wrong with your hip there, Randy?"

"None of your business, Mikela."

"Damn, and here I am trying to make small talk."

"Don't bother."

"Kristen would be so upset if something bad happened to you. Make sure to look both ways before you cross the street."

My jaw clenched as I put together her warning with what had happened to me. I hissed at her through my teeth, ready to lay into her. "You fucking—"

Kristen swooped back in. She sat on the edge of the futon and handed me a glass of iced tea. She leaned gently on me and rubbed her hand in slow circles on my back.

"Isn't this great? I am so happy to finally have time to have people over. It was so hectic through the holidays. It's nice to be able to breathe a little and relax."

I released my jaw, looking away from Mikela, and nodded, resting my hand on Kristen's thigh. Keeping Mikela in my peripheral vision, I sipped some sweet tea and adjusted the bag of ice.

"Are you going to tell me what happened, babe?"

"Later. I don't want to talk about it with an audience," I said and turned to Mikela, who narrowed her eyes at me, got up, and strutted out of the door. Her silhouette was visible just outside the kitchen window. I watched as she dialed a number on her cell phone and held it up to her ear.

"I had hoped that you and Mikela could be civil. I see

I was wrong about that." Kristen's voice was heavy with annoyance.

"I am trying. I promise." I wanted to scream out that Mikela had tried to run me down with her car but knew it would come out as me sounding paranoid and would just irritate Kristen more. A feeling of helplessness settled.

"I need to circulate. Do you need anything?"

"I'm good. Thanks."

Kristen rose and went to talk to two guys near the window who were smoking from a bong. The easy comfort that she seemed to have with all her friends and coworkers was nice, and I relaxed a bit since Mikela was out of the room.

I looked at the person sitting next to me on the couch. She was wearing a cap knitted to look like a bunny's head. She sat cross-legged, earbuds in her ears, knitting. I was curious what she was listening to, but figured it'd be rude to interrupt her and ask.

I got up slowly, hobbled over to the food table, and picked up a paper plate. I loaded the plate up with deviled eggs, sausages smothered in barbecue sauce, squares of spanakopita, and little pieces of bread with something that smelled like artichoke dip. I realized I could hear Mikela's voice drift through the kitchen window. She was speaking in an angry hiss.

I checked the room, seeing that nobody was paying me any mind, and sidled over to the counter, near the sink. All I could see was the back of Mikela's shoulder through the window, because she was turned away from me. To keep up the ruse, I nibbled on a piece of bread dipped in the white stuff, and sure enough, it was artichoke dip. A damn tasty one too, tangy and rich. I strained to eavesdrop on Mikela and tried to play it off like I was hanging out in the kitchen eating snacks.

I pushed out the noise from the party and closed my eyes, trying to catch her words.

"…Goddamn it. How long do you think you'll be able to keep this up? You think just cuz you've got dirt on me that I won't throw you under the bus? I'm the goddamn bus driver. Listen here—" She paused, lowering her head. "Fine. That's your opinion, and you can shove it up your ass. I've got you by the balls and you know it. You'll do more prison time than me. I mean come on, grand theft embezzlement is a state charge, and you'll do maybe three years. But the money laundering, that's federal, baby. You're looking at twenty years at least. And maybe life in prison for the other thing. What you have on me… I'll be out in under five. So, just sit and think about that before you keep lording this over my head."

Holy shit.

There was a long pause as Mikela listened, scuffing the heel of her shoe on the ground and rubbing the back of her neck. "Ey, are you threatening me right now? Because if you are, you better rethink that. I will end you and sleep just fine at night."

A hand on my lower back startled me, and I nearly jumped out of my skin. I turned, a half-eaten piece of bread in my hand. Kristen had a worried crease between her eyebrows.

"You okay? Do you need to lay down or something? I can make up a little nest for you in the walk-in closet till people leave."

"I'm fine. It's just been a day. I should probably sit

back down."

I took one step and pain exploded in my hip. I flinched and grabbed the edge of the counter, stifling back a groan. Kristen took my plate before I dropped it.

"Hun. Do you need to go to the hospital? I can drive you right now."

"No, no. I just need to sit."

I leaned heavily on Kristen and hobbled the few steps across the living room to the couch, sitting gingerly. I got myself situated with the bag of ice, which had made a big wet spot on the couch and my pants. Kristen rested my plate of snacks on my lap and kissed the top of my head before wandering off again.

A gray cloud settled around me as I realized the predicament I was in with Kristen and Mikela being friends, all while Mikela was still a threat to me. I knew I couldn't say anything about it to Kristen without pissing her off.

Dammit.

The woman sitting next to me removed her earbuds and stopped knitting long enough to extend a hand to me.

"Hey. I'm Gladys." Her glasses slid to the end of her

nose, and she pushed them up with a knuckle. I realized she was closer to my age, compared to the younger crowd in the room.

"I'm Randy. Nice to meet you. Do you work with Kristen?"

"Nope. I shop at her store. She is so warm and welcoming to the customers. I envy you."

I smiled, not sure what else to say. It seemed weird to me that Kristen had invited a customer to her home for a party.

"So, uh, do you guys spend any time with each other outside of the store?"

"Oh yeah. We go on hikes and walks mostly. She talks about you nonstop, just so you know. She is like, totally besotted with you."

"Can you define that for me? Besotted?"

"Oh my gosh. I love that you just asked me that and aren't one of those people who just nods along when they don't understand something. Besotted is like…she's drunk on you."

"Well, I'm flattered, I guess. Hopefully it's not a total

snooze hearing about me."

We both chuckled and she briefly placed her hand on my forearm. "Not at all. I see what she sees in you."

I held my drink up to her, not knowing what to say. I had never been good at telling if someone was flirting with me, and I sure didn't want to assume anything, so I just took the compliment and left it at that.

I worked my way through the food on my plate and finished off the tea, watching Gladys' hands as she knit.

"If you don't mind me asking, what were you listening to earlier? Whenever I see people with headphones, I get so curious."

"An audiobook version of *The New Jim Crow*, by Michelle Alexander."

I hadn't heard of it and shook my head.

"Every single human in this country needs to read it, including you."

"Oh yeah? Is that something they'd have at the library?"

"Definitely."

"What's it about?"

"To sum it up, it's about criminal justice reforms, and how the system is inherently racist. Though that doesn't even begin to cover everything she talks about."

"That sounds intense."

"It is, as it should be. I hope you will consider reading it. Or listening to it," she said as she popped her earbuds back in.

Mikela stormed back into the house, walked up to Kristen, and whispered something in her ear. Kristen nodded, they exchanged a quick hug, and Mikela left, grabbing her keys off the table as she went. I certainly wasn't sad to see her go, and her leaving seemed to be the trigger that made the party wind down. People started gathering their stuff and saying goodbye to us.

After the last person eventually left, Kristen locked up and closed the shades. I started to get up, intending to help her clean up in the kitchen, but she waved me down.

"Sit, sit. There's hardly anything to do. You rest." She cleared dishes off the table and put food away in the fridge and cabinets. Her voice drifted out to me. "So, did you have a nice chat with Gladys?"

"She seems nice. Says you're besotted with me!"

Kristen let out a big belly laugh. "She's not wrong."

"So, do you spend time with other customers outside of work too?"

"Oh yeah. I meet all kinds of people there, and some seem interesting. Can you believe she knit that cute bunny hat herself? It's adorable."

"That's definitely some skill. But uh, do you think it is safe to do that? Hang out with strangers like that?"

Kristen stepped out from behind the cabinets, giving me a measured gaze. "Randy, we have been through this already. I do not need you to protect me, okay? I can decide for myself who I spend time with. I am around people all day long, so I think I am pretty good at picking out who is a creep and who isn't."

Except for Mikela. "Okay, fair enough. But, just cuz I'm nosy, have any of them ever actually turned out to be a creep?"

"Oh yeah, this one older guy who is an extreme couponer, he invited me to go shopping in his garage. When I got there, he literally had shelves lined with products, just like a store. He had so much stuff and said he'd hardly paid anything for it. He was really proud of himself. It was actually kind of impressive."

"What made him a creep?"

"Well, he started rambling about his job. He was a retired engineer. Worked at nuclear power plants down on the central coast or something. Anyway, he invited me to see his office. He said he thought I'd like it. I felt safe because the garage door was open to the driveway, so I could run out or scream if something got weird. His office was just off the garage, and when he opened the door, I was shocked. The walls were covered in Nazi flags and banners and there were big pictures of Hitler. He even had an old KKK outfit on a mannequin in the corner. I kept taking baby steps backward until I could get out of there. I think he was trying to recruit me or something." She shuddered. "He kept going on about my good genetics."

"Wow, that's really sick…and scary that there are still people like that."

"I know. He just looked like someone's sweet old grandpa."

"Any other stories?"

"Yeah. This guy wasn't a creep though. He invited me to his place. He said there were great hiking trails nearby and wanted to show off the amazing view from his deck. I didn't see the harm in it. Seemed harmless, like some computer guy or something. Anyway, when he opened the door, he was dressed like a baby."

"What?"

"Yeah. He was a big guy, like six foot five, and easily thee hundred pounds. But there he was, wearing nothing but an adult-sized baby diaper and sucking on a pacifier."

I raised my eyebrows at her. "So, did you go inside or what?"

She cleared a few more dishes and wiped off the table.

"Of course. I had to know what the deal was. So, I went in, and he had his whole living room set up like a nursery. He even had a custom-made crib for himself. So, I rocked him and gave him a bottle and put him to bed. He was totally harmless. Very sweet, actually. And he wasn't lying about the view, it really was incredible. I could see the coastal range and the bay."

I sat there, my mouth hanging open, not knowing what to say. It hit home how truly different Kristen and I were. While I would have turned and walked away at the sight of that man dressed as a baby, Kristen didn't. She seemed to have no fear, boatloads of curiosity, and sought out different experiences. I appreciated that about her, but it also worried me.

I stood up carefully, grimacing, and carried the dripping ice bag to the kitchen sink.

"Sorry, I got your bed all wet." I emptied out the water and what was left of the ice. My pants were soaked too, and I wasn't happy about it.

She pulled the futon couch out into a bed and put on fresh sheets. "Why don't you get changed into your sweats. You still have some in my closet. Get comfortable. You wanna stay the night? You're so much closer to work here and you have to be up so early."

I pursed my lips, realizing I didn't have any of my stuff to get ready for work. I hadn't packed a lunch or left any food out for Porkchop.

"I know you're thinking about Porky right now. He'll

be fine missing one meal. And I'll bring you some lunch on your break since I am off tomorrow."

I couldn't really argue with any of that, and I was so darn tired. I nodded and went into the closet to get changed. I hung my pants and underwear up so they could air dry during the night. Once I was in my comfortable sweats my stress level lowered.

In the bathroom I flipped on the light and lowered my pants. I got up on my toes so I could see my hip in the mirror. A deep-purple bruise wrapped around from my butt cheek to my hip. I knew it would continue to settle in and would look worse by the morning.

I opened the medicine cabinet and dry swallowed two acetaminophen. I didn't have a toothbrush at her house, so I swished with some of her antiseptic mouthwash before shutting off the light and settling in bed.

I begrudgingly set my alarm for two in the morning and lay down. I fell into a light sleep while she went about getting ready for bed. Eventually she slid in under the covers and cuddled up to me, putting her head on my shoulder and her hand on my chest. I closed my eyes, ready to nod off again, but she spoke, pulling me back awake.

"Can you please tell me what happened to your hip?"

I cleared my throat, trying to wake back up enough to have a conversation. "Yeah. I got hit by a car." She started to sit up, but I hugged her back down to me. "It's okay. Thanks to Darcy yanking me out of the way, the only part of the car that hit me was the side mirror. They took off. Probably a drunk driver or something."

Or your best buddy, Mikela.

"Oh my gosh. Did you call the police?"

"No, I was too shaken up, but Darcy did."

"Okay, good."

I felt bad about letting her think that we had reported my being hit, and not just an erratic driver, but I knew she would disagree with my choice, and I was too tired to argue.

"Are you going to go to the doctor? Actually, let me rephrase that. I think you should go to the doctor and get checked out."

"Maybe. I'll see how I do at work tomorrow."

"Babe, you can barely walk across my studio."

"Well, I'm going to give it a try."

"I'd say getting hit by a car is a reason to call out."

"It just grazed me. I will see how I'm feeling when it's time to get up."

"Well, just know that you don't have to be so stoic. You're allowed to admit you're in pain and maybe need to take a day off and see a doctor."

"Noted." I started to close my eyes when Mikela popped back into my head. "I saw that Mikela left early and seemed upset. Is she okay? I hope it wasn't me who made her leave." I was bullshitting Kristen and hoped she didn't see through it.

"No. It wasn't you. She said something about a friend being stranded with car trouble."

I worked up the nerve to keep pushing about Mikela even though I knew it would probably piss Kristen off.

"Babe, listen, I know we've already talked about this...but I really need to say it again. Mikela is dangerous. She may play it down with you, but something just isn't right, and I don't trust her."

Kristen heaved a big sigh and pulled a few inches

away from me, looking at me in the dark.

"Randy, other than how she acted at the warehouse during peak season she has been totally respectful and, yeah, I'll say it, fun. We have fun together. She's my friend and I enjoy getting outdoors with her. I hear you that you feel differently about her, but my experience with her has been fine."

My heart sank. *Well, that's that.* I zipped my lip, nodded to her, and closed my eyes. It was clear there was no more point in trying to convince Kristen that Mikela wasn't safe to be around. I winced as I felt a small wedge drive itself home between us.

Frustrated as I was, I kissed the top of her head and rubbed her back until her breathing evened out and slowed. Talking to Kristen had woken me up and I wasn't able to fall back asleep, so I watched reflections from the creek dance along the ceiling.

I ran through what Mikela had said on the phone earlier when I had been snooping in the kitchen. It sounded to me like she was blackmailing someone who was also blackmailing her. I wanted to know who she had been talking to, and what dirt they had on her.

I eventually fell into a half-doze while Kristen snored daintily on my shoulder until my alarm went off. She woke enough from the alarm to roll over, freeing me. I took my time getting up from the futon and testing my hip, which was stiff and sent spikes of pain down my leg and up to my lower back.

I hobbled into the closet, closed the door behind me, and dressed in the faint glow of the streetlight coming through the high stained-glass window.

My pants and underwear were damp and a little stiff where they had been soaked the night before. Sliding them on, I shivered. I sat on the floor to lace up my boots because it hurt too much to bend over and do it. I certainly couldn't squat in my condition.

I moved from the closet to the bathroom as quietly as I could, splashed water on my face and rinsed with mouthwash, then pulled a beanie down over my jumble of hair, noting that I was long overdue for a haircut.

On the way out I gave Kristen a kiss on the cheek. She stirred, then settled. A chill went up my spine as I walked outside into the crisp early morning. I had just the faintest sensation of being watched. On guard, I slowly made my way down the stairs, biting back the pain. I scanned the sidewalk and my truck before approaching but found everything quiet and still.

The seats in my truck were cold and the windshield had a layer of ice on it. I started up the engine and blasted the defroster. The inside of my truck held the leftover smell of years of cigarette smoke in it, though it was fading over time.

It would take a few minutes for the defrosters to blow warm air, so I pulled out my phone and checked my messages. I had a few more in the group text with Buck and Bear, both checking on my status. I sent a text back telling them I was still alive and was heading to work. They both responded right away, and I remembered that neither one of them went to bed until at least three or four in the morning.

We texted until my windshield defrosted. Whatever feeling I'd had of being watched had passed and I cranked up the radio, listening to Alice Cooper sing "School's Out" as I drove through the quiet streets of downtown Marsh-town.

I made a quick stop at the gas station near the warehouse to grab some coffee and snacks. Arriving to work earlier than normal, I had my pick of parking spaces. The only cars in the lot were the sports cars and shiny lifted trucks of management. I sipped on the scorching hot coffee and ate a Pop-Tart while watching the beat-up cars and trucks of the hourly employees pulling in, one literally dragging a rear bumper.

The guys got out of their cars one by one, stretching and scratching, chugging canned energy drinks, smoking, and stuffing gas station burritos and cheeseburgers in their mouths as they stumbled to the guard station.

I got out and hobbled across the lot to join them in line.

"Damn, Randy, you look rough…er than usual. You all right?" asked the guy in front of me as he belched and took another swig from his drink, which smelled like sweet chemicals.

How the hell does he drink that thing?

"Yeah. Just didn't sleep."

"Well, don't fall asleep up there in the crow's nest, it's a long way down." He chuckled and thumped me on the back cheerfully.

"Safety first. Don't you worry about me."

The door closed quietly behind him as he went into the security station. I waited until Granny called out, "Next!"

Stepping into the shack, the metal push plate sticky under my fingers, I saw that Granny had on a black plaster cast from her hand up to her elbow. The cast matched her black security uniform.

"Oh no. What happened?"

She gave me her usual salty frown. "I tripped over one of those damn parking blocks in the customer parking lot."

"Well, that sucks."

"Sure does."

When I passed through the metal detector, it beeped so I lifted the bottom of my sweatshirt, showing her my belt buckle. She waved me through without using the hand-held wand.

"Have a good one, Granny. I hope you heal up quick."

"Yeah, yeah. Next!"

After clocking in, I tucked the flimsy gas station coffee cup into my jacket and climbed slowly up the ladder to the crow's nest. It took twice as long because of my hip and the cup of steaming coffee.

Given how hard it was to walk with my hip all banged up I was glad I had enough seniority to be a splitter and wasn't down below in the load. When I was lower seniority and a loader, I used to wear a pedometer to see how far I would walk. It usually fell somewhere between five and seven miles per shift, all just inside the warehouse and trailer.

I still had to be on my feet the entire shift, and use my body, but figured I could tough it out up there for eight hours, then go home and rest. The buzzer blew overhead, startling me enough that I spilled a few drops of coffee through the grating. I watched as the drops fell and splatted on the concrete floor far below.

I took a deep breath, set down my cup, and turned to face the conveyor belt, ready for the steady onslaught of packages that would soon head my way. By trial and error, I figured out how to do my job with the least amount of pain, but it was a long shift and it ground me down despite having a visit during lunch break from Kristen.

By the end of the shift, I was shaky, and climbing down the ladder was the worst part. My entire body was ready to give out, and I took it one rung at a time. A few of the guys passing by below gave me some friendly ribbing.

"Come on, Nana, you can do it."

"Hey, someone call Life Alert, cuz she's about to fall and not get up."

"Ey Randayyy! Slow down! Don't forget, three points of contact on the ladder!"

"Oh, I see what she's doing. Trying to milk the timeclock. Nice strategy, Randy."

I smiled. "Oh, fuck off, you guys. Safety—"

"—first. Yeah, we know."

Finally, my boot touched the concrete floor and I let out a sigh of relief only to suck in another breath as I turned and found Shelly waiting for me.

"Randy, that type of language is unacceptable in the workplace."

I thought back to what I had just said to the guys. *Oh.*

"My apologies."

I started walking away when she piped up again. "I notice you are limping. If you got hurt at work, please let us know so we can get the appropriate paperwork started and send you to the occupational health clinic."

"No need. I'm fine."

"Very well." Her high heels clicked away in the opposite direction.

I clocked out and headed for the guard station, surprised to see that Granny was still there.

"Hey, what're you still doing here? Don't you get off at eight?"

"Yeah, but the day shift guy didn't show up and my boss doesn't have anyone to cover me so I'm pulling a double. Mandatory overtime, they call it." She rubbed at her cast.

"You need anything? I can run to the store for you."

"Nah." She pointed to an ice chest on the floor. "I packed enough last night to hold me over. But I think this just about does it for me. I'm sick of this shit. Gonna put in my papers to retire."

"Well, good for you. You deserve it."

Granny patted at her white, wavy hair. "You got that right."

"Okay then. Have a good one."

"You too."

On the way home I made a pit stop at an urgent care clinic inside the pharmacy near my house. There was hardly a line, and I was seen quickly. I wasn't entirely sure if the person who treated me was even a doctor, but I didn't care. I just wanted to know if any bones were broken, and thankfully, none were.

Talking to Granny earlier about her situation got me thinking. I spent the rest of the day on the computer and phone with a rep from the pension fund seeing what kind of money I'd pull down if I retired early. I had two more years to go for a full pension but wanted to see if early retirement was possible.

There was a little bit of an adrenaline rush while I was waiting on hold with the benefits rep as she ran the numbers. The thought of being done with the job sooner was a relief. The hold music wasn't too bad, and I watched branches sway outside the window, smiling and hoping for good news.

She took me off hold and went through the numbers for me, which I jotted down. My stomach dropped when I realized I just couldn't afford to retire yet. I thanked her for her time and ended the call.

I'd had a few hours of excitement, but I was brought back down to earth by the reality of my mortgage and the high cost of living in the Bay Area. I'd always loved my job, and until then had never even considered retiring early, but things had changed and seeing a glimmer of hope to get out was enough to make my palms sweat.

I already lived frugally, and no matter how much I tried to crunch the numbers myself, it all came down to me still having to hang on until I was fifty-five as originally planned.

"Oh well, back to work," I said as I ruffled Porkchop's fur, and went around the house locking up for the night, careful not to tweak my hip.

Chapter Seventeen

Adamant

WHILE MY HIP healed, I carried on working like usual and the brief California winter grew milder as spring approached. I was grateful for the warming temperatures and return of the sun and blue sky.

Kristen started to spend more time with Mikela and less time with me, which I didn't fight. We drifted slowly apart until it was clear that we were no longer really girlfriends. Without ever really discussing it we shifted to being friends and not in a romantic relationship any longer.

Just after Granny's cast came off, we threw her a party and sent her off to a well-earned retirement. She had worked for decades in that tiny little guard shack, putting up with all of us roughnecks, never backing down to any of us, dishing it out just as well as she could take it.

The kid they replaced her with was timid, so the guys had their fun with him.

*

FINALLY PAIN FREE, and happy the temperature was above fifty degrees that morning, I strode to the guard station with confidence. Even though it was well before sunrise the sidewalk and yard were lit up so brightly they caught my attention. The building always had exterior lights on, but it seemed like the brightness was doubled.

When I was next in line to enter the guard station, I waited and waited for the call of "Next!" but it never came. I opened the door and the meek new guard stood there waiting for me, his ill-fitting uniform still creased from being brand new out of the bag.

"Company ID card, please."

Shit. I hadn't been asked to show my company ID in years. I pulled out my wallet and dug around in it, eventually pulling out a cracking, faded laminate ID card.

I showed it to him, and he nodded. "Empty your pockets, please," he said, his Adam's apple bobbing. He slid the plastic basket down the counter to me. I went through the ritual I had been through thousands of times over the years, emptying out my pockets and walking through the metal detector, which beeped at me. I reached for the basket to start loading all my stuff back into my pockets.

"Just a moment, please. Raise your arms."

He stepped forward and ran the metal detector wand over me more thoroughly than I had ever been wanded before. As expected, it beeped at my waist. I reached to raise my jacket and shirt to show him my belt buckle, but he jumped back like I'd hit him.

"Freeze. Just hold it," he said, his voice trembling.

With my arms still raised up at my sides I chuckled. "I'm not carrying a gun. It's just my belt buckle. May I show you?"

He nodded and I slowly lowered my hand and displayed my belt buckle. "There, see?"

He stepped forward and ran the wand over my belt buckle, just to double check, and sure enough it beeped. "Okay, you can get your stuff."

"Hey, man, you need to relax a little bit. We don't bite."

"Yeah, well, maybe you don't, but bad things happened at my last job site at one of your other warehouses." As I scooped up all my crap from the basket and dumped it in my pockets he leaned forward. "In case word hasn't gotten here yet, one of the unloaders at the other warehouse shot a supervisor in the face and back…in the guard station, right in front of me."

Shocked at the news, I paused. "Oh shit, I'm sorry to hear that. What happened to the supe? Are they taking care of you?"

"Yeah, I've been off on stress leave for a while and getting therapy and stuff, plus the transfer here. The supe survived, barely."

"Sounds like Granny retired just in time. Lucky you."

The buzzer rang inside and the rest of the guys outside waiting to get in grumbled. I popped my head out the door.

"Hey, guys. I'll go tell the supes that it's my fault you're late, okay?"

More grumbling as the door shut behind me and I finished loading up my pockets.

"Your ID says Miranda Cox on it, right?" the guard said.

"Yeah."

"Do you know a Randy Cox?"

"That's me. Why?"

He blanched. "Oh. Well…there was a cop in here asking for you earlier."

I stifled a groan. "Great. Thanks. Have a good one."

I jogged inside and clocked in and found Justin.

"Hey supe, a couple of the guys are gonna be a minute or two late. There was a backup at the guard station. My fault."

He frowned. "Get your ass up to your station, Cox. The belts are already rolling."

I hustled up the ladder, glad to be able to do it without pain, the spring back in my step. Only a few packages had made it past my station when I got there, and I was able to get into the flow of things quickly. The anxiety seemed to have taken a back seat that day and I was feeling a little better about things. I smiled as the guys farther down the belt from me scream-sung their favorite songs.

A little after seven the belts shut down for lunch. I was dilly dallying, drinking the dregs of cold coffee and putting my earplugs back in their case when a commotion started up down below. I peered over the railing and saw a row of uniformed police filing from the management offices toward the exit door.

A chorus of shouts from the rafters and along the load wall echoed as employees notified one another that the cops were in the building.

"Five-ohhh, five-ohhh."

"It's the po-po!"

I watched the line of cops, a cluster of them escorting someone. I couldn't make out who it was yet. As the group got closer, I heard the sound of heels clacking and saw

Shelly, her chin held high and hands cuffed in front.

The murmurs turned to shouts as the other employees recognized what was happening. It was like a string of fire-crackers went off as the guys down the load wall had their fun shouting down at the cops and Shelly. I knew her arrest meant something big had happened with the investigation, and I smirked in satisfaction.

They led Shelly to the customer parking lot out front and put her into a police SUV, its fresh paint shining under the bright lights. At the tail end of the column was Joe from security. As he walked under my station, he looked up, his faced squashed in a grim expression. He gave me a brief salute and went out to the lot to talk to the kid in the guard station.

I decided to make a quick run to the restroom and eat my lunch up in the crow's nest. Out of sight, out of mind. I didn't want any cops looking for me or asking me any more questions.

It worked, because nobody bothered me. At the end of my shift, I climbed down and clocked out, taking a detour to pass by the management offices. Shelly's office had police tape across the door and one of those seals on it, so they'd know if it had been opened.

In a haze on the drive home, I barely registered that my phone was blowing up with text messages. Just as I pulled into my driveway the phone started ringing relentlessly, so I pulled it out and answered.

"Hullo."

"Randy, it's Darcy."

"Hey, Darce. Are you at work?"

"Nah, I was furloughed today."

"Well, that sucks. So, what's up?"

"Have you seen the newspaper or TV news?"

"Nope. I've been at work since three this morning. What's going on?"

"Why don't you jet on over here. I've got something I think you'll want to see."

"All right. I'll be there in a minute."

I backed out of the driveway and drove the couple of blocks to her alley. I figured whatever it was she wanted me to see had to do with Shelly's arrest.

Darcy greeted me at the back gate and gave me a hug. "Come on in."

I followed her inside and hesitated before sitting. "Uh, I just came from work, so I'm kinda dirty."

"Sit, sit. The cover is washable. Can I get you something to drink?"

"No thanks." Sitting, I tried to shake off the tension in the air. "So, what's going on, Darcy?"

She turned on the TV and scrolled through the recordings in her DVR menu. She stopped on a news report and pressed play. The news announcer wore a sharp blazer and blouse, hair coiffed and sprayed to perfection, her face drawn. A red banner across the bottom of the screen said "Breaking News: Officer Misconduct Leads to New Development in Death…"

The reporter spoke, her voice serious. "This is Nance Powell, bringing you a special report. A press conference was just held at the Sheriff's Department. Public information officer Darryl Hardey announced that a recent internal investigation uncovered substantial officer misconduct, which required the reopening of a case. It was discovered that a death was incorrectly deemed an industrial accident. The incident involved the death of a worker who was crushed at a loading dock in Diablo. The district attorney's office has filed charges against corporate Human Resources manager Shelly Barstow, and her brother Sergeant Chester "Chip" Cleese, who was the lead investigator on the case. Sergeant Cleese is a seventeen-year veteran with the department. Both Barstow and Cleese have been arrested, though their charges have not yet been released. There was mention of a third person, Mikela Gunnarsdottir, who was placed under arrest, though details on her involvement are not yet clear."

On the screen behind Nance, video played of Shelly in handcuffs being unloaded from the sheriff's SUV and led into the jail booking door. Then a picture of Bryant, prideful and exhausted, holding his newborn baby, flashed on the screen.

"The victim, Bryant Green, left behind a wife and baby. He had worked for the company for five years. Mister Green's family has not responded to requests for an interview or released a statement. We will continue to follow this story as it develops and provide updates."

Darcy pressed the stop button and shut off the TV. I stared at the black screen, digesting what I had heard. Shelly, Cleese, and Mikela had been arrested. Charges not yet announced. I turned and met Darcy's gaze. Deep creases formed around her mouth and eyes.

"I'm okay," I said, trying to convince us both. "I saw them arresting Shelly at work today. But I didn't know about Cleese and Mikela." I ran my sweaty palms along my pant legs.

"I hear you saying you're okay. But are you really?"

I nodded. "Yeah. I'll be okay. I just need to let it all sink in. And I need to find out who was charged with what. I think I'm gonna head home."

I stood, the room swaying around me. Darcy rose quickly and held out a hand to steady me.

"You sure you're okay? You want me to drive you home?"

"Nah. It's just a couple blocks. I can manage."

"Okay. Let me know if you need anything. I mean it."

"Thanks."

I walked blindly to my truck. The drive home was a blur. As soon as I walked in the door I changed into sweats and took a shot from a dusty bottle of tequila. I knew I should eat some food to absorb the booze, but I took two more shots instead and flopped down in my recliner. I switched on the TV and took a few minutes trying to find the local news station. I barely watched live TV, and when I did it sure wasn't the news.

I opened my computer, propped it up on a pillow on my lap, and went to the website for the county jail. It took some clicking around, but I was able to find the page for inmate booking information. I searched for each one of them by name to see their arrest information. Something must have changed since Darcy recorded that news report, because Shelly and Mikela's charges were listed. Cleese's were not, though he did show as being in custody.

Barstow, Shelly

DOB 06/10/1968

Booking #MV34VG21

Bail Amount: $0

Arrest Type: Agency Warrant

Charge: 503 PC Embezzlement

Charge: 186.10(c) PC Money laundering

Charge: 653(f) PC Solicitation of murder

Charge: 187 PC Murder

Charge: 182 PC Conspiracy

Holy shit. There it was, plain as day. Charges of conspiracy, solicitation, and murder. I looked out of the window trying to absorb what I had read.

I wasn't sure about conspiracy and solicitation, so I did internet searches for each of the penal codes to see exactly what they meant. I learned she had been working with someone else on the murder of Bryant. Sighing, I pulled up Mikela's arrest report.

Gunnarsdottir, Mikela

DOB 11/09/1996

Booking #MV34VG26

Bail Amount: $0

Arrest Type: Agency Warrant

Charge: 503 PC Embezzlement

Charge: 187 PC Murder

Charge: 182 PC Conspiracy

Charge: 148(a) PC Resisting Arrest

Charge: 243(c)(2) Battery on a Peace Officer

Things weren't any better for Mikela, though I'd heard plenty of stories about the district attorney dropping charges or cutting a plea deal. Maybe even in her case they would try to get her to turn on Shelly and become a witness in exchange for a lighter sentence. It was hard to know how it would all unfold, but I was glad that at least Joe's complaint and my statements had been enough to get things moving in the right direction.

I closed my laptop and looked at Bear's painting, letting my pupils and brain go out of focus. The tequila dulled my emotions as I had hoped it would, but it also made my thoughts muddy. I belched up a bit of tequila fumes and bile and quickly swallowed it down.

My phone buzzed and I remembered that it had been blowing up with messages earlier. Even though my phone was only in the next room, the thought of having to get up and walk to get it seemed like too much. I lowered the leg rest of my recliner and heaved myself up to standing, causing the room to spin briefly. Steadying, I went on a search for my phone, which I found on the kitchen counter.

There were texts from the usual suspects: Bear, Buck, and Darcy. I also saw texts from my shop steward Brody and Joe. I started with the text from Joe. He simply asked if I had seen the news. I responded that I had and threw in a thank-you to him for his help in getting some justice for Bryant.

Next, I opened the text from Brody. His was vague, just asking if I'd stay after my shift the next day to meet with him. I told him I would.

Bear, Buck, and Darcy were all checking on me since the news was out about the arrests. I was too buzzed to do much texting, but I let them know I was okay and going to bed early. I tossed some kibble into Porkchop's bowl, though he didn't come out of wherever he was hiding.

*

TEQUILA CHURNED IN my belly and thoughts circled in my mind, giving me a long night of no sleep. The alarm clock greeted me at two in the morning, and I peeled myself out of bed, worried about how I would survive my shift with a headache, sore muscles, and a foggy, sleep-deprived brain.

My stomach ached in protest of my dinner of booze and breakfast of coffee, so I stopped at a drive thru for some food. Since it was so early in the morning, they hadn't switched over to the breakfast menu yet. I ended up scarfing down a bacon cheeseburger and a flimsy bean and cheese burrito as I drove the last few miles to work.

My shift wasn't anything special, though there was a lot of talk rolling around the building about Shelly and what she'd been arrested for. Other hushed conversations stopped abruptly when I walked by.

After I clocked out, feet dragging, I walked out to my truck, and was startled to find Brody leaning against my back bumper. Somewhere in the mist of my brain I remembered that I was supposed to meet with him after work.

"Hiya, Brody. How's it hanging?"

"A little to the left. Hey, you still able to talk?"

"Sure. Hop in."

I went around to the passenger side and unlocked the door for him before settling my own bag of bones in the driver seat. I rolled the window down just a hair so the windows wouldn't fog up. Brody got in and sat sideways so he could face me.

"Jesus. Randy. You look and smell like roadkill."

I chuckled weakly. "Thanks. I feel like it too. What'd you want to talk about?"

"Well, obviously there have been some big things happening around Bryant's death and who did it."

"Yup, sure seems that way. You recording us right now?"

"Nope." He pulled out his phone and showed me that the recorder was not running. "So, I just wanted to check in with you and see if there's anything you know that I, and the union, might need to know about what's unfolding."

"Well, despite working in a different hub, Mikela is in our union so hopefully the steward at the air hub knows what's going on."

"He does."

"Have you talked to the yard truck driver?"

"Yeah. I visited him at the jail this morning. He is adamant that he had nothing to do with this and his part in it was just an unfortunate accident."

"Adamant. Can you define that, please?"

Brody gave me the look I had gotten my whole life when asking people to define words. His face somewhere between surprised and defensive, as if I were messing with him.

"Uh, well, adamant meaning he is absolutely rock solid and unyielding in his insistence that he was not involved in whatever Shelly and Mikela were planning."

"Okay. Thank you. Well, then I hope that's true and

they let him out."

Brody looked out of the windshield at the yard beyond the chain-link fence. He scratched at his whiskers and returned his gaze to me but didn't say anything.

"Brody, I'm really exhausted. Was there anything else?"

"No, just wanted to check in with you."

"Okay. Have a good shift."

"Get some rest and eat a good meal, you need it."

"Sure."

"And I hope this isn't too forward, but maybe try doing some laundry. Looks like you've been wearing the same clothes for a week."

"That's fair."

He got out of the truck, the heavy door slamming behind him. The sound alone hurt my entire body, and my hands shook on the steering wheel. I went straight home and got out of my nasty work clothes, scrubbed the grease and dirt off my hands as best I could, and fixed myself up a bowl of oatmeal, and some scrambled eggs with toast. I ate the food without thought. There was no taste to any of it.

Afterward, I washed up the dishes and put on some slippers before going out to the backyard. I sat on the deck chair and reached to my pocket for a smoke, disappointed when I came up empty. I realized that I would continue reaching for and craving cigarettes for the rest of my life. I listened to the whir of hummingbird wings buzzing nearby, and the caws from the neighborhood crows.

There was a rustling in the bushes as Porkchop slunk out, staying low to the ground as he stalked a dragonfly. I smirked, knowing he wouldn't be able to catch it, but appreciating that he still tried to do young cat things even though he was clumsy, old, and a little chunky.

After another minute of stalking the bug, he gave up and lay down in a sunny spot in the corner of the garden. "You've got a good life, Porky. Sometimes I wish we could trade places for a few days." He looked up at me over his belly fluff and blinked a few times before resting his head back in the woodchips.

"You've got the right idea."

*

NAPPING HARD, I did not have any dreams. Slowly I swam back to the surface when my bed rocked lightly. I thought we were having a little earthquake, so I sat up on my elbows in the dark, waiting for an aftershock, but none came.

"Hey."

My heart leaped into my throat and I jumped out of bed, fists up and ready to fight. The bedside lamp flicked on and I saw that Kristen was sitting on the bed. I lowered my fists and let out a big gust of breath, blood pounding in my ears.

"Jesus, Kristen, you really scared me." Dizzy, I sat on the bed and rubbed my throbbing head.

"Sorry. I just needed to talk and couldn't reach you on your phone."

"Yeah, I turned my ringer off because I really needed to get some solid rest before work tomorrow."

I wondered how she had gotten in, since I had never given her a key.

"Your front door was unlocked and I could see that

lights were on inside. You didn't answer the doorbell so I just let myself in."

"The door was unlocked and lights were on?"

"Yeah."

"I must have crashed so hard that I didn't lock up. Dang, that never happens."

I was annoyed that she had woken me up but looking at her, I could see she was sad. And tired or not, I wasn't one to turn away a friend who needed help. The clock said it was only nine, so I'd gotten about five hours of sleep, which wasn't nearly enough for what my body needed.

"What's going on?"

Chin to chest, a tear dripped down the bridge of her nose and landed on her thigh, her denim jeans soaking it right up. She sniffled and wiped her wet eyes on the collar of her work hoodie. "Uh…a lot has happened."

"You've got that right," I said with a huff. "What happened with you?"

"Well, you probably already know it, but Mikela was arrested."

"Yeah."

"They arrested her right in front of me. It was scary."

I raised my eyebrows, but kept my mouth shut.

"She fought with the cops and even ran away, but the dog got her within a few yards. She tried to fight the police dog too, so he ripped into her. It was…messy." She paused, chewing on her lip and finally turned to me. "I think maybe you were right about Mikela not being a nice person."

Fucking finally! I bit back the "I told you so" that desperately wanted to come out of my mouth.

"Were you hurt during all of this?"

"Well, the police weren't sure who I was, but since I was with her, they detained me for a bit. I didn't struggle with them or anything, so they were mostly gentle." She sniffed. "No, I'm not hurt."

I had so many questions but pushed them aside. "Sounds like it was really intense."

"It was." She sniffed some more and scooted across the bed. She rested her forehead on my shoulder. I stiffened, but realized she needed some comfort. I rubbed her back while my mind raced. "Can I stay with you tonight?"

Her request took me by surprise. We certainly weren't

in that kind of place anymore. But I wasn't going to turn her away. "Of course. I really do need to get some sleep though, so if you're not tired yet you're welcome to go watch a movie in the living room or something."

"No, no. I'm ready. I'll let you sleep, I promise."

I stood up and grabbed a blanket and pillow when she started getting undressed. I did my best not to look but recognized the panties she was wearing.

She paused as she started sliding into my bed. "Where are you going?"

"I'll just set up on the couch with Porkchop." I started to close the door.

"You really don't have to go."

"Goodnight, Kristen."

Her face sagged as I closed the door. As much as I wanted to stay and comfort her, I just couldn't do it. I truly needed to get some more sleep, and I also wanted to make sure she understood where I drew the line around our friendship.

I crashed out on the couch, with Porkchop sleeping in a ball next to my head. When the alarm woke me up, I shut it off as quickly as I could, hoping it didn't wake Kristen. I needed to get some fresh work clothes so I tiptoed into my room. Kristen's silhouette rose and fell gently. She lay on her side, head on the pillow, sheets pulled up to her chin. It took a moment for me to realize that her eyes were wide open, and she was staring at me.

"Have you slept?"

"No."

"Dang."

"It's okay. I was glad to be here, instead of alone at my studio. Go get ready for work. I don't want to make you late."

I got some fresh clothes from the closet and dresser and pulled them on in the dark before heading down the hall to wash my face and brush my teeth. Having slept some, I was a little less shattered, but still wasn't running on all cylinders. I felt and looked haggard but did the only thing I knew how to do, which was to just carry on.

When I came out of the bathroom Kristen was gone.

The drive to work was spent worrying if I would have

to go to court. I hadn't heard anything from the district attorney's office yet but figured that call would be coming. The idea of getting up in front of a courtroom and reliving everything brought on a fresh bout of anxiety.

Chapter Eighteen

Are You the Person In This Picture?

MY DAY IN court had arrived. I'd had to take the day off from work, which irked me because I was trying to save up my accruals for retirement service credits. Freshly showered, I put on my best jeans, cowboy boots, and dress shirt. I was in all black except for the abalone snaps on my shirt, and my turquoise ring.

I fussed in the mirror, trying to get my hair to

cooperate, but it was as unruly as ever even though I had gone in for a trim. I decided to put on my favorite bolo tie, made of black braided leather. I slid up the clasp, which had been handmade especially for me by Bear. It was silver in the shape of a bear paw, the claws etched into the metal, and a hunk of turquoise inlaid as the center pad of the foot.

I smiled, feeling all the love Bear had poured into that piece of jewelry when she'd crafted it for me years ago. She'd said it would protect me, and I believed her. I needed her strength, nervous as I was about being in a courtroom and speaking in front of people about what had happened.

Traffic was heavy, which made the drive across the bridge and through the city streets challenging. So was finding parking near the courthouse. I wound up pulling into a spot several blocks away and hurrying, my boots clicking on the pavement. When I rounded the corner of the old granite building, several news reporters talked to cameras, and people formed a line out of the door, waiting to pass through security. I got in line, checking the time on my cell phone before powering it down and tucking it into my breast pocket.

Sweat formed on my forehead and in my armpits. The breeze rattled an empty soda cup down the sidewalk. The air downtown smelled a little bit like low tide. Ahead of me, I recognized a few management folks from work, all dressed up in business suits and talking in a huddle, their heads close.

Eventually I made it through security and into the courtroom. I took a seat in the gallery behind the prosecutor's table. I wiped at my sweaty top lip with a handkerchief and tried to sniff my armpits as slyly as I could. My deodorant was failing.

Both the prosecuting attorneys turned and smiled when they saw me. I'd spent a lot of time in their office over the last few weeks preparing for my testimony. It had helped me get a better idea of what to expect, but I was still scared shitless about getting up on the stand.

The attorneys and court staff seemed so comfortable in that place. Sitting there, I felt like a triangle peg trying to fit in a round hole. The last time I'd had to get up and speak in court was when I was a kid. I'd been a witness to my mom killing my dad and had to tell everybody what I saw.

Being in court was just as scary to me as an adult as it had been when I was a kid.

At Shelly's trial I spent most of the time listening with my eyes closed, trying to keep my heart rate and breathing down. The room smelled like floor wax, old books, and armpits. After a few hours my heart leaped as I was called as a witness.

On shaky legs, I walked up to the front of the room and was sworn in before I took a seat on the witness stand. I did my best to keep my eyes on the familiar face of the prosecutor, but in a moment of distraction I glanced at Shelly. She scowled at me, her eyes narrowing, hands steepled under her chin. In the gallery sat the folks from corporate and I was surprised to see they were on Shelly's side of the room. I wondered then if corporate was throwing their money in to hire her a ball buster of an attorney.

The first bit of questioning from the prosecutor ran through the details I had already shared so many times. Just the basics about the day Bryant died, like what door I was working on, what time I'd done the belt walk, and what I had seen and heard after he had been pinned.

My nerves really ratcheted up when it was time for Shelly's attorney to question me. The lady looked like Shelly's clone, with equally high heels, sharp features, and perfectly tailored skirt suit. As she shuffled some papers around on the table and prepared to ask her first question, I closed my eyes and shut out all the sound. I listened only to my heartbeat and my breathing. My dad's voice came to me.

This lady is no better than you, Randy. Don't you be intimidated by her. Do not let her get under your skin. Remember what they told you: only answer exactly the questions she asks, nothing more.

When I opened my eyes, the entire room was watching me, expectant…waiting. I touched the bear paw clasp on my tie, trying to draw some strength from it. My stubborn self woke up and I heartened, knowing I'd get through the day.

The attorney took a step forward. "Miss Cox, are you ready?"

I scanned the jury box. Some seemed bored while others were alert and curious.

I let out a breath. "Yes."

The corner of her lip curled, and I knew right away that she was not a good person. She liked scaring people. I doubled my resolve and clenched my jaw. People in the gallery shifted, waiting for her to get started.

"Bailiff, dim the lights, please."

I did my best to keep a good poker face, but I had no idea what to expect, and I didn't like being off footed. The lights dimmed and a projector turned on. Everyone in the room turned to face the projection screen, which was on the wall across from the jury. The attorney started asking me questions as she fiddled with a keyboard, trying to put something on the projector.

"Miss Cox, you are aware there was video surveillance on door seventy-six on the date in question, correct?"

"Yes."

"When did you become aware that there was video?"

"Not until much later."

"And how did you first become aware of the video?"

I cleared my throat, not liking to name names, but knowing I had to. In the dim gallery, Joe nodded at me.

"Joe Rawlins showed it to me."

"Okay, we will get back to that part later. Have you seen the video in its entirety?"

"I don't believe so. No."

"Why not?"

"Well, the two times I saw it, I asked that I not be shown the part where Bryant gets…pinned." Bile crept up the back of my throat.

"Are there other parts of the video you have not seen?"

"I have no idea. Well, yeah probably, because both times I saw it the bulk of the shift got fast forwarded."

"Okay. I am going to show you a section of the video that you may or may not have seen."

I nodded and turned back to the screen. A grainy freeze frame of the video was on the large screen. She pressed play and the video began running silently. I recognized it as the usual hustle and bustle of the loading dock as people were cleaning up after the shift. Bryant passed by a few times, giving direction to the loaders and picking up a stray hub snake, which he tied in a knot and tucked into his back pocket. I'd done that plenty of times myself, saving it until I was near a trash can to toss it out.

We continued watching while Bryant put load straps and load bars into the back of the trailer. I had seen all of that before, in fast forward. The dock grew calm as people left to go clock out, and we all sat there staring at a loaded trailer ready to be pulled.

What came next was not something I had noticed before because it happened so quickly, and I watched with interest while, in the bottom corner of the video, we saw the back of someone's head as they walked by on the floor level and placed some packages on the dock grating. I blinked, confused. We all continued watching as the person pushed the neat stack of packages across the grating to door seventy-six.

Clear as day, the person in the video was me.

I took a quick glance at Joe, and he sat with his forehead buried in his hands.

"Miss Cox, please return your attention to the video." The attorney pointed to the screen sternly.

I swallowed and looked at the prosecutors, who were

in a huddle, whispering, then back at the screen. The video continued in silence, though I could hear the occasional foot scuffing and stifled coughs from the gallery and jury box.

We watched as nothing happened for a while, then the familiar jostling as the Yardbird backed up and coupled with the trailer. Then the trailer was pulled away and blinding light shone through the door. I'd seen it before and knew what came next, though was less shocked by it that time, as I watched the outlines of Mikela tossing packages into the yard while Shelly appeared to tell her what to do. I knew who the silhouettes were, but the jury did not, and I knew that wasn't the point of showing the video that day.

My stomach sank as I realized the packages I had placed on the dock were the same packages used by Shelly and Mikela to lure Bryant out into the yard. Once Mikela had dropped the last package into the yard, the attorney stopped the video. I was destroyed by the realization I'd just had. I could hardly breathe.

"Bailiff, please turn the lights back on." The lights rose

and everyone blinked briefly, before turning to face me.

Sweat dripped down my temple, tickling my jaw before continuing down my neck to be wicked away by my shirt collar. It took everything I had not to break down crying right there in front of everybody. I closed my eyes and touched the bear paw on my bolo clasp again, drawing all the strength from it I could.

Despite the lights being back on, the defense attorney pulled up a picture on the projector screen. It was a clear picture of me placing a stack of packages by the load door.

"Miss Cox, are you the person in this picture?"

I started to speak, but my voice didn't work. I cleared my throat a few times and took a sip of water from the little plastic water bottle on the stand. "Yes."

"And what is it that you are doing in this picture?"

"Well, as you saw in the video, most everybody else had left by this point. I am the sweeper, which means I stay after and find all the packages that got left behind or missed in my area. Those packages were due to be loaded in that outbound trailer you saw there." I pointed to the screen.

"Well, why didn't you load them, then? Instead of just putting them on the dock like that?"

Talking about work was easy for me, so I relaxed just the tiniest bit.

"Company policy, ma'am."

The corporate suits in the gallery began whispering to each other again.

"What does that policy say?"

"Basically, any packages that don't make it into the trailer before the load straps go on must be logged, and someone held accountable for them not making it on the truck on time. See that clipboard hanging on the wall there?" I pointed to the picture.

Everyone leaned forward, squinting at the image.

"Well, on that clipboard is the sheet where the supervisor is supposed to log all the packages that got left behind. Unless they are air packages, those go straight to the clerks. But ground packages like those, they get logged."

"In the video we see that Bryant does not come back to log those packages. Do you know why that is?"

"I have no idea."

"Did anyone instruct you to put those specific packages on the dock that day?"

I frowned at her, not understanding where she was going with it.

"Um. No. I was working solo, like usual. I found the packages and put 'em on the dock, then went up to walk the belts. Just my usual routine."

The attorney shot a quick, triumphant glance at Shelly.

"So, is it possible that had you not placed those packages on the dock at door seventy-six, Mister Green might still be alive today?"

My jaw dropped and the prosecutor shot out of his seat. "Objection!"

*

THE REMAINDER OF my time on the stand was a damn circus. Shelly's attorney had gotten under my skin, and I lost my temper, which was probably exactly what she had wanted. It took me time to get myself composed again once I realized that if me placing those packages on the dock was part of the setup to kill Bryant then I would have been charged too. The damn attorney was just trying to rattle me, and I didn't want to let her play me like that.

The rest of the trial unraveled over the next few weeks, but I didn't bother keeping up with it on the news or internet. I couldn't handle it. Darcy had promised me she would keep an eye on it and let me know if anything important happened.

I made another halfhearted attempt at finding a therapist, but never connected with one who felt right for me. I decided to only spend time with people I cared about and try to take better care of my body. Spring sprung and I spent most of my free time fishing with Darcy, riding my motorcycle with Buck and Bear through the hills, or exploring some of the regional parks in the area. Aside from work, those things were about all I could bear as I digested my role in Bryant's death.

Kristen's love of exploring the outdoors had worn off on me and I started doing some beginner level hikes. I cut back on booze and traded out the sweets and fast food for healthier stuff, which Kristen helped me find. She had an entire grocery store at her fingertips, and she was good about getting me to try new things. I even went in for a mammogram and a colonoscopy, both of which I was way overdue for. Thankfully, both came back fine.

*

I FOUND DARCY on my doorstep one evening after work. She was smiling and clutching a bouquet of wildflowers.

"Hey there," I said as I walked up the path, noticing new weeds that needed pulling in the flower bed.

"Hiya, Randy." She stepped to the side so I could unlock the door.

"Come on in. You on furlough again?"

"Nope. I knocked off early so we could talk."

"Oh? That doesn't sound good." I stepped inside and unloaded my jacket, keys, and lunch pail.

"Well, I promised you I'd let you know when something important happened with the trials, and something did." She handed me the wildflowers, which I put in an old wine bottle vase and set on the kitchen windowsill.

I motioned for her to follow me into the garage and turned on the overhead lights, which lit up the garage like a showroom. I dusted off a chair for her and pulled chamois and a spray bottle off a shelf. She took a seat and watched as I went about debugging the windscreen and front faring of my bike.

"This is a really nice setup you have here. Great lighting and, I'll be honest, this is one of the most organized garages I've seen."

"Yeah, thanks. I installed those lights when I first bought the place and took my time building the custom shelving. I like to have my tools and stuff handy. Buck helped me build the shelving."

"It's nice to have friends like that."

"Sure is."

I scrubbed at a stubborn patch of bug splatter on the fender, and decided I was ready.

"Okay, what's the news?"

"Well, Shelly was found guilty on all counts. Sentencing is in a few weeks."

I went back to scrubbing at the fender as I let that information settle in.

"Anything on Mikela?"

"Mikela turned on Shelly and became a witness for the prosecution. In exchange, she accepted a sweet plea deal, and got most of her charges either dropped or reduced. She claimed she was young and impressionable and was under the control of her mentor."

I guffawed. "Well, that's a stretch. Mikela knew exactly what she was doing." I stopped scrubbing and pointed a filthy finger at Darcy. "Calculated, that's what she is. And a manipulator."

I snapped the chamois and squatted back down to inspect the fender, biting back my rising temper.

"Oh, it gets better. Mikela admitted, in court, that she had been blackmailing Shelly because Shelly was stealing from a charity she was on the board of. And to top that off, Shelly was then laundering the money."

"So, Miss Holier-Than-Thou Shelly, who was fronting as some kind of good guy donating time to these nonprofits, was actually stealing from them? Well, shit."

"Mm-hm. Aside from that, Shelly figured out that if she got Mikela to drop those packages off the dock, then she'd have dirt on Mikela too. They were in a bit of a black-mail standoff. If Mikela ratted on Shelly for stealing the money and doing money laundering, then Shelly could turn Mikela in for setting it up so Bryant would be killed." Darcy brushed at the front of her pants and sighed. "Sloppy. Have neither of them ever watched a true crime show? Either way, they are both screwed. Shelly more so than Mikela. But they both got popped and will do some prison time."

Satisfied with the bug removal on the front end, I stood up, groaning as my back protested, and grabbed a fresh chamois. Thinking about what Darcy had said so far, I ran the rag gently over the gas tank, hard bags, and rear fender, shining up the black paint.

"I do want to know this…but I also kind of don't. Did anyone ever explain why Bryant was targeted?"

"Well, Shelly denied everything right up to the bitter end, so she didn't explain anything. But when Mikela was on the stand, she said it had something to do with a law-suit…and sex. For the lawsuit part, apparently Bryant was suing corporate, and Shelly, for age discrimination. He claimed he was passed up for a promotion because he was too young. Not sure if that case had any merit, but Mikela insisted that Shelly was irate about it and obsessed with how the lawsuit would ruin her career advancement."

"And getting busted for grand theft, money laundering, murder, conspiracy, and solicitation wouldn't ruin her career? Jesus."

I formed the chamois into a tight spiral and snapped it. The tip let out a crack and all the dust exploded out in a cloud. I watched the particles slowly settle on the garage floor.

"Well, from what you've said about her and what I saw on the news, she seems like the kind of lady who thinks she is really clever, bulletproof even. And honestly, she probably would have gotten away with it if the guy from security—"

"Joe."

"Right. If Joe didn't happen to have surveillance on the trailer that day."

I nodded and stood back to check out my bike. There were a few boot scuffs on the exhaust pipe, so I pulled a bottle of spray from the cabinet. Kneeling next to the pipes, I spritzed the melted boot scuffs and got to work scrubbing them with a soft shop towel.

"And…how does sex tie into this?"

"The prosecution explained that part of Bryant's lawsuit alleged that Shelly tried to trap him in a quid pro quo type situation and that corporate completely ignored his complaint about it, which is why he sued."

"Quid what?"

"Quid pro quo. It means 'this for that.' Basically, Shelly demanded sex from Bryant in exchange for approving his promotion. He refused, so Shelly blocked his promotion."

"Well, that's gotta be illegal."

"It is. And it was all outlined in the papers he filed to sue Shelly and the company, so they were able to put it on blast during the trial."

"How did Shelly's attorney handle that?"

"She said there was no merit to any of it, and since the lawsuit hadn't seen the light of day in court yet, they were kinda stuck."

"Jesus. Did Shelly's attorney try to throw me under the

bus to the jury?"

Darcy looked down at her hands for a moment. "Yeah, but don't worry, the prosecutor cleaned that mess up in his closing statement. He made sure the jury knew that you were just doing your job by cleaning up those packages and putting them on the dock, and you had no way of knowing what was going to happen."

"Anything else?"

"Well, they went into detail about how Shelly set it all up. Dropping the packages into the yard was just one piece of it. There was record that day of her going up into the control tower and checking the schedule to see which trailers would be pulled and parked, and when. Someone also saw her removing the traffic cones and safety vests from the safety station on that load wall. And the person Bryant was on the phone arguing with when this all happened…was Shelly. They traced it back to his company cell phone records."

"No shit? How'd Shelly try to explain that away?"

"Well, she said it was just a routine call about his performance."

"That doesn't even make sense."

"Yeah, her explanation was pretty flimsy. The prosecution punched holes in it."

"And Cleese?"

"They aren't saying anything about him. The internal investigation is still going on. He is off work on paid administrative leave, but that's all I have been able to find out."

I let out a sigh and took one last swipe at the exhaust pipes before putting my supplies away. I eyed my fishing gear.

"Tide's in. You wanna go fishing?"

She checked her watch. "You don't have to ask me twice. Let me run home and grab my stuff. The pier is going to be too crowded. Meet me under the bridge?"

"Sure."

I opened the garage and Darcy took off while I loaded up my truck. I had plenty of chores around the house and yard that I'd planned to do but decided they could wait. I made the short drive down to the road running past the port and along the shoreline. Several other people fished under the bridge already, so I had to find us a spot farther down. By the time I'd set up my chair and was baiting my hook, Darcy pulled up and hopped out, clearly excited to fish.

"It's so nice to drive right past work instead of pulling into the lot to start a shift. I mean, don't get me wrong, I like my job, but it's such a nice day and you know how much I love it out here."

I nodded and cast my line. While the fishing was plentiful near the bridge, it was not as peaceful as some of the other places across town. The bridge was a heavily traveled freeway, so the constant sound of trucks and cars rumbling by overhead annoyed me. I liked peace and quiet and time to contemplate when I fished.

Darcy cast her line and handed me a cold bottle of beer.

"Thanks."

I watched as two massive sea lions swam by, splashing and playing. When they reached one of the side docks near the port they popped right out of the water onto a small, runabout motorboat, nearly submerging it with their weight.

Darcy shook her head. "They are such pests. And there's no way to keep them off our gear, so they have the run of the equipment that is on the water."

I watched the sea lions spread out on the boat to sun themselves. Out in the water I saw several small eddies in the middle of the strait. Across the water was downtown Marshtown. I scanned along the buildings until I spotted Kristen's brick apartment building nestled in among the other historic buildings.

"Darce, what are your thoughts on marriage?"

She looked up from a notebook she'd been writing in. "It's not for me. But I can see why others might want to do it."

"Why isn't it for you?"

"Well, I like being on my own. I can come and go as I please and can make all the decisions about everything from where I live to what I eat. While I have enjoyed having partners in the past, I am always happier on my own. I have my friends and my hobbies… It just works."

What she said made perfect sense to me since I'd been

contentedly single for twenty years. My fishing line twitched, and the tip of the rod bent briefly, then straightened out again. I reeled in my line and saw that something had swum by and stolen my bait. I loaded the hook up with another hunk of sardine and cast my line.

We watched as a woman on a paddleboard passed by, fighting the current. She had a Bluetooth speaker clipped to the cargo net on her board, and I nodded my head along to the beat of Bob Marley's "Could You Be Loved" until she'd paddled far enough away that the road noise overhead ate up the song.

"At one point I thought someday I might ask Kristen to marry me."

Darcy stopped chewing on the tip of her pencil. "Now that's a surprise."

"How come?"

"In the time I've known you, you always seemed to be like me. Content on your own, I mean."

"I am. Have been for a really long time, in fact. But something about her drew me in, made me want more than I'd given myself permission to want in a long time." A big rig rolled by overhead, rattling loudly. "And I think the whole thing with Bryant and Shelly and Mikela…it shook me up. My connection with Kristen was a good one, but then the whole Mikela thing happened and…well…"

Darcy nodded and dug around in her tackle box. I watched the spot where my fishing line met the surface of the water.

"I'd stayed single so long exactly because I couldn't find anybody I trusted, and eventually I gave up." I chewed the inside of my cheek for a moment. "I mean, I like feisty women who stand on their own two feet, which Kristen sure is. But…I guess there's a limit." I looked across the strait at the massive fuel storage tanks on the shore of Marshtown. A motorboat sped by, its wake eventually reaching us as little waves breaking at our feet.

Darcy paused from her tackle box and gave me a genuine smile. "I'm glad you two were able to at least salvage it as a friendship. Here's to life as old maids," she said with a chuckle, clinking the neck of her beer bottle against mine.

"Amen."

Chapter Nineteen

It's Back

IN THE EARLY days of summer, Darcy told me that due to some loopholes in the police union contract, out-of-date department policies around officer conduct, and some clever work by his high-class union-sponsored attorney, Cleese was returned to full duty with no loss of pay or seniority. Whatever happened with the internal investigation was confidential, and I went on about my life with a growing chip on my shoulder because a dirty cop got away with a cover-up even after being caught. After all my scuff-ups with cops raiding gay gatherings in my youth, I already didn't trust law enforcement, and the outcome of Cleese's case made it worse.

But a day finally came when I decided to let all the anger go. The burning rage at Cleese, Shelly, and Mikela had done nothing but harm me, and I was sick of it. To top it off, the anxiety had set down some deep roots and was a constant backseat driver as I went about my days. So, one day at work I sent some respect up to Bryant, and as I shoved a large package down a chute, I let my anger go with it.

*

DARCY WAS AT the kitchen counter arranging several vases of wildflowers while I stirred a pot of jambalaya on the stove. I was swaying along to a Ray LaMontagne song on the stereo when someone knocked harshly. I nearly jumped out of my skin because it sounded like the cops pounding on the door.

Darcy paused, flowers held midair, looking at me questioningly. I raised a hand to her, motioning for her to stay there, and grabbed a kitchen towel. I dried my hands as I went to the door.

"Coming," I shouted as the pounding continued.

Hand on the door handle, I waited a beat, drawing in a breath. I twisted the handle and pulled the door open. Standing on my step was Bear, her arms opened wide.

"Get over here and give me a hug, beezy," she said between laughs.

Relieved, I stepped into the hug as she thumped me on the back lovingly.

"Jesus fuck, Bear. I thought you were the cops. Here, gimme that."

She chuckled and handed me her overnight bag. Buck stepped up behind Bear.

"Buck! Get on in here," I said.

She gave me a smirk and a hug.

I looked back and forth between Bear and Buck. "Are you sure you two don't mind sharing a room?"

"Nah. Buck's heard me sleep-fart and snore plenty of

times. Nothing she can't handle."

Buck rolled her eyes, tossing a set of truck keys back and forth between her hands before clipping them to her belt loop. They followed me down the hallway and I flipped on the light in the guest room and put Bear's bag on the bed.

"You have a good drive up?"

"Yup. Only a few crazies on the road, but Buck got us here in good time. Now, you two get out so I can get all gussied up. I'll be out in a few."

"All right, all right."

The doorbell rang as Buck and I walked down the hall-way. Opening the door, I saw an older woman standing on the porch, admiring my potted plants.

"Lovely marigolds and zinnia you have here." She extended a hand to me. "I'm Bear's Aunt Jane." Her grip was solid as a rock.

"It's a pleasure to meet you, Jane. I'm Randy. Come on in. This is my friend, Buck."

"Oh, no need to make introductions. I know Buck." She extended a hand to Buck, who took it and kissed her knuckles with a smoldering grin.

"It's a pleasure to see you again, Jane."

"Hello again, Buck…" Aunt Jane faltered, flustered and flushing.

"Well come on in, make yourself at home. We're setting up out back."

Aunt Jane swished through the house, headed for the back garden, her long skirt flowing.

"You old dog," I muttered jokingly to Buck. "She's widowed and at least fifteen years your senior."

"The riper the berry, the sweeter the juice, my friend."

"Jesus, you're too much sometimes. You hardly ever open your mouth, but when you do, I never know what's gonna come out. Come help me set up."

Out back, we set up chairs and strung fairy lights. She pulled some coolers full of ice and drinks onto the back patio and I set up the Bluetooth speaker. It was a nice evening, but I was sweating through my undershirt. I took a break, pulling a bottle of water from the ice chest.

It was Bear's birthday, and we were having a small party to celebrate. I wondered at the fact that my friend was turning sixty. The same friend I had raised hell with back in our twenties and thirties.

Eventually, when my heart slowed and the sweat dried, I pushed up out of the Adirondack chair, ready to get back to work.

"Hey, uh, Vivian and I made Bear something for a birthday present. I think we might be able to use them for the party tonight. You want me to go out to the truck and get 'em?"

"Sure. You need a hand?"

"'Nah. Be right back." She strode out through the side yard and the squeal of the gate hinge told me when she left and when she came back. Coming around the corner, she had one big wooden thing up on her shoulder and the other against her hip.

"Holy crap. Those look heavy. Lemme help." I hurried over and took the one that was up on her shoulder. We set them down in the grass so I could see what she'd made.

"Cornhole," she said around the toothpick clasped between her teeth.

I stepped back, taking it in. "Well yeah, I can see they

are cornhole boards. But these are… Man, they look great."

The set was solidly constructed. Her carpentry skills had only gotten better over the years and the craftsmanship was amazing. Each of the boards was custom painted with Bear's initials over a deep-blue background, with classic motorcycle style pinstriping in yellow. The paint jobs were topped off with a layer of rich varnish that would protect the wood and paint from the weather and would also make the playing surface slicker.

"Gosh, these are really incredible. Bear is going to be so stoked. Who painted them?"

"Viv."

"That's really amazing. Hey, do you wanna go get that diva out of the bathroom so we can get started?"

"Sure thing."

Buck went inside and let everyone know it was time. The small group filed out and took seats in the chairs we'd set out in the grass. For years my back porch had been nothing more than a concrete slab I had used for smoking. With a lot of time and patience, Darcy and I had decorated it with potted flowers, some wall art, and had hung an outdoor curtain for a bit of shade and privacy. We had sanded down and refinished my wooden chairs. Everything looked fresh, which made me feel good.

Off to the edge of the yard, we'd strung up a hammock between two oaks. I'd spent plenty of afternoons looking up at the canopy of the trees and thinking about the roller coaster ride I had been on.

"All right, we're ready," Buck said from the doorway before taking a seat in the chair next to mine.

The song on the outdoor speaker stopped abruptly and switched over to "Kiss" by Prince. Bear stepped through the slider onto the porch with a flourish and did her signature shimmying dance moves as she lip-synced the lyrics and walked through the group. Her hair was in a perfect pompadour, and she wore a dark-blue crushed velvet suit with ruffled collar and long ruffles on the shirt cuffs. Prince fan that she was, she looked like she had just come from shooting one of his music videos.

I caught myself grinning and tapping my toes to the beat. I was grateful to be celebrating her birthday, and grateful that, given our rowdy early years, we had all made it this far. Watching Bear being her larger-than-life self made my eyes well up. I dabbed at them quickly with my bandana handkerchief, Buck giving me a knowing nod.

When the song faded out Bear cleared her throat and gave me a wink.

"Aw heck, are we in for another one of your speeches?" I chided jokingly.

"You're damn right you are. Zip it, Randy. We are here to celebrate me! I made it to sixty. I never imagined that I would have this honor. Most of you know I lived hard and fast back when I didn't have all this gray in my hair. Plus, the damn cancer tried to take me out. Fuck cancer." She paused, looking at each of us in turn.

"Yup, fuck cancer," echoed Aunt Jane, holding her open hand up to the sky the way people do at church sometimes.

She went on. "But here I am, still raising hell." She chuckled. "Well, if playing video games in my underwear is considered raising hell, that is."

Everyone chuckled with her. Small beads of sweat had

started to form on her forehead, though her smile never faltered.

"You guys are the fucking salt of the earth, and I wouldn't want to spend this day any other way. Now, let's do it up right!"

"Hear, hear," I said, and everyone clapped and cheered for Bear.

She pulled out her phone and poked around on it until the music started back up again, this time a Journey song coming on. Dusk had settled and the fairy lights danced in the gently swaying trees.

Stepping up to the food table, I rubbed my hands together as I looked at the spread. My stomach growled. I grabbed a plate, piled it high with rice, and ladled jambalaya over the top. I added a few edge pieces of cornbread and a hearty wedge of fruit tart.

As I sat down at one of the tables, the legs of the chair sank down into the grass about an inch. Tempting as the food was, I waited to start eating until everyone else at my table was seated. Bear was to my left, at the head of the table. Darcy anchored the other end of the table. Buck and

Jane sat shoulder to shoulder across from us. I smirked at Buck, but her poker face gave up nothing.

I stood, lifting my sweating glass of iced tea. "I just want to thank each one of you for making the trip out here today to celebrate Bear. Now, dig in."

Everyone clinked glasses and got busy eating. I was impressed with the jambalaya I'd made. The chicken and kielbasa balanced well with the vegetables and seasoning, and it had just the right amount of kick to it. I did my best to have some sort of table manners, but as hungry as I was, I plowed through the jambalaya in no time. I sopped up the remnants with cornbread and went to lick my fingers, but for Aunt Jane's sake, I stopped and used the napkin from my lap.

Darcy and Jane chatted quietly while they ate. Bear talked shit to me and Buck throughout the meal because that was how our friendship worked. Sitting back in the chair, I was so happy to see our friends enjoying themselves and tears threatened to well up again. While the anxiety I had picked up after Bryant's death hadn't completely gone away, on that day it was an echo in the background.

A feeling of joy settled over me and I took a second to feel smug about the fact that Shelly and Mikela were in prison while I was free, in my own yard, living my life and surrounded by my friends.

Bear's voice brought me back, and I realized she was standing up and speaking to the crowd.

"Folks, I hope you all are enjoying your dinner and drinks. Please don't be afraid to help yourselves to seconds and thirds. After that we'll clear out a space for dancing, and Randy…you better report to the cornhole boards for an ass whooping."

"You think you can whoop me at cornhole? Yeah, we'll see about that."

*

PEOPLE HEADED TO the food table for seconds while Bear and I meandered over to the cornhole boards. Porkchop woke up from his nap in the bushes, gave a big stretch, and wandered over. He brushed against Bear's legs and flopped down in the middle of the game.

"Jesus, Porkchop." I bent down and picked up all the

bean bags. "You want to play red or blue?"

"Red," she said and blew out a drag from her vape pen in two jets from her nose. "It's back," she said as she held out her bear paw of a hand to me.

I froze as I placed the bean bags in her hand, closing my eyes as those two words sank in.

It's back.

She'd said those words to me once before, during a particularly hot summer evening when she'd been swimming topless in her apartment pool. She had done slow laps, at one point popping her head out, arms resting on the pool deck, to talk to me. "My streamlined body makes swimming feel so smooth. Like a river otter in a dream state or something." She had angry purple scars left behind from radiation treatment and her double mastectomy, but none of it seemed to bother her in the slightest. And then she'd said it: *It's back.*

It. Fucking it.

"Does Buck know?"

With a steady hand, she took the red bean bags from me and stepped over to her cornhole board. "Yeah." She tossed one of the bean bags lightly, as if testing its weight. "It's, uh, causing me some problems. That's why Buck drove. I'm going to have to stop riding too."

I grit my teeth. *It's not fucking fair!* I closed my eyes as a sad sort of anger came over me. Bear didn't seem bothered by the news, so I tried to follow her lead.

"Well, shit." I stepped up and gave her a hug, the ruffled collar of her shirt tickling my cheek. She gave me a true bear hug back, nearly squeezing the air out of my lungs while rocking us back and forth.

She eventually let me go before tossing the bean bag lightly again. "You ready to lose?"

"Uh, that's where you're wrong. I'm about to school you at this game, punk. Let's go."

Epilogue

AT HER SIXTIETH birthday party Bear had asked me if I was ready to lose. We were about to play cornhole, so I thought that was what she had meant. I wondered afterward if she wasn't asking about cornhole at all, but actually asking me if I was ready to lose her.

It wasn't long before the cancer wormed its devious self throughout Bear's whole body, the final sticky fingers of it grabbing hold of her brain. Modern medicine had worked wonders for her in the past, but that time was different. No amount of radiation, surgery, or chemo could stop it.

Bear responded to text messages less and less until one day my phone rang. I was taking a break from a motorcycle ride, sitting in the dirt with my legs dangling over the edge of a creek. My phone vibrated in my pocket, and I almost didn't answer it. I hadn't wanted to break the quiet moment I was having, but something urged me to answer.

"Hullo."

"Ey, Randy."

"Bear. It's good to hear your voice, you old fart."

It was good to hear her voice too, though she sounded exhausted and drugged. Not her usual self at all.

"I'm making Buck drive me up to the wetlands to look at birds. You remember the place we took a pitstop at one time and got bit all over by no-see-ums?"

"Ha! How could I forget. Dang, you guys are driving all the way up there?"

"Yeah. She has me all bundled up in here with my blanket and some pillows. Nice and cozy."

"Well, don't overdo it. Just take it easy today, okay."

"You know how Buck is, like a mother hen to me. I'll

be fine."

I heard Buck chuckle in the background.

"I want to run away from home, Randy."

I looked at the far bank of the creek, where the spring grasses were starting to die off and turn brown.

"What do you mean run away?"

"I don't like it there. So many pills, and a hospital bed in the middle of my damn living room. Nurses coming and going."

"When did the nurses start coming?"

"Last week. I'm technically on hospice now, but I got Buck to break me out of jail for the afternoon to go look at the birds. We're going to the wetlands. You remember the place we took a pitstop at one time and got bit all over by no-see-ums?"

My heart lurched and I closed my eyes, biting back the sadness.

"You remember, right?"

"Of course, Bear. Of course. I'll never forget. But hey, no running away from home, okay. And be nice to your nurses. I'll come up next weekend to see you, okay?"

"Yeah, come on by any time. I love you, Randy."

"I love you too, bud. Have fun with Buck."

After we hung up, I lay down in the dirt and sobbed, sad not only for my friend but also at the loss I knew was coming. I didn't know it then, but that was the last time I would ever hear Bear's voice.

*

BEAR, WHO WAS larger than life, who had felt so deeply, lived so bravely, and fought for every last second, was gone a few weeks later. I was at her bedside on her final day, but the details of that I have chosen to keep for myself. I will only say that she spent her last day surrounded by people who loved her, and that she died with dignity and respect.

My promise to her that I will never forget is one I take seriously. She rides with me every time I take my bike out and is a constant reminder by the painting she blessed my home with.

It has been a rough couple of years, and I know that I am getting to the age where my friends will start to pass away. But losing Bear to the cancer she had beaten once be-fore, and Bryant to some corporate hack trying to save face, feels like the world has been robbed.

My father had told me that the only guarantee in life is there are no guarantees in life. I hadn't really understood it as a child, but as a grown woman it makes more sense. Life doesn't always have a happy ending and neither does this story.

Acknowledgements

Authors do not create novels in a vacuum. While writing is mostly a solitary endeavor, other people play a key role in making a tatty first draft manuscript into an amazing novel.

I'd like to thank my mentor, Pat Henshaw, for her tough love and insight. Landee Linn, one of my beta readers, provided some good feedback for me to consider, which helped redirect a big part of the storyline. My writing pal, RL Merrill, generously spent time helping me get "unstuck" when this storyline was mired in the mud, and I had all but given up hope. J. Scott Coatsworth and Marco Guzman have been great at helping get the word out about my books.

As always, I want to thank my editor, Elizabeth Coldwell from NineStar Press, for her thoughtful and thorough work.

About Liz Faraim

Liz has a full plate between balancing a day job, parenting, writing, and finding some semblance of a social life. In past lives she has been a soldier, a bartender, a shoe salesperson, an assistant museum curator, and even a driving instructor. She focuses her writing on strong, queer, female leads who don't back down.

Liz transplanted to California from New York over thirty years ago. She now lives in the East Bay Area of California and enjoys exploring nature with her wife and son.

Email

liz.faraim@gmail.com

Facebook

www.facebook.com/liz.faraim.9

Twitter

@FaraimLiz

Website

www.lizfaraim.com

Other NineStar books by this author

The Vivian Chastain series

Canopy

Stitches and Sepsis

Concussion and Contentment

Connect with NineStar Press

WWW.NINESTARPRESS.COM

WWW.FACEBOOK.COM/NINESTARPRESS

WWW.FACEBOOK.COM/GROUPS/NINESTARNICHE

WWW.TWITTER.COM/NINESTARPRESS

WWW.INSTAGRAM.COM/NINESTARPRESS

www.ingramcontent.com/pod-product-compliance
Lightning Source LLC
Chambersburg PA
CBHW060259100726

47907CB00002B/209